P9-CRV-432

Aloha, Mr. Lucky

Aloha, Mr. Lucky

Corson Hirschfeld

A Tom Doherty Associates Book
New York

This is a work of fiction. All the characters and events portrayed in this novel are either fictitious or are used fictitiously.

ALOHA, MR. LUCKY

This book is printed on acid-free paper.

A Forge Book
Published by Tom Doherty Associates, LLC
175 Fifth Avenue
New York, NY 10010

www.tor.com

Forge® is a registered trademark of Tom Doherty Associates, LLC.

Design by Lisa Pifher

ISBN 0-312-87002-7

First Edition: March 2000

Printed in the United States of America

0 9 8 7 6 5 4 3 2 1

For Thelma, Sherri, and Koko

ALOHA, MR. LUCKY

PROLOGUE

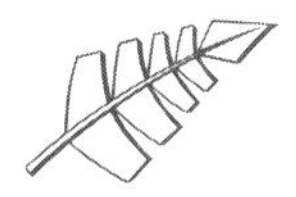

It might have been the moon. From horizon to horizon, all McWhorter could see was gray lava. Everywhere: fossilized, monochromatic chaos.

"Friggin' place." Mumbling. "Must be a mecca for the colorblind."

"What was that?" asked Kapono, the young Hawaiian.

"I said Mecca'd be no match for this place. Yessir, one hell of a holy land you've got here."

Kapono and McWhorter had hiked deep into the caldera of Kilauea volcano on the island of Hawai'i, by the cliffs rimming the Halema'uma'u fire pit. Halema'uma'u was sleeping, but its scarred crust, two hundred feet below, looked black, burnt and fresh.

Kapono muttered a curse in Hawaiian at the man's sarcasm and turned his back to him. Not that McWhorter was easy to ignore. Though slight, and half a head shorter than Kapono, he wore a pair of hot pink plastic sunglasses, and practically swam in a baggy purple aloha shirt spangled with yellow birds of paradise.

Kapono clutched a sprig of *'ohelo* with red berries to his chest, walked to the jagged edge of the precipice, and stretched to full height, a chiefly six feet. Bare from the waist up, his skin glistened like oiled mahogany in the late afternoon sun. He held the branch high and tossed it into the fuming crater. "For Mother Pele," he said, and, with palms upraised, began to chant, *"A ka luna i Kilauea . . ."*

Six paces behind, McWhorter fidgeted, finally yelled, "Don't screw it up—I'd hate to see you steam up Mother Pele, make an ash of yourself." That put an end to the chanting. McWhorter snorted and slapped his thigh, knocking off the sunglasses.

Silent, Kapono kept his back to him. A gust of fetid, superheated air rose from below to flutter the scarlet cloth at the tip of his long black braid.

McWhorter stooped to pick up the glasses. "Smells like the old gal's got a hygiene problem to me," he said, and laughed again.

When Kapono turned, cocked an eyebrow at him, McWhorter began to cough. Glasses in hand, he gripped his neck in a strangle-hold, bugged his eyes, stuck out his tongue, and rocked his head from side to side. Then his eyes sparkled and the choking noises turned to chuckles.

Kapono glared. "Beware the goddess, old man. Mother Pele may be sleeping, but she listens."

"Sorry, son, no disrespect intended." Still smiling. McWhorter put the sunglasses back on and ran a hand over his short gray flattop. "Sulfur doesn't agree with these old lungs. Hate the stuff. Brings back memories of chemistry class, way back, and those stinkin' attacks." He took a healthy gulp of orange soda, scanned left and right. "Those tourists on the far rim are small as fleas on a hog's back," he said. "We must be a mile from nowhere. Maybe two."

"As it should be," said Kapono. "You know, a haole like you ought to be careful up here." He looked over his shoulder, watched Mc-Whorter peel waxed paper from an enormous sandwich, half as long as his arm, then work his mouth over the end of the oily loaf like a snake swallowing a lizard.

Kapono shook his head. "You aren't the kind of writer I ex-pected—not that I don't appreciate your paper finally taking notice of our problems." He closed his eyes for several calming seconds be-fore curling his fingers into fists, a new anger rising. "How can these people consider destroying something so sacred? It's a travesty. This calls for strong action!" He spit out the words.

"No need for you and your Sons of Pele to throw a hissy fit," said

McWhorter. "It hasn't happened yet." A crinkled sheet of waxed paper floated from his hand, fluttered like an irreverent ghost past Kapono's ankles and over the crater rim to disappear from view. "So, you've told me everything?"

"I told you the story of Pele," said Kapono. "Did you listen? I told you everything I saw, and if I'd been with Dr. Finch in the Pali-uli the day he found it, I'd know exactly where it was, too. I can tell you this—he has a map and photographs, all the proof he needs."

"I'll keep nosing around, find out what I can about this Dr. Finch," said McWhorter, now with a hard-boiled egg in his palm. "Whoa. Look at that," waving the egg at a hundred-foot plume of steam rising half a mile away from the cylindrical pit's sheer wall. "You know, ever since I was a little tyke, I've wanted to eyeball the bowels of a sure-as-hell live-ass volcano."

McWhorter watched Kapono hopping from one foot to the other along the broken ledge, fearless, in ragged shorts and flip-flop sandals, toes out over space. "Whew! Some nerves you got, son." He thumped his heel on the syrupy swirl of frozen lava beneath his feet. "I'd love to have a look straight down. You feel safe dancin' around out there?"

"It's solid enough," Kapono said. "You spend time here, you get a sense of what's safe, what's not. And Mother Pele takes care of her own."

McWhorter placed most of the sandwich and half the egg in a brown paper bag, set it by the bottle on the ground. He walked toward the edge, testing his footing with each step, squinting at the stone beneath him like it was melting ice on a spring pond. When he reached the lip of the chasm, he rested his hand on young Kapono's muscular shoulder, perhaps fearful to stand alone with all that emptiness before him.

Kapono rippled his shoulder at the touch, but McWhorter tightened his grip and leaned forward, craned his neck to peer into the simmering pit.

"Fire, air, earth, and water," said Kapono. "Take a good look. Below you is Halema'uma'u, the home of Mother Pele." And for a moment they stood motionless, side by side, in awe of the grandeur.

High in the distance, a white-tailed tropicbird soared on a thermal. In the crater, huge crevasses had fractured the congealed lava, silent, unmoving, streaked with yellow sulfur, or obscured entirely by clouds of vapor and gas. It was easy to imagine the hissing and crackling at the bottom, where sinking groundwater sizzled on hot rock. Even deeper, unseen, magma seethed.

Standing as they were, it was surprisingly easy. McWhorter merely straightened his fingers to throw young Kapono off balance, then tapped his back with the flat of a hand to send him over the edge. The move was so fast there was no scream, only a sharp intake of breath and a whirl of flailing arms.

Suddenly agile, McWhorter jumped back, extended the toe of his shiny combat boot to nudge off the sandal still teetering on the rim. "Say hi to your mama for me," he said with a quick salute, and flipped the pink sunglasses the way of the sandal.

He stripped off the aloha shirt and stuffed it in the bag, exchanging it for an olive drab T-shirt, then sat on a hump of lava and finished his meal under a golden sky, watching steam billow silently from the crater. Ten minutes later, he stood, fingers wrapped around the neck of the empty orange soda bottle. He tossed it from one hand to the other, leaned back and pitched it, high and far, end over end. At the apex of its arc, the glass glinted in the hard yellow light of the setting sun, then winked away, swallowed by the shadows of Halema'uma'u.

"If there's two things in this world I can't stand," McWhorter said to the still air, "it's friggin' volcano lovers and a man with no sense of humor."

1

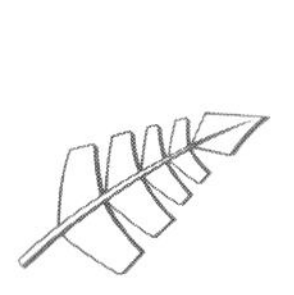

LADIES, MEET MR. LUCKY
Married. Thirties. Good-looking. Fit. Seeking lively companion for discreet fun and games. #3405

Star Hollie took another sip of coffee, reread the ad, and winked at his reflection in the plate-glass window. "You sneaky devil," he said, running his fingers through his hair. It was good hair: shiny, light brown with sun-bleached highlights, hanging in waves to his shoulders. The ladies liked that hair. And the green eyes. Knock 'em dead, he thought, and smiled.

He looked through his reflection onto Kuhio Avenue. Tourists streamed by like butterflies. Or brightly colored fish. Perceptions mingled with memories, and he thought of a glass-bottomed boat gliding over a sunlit reef.

Lavender sea fans and plump pink anemones swayed with the current. See-through jellyfish pulsed over black urchins while blue parrot fish nibbled at coral. Then a hundred shadows flickered across the sand as a school of silvery mackerel flashed their tails at a hammerhead shark. Floating and crawling and swimming things. Big fish eating little ones. The watchers and the watched.

He blinked as two young Japanese couples blocked the sun, milling, three feet away, admiring the restaurant's ten-foot deco sign: three green neon palms with yellow coconuts, flanking a lavender ukulele and red script, "Papa's Coffee Shop, est. 1935."

Cameras materialized from fitted cases and purses. He watched the girls wobble on high heels, posing, little bodies up on stilts like Minnie Mouse, and wondered what they'd be like in bed. Did they bow before they hopped in the sack? Japanese girls were always tittering. Did they keep it up under the covers? Must like sex—how about those Japanese art prints of all the positions? And the Tokyo businessmen sure kept the Waikiki hookers busy.

Hookers. He thought of fishing. Of a sailfish leaping off the coast of Baja. Of freedom and blue ocean. Then he thought of the gaff and the taxidermist's knife, and the same fish, now a plasticized husk gathering dust in some car salesman's cubicle.

That fish and I have a lot in common, he decided, and cringed at the prospect of violence just around the bend.

He rested his head against the cool window, felt his mind wander again. What had he been thinking about, just before? Something about sex, he was pretty sure.

"Wake up, honey. Just brewed a fresh pot."

Star rolled his forehead from the plate glass and squinted. He held out his cup, face brightening at the friendly face under strawberry blond hair. "Best damn coffee in Waikiki. My only vice."

"Right, sweetie." She patted him on the head. "Thought we'd lost you there."

"No way." He sipped coffee.

"So, tell mama how baby's new scam is coming along." Coasting through life on the experienced side of fifty, Doris had seen them all. "Burned your fingers yet?"

"Don't worry your pretty head about me. The Star man's in control."

"Sure, honey." She turned, wagged her rear at him on the way back to the kitchen.

Star checked his watch. Tammy, his three o'clock, would be there soon.

He usually kept it to "Let's meet at Papa's Coffee Shop on Kuhio, a block from the beach, near the International Market Place. We can talk and get acquainted. I'll wear a black aloha shirt with red hibiscuses. Booth by the window."

He closed his eyes, inhaling fry-griddle and coffee-brewing smells mixed with scents of aging wood and coconut suntan lotion, then exhaled slowly. Papa's was comfortably busy, a pair of cops on break, elbows on the counter, grandparents exchanging snapshots of children's children, two old Chinese men, wishbone-thin, in dirty armless white undershirts arguing in singsong Cantonese, and here and there, pods of tourists and locals. Hawaiian music played in the background, as always.

He checked his watch again. Five after, and there at the register, eyebrows raised, nodding toward the door, was big Papa, middle-aged, Hawaiian—not the original Papa, but his son.

Could that be her in the shadows? With the sun in his face, he couldn't get a good look, but when she stepped into the light, checking the booths, he pursed his lips and whistled. Lordy. It's Barbie herself. Skin all over the shade of and, whew, the firmness of a ripe apricot. Natural glow at her cheeks, no makeup. Blue eyes, incredible golden hair, sunlit, shining, swaying halfway down her back. Nice body. Still a little baby fat, the kind she'll be losing in a year or two. Somewhere between her mid and late teens. A real honey pot.

A smile of recognition and there she was walking toward him in open-heeled, cork-soled shoes, wearing denim shorts, cut high to show off long thighs and, no doubt, a glimpse of cute cheeks had she been going the other way. A little higher, the hem of a peekaboo T-shirt, Easter-chick yellow, danced around her navel to reveal a soft and slightly rounded tummy.

"Hi. You Star?" A high little-girl voice but far more sure of herself than he'd been at her age.

"That's me," he said, smiling, "and you must be Tammy."

"Uh-huh." She sat. "Star. That's your real name?"

"Yeah. It's a nickname I picked up when I was little. Now I'm big and still Star."

"You were a little star and now you're a big star, huh? I like it."

"Thanks, honey." What a cutie pie. "Tammy is a nice name too."

"Yeah, maybe. I've been thinking about changing it though. You know, like to something different, older, more sophisticated."

"How about Tamara. That's your given name, isn't it?" Enjoying the small talk, enjoying looking Tammy over up close. He leaned toward her, close enough to notice a zit on the point of her chin, lurking beneath a dab of fleshy Clearasil. Then he saw another one firing up on her left nostril. Baby's been eating too much chocolate, he decided, and slid back in the booth.

"No," she said. "I told you my name's Tammy, T-A-M-M-Y. I've been thinking about Sheri, with an *i*, S-H-E-R-I. Sounds French, don't you think?"

"Oh, definitely French. Unusual. People will think you're older, too, European for sure." No, she's not local and not kidding either. I'll bet she's from California, L.A. without a doubt, and here with her parents. Sure not with a man, and if she's with girlfriends it's not likely she'd answer my ad or be alone. Unless this is some kind of a dare. Let's try the direct approach.

"Where are your parents today, Tammy?"

"Oh, Daddy's doing business and Mommy's at the bishop's museum, I think, probably buying out the gift shop."

"Business and Bishop Museum. You're all alone?"

"That's right, Mr. Star. You and me."

Doris set a glass of water in front of Tammy. "So, Star, this is your daughter, huh? Looks just like you, with the long hair." She tossed a child's menu on the table, little cartoon fish smiling up at him.

"No, Doris, Tammy is a friend. Something to drink or eat, Tammy?"

"Cherry Coke."

"Cherry Coke, thank you, Doris," he said.

Doris walked away but stopped at the end of the aisle, waited until he saw her, then crossed her arms, hands on elbows, and began rocking them, head down, mouthing coochi-coo's.

Star shot Doris a glare, looked again at Tammy, now prodding the pimple on her chin. He stared at tiny flakes of dried Clearasil stuck to her fingertip, at a nail bitten to the quick, a chewed wart clinging like a tenacious pink tick to the knuckle of her thumb. He dropped his eyes to his cup and took a sip of coffee. Cold. His mind went blank.

He looked again at the coffee. What he saw this time, swimming near the bottom of his cup like a Gypsy's tea-leaf vision, was this: He was in a hospital bed, flat on his back with two broken legs packed in plaster, raised off the mattress by pulleys, like in the movies. Maybe a broken arm or two as well, he couldn't make that out, but it was possible. What was clear, much too clear, was that he was twenty-five hundred dollars shy of keeping that glimpse of what might be from turning into a grim reality.

Twenty-five hundred dollars, he thought. Jeez. Where the hell am I going to come up with twenty-five hundred dollars?

"Hey!" said Tammy. "Hey, you there?"

Star blinked, saw little Tammy again, raising her eyebrows, twirling a hank of bleached hair around stubby fingers. Waiting. Expecting him to say something clever. "Ummm . . . So . . ." He remembered the ad. "How come you answered my ad, honey? Why me? Aren't there enough boys around here your age? Tourists, local boys?"

"*Bo*-ring. The tourist boys are as immature as the ones back home, and the local ones care more about their surfboards than showing a woman a good time. And you? You sounded like fun in your ad. I've been looking for real action since I got here, and I've always wanted to do it with an old guy or a foreigner. And you're both. Or close enough, huh? Hawai'i counts as a foreign country, doesn't it, Mr. Star?"

"Sure, Tammy." He sounded tired.

"Hey, no offense, you're really good-looking for your age. Great hair, sexy eyes, nice bod. A real stud, I'll bet." She slipped a foot out of her right shoe and raised it under the table, slid it fast along Star's thigh to his crotch. She wiggled her toes. "I want to meet Mr. Lucky." Giggling. "Is that Mr. Lucky in there? Wake up, Mr. Lucky."

"Jeez!" He jerked away, bumped against the back of the seat, grabbed her foot and pushed it down. "We're in a restaurant."

"Big deal. No reason to stay, is there? My hotel's only three blocks away and my parents won't be home till after dinner. I've got my own room anyway. Real neat, with a king-size bed, a VCR, and a bitty fridge with beer and minibottles of booze. Let's go. I want to see Mr. Lucky."

"I'm sure he wants to see you too, honey, but maybe we should talk first, huh?"

"Talk?"

"Yeah, like, uh, what's your father do for a living?"

"Are you serious? He's a lawyer. Now let's get a move on."

"A lawyer. That's interesting."

"Interesting?"

"I mean, I'll bet he makes a lot of money, and it's interesting that you all travel together."

"Yeah, sure, fascinating. What do they say, the family that travels together unravels together? Daddy took us on this trip 'cause Mommy threw a fit and was gonna hit the road. *Adios, mamacita*. So . . . Aloha, Honolulu. But the trip's just like home, Daddy does his business all day and Mommy shops all day, then they fight all night, unless they're making up, then they you-know-what all night. It's a lot easier on me though when he's on one of his trips to those foreign countries—really foreign countries, not like here—and I'm on my own."

"Really foreign countries, huh? Well, when you change your name, maybe you can go with him to Paris, learn the wicked ways of the French."

"Yeah, except he hardly ever goes to posh countries like that, only to beaner places like Colombia and Bolivia or Mexico or Turkey. Mr. Big Attorney's going to Thailand from here, sending Mommy and me home alone. But, hey, long as I'm here, we can hang out, right, Mr. Star? I can give the driver the slip any time I want, then I'm on my own. You and me, baby."

"Tammy, what do you mean, 'driver'?"

"Some greasy weasel, works for Daddy. Drives me around, supposed to keep me out of trouble. But I like trouble—does Daddy good to worry about his little girl."

Her foot slid up his leg again, but this time he caught it at his knee, held it to the seat. The foot felt damp.

He looked out the window to see who might be idling around out there, looking his way, and had a fleeting vision of a reluctant drive to the pineapple fields for a meeting with the itinerant father to discuss his intentions toward little Tammy. Little Tammy the minor who couldn't be more than fourteen or fifteen. Jeez. As if he wasn't up to his chin already.

"Uh, Tammy, how old are you, honey?"

"Nineteen, twenty next month."

"I'm not so sure, sweetheart. You wouldn't mind showing me some ID, would you?"

"Excuse me, ID?" Voice rising.

"Yeah, driver's license. ID with your age on it."

"ID? ID?" An angry flush ran up Tammy's neck, across her face. She rooted in her purse, fished out a driver's license, handed it to him.

Star stared at a sorry counterfeit. "Ummm. I don't think so." He passed it back. "Could be we started out on the wrong foot here, honey. Maybe it's better we just . . ."

"Wrong foot? I'll show you wrong foot." Tammy's foot, the sweaty, bare, intercepted one that had crept up his leg a moment before, now resting against the seat between his legs, lifted six inches and kicked. Connected.

"Umpff!" *Thump!* Star's forehead slammed the tabletop. *Thump, bump!* His knees jerked into the table's underside. He toppled sideways onto the seat in a fetal crouch, then rolled onto the floor. With an agonized moan, arms clutching knees, he twirled on the linoleum in an anguished break-dance backspin.

That got everyone's attention.

Through watery, half-closed eyes, ear to the floor, he caught a fleeting glimpse of Tammy's teenage can flashing over his face as she twisted from the booth and stomped away.

She hadn't gotten her right foot entirely back into her shoe, however, and it fell off under the table, requiring a return visit. Doubly affronted, she marched to the front door, shoe in hand. She halted beside Papa at the register, wheeled around, lifted a chubby young arm, and pointed a finger, the one with the abbreviated nail, back at Star on the floor. Tammy's finger trembled. Papa's patrons were all ears.

"Just wait till Daddy hears about what you wanted to do to his little girl, mister." Big baby's tears began to roll down her cheeky cheeks. That was it for Tammy. Shoe in hand, she trotted out the door and away, with a rocking gait: up left, down right, up left, down right.

Silence. Not a tinkle of steel on china. The tones of the Hawaiian slack-key guitar sounding over the speakers behind the counter faded as a song ended. One of the cops started to get up, looked at his half-eaten burger, glanced at his watch, and sat back down.

Star staggered to his feet, sick in the gut, blushing at the same time. Damn.

He eased into the booth, pretended to read the newspaper, saw headlines: SIX MILLION TO VISIT ISLANDS BY YEAR'S END. HAWAIIAN BURIALS HALT HIGHWAY CONSTRUCTION. VOLCANO DEATH STUNS BIG ISLAND. He feigned interest, but couldn't muster concentration.

Diners returned to food, conversations. Words came to his mind: "Hell hath no fury like a woman scorned." A line from an old pirate movie? Then he thought of a long-forgotten textbook image, a Greek goddess, one of the moody ones, wearing a breastplate rimmed with snakes and the face of a Gorgon, a monster who turned men to stone. And in Hawai'i? Pele rules. The volcano goddess. Known for her capriciousness and dark furies. Burns to a crisp men who cross her. Even closer to home, he remembered the temper fits hurled by his own sweet Cindy. He shivered. Women.

Fortunately, Doris had yet to bring the cherry Coke. He dropped two dollar bills by his cup to lessen the sarcasm he'd earned, grabbed his day pack, and hurried to the counter to settle up.

"Sorry about the outburst, Papa."

"Hey, no problem, Star boy. People here, they'll be back tomorrow, hoping for more. You're better than the talk shows."

"Yeah. The ladies are wild about me, huh?" Still a little nervous, talking too fast. "Going for a swim. Cool off. Clear my mind. Got to get home to feed my boy soon anyway. Looks like we may be alone again tonight."

He stepped outside, shook his long hair in the sun, and said to no one in particular, "Way to go, Romeo, dig the hole a little deeper."

2

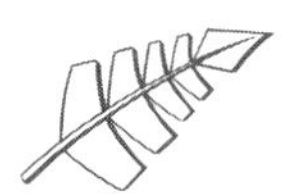

Long after his colleagues from Bishop Museum had left the lounge, Stan's Mr. Meat, All You Can Eat, Artemas Finch had remained, humming along with the piano, flirting with the lingerie models, enjoying those extra manhattans.

Artemas shuffled to the rear door, muttering, "Car keys, car keys, car keys," digging through his pockets. He found them—"sneaky little buggers"—in the cuff of his trousers, and squinted through the glass. It was dark out there. Really dark.

He pushed open the door and peered out. As if urging him to stay, the warm yellow light hugged his shoulders, then shot across the black asphalt of the parking lot in a long white dagger probing the night.

Artemas stepped onto the back stairs, momentarily blinded as the closing door sucked back the light, but reassured by the muffled laughter and tinkly piano music. He took a deep breath, smelled night-blooming jasmine over the lingering scents of tobacco smoke, alcohol, and the *kiawe*-wood grill. Eyes closed, he listened to the trade winds rustle the palm fronds.

He frowned, remembering that morning, when he told Bernie Bergen from HydraCorp about his find. Not that he wasn't grateful for HydraCorp's philanthropy in underwriting the survey for the Ka Pono Foundation. But this Bergen was crude, devoid of intellectual curiosity. When Artemas told Bergen how the survey would have to be amended because of his marvelous discovery—not the details, of course, but its significance—the man simply stared at him, made a note or two, then boldly asked how much it would all cost. Knowledge? Curiosity? Ha! Try money. Artemas said the name aloud. "Bernie Bergen." Then, "Philistine."

Just wait, he thought. Tomorrow I'll release a public statement; then, once my findings are presented in a professional journal, Artemas Finch will receive his due.

He grabbed the railing and scanned the parking lot, large and dimly lit. "Damn it, car. Where are you hiding?" He wandered on autopilot down the rows of automobiles toward the rear of the lot.

Bingo. There, near the light. But what's this? Two men *sitting* on the *hood* of his brand-new white car, legs extended, backs against the windshield like it was a TV-room recliner. Big men, too, big as bears. In western boots and denim. Wait for them to leave, he decided, or better, find one of Mr. Meat's employees to send them packing.

Curious, however, he watched from the shadows forty feet away. Look—identical twins. Young, late twenties, with rough, sunburnt faces from years of work in the sun, like digging ditches, the sort of thing construction workers do.

Quite the specimens, he decided, anthropologically speaking. Not the body-beautiful types—their stomachs protruded too much for that—but tall, virile, powerful. Hardly Greek gods, but yes, Vikings. He imagined them cloaked in homespun tunics with fur capes and iron helmets, wielding broadswords or head-splitting battle axes.

They had light blond hair, almost white, so the Viking analogy was apropos, although their eyebrows were dark. Was it possible they bleached their hair? Clean-shaven, hair short, but when they turned, matted clumps hung past their shoulders. Disturbing.

Artemas closed his eyes and rolled back the centuries in his mind, imagining events at the close of the first millennium, the days of Viking marauding. He imagined eleventh-century Irish monks confronted by Vikings, face-to-face at the monastery gate. How would men of peace—scribes, horticulturists, intellectuals—have reacted to an encounter with such barbarians?

He shuddered, opened his eyes.

"Howdy," said one of the Vikings, three feet away.

Artemas stumbled, fell to his knees.

The Viking lifted him to his feet with one hand. "We was wondering what you was doin', standin' there all alone. Join the party." He draped a massive arm around Artemas's slight, seersucker-clad shoulders and gave him a squeeze. The man smelled of booze and, yes, lemons. "I'm Ray Don," he said, "and that's my little brother over there." With Artemas in tow, he walked to the car.

Ray Don jumped back onto the Buick and the second one extended his arm from the hood to shake Artemas's hand. "How do," he said, "I'm Bobby Lee."

Artemas straightened his shoulders, affected confidence. "Pleased to meet you, I'm sure," he said. "I'm Dr. Artemas Bingham Finch."

He wrinkled his nose at an overpowering odor. Not the lemon scent, or the alcohol, but some cleaning smell. Aha, he thought, I'll bet they washed my car, like the boys in the big cities with the squeegees and buckets. No doubt they'll ask for money next. He looked around for the water and brushes, but the ground was dry. "What *is* that odor?" he asked.

"Bobby Lee's smell-good," said the first one. "Strong, ain't it?"

"Pine Sol," added Bobby Lee. "Manly, huh? Goodly down-home smell. I ain't seen a real pine tree in these islands yet, and I miss 'em somethin' awful. Now Ray Don, he goes for the sweet stuff. Don't you, brother?"

"Lemon Pledge," said Ray Don. "Not only smells fine, it's great for that rough skin on the back of your neck, too."

"And both of 'em's a far sight cheaper than those smell-goods they sell in the fancy bottles," added Bobby Lee.

All Artemas could think to say to that was, "You know, I believe that's my car you're on."

"Your car?" said Ray Don. "The man says this here is his car, Bobby Lee."

"No, Ray Don, the man said he *believed* it was his car."

"Well, mister, I *believe* I'm goin' to heaven, but that don't mean old Satan ain't stokin' up the fires of hell in anticipation of my company."

Artemas cocked his head to better understand the man. Ray Don's "fires of hell" sounded more like "fahr-ez uh-va hey-all."

"What proof has you got it's yours?" said the other one, Bobby Lee.

"Proof? Why that's preposterous." Then, thinking it wise to tread softly, Artemas said, "Perhaps you didn't know it was my car, but it is. Look, I have the key."

Ray Don laughed, slapped the Buick's hood. "No offense. We was just funnin', warn't we, Bobby Lee?" He punched his brother hard in the triceps with two extended knuckles. Bobby Lee scowled, kneaded the back of his arm.

What atrocious English, thought Artemas. And those incredible Appalachian accents? Lord, they're fortunate they have one another to talk to.

Ray Don slid off the hood with a *rsssp* as a rivet on his wallet pocket gouged a long furrow in the white paint of the Buick. "Whar the hell's the bottle?" he asked, rooting around the wheel well. He bounced back up with a half-empty fifth of bourbon, took a swig. "Here you go, Doc. Have a drink on us."

"No thanks," said Artemas, backing away. "I've had more than my quota." He looked around the lot, but the three of them were alone.

"Doc, where we come from," said Bobby Lee, slipping off the hood himself, "saying no to a drink what's offered in friendship is the worse kind of insult."

"Very well," Artemas whispered to the towering Vikings. "Very well." He took the capless bottle and stared at it, then leaned forward, hid his mouth, tucked his lips inward, pinched tight so their moist inner surfaces would stay free of the glass, and raised the bottle, up and down, quick. "Very good," he muttered and wiped his lips with his sleeve. He passed the bottle back. "I really must be getting home."

"Shit fire, take a man's swig," said Bobby Lee. "You some kinda pussy?"

There was the bottle again, and with both of them eyeing him, there was no alternative. Artemas took a gulp and felt the bottom-shelf booze sear his throat and stomach.

"There, warn't that good?" Ray Don took a nip, passed it back.

Bobby Lee set a weighty paw on Dr. Finch's shoulder. "Doc, now that we is drinkin' buddies, mayhaps you can help me out. I got this problem, see."

Aha. Here it comes, thought Artemas—hit the old man up for cash. Fine enough, it's worth twenty dollars to be done with them.

But apparently, money was not the problem. Bobby Lee groped his crotch, scratched the pavement with a boot heel. "Doc, whenever I take a pee, my pecker burns somethin' terrible. It's real swole up, too. There's some pills or a shot you could give me, huh? Fix my ol' pecker up?"

"Tell him about the green stuff," said Ray Don with a snort. "Better yet, give him a look at it."

"No, no, no," said Artemas, relieved that money wasn't the issue, enjoying the man's naïveté. "I'm an archaeologist, not that kind of doctor. You need to see an M.D., a medical doctor, a urologist."

"Ark . . . arkol . . ." It was too much for Bobby Lee.

"Specialist," said Ray Don. "This here ain't a pecker doc, he's a somethin' else doc, right?"

Artemas took a drink. "Thash it." The pavement shifted. "Forgive me, I've had too, too much." Everything blurred, slurred, blended together: the hulking Vikings, their strange speech, raucous laughter, and powerful odors, the bitter taste of the bourbon, his shiny new Buick. Eyes flickering, Dr. Finch dropped, lay sprawled across the nose of his own car like a shot deer.

Down, but not out, he raised his head, placed both hands on the hood, and pushed up. "Lord," he said, "I'm in no condition to drive. I can barely stand."

"Stand?" said Ray Don. "Hell, reason they's got seats in cars so's you don't have to stand—man can still see, he can drive. How far away you live?"

"Kailua, other side of the island."

"No big deal," said Bobby Lee. "You're three blocks from the Like-like and it's practically straight across."

Bobby Lee referred to the Likelike Highway, one of two direct routes across the central mountains to the other coast. He pronounced it as it appeared in English, "like-like," although from Bobby Lee it came out "lack-lack." Everyone else pronounced it the Hawaiian way, "leeky-leeky," but to the twins that was sissy foreigner talk. Ray Don and Bobby Lee believed in talking American.

Dr. Finch centered himself behind the wheel and turned the key.

Bobby Lee yelled, "Seat belt, Doc," as the car lurched forward, but the archaeologist ignored him. It was all he could do to get out of the lot.

Once on the road, Artemas felt better. Light traffic, cars passing without incident. Though halfway up the mountain a yellow Mustang convertible full of teenagers and a blue van, racing, passed him at nearly three times his cautious twenty-five miles an hour. The teenagers lay on the horn as they flew by and shouted obscenities. "Serve them right if they have an accident going that fast," Artemas said to the steering wheel.

He cleared the tunnel at the top and began the descent to the island's windward side. Ahead, to the right, yellow warning lanterns winked out of the night. He recalled that a stretch of concrete roadside barrier was being replaced. And right there. Trouble. An accident. Hazard lights flashing. Either the kids or that blue van.

He knew it—the van, practically sideways, nose to the center rail, back doors open, big boxes lying all over, blocking both lanes. Kids long gone.

At any other time he would have stopped, but not tonight, not in his condition. No time for guilt. Slowly, he pulled onto the shoulder to drive around the obstruction.

Bang! The car shook. Artemas punched the brake pedal. What the hell? He glanced at the rearview mirror and saw a black Dodge pickup, one of those big bulbous models like the one at the museum. Followed him onto the shoulder, ran right into him.

Your fault, not mine. So there.

Sit tight, he thought. Don't get out and stagger or it'll be handcuffs and a Breathalyzer for Artemas Finch. Maybe they'll check the bumpers and wave, "Sorry, no damage done."

In his mirror Artemas watched the truck reverse, back up, at least ten feet. The driver intended to flee! Well, go ahead, turn tail, suits me fine.

Then he heard the truck's engine scream and saw the headlights charge.

Wham! The pickup butted the car like a jackhammer on concrete, pitching it forward a full four feet. Dr. Finch's forehead bounced hard off the steering wheel and his world exploded in a flash of white light.

Amid cries of metal on metal and clouds of blue smoke, the black Dodge pickup battled inertia for the soul of the white Buick. Inevitably, the big truck won out. Dr. Finch's Buick crept, then raced forward to splinter the construction barrier and plummet down the mountain.

The blue van at the center rail sprang to life, darted to the side of the road. The driver, a tiny Filipino, ran to the punctured fence just as the murderous black Dodge skidded to a stop on the shoulder. Before the exhaust cleared, the two occupants of the truck stood shoulder to shoulder with the Filipino, transfixed, listening to the Buick swish and crackle through the dense tropical growth. Every now and then one still-lit headlight beamed back up at them.

One of the men from the truck ruffled the little one's thick black hair. "Way to go, Mongoose. Them boxes was a fine touch. Nowhere to drive but the shoulder." He turned to his companion. "An' you too, Ray Don. That first little tap stopped him right where you wanted, huh? Jest like settin' up a cue ball on break." He scratched his chin, considering. "Though I don't expect ol' Doc shifted into the park gear there or you wouldn't of given him the heave-ho so easy."

"Yeah. He must'a left it in D for 'down,' huh?" Ray Don guffawed, slapped his brother hard enough behind the head to make his teeth clack.

Bobby Lee waggled his jaw, rubbed his smarting scalp, but didn't say a word. His attention was somewhere far below. After a good fifteen seconds, he spit. "Hell, Ray Don, no fireball. I thought there was always a fireball at the bottom."

"You been lookin' at too much TV, Bobby Lee." Ray Don clapped his brother on the back and smiled. "Shit happens, little brother. And then, sometimes it don't."

3

Star threaded through sunbathers yapping and milling like breeding seals.

To his right, high, from the lifeguard tower by Kuhio Beach Park, a male voice shouted, "Hey, Star, where's my money?" Star kept his head down, veered to the left, toward a cluster of surfboards standing upright in the sand a hundred feet away. On the ocean side of the boards stood a hefty brown beach boy with a bulldog face. A hand-painted sign at his back posted prices for surfboard rentals and lessons.

"Hard of hearing?" said the stocky Hawaiian. "I could hear Crabs from here. Something about money?"

"Yeah, yeah, yeah. You know damn well what he wants, Koki," said Star. "His prize money."

"It's not Crabs, it's his *ipo,*" Koki said. "She's been bitching ever since he won the contest to take her to Kaua'i."

"The contest. Damn the contest. I wish I never heard of the contest."

"Okay, forget the contest. You free later? I got a couple of girls lined up."

"Girls? Like the hairdressers from Buffalo, the ones who tied you to their bed, painted red barber-pole stripes on your prick with nail polish, and shaved your pubies?"

"No. These are sweet girls, musicians from L.A. Five days in town and looking for a good time."

"Koki," said Star, "you know what a praying mantis is?"

"Big bug, huh?"

"After they mate, the female eats the male. Black widow spiders do the same thing."

"So, what's that supposed to mean?"

"Nothing, just a thought."

"You're nervous. That personal-ad scam's gone bad. Women put the fear in you."

"No, I just feel like watching TV with my boy tonight is all."

"Right. Wait—I know. It's our friend Mr. Smiley, isn't it? Mako."

"Mako. Jeez. You haven't seen him, have you?"

"Matter of fact, he left you a present." Koki pulled a box wrapped in newspaper from behind an ice chest.

Star took two steps back.

"Don't imagine it's a bomb. You've still got time before the loan's due, don't you?"

"Nowhere near enough." Star took the package and shook it. It rattled. "What do you think?"

"What I think is, you're not gonna find any money in there. Open it."

Star untied the twine, teased away the paper, and pried open the box's end flap. He reached in with two fingers and lifted out a Ken doll in red swimming trunks. Ken's legs were broken off at the hips.

"Jeez!" Star dropped the box in the sand. One of Ken's legs bounced out of the box onto Koki's foot.

"That Mako's a million laughs," said Koki. He picked up Ken's leg with his toes and flipped it to Star. "I don't suppose you've heard from Trots?"

Trots—so named for a parasitic digestive disorder he picked up on a surfing safari to West Africa—and Star had become collaborators in an ill-fated enterprise. Trots had declared an impromptu peeing contest. The contest had been so popular, he decided to expand it into a commercial event, and invited Star to buy in as a partner. It looked like easy money. Star borrowed two thousand dollars from Mako Ramires, a ready but risky source of cash, to underwrite their expenses.

The plan called for Star and Trots to clear eight hundred dollars each. More like a thousand apiece when they saw the crowd. Spectators packed the site of the peeing Olympiad at five dollars a head. Thirty-one contestants entered at fifty dollars each. Star and Trots provided fifty-cent beer, cheap food, music, a betting pool, and a wet T-shirt contest. The partners also sold out their three dozen Beefy-Ts silk-screened with the contest logo: a yellow rainbow arced over Waikiki.

With an assist from three quarts of beer, Crabs the lifeguard won, peeing an impressive seven feet four inches. He should have received the three-hundred-dollar prize.

Trots held the money. After Crabs had been declared winner, Trots told Star he "had to go." No one questioned Trots when he had to go. No one wanted to be anywhere in the vicinity of Trots when he had to go. The problem was, Trots didn't just go, he kept going, all the way to the Cook Islands on a freighter out of Honolulu Harbor the same night, with a stolen custom surfboard and every penny from the event. Star was left owing two thousand dollars plus interest to Mako Ramires, and three hundred more to Crabs the lifeguard.

"Trots. Jeez. Who'd have guessed? I'm thinking of selling blood, maybe my hair. You know, like in that Christmas story? Can you believe getting your legs broken over a peeing contest?"

"Means zip to Mako. The story on the beach is, he's got too many slow payers, wants to set an example with somebody everyone knows—show the deadbeats he means business."

"Jeez." Star scowled, ran his fingers through his long hair, flexed his right leg and then the left, both still intact.

"Ke hoa," said Koki, "you've still got time."

Star stared at his legs. "I guess." Then he looked up at Koki's grin and laughed. "Hell yes." They slapped palms. "Screw Mako," said Star. "Something'll come up. Today, I swim."

He stripped off his shirt, stepped from his Levi's, wearing trunks, left the clothes and pack with Koki, and ran to the surf. He took three steps into the surge, dove through a wave, and swam fast to sea past bobbing heads, surfers, and most of the beach noise, then flipped onto his back and enjoyed the play of clean, cool salt water over warm skin.

Seconds later, a familiar fear wormed its way into his tranquillity.

Thanks to the movie *Jaws,* every time he swam offshore, he'd catch a glimpse of that shark's-eye view of pale legs kicking, he'd hear *da-dump, da-dump, da-dump,* and spin around, scan the surface for fins, and look below for the Big One.

Now, as he did every day, he forced himself to swim—stroke, kick, breathe—to conquer the demon predator, drive it back into the cave of his subconscious. Only then did he begin swimming long laps parallel with the beach.

After three-quarters of a mile, Star floated on his back, put his feet together, porpoiselike, and flipped his toes to splash a fountain of water high in the air. He watched the sun glint off the falling droplets, sparkling jewels against a china blue sky.

"Here's to freedom," he said to the gulls overhead. "And to keeping the sharks away."

4

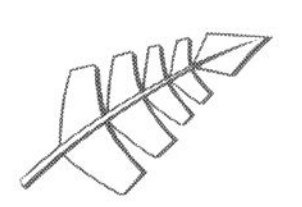

Mulling over escape and freedom, Star walked the three miles from Waikiki to the office of *Pacific Rainbow* magazine.

He dropped into a butter-soft Italian sofa, lay back, arms behind head, and crossed his ankles on the coffee table, messing the neat rows of magazines the receptionist had aligned minutes before. "Hey, beautiful," he called to the middle-aged Chinese woman filing in the next room. "Is the big man in a good mood?"

Before she could answer, "Star boy!" sounded up the hall. Star jerked his feet from the table and sat up straight.

A neckless bull, Dan Capistrano stood five-eight. Three years past sixty, he had a prominent, in-your-face Mediterranean nose, bulging black eyes, bushy salt-and-pepper eyebrows, gray fleece for hair, and a close-cropped white beard.

Dan grabbed Star by the shoulders, shook him like a dog with a stolen sock. "Get up, boy," he said. "Let me see you." Star didn't move fast enough, so Dan hauled him to his feet by the upper arms and gave him an Indian burn on the scalp with rocklike knuckles. "Well, how are the ladies treating you?" his New Yorker *r*s still soft, the syllables clipped, despite twenty-five years in Honolulu.

"We need to talk."

“That’s what we’re here for, boy. Go ahead, talk.”

Star nodded at the receptionist, hovering.

“Man to man, huh?”

Two employees materialized from an inner office, stood eight feet away, whispering, shooting one another dirty looks. Dan, publisher, arbiter of subordinate disputes, raised an eyebrow. “Star,” he said, “my office. Catch you in sixty.”

Star sat in the chair facing Dan’s massive English partners desk, imported, Dan had once explained in excruciating detail, from London in the nineteenth century by a Hawaiian sugar merchant. Twenty drawers on Star’s side pleaded, Open me. Star interlocked his fingers and looked away.

Stacks of magazines, books, and file folders jammed the room. Rolled maps filled a brass umbrella stand like calliope pipes. Centered on the desk, within a bare patch of polished mahogany surrounded by desk clutter, stood a gold-framed photo of Dan’s wife, Angela.

An elevator-size birdcage, a new addition, filled one corner. Inside, a scarlet macaw sat on a swing.

Star called to the bird, “*Wraack!* Polly want a cracker?”

The macaw preened, ignored him.

Star looked from the bird, across Dan’s desk to a chiseled coconut on the far side, its carved face a ringer for the big man. What the hell is that? He couldn’t read the brass baseplate from where he sat, so, eyes to the door, he leaned sideways across the five-foot-wide desktop, far enough to wrap his fingers around the crown of the coconut and lift it.

“BASTARD! THIEF!” screeched the macaw.

“Jeez!” Star stumbled, dropped the head, tipped a canister of pencils. He grabbed the coconut before it rolled off the desk, realized he had separated the head from its base, still on the other side. He wheeled toward the brass cage, jabbed a finger toward the macaw. “Stupid parrot, you broke the thing.” He stretched across the desktop for the second time, wiggled the head onto its spiked base, scooped up rolling pencils, straightened papers, and sat on his hands.

Glowering at the bird.

The macaw rocked on its swing, watched his every move, said nothing.

Star looked around the room. Lots of bird stuff, Dan's passion since he left the concrete jungle for Shangri-la: a mallard duck phone, a Tweety Bird figurine, antique ornithological prints on every wall, and photographs, either of birds, taken by Dan, or of famous people. Star recognized the governor, Jacques Cousteau, President Kennedy. He saw fat people in old clothes, decided they were opera singers, and a vaguely familiar man wearing a small cap—either the pope or a famous Israeli, he was sure. There's my favorite, he thought: Jack Lord looking down with a smug smile from the balcony of Iolani Palace, Five-O headquarters in the old TV series. Signed in a strong hand, the inscription read, "Book 'em, Dano. All the best, Jack."

Plenty of editorial awards. Over the years, Dan had turned the once sleepy local bimonthly into a force throughout the Pacific Rim. Star counted picture frames, ceiling tiles. He slumped, began to doze, then nearly fell from his chair at the booming "Okay, boy, I'm back."

"BASTARD! THIEF!" yelled the macaw.

"Jeez!" from Star.

"That must be you," said Dan. "He calls me Chicken Shit. Star, meet Ernest Hemingway. I bought him from a Hotel Street barkeep who retired to Las Vegas. I thought he'd keep Angela company, but Ernest has such a foul mouth, she threw him out of the house. So here we are. Actually, he's not a bad watch-bird. Anyone fools around in here, I hear about it."

Star squirmed, thought about the coconut head.

Dan lifted a framed bird print leaning against the wall. "New acquisition," he said. "Hawaiian *'o'o,* now extinct. This is a watercolor painted by William Ellis—not the missionary Ellis, but an assistant surgeon on Captain Cook's third voyage. Hell of a discovery, and I picked it up for a song. Absolutely priceless."

Dan dropped into a high-backed executive chair and scratched his beard. "Things haven't gone as expected, eh? I remember when you came in last month, 'Dan, I've got this great idea for an article. I'll run an ad in the personals section, say I'm married, see what kind of women respond, what they're up to.' I wasn't at all sure, but you smooth-talked old Dan into it, right? What went wrong, boy?"

"I did run the ad. And they did respond. Still are. But, jeez, they give me the creeps." Star faked a shiver. "Hey, women are great, even if there's no action. But I'm used to being the one in the driver's seat, see?"

His hands wiped an invisible slate. "Forget that. All they want now is to get down to business. And business is what's between my legs. I try to dig out a story, but their eyes drop to my crotch, they lick their lips and I get the willies."

"I'm enjoying this. The tables turned. There's the title for our article: 'The Tables Turned.' "

"Yeah, yeah." Star ran his fingers through his hair. "You know what else? I'm feeling sneaky."

"SNEAKY! THIEF!"

"Hey, you *are* sneaky."

"Maybe. But I'm not sleazy."

"No, not sleazy. Cheer up. These women are coming to you expecting to ball another woman's husband, right? Most of them are no doubt married themselves. You're not cheating on your wife,'cause there is no wife. I'm sure you're charming, and you're treating them to a fancy dinner, after all.

"By the way, how's little Miss Hot Pants, the Maidenform maven, doing? What's she think of this caper?"

"Cindy? Jeez. She doesn't know anything about it. She sees me wink at another woman, my ass is in hot water."

"ASS, BUTT, BUM!"

"Filthy bird!" Dan shook a finger at Ernest Hemingway.

Star made a face at the macaw.

Dan's finger moved to Star. "Watch what you say around him, please." He settled back in his chair. "I'll give you this, boy, you have a unique penchant for courting trouble. As to the article? You simply haven't found the hook. Find the hook and it'll fall into place. Remember when you first came to the magazine wanting to write about the 'thrill' of surfing? Had 'boring' written all over it, and you, with no experience. I told you to go back to the beach and dig up a real story, one with human interest. And you did. There was that shark scare on the windward side of the island. Shark bit a chunk out of a surfer's board. Kid's an average surfer, a nobody, but he kept surfing—on the same board, with the bite out of it. Until the next time, when the shark got a bigger piece of the board—and the boy's foot.

Then he surfed one-legged. He was still a crappy surfer—what would you expect from a man with one foot?—but now he was a somebody. That boy had heart. Our readers loved it.

"And how about the pineapple hormone piece? Who else would have noticed the disparity in breast size between girls on the island of Lana'i with the pineapple plantations and on Moloka'i, with none? You did it, boy. Won a Robert Louis Stevenson Award, didn't you?" Dan pointed to the plaque on the wall. "Let's not get a big head, though. You're still a crummy writer, truth be told."

"Guess that's what editors are for, huh, Dan?"

Dan had drifted off, stared at the gold-framed picture of his wife.

Star compared the publisher's features to the carved coconut head, mouthed an Uh-oh, and thought, Damn, I put the thing backward on the base. If he sees I've been rooting through his stuff, I'm dead meat.

"Where was I?" asked Dan. He cocked his head. "There's something else you haven't told me. I can see it in your face. You in trouble, son?"

"BASTARD! THIEF!"

Star shot the bird a dirty look, glanced at the broken, backward coconut head. "No, no. Well, sort of. Look. Dan." His voice dropped to a whisper, his eyes played over the wall. "I've, uh, been thinking of going away for a while."

"*What?* Where? How long?"

"Not sure. Months. I don't know." Until Mako forgets I exist. "I have friends in Darwin, Australia, who've set up a rafting trip in New Guinea. They got permits, funding, everything. . . ."

"So. Running away again? I thought after all that sailing around the Pacific with your uncle, you decided to put roots down here. What about the Townsends? Their house? Your home now for five years?"

"Maybe we could get someone else to stay there."

"Star, it's been almost two years since they've been here. Did it ever occur to you the Townsends don't need that house, with Anna's health so poor. That maybe they're keeping it for one reason: that it's become your home? Did you ever think of that?"

"Jeez. Not really."

"You have friends here, obligations, a future. Hold on. There's more, isn't there? Trouble. Someone after you? One of those beach people?"

Star studied his sneakers, thought, The old goat can read minds. "I do owe somebody money."

"Aha! How much?"

"I don't want to talk about it, okay?" Next he'll be asking about the peeing contest. Or "Why don't we talk to this Mako, explain your financial predicament? I'm sure he'll understand."

"Hey, boy, I told you I'm here if you need me. Tell you what, let's not get in the habit, but I'll have Mrs. Kaluau cut you a check for an advance. How's five hundred dollars sound? I already gave you three hundred for expenses, to entertain the women answering your ad. Any of that left?"

The expense money had gone for engine work on his car. Star had decided the women didn't need fancy dining—Papa's was adequate. An advance? Something for Mako? No, he thought, I can't take Dan's money for an article going nowhere.

But when he spoke, a "Yeah" came out, and, "the expense money was useful. And an advance would be great, thanks."

"But I want to see a manuscript come out of this, hear? Hey, there's more?"

"I wasn't gonna mention it, but I've been having this recurring dream. A nightmare."

"A nightmare. Sometimes it helps to discuss bad dreams in the rational light of day. De-emotionalizes them. Care to tell me about it?"

"Not a word to the women around here?"

"Confessor's confidentiality." Dan glanced down at the coconut head and frowned. It's chiseled, backward eyes stared straight at Star.

Star considered a dash for the door.

Dan gripped the head with a thumb and two fingers and spun it around. "Damned thing's loose," he said. "Got to put some glue on it sometime."

Jeez. Star took a relieved breath, shot the bird another dirty look.

"All right." Star raised an eyebrow. "This is serious, okay? The dream starts with me in Papa's. This black cat, big as a rottweiler, rubs against my legs. It looks up at me with yellow eyes the size of moons, blinks, jumps onto my lap. It's got thick fur and I'm stroking it. I feel good, it feels good. It's purring, extending its claws in and out, in and out. Now the claws bite into my legs. I try to lift it off, but it digs in. Its claws hook my *balls*." He checked to see if Dan was laughing.

Dan's chin rested on his fist. No expression. He raised a thick finger, curled the air for more.

"Man, my balls hurt—in the dream, see?"

Dan nodded.

"I panic, run to the beach, try to reach the surf, but the cat's hanging on like some kind of torture truss. I dive in, screaming. Then I swim into deep water and the cat drops off. The pain's gone. I'm underwater, holding my breath. It gets darker and darker. I'm swimming down, deeper, but instead of getting cooler, its hotter. I see predators off the edge of my vision. Scary things I can't make out, squirming and wriggling like parasites. I know they're there, but I keep swimming, looking for something.

"Then I see it. It's a monstrous giant clam. Wide open. You know, a *Tridacna gigas*, from the South Pacific. I've seen the real McCoys in the Coral Sea—whoppers, but tame old guys. This one is something else, pink inside with big blue eyes rimming the edges. And all of the eyes are waving, watching me. Deep in the center is a huge red pearl, big as your fist. The predators are closing in, but I have to have that pearl. I get closer to the clam. It's much bigger than I thought, really humongous. But I don't stop. I swim down into it, into the warm wet flesh, reaching for the pearl. The jaws of the shell clamp shut. *Whop!*" Star clapped, then crisscrossed hands and arms over his face. "I'm trapped inside, it's dark, suffocating." He writhed in his chair.

"Then I wake up, heart pounding, sweating."

"Boy, I can't imagine what any of that means." Dan finally laughed.

"Sure." Star picked up an imaginary telephone: "Hello, Dr. Freud?" His smile vanished. "But it scares the hell out of me at night."

"Star, you want to back off from this article? It's not that big of a deal. I could find something more tame. We've got a feature on ikebana flower arranging coming up. Another one on Korean kimchi sniffing . . ."

“No, I started this and I’ll finish it. Maybe it’s a guilty conscience. All those ladies over the years, haunting me.”

“You’ll be all right, son.” Dan walked around the desk, lifted him from his chair in a bear hug, and led him to the hall. “You’ll do fine. But forget this running-away crap, okay? I can’t stand a quitter.”

Star walked down the corridor, didn’t look back. But before he reached the reception desk, he heard Ernest Hemingway shout a good-bye from Dan’s office: “BASTARD! THIEF! QUITTER!”

5

At least once a block on the way back to Waikiki, Star muttered, "Quitter," and kicked a palm trunk, swatted a flower along the sidewalk, or stomped a soft-drink can in the gutter.

He stopped for a carryout pizza, and followed the Ala Wai Canal, paralleling Waikiki Beach, to his car, a salt-stained, seven-year-old, slightly rusty green Geo Metro nicknamed the Turtle. For twenty a month, slipped in cash to Scooter, the boyish female manager of a small, aging apartment complex, the Turtle had its own unofficial parking space behind the sun-bleached buildings, between a Dumpster and a Cyclone fence, shielded from the sun by a tall mango tree.

Star shrugged his shoulders, decided the quitter decision could wait until the next day. He waved to Scooter unbolting the frame of her go-cart, picked up a few ripe mangoes, and dropped them in his bag. The fruit was free.

He rolled down the windows to let the warm air blow the worry from his mind, and drove up the mountainside to his house, a one-story pink cottage with a red-tiled roof, a fenced-in yard, and a partial view of the ocean. He left his car in the drive, blew through the front door, tossed the pizza box on the seat of an armchair, flopped onto the couch, and waited. Nothing. Waited some more. Nothing. Finally he yelled, "Hey boy, I'm home."

Thump! in the bedroom. Sleeping on Star's bed again. Star smiled at the sound of him running down the back hall, around the corner, not quite making it, bouncing off the far wall by the kitchen.

Down the home stretch, Mr. Lucky leapt in the air onto Star's chest. Squealing, out of control, twisting and spinning in a blur of white and black fur, the wiry border collie licked Star's face and neck, knocked him to the floor.

They wrestled, tipped over the coffee table, finally came to rest with Star on his back, Mr. Lucky quivering on his chest.

"Hey, Mr. Lucky, how's my boy?" Star righted the table and dabbed a paper napkin at a wet yellow stain on the corner of the couch. "Bad dog. Look what you did again." Mr. Lucky's ears flattened. "Sorry's not good enough. I'll try that bleach I got, but if you keep this up, the Townsends are gonna throw us out, hear?"

Star recalled what Dan had said about Mrs. Townsend's health. The elderly doctor and his wife lived in Omaha, had purchased the house as a getaway. Dan had arranged for Star to house-sit five years ago. Five years I've lived here, Star thought. Five years. Man, time flies fast.

Woof! Mr. Lucky, a Frisbee in his mouth, brought Star back to the present. He wrestled the disk from Mr. Lucky's jaws and pitched it in a high ricochet off the dining-room wall.

Ten minutes later, he and Mr. Lucky settled in with the pizza before the TV. Star's mind wandered to Australia and New Guinea. He blinked and realized he was watching a religious show, the kind with hallelujahs, crocodile tears, and flashing send-cash-now numbers. He waved bye-bye to the screen and lifted the remote to zap the set, then set it down again when the camera shifted to the perky, ponytailed teenagers sitting at the feet of a gold-ringed, white-haired televangelist reading Bible stories from a gilt throne. The preacher, Star decided, was a near double for the colonel of chicken fame. At the bottom of the screen a phone number alternated with "Please help the Reverend Jaycie Pitts continue the Lord's work."

"My little Cheerleaders for Jesus," the Reverend crooned, patting the girls' impressionable young heads. Dressed in saddle shoes, ankle socks, virginal white skirts, and cotton sweaters with JESUS printed in big blue letters across the back, the cheerleaders stared up at their spiritual mentor with wide-eyed rapture.

The TV show moved from Bible stories to "Delilahs of the Beach" as three bikini-clad, face-shadowed, voice-altered sinners aired soul-stirring confessions. The Reverend followed with a prayer for forgiveness and shifted into a tirade about parsimony. Without the Cheerleaders for Jesus or the Delilahs of the Beach to hold his attention, Star dozed off.

Sometime in the wee hours, Star's girlfriend, Cindy, showed up, tipsy, but free of her normal late-night alcohol-inspired temper. In fact, Cindy appeared more than a little friendly. She gave Mr. Lucky a perfunctory pat on the head, Star a kiss on the forehead and a tickle under the chin with long polished nails, then stood between the boys and the TV, kicked off her heels, slipped off her blouse, dropped her short skirt to the floor, and began a slow dance in a black lace bra and panties. Cindy had a dancer's body and knew all the moves.

She held a franchise for Teddies of Times Square lingerie. Cindy and the other Teddies Girls modeled their wares at private parties and lingerie shows at Honolulu's popular Stan's Mr. Meat, All You Can Eat. Evidently, Cindy had had a show tonight, because her crotchless panties were still stuffed with a pelt of white Angora rabbit fur, a nod to modesty and the Teddies slogan, "Naughty but Nice."

With her long muscular back to Star, Cindy peeled off her Teddies Reach for the Sky Underwire Superlifter and stretched. Weaving ever so slightly, she headed for the bedroom, flopped on her back at the center of Star's bed, and spread her legs. Long, dark red hair streamed over the pillow, while lower, a tiny tuft of red curls peeked from the side of her Angora crotch pelt as Cindy cocked her knees and wagged them, slowly, in and out.

In case Star missed the body language, she gave him a lascivious wink. Cindy didn't wink well sober—the open eye always squinted—and now, with impaired motor control, both eyes closed entirely.

But Star got the message. He winked back. "Don't go anywhere," he said, "gonna brush my teeth," and backed into the bathroom.

Thirty seconds later he returned, minty-mouthed.

Cindy hadn't gone anywhere, but she had passed out.

Staring at her snoring softly, knees fallen to one side, he faced a crisis of conscience. Should he tuck her in? She certainly looked restful. Or attempt amour? How would she react if he awakened her? With affection? Passion? Would she turn on him? Or throw up, as she had the week before?

Best to let sleeping dogs lie, he concluded, with no reference to Mr. Lucky, still asleep on the couch. So he turned off the TV and lights, covered Cindy with a sheet, and lay down on the bed himself, facing the wall, aroused one minute, angry the next.

6

"Friggin' volcano lovers!" D. L. McWhorter swiped the fatigue cap against his thigh.

Barely five-eight, 160 pounds, the HydraCorp chief of security and contingency operations wore a neatly trimmed, blunt mustache, his hair in a flattop. His lean sinewy body suggested a man in his thirties, but the deep lines etched in his face and the gray hair said at least twenty years older.

D. L. sighed, ran a forearm across his brow—less from the heat than to wipe away residue of the civilization he had left behind in Honolulu two hours before—then coughed and spit out a mouthful of the gritty ocher construction dust powdering the leaves and everything else in sight like cayenne pepper.

He replaced the hat, removed his metal-rimmed sunglasses, looped one of the ear pieces into the button hole of his fatigues, and squinted into the distance toward the summit of Mauna Loa volcano, tracing the path of the double-track dirt trail as it ran up the green ridge into the shade, then back the other way, down to the dozers and trucks lying idle, impotent. Beyond the equipment, the track became a forty-foot-wide cleared and graded roadbed, a blood-red swath cut from the heart of the forest, snaking toward the sea. Three thousand feet lower and seven miles away, blue ocean dazzled in the noonday sun. Again he looked upslope. Somewhere up that path, in the violet shadows, lurked the source of his trouble.

"Volcano lovers," he muttered. "Has to be."

He looked downhill and frowned at the big man puffing toward him. "When was the shooting, Frank?"

"Eight-thirty this morning," answered the panting construction boss, Frank Stevens, a burly ex-longshoreman. Frank stopped several paces away. He had heard stories about the unpredictable gray-haired man who might poke you in the ribs, joking, one minute, and rip out your heart the next. He stared at the holstered gun, a military .45 automatic, carried, no doubt, without a permit.

On thin ice, Frank swallowed. "I was below, in conference with the Mitsubishi people when it happened, sir," he said. "I called you in Honolulu the second I heard about it."

"Okay. Fill me in."

"The last few weeks we've had an awful lot of flat tires, two of the earthmovers sabotaged—you know about that. Another one turned up busted yesterday, hydraulic lines cut, 'Sons of Pele' scratched in the dirt."

"Volcano lovers. I knew it."

"Right. Then this morning they shot Jed. In the leg. He was driving an open Jeep a mile up the track. He made it back to base, blood all over, white as a sheet. Hospital confirmed he'd been shot. Small caliber, twenty-two they think."

D. L. nodded. "And . . . ?"

"Police think it was kids or hunters, an accident."

"Police?" D. L.'s face reddened. "Security's my job, Frank. The fewer people see you're building this friggin' highway instead of a dinky access road, the better."

"Sorry, Mr. McWhorter"—Frank stepped back—"but hospitals report gunshot wounds. It was unavoidable."

"Cops think it's an accident," said D. L., "that's fine with me. Fact is, I can't imagine kids way up here, and if the shooter was a hunter you would have seen his vehicle. No one walks anymore. A hunter sure as hell wouldn't have been using a twenty-two, and you would've heard other shots. With a lame explanation like that, I think the boys in blue don't want to get off their duffs, come way the hell up this mountain to beat the bush."

"Then Willy got caught in the bear trap."

"Holy shit, a bear trap! When did *that* happen?"

"Probably while you were on your way to the Honolulu airport."

"What did the police say about *that?*"

"Don't know about it. We told the hospital it was a dozer accident—I'm not sure they believed us, but what could they say? Paco and him was surveying a mile and a half ahead. Willy had to take a dump and walked off the track along a trail. I guess he was squatting, scoonchin' around . . . set it off anyways, and it got him. He was lucky Paco was there, 'cause Paco heard him scream and Paco's a big man. He carried Willy out over his shoulder with the bear trap clamped on his butt. It took two men with pry bars to get the bastard off."

He saw McWhorter wince. "Yeah"—Frank nodded—"I'm afraid old Willy won't be doin' no sitting for a long time to come."

"Stinkin' volcano lovers!"

"Maybe."

D. L. shot him a glare. "What do you mean, 'maybe'?"

Frank shifted his stance, edged away. "Well . . . we've got this good ol' boy on the crew who's been telling the men there's bears here. Grizzly bears. He's from some town called Eek—no shit—Alaska. Says he knows all about bears. After he saw the trap, he found tracks. Way up here in the boonies, who knows? He claims it's a federal plot, one of those endangered species restoration things, like stocking Yellowstone with wolves. He's got stories about bears in Alaska running men down, tearing their heads off. Awful stories. Says there's so many wild pigs up here for food, the bear population's gotten out of control and the feds are afraid they'll head for the coast, dine on tourists—that's why the traps.

"Don't look at me like that, Mr. McWhorter." Frank took another step back. "Fact is, the crew is really spooked. I saw the tracks myself. Big mothers. Anyway, it's not just the bears. They've found five bullet holes in other vehicles now that they've started looking. Between the shooting and the bears, everything's on hold, which is a bitch, because Mitsubishi's ready with the wind generators and we're ready to start the spur into the valley soon as we get the okay."

"Bears. What a crock. Listen, you get Paco and a Jeep. Drive me up there. I want to see where your man walked off the road."

"You think that's safe?"

"Afraid the grizzlies'll get us, Frank? Hows about a police investigation? Maybe we invite Channel Seven up? Phone the Honolulu Zoo? You know, right now you're paying your men for sitting on their asses doing nothing. Think of your speedy completion bonus."

D. L. thought of his own dream going up in smoke. One month after initiation of construction on the second phase of the project—if they kept to schedule—he was to receive a very large cash payment, large enough to set in motion the plan he'd been dreaming about for years.

"No sons of bitches are going to screw around with *me*. You get that Jeep, find Paco, and bring me a sharp machete and a canteen. Pronto, mister."

"Yes sir."

The three men drove up the dirt track, big Frank nervous, eyes darting, bigger Paco hunched down in the seat trying to look small, sweating like a cold beer in the sun, and D. L. McWhorter sitting straight, craning his neck and scanning the forest, eager for action.

"Right there. That's where Willy went into the woods," said Paco, pointing to the next bend and a tall *'ohia* tree.

"All right, go by, don't look over, don't slow down. Drive half a mile past, drop me off, go back to camp, and wait."

"Crazy bastard's gonna get shot," said Paco as soon as they were out of earshot. Then added, "No way I'd face a grizzly with a pistol either, even with a forty-five. No way."

D. L. slipped into the forest, a stalking cat in slow motion. He moved parallel to the small path, recalling the time he tracked a man into the Everglades who'd run off with an air-dropped special delivery for a previous employer.

Thirty feet back he saw trampled vegetation, blood on the ground. Two quarters and a nickel lay on the leaves. D. L. cocked his eyebrow at the roll of toilet paper unraveled across the narrow path and ran a hand over his own, intact, posterior. Poor Willy. He took a deep breath and moved on.

Seventy-five feet ahead, he saw a wire, thin as a spiderweb, six inches off the ground, taut across the path, one end tied to the base of a tree. He followed it the other way to a large tree fern. Under a layer of dead fronds camouflaging a sheet of polyethylene lay a shotgun, staked into position and pointed at the trail, the wire tied to the trigger. He released it and thought, Son of a bitch, this feels good. Early this morning I was sitting in a damned *meeting*. In a *corporate office*. Un-frigging-believable.

Ten feet ahead, the forest opened along the sunny edge of a small escarpment, and D. L. saw what he had expected: a well-tended marijuana plant. And then another, and another, interspersed with mountain vegetation. The plants had healthy buds, no more than a week from harvesting. He stopped counting at twenty bushes. At a street value of from twelve hundred to two thousand dollars a plant, someone had a serious investment along the ridge, well worth delaying the road crew until the crop could be gotten in.

He stroked the .45 at his hip. The friggin' volcano-lovin' pot farmer was here this morning when he shot our man. Where is he now?

In the next hundred yards he found another bear trap and a pitfall with the necks of broken beer bottles poked in the ground at the bottom, jagged edges up.

Not far past the fourth clearing, he heard voices. He stepped over trip wires attached to a tin-can alarm and edged toward two men sitting on the trunk of a fallen tree.

Behind them, marijuana plants, sun-kissed Hawaiian *paka lolo* with gnarly buds like alien seedpods, hung upside down, suspended from a pole lashed between two tree trunks. Dried pot lay in small piles on plastic sheets. To one side, camouflaged from air surveillance, sat two small tents with sleeping bags and a clutter of empty food tins, jerri cans of water, and cases of beer.

He sat on his heels, Asian-style, and studied them. Part Hawaiian, he decided, part something else. Smelly. One was muscular and shirtless, huge, with a big hard belly that shone in the sun, barefoot, with clown's feet, toes splayed out from years of going without shoes—so much for Frank's bear tracks.

The man rocked on the log, sucking on a huge joint. D. L. smiled, thought, Why not?—one of the perks of the farming life.

The other one, skinny and quick, D. L. judged, wore a dirty red T-shirt, canvas shorts, and shower clogs. His Adam's apple bobbed in time with a stringy goatee as he drained the last of a warm beer.

". . . when we went to that Grateful Dead concert? Was Philadelphia in eighty-seven."

"No, New Jersey, eighty-nine, when that kid got beat to death. Was a cold mother, I remember that . . ."

D. L. took careful note of the big one's holstered revolver, a .38, and a twelve-gauge pump shotgun lying against the log at the small man's side. A .22 rifle leaned against one of the tents. D. L. unholstered his .45, wrapped his fingers firmly around the handle of the machete hanging in the scabbard at his waist, and stepped into the sun.

He rang the tip of his gun hard against the blade of the machete, said, "Smokin' and drinkin's bad for your health, boys."

The little one's head bounced. Without turning, he grabbed for the pump shotgun, arm a blur. Before his fingers touched the stock, D. L. slammed the flat blade of the machete hard across his head, slicing off an ear. The man screamed, tumbled to the ground, gripping his head.

The big one fumbled for his revolver, sluggish, dulled by the pot.

"Don't even think about it," D. L. said.

Adrenaline and reefer wrestled for control of the big man's brain. He stared at McWhorter, then at his friend, writhing, wailing in the dirt six feet away, his hands and face awash in blood, the dust stained red.

"Hey!" D. L. motioned the big man to stay on the log, looked at the injured man. "Criminy," he said, "what a crybaby. Better your ear than your dick." He retrieved the shotgun. "Now you. Hand me that thirty-eight."

The man passed the gun, handle first. His eyes scanned the clearing. Where were the others? How had this man gotten to their camp? No helicopters, no dogs, no warning. "You DEA or state?" he asked.

D. L. ignored him, turned instead to the man on the ground. "Cut out that caterwauling," he shouted. "Can hardly hear myself think. I want to talk to your friend here."

The wounded man howled even louder.

"Whatsa matter, can't hear me, boy? Cat got your ear?" With no warning, D. L. shot him three times. The small man's body jumped with the impact of the bullets.

"Ah, ain't silence golden?" D. L. said, turning to the large man, now blinking, trembling. "Listen up. I'm not gonna fart around—you sabotaged our equipment, shot one of my men."

"Wasn't us," said the man. "Not the equipment, anyway." He watched D. L. raise his gun, and spoke fast. "I didn't mean to shoot him. Was just trying to flatten his tires, scare him. Wanted them to stay down the hill."

"Who sabotaged the equipment, then? Was it volcano lovers? Friends of yours? Was volcano lovers, wasn't it?"

The man looked down at his dead friend and flushed with anger. "Fuck you, old man."

"Old?" D. L. raised the gun, pointed it, but it didn't fire. "Damn," he said. "It must be jammed."

The big man stared at him.

"I *said,* it must be *jammed.*" D. L. hammered at the barrel with the butt of his hand.

The grower jumped up and ran, crashed through the brush like a derailed train.

D. L. let the man get forty feet away before taking up the chase. "See what smokin' and drink'll do to you?" he shouted. "Bet you wish you'd stayed with Weight Watchers and shed some of that lard, huh?"

The bare-chested man bulled through the mountain vegetation, slammed into trees in a blind rush to escape. D. L. stayed thirty to forty feet behind. "Run faster, you bastard," he yelled, "I could use some exercise myself."

Sixty yards from the men's camp, thirty feet behind the runner, D. L. shouted, "Did I say jammed?" He laughed. *Kbang!* Fired over the man's head.

Five seconds later, he said, "Hell. This ain't no hunt, it's a barrel shoot," and fired three shots. The first and the third hit the man in the back. He crashed to the ground, writhed in the bushes, then fell still.

D. L. poked at the man's bare shoulder with the toe of his boot.

"I guess two out of three ain't bad with a forty-five on the run," he said to himself. "But hell, with a target like that, how could you miss?"

D. L. was whistling when he walked into the construction compound. He tossed the .22 rifle at Frank's feet.

"What happened, Mr. McWhorter? We heard shots."

"Grizzly tried to rip my head off, Frank." He winked. "Naw, was just a coupla kids growing pot. Juveniles. Police weren't far off. Better we keep this business out of the courts—they wouldn't do nothing with them, anyway. I took their rifle, slapped them around. Fired over their heads—scared the hell out of them. I guarantee they won't be back." He smiled.

"Frank, in the future, if your men need to take a leak at the side of the road, fine, but if they have to drop their pants and want privacy, tell them to hold it till they get back to the Port-o-lets. Keep them out of the woods. That's where those grizzlies hang out, right?"

"Yes sir."

"Now get me a shovel, a can of gasoline, and a Jeep. I found more of those traps. I'll bury the suckers, then burn the pot. While I'm doing that, you get the men moving. Savvy?"

"Right, Mr. McWhorter."

D. L. disposed of the growers, doused their camp and harvested pot with gasoline and set it afire, dismantled the traps, and uprooted the growing hemp.

On the drive to the Hilo airport, he listened to a cassette of Beethoven's Fifth Symphony and thought about the cold beer awaiting him aboard the company plane.

At the construction camp, gearing up to full activity, there was plenty of talk of traps and grizzly bears, of the small brave man with the gun at his side, and the kids who got the hell scared out them.

But of the blood he'd seen smeared on the scabbard of D. L. McWhorter's machete, Frank Stevens said not a word.

7

Bonnie and Dale Perkins from Pigeon Forge, Tennessee, had honeymooned in Hawai'i the previous year. Now they were back, celebrating their first anniversary. Freckle-faced Bonnie in the Dutch-boy haircut was telling Heather and Tommy McDougal and the others waiting for the luau bus what fun they were in for. "We went to a luau *three times* our last trip," she said. "It's something else! They take you to this beach way out in the boonies away from the hotels. Lots and lots of friendly people, just like us. There's fire eaters and hula dancers and warriors blowing on shells and climbing palm trees and a Hawaiian wades out in the water and throws a net for fish like they used to do, and if he catches one he bites its head off with his teeth, and there's all you can eat Hawaiian cooked pig with its head and tail still on it, and French fries and lots of other stuff—"

Husband Dale interrupted. "And all you can *drink* too." That got the guys' attention. "Stainless tanks, bigger than full kegs, of margaritas, mai tais, sangria, and daiquiris. Man, I got so plastered. What a blast."

"But like they tell you on the bus," clucked Bonnie, wagging her finger at husband Dale, "don't drink so much you puke all over your neighbors on the ride home. Right, honey?"

Excitement rippled through the four waiting couples when a shiny maroon bus rolled to a halt amid screeching brakes and a puff of diesel fumes. On its side, reminiscent of the velvet pirate-ship painting hanging over the mantel of Bonnie and Dale's new Pigeon Forge home, a colorful airbrushed island sunset surrounded the orange and purple Sundowners Luaus logo. Sundowners had fourteen buses in service that night. Added to the twenty-one buses representing Sundowners' competitors, that made for over fourteen hundred tourists eager to experience the folkways of old Hawai'i.

The doors opened with a hiss, and the Perkinses, the McDougals, and two other couples in their early twenties climbed aboard. It was a full house, all couples except for a single man on the bench seat at the back of the bus.

A slight Filipino around thirty, no more than five and a half feet tall, with a round, childlike face, clapped his hands at the front of the bus. "I am Pan-dak," he announced, a little too loudly, into a small microphone. Pandak had a heavy accent and a gracious, although somewhat nervous, smile. He wore glossy white platform shoes with gold buckles and a bright yellow aloha shirt hanging almost to his knees, over chartreuse trousers. "Welcome to Sundowners Luaus. I am your tour guide. We got special plans for you tonight, folks. We having whole lot of fun, you see." Then he sat down on a single seat next to the driver and the bus set out for a night of adventure.

"Don't you want our vouchers?" Bonnie chirped to the guide.

"Yesss, of course," said Pandak, and collected them. The bus weaved through traffic.

"Aren't you going to ask how many of the couples here are newlyweds?" asked Bonnie. She knew the routine from last year and was eager for the fun to begin.

Pandak stood. "How many newlyweds?" Everyone shielded their ears from a punishing whine—feedback from the mike—but when it subsided, twenty-eight honeymooners raised their hands. That was everyone, except for three unmarried couples traveling in sin, the single man at the back, four old folks, and Bonnie and Dale from Pigeon Forge.

"We're here on our first anniversary," Bonnie explained to the people across the aisle. "Well?" she called to Pandak. "Don't you want everyone to introduce themselves?" Bonnie was beginning to think they'd gotten a dud luau guide. Last year the guides had been perky young females who had everyone in the mood to party long before they arrived at the beach.

"I'm sorry," said Pandak, forgetting the microphone this time. "This all new for me. Why don't you introduce yourselves?" But Pandak didn't seem too sure how they should go about it.

Born to lead, there was no way Bonnie was going to simply sit there and watch poor Pandak let the evening fizzle, so she stood and walked to the front. "Do you mind if I show them how to do it?" she asked. Pandak shrugged his shoulders and handed her the mike.

Bonnie grabbed the pole next to the door for support. "Hi, y'all! I'm Bonnie from Pigeon Forge, Tennessee. That's my husband, Dale." She waved to Dale. "I was a drum majorette and senior class president at Andrew Jackson High. At college, University of Tennessee—just graduated—I was a cheerleader for the Volunteers, as well as captain of the Rhythmettes women's drill team. Last summer I was a greeter at Dollywood. And after this trip? I'm gonna be a junior account executive with the second largest advertising agency in Knoxville!

"So there, neighbors, y'all know about me. Now, who are y'all? From the front at my right, and around the bus, either the boy or the girl tell us your first names and where you hail from. Speak up, folks, we're all friends and neighbors tonight!"

The first couples shifted in their seats, coughed, barely got their names out, "Jeanine and George from Sioux Falls," "Patata and Jesus from Los Angeles," "Darla and Frankie from Atlantic City . . . ," but with Bonnie's encouragement, the rest of them were soon outshouting one another.

"Friends," said Bonnie, "y'all know that in Hawai'i 'aloha' means both hello and good-bye. We'll save our good-byes for later"—she waved bye-bye with her hand—"but right now, let's give our neighbors a rousing a-lo-ha hello. C'mon, A-LO-HA! Let's hear it."

"A-lo-ha," said the bus, "A-lo-HA, A-LO-HA!"

As it picked up speed out of the city, the bus began to rock and sway, inspiring Bonnie to sing. "Row, row, row your boat . . ." A few voices, female, chimed in, and by the last chorus, all but the most macho of the men were getting with the program. Bonnie followed with "John Jacob Jingleheimer Schmidt," "The Bear Went Over the Mountain," and "Michael Row Your Boat Ashore," then asked if any of the friends and neighbors had special favorites.

The single man at the back, a strapping fellow, lit up. " 'Ninety-nine Bottles of Beer on the Wall,' " he yelled, and began, "Ninety-nine bottles of beer on the wall, ninety-nine bottles of beer, if one of those . . . "

Bonnie admired his robust baritone. The husbands could get into music like that. And did. Ten or twelve rousing choruses shook the bus, although by eighty-one bottles of beer on the wall, enthusiasm, even among the men, had waned. The single man, however, kept it up, with spirit.

"I think that's enough," said Bonnie.

But the man kept singing. He obviously knew the words and the melody and seemed challenged by the subtraction, and damned if he was going to stop. It might be the only fun he'd have that night, everyone else being with someone.

"ENOUGH! ENOUGH! ENOUGH!" Bonnie shouted into the mike. The feedback was awesome.

The man stopped. At seventy-nine bottles. He glowered, making it clear he didn't want Bonnie for a friend or neighbor anymore.

But Bonnie got right back into the aloha spirit, initiating a round of guessing games that kept everyone jumping until the bus rolled to a halt at their destination.

Pandak stood. "Everybody up," he called.

Bonnie looked out the window. Darkness. No flaming torches, no milling tourists, no troughs of food or tanks of booze. "What?" she said. "Where are we? All I see is sugarcane." She looked again at Pandak, and gasped. His face was horribly pinched together. Suddenly he had a nightmare case of acne.

Pulled tightly over Pandak's head was the leg of a pair of red paisley panty hose, one foot flopping down his back like a scarlet ponytail, the other dangling to the floor, brushing the toes of his white patent leather shoes.

"I mean, everybody's *hands* up!" Pandak yelled, louder, his voice muffled by the panty hose. Now he was waving a .45 automatic pistol in the air.

"My God," said Bonnie, echoed by many of the friends and neighbors. The driver, bigger than two Pandaks, was standing also, a .45 automatic tucked in his belt, a pair of black fishnet panty hose compressing his face into a thousand tiny diamonds. Panty legs clung to his shoulders like withered vines.

The man at the back of the bus, the singer, stood next, pink lace panty hose on his head, the legs tied under his chin in a bow, like a cartoon *bandido* with a toothache. The handle of a gun peeked over the waistband of his jeans. He was every bit as large as the driver. In fact, their size and clothing down to their Tony Lamas—except for the color of the panty hose—were identical. "See this here bag?" he said, holding a flowery pillowcase high. "I want yore pocket change, wallets, purses, watches, jewelry, rings—"

"Not my rings!" a chorus of women wailed in unison.

"Bet yore asses. Get 'em off," said the man at the back, "afore I bite 'em off." He bared his lips and clacked his teeth together ominously. Sensing reluctance, he nodded to little Pandak, who fired two rounds through the roof of the bus, knocking himself to the floor with the recoil. The sound was deafening.

The big man, reeking of—what was that smell, pine trees?—worked his way forward, holding the bag open for the requested valuables. Now and then he would spy an empty ring finger with a telltale reddish impression and tap his gun against the bare hand until the overlooked donation materialized.

When he got to Bonnie, he stopped. "Sorry?" he asked. Bonnie dropped her rings in the bag, but refused to look at him. She clenched her teeth, stuck her lip out, and stared at the seat back in front of her. The man balled a fist and rotated it a foot from her face. "Sorry?" he asked again. Silence.

Boff! He rapped his burly knuckles into Bonnie's freckled nose. Blood gushed from her nostrils and then onto her husband and neighbors as she shook her head, a screaming blur. A former glee club member, Bonnie had an exceptional set of lungs.

"Enough," said the man. "Remember *that,* Missy? ENOUGH! ENOUGH! ENOUGH!"

Bonnie's terrified husband pulled a McDonald's napkin from the pocket of his cutoffs and pressed it tightly to Bonnie's upper lip to stanch the bleeding and her wailing. From under the scarlet wad, Bonnie blubbered the word "Monster," then fell silent, closed her eyes, and rolled her head back against the seat. Satisfied, the big man worked his way through the rest of the bus.

"*Gracias* and thank you so much," said Pandak. "Now, everybody out, plees."

The driver opened the doors and the passengers scrambled into the night, encouraged by shouts of "A-LO-HA!" from the big man with the pink panty hose. With a swish the doors closed, and the Sundowners bus drove into the night, trailing a familiar chorus, "Seventy-eight bottles of beer on the wall, seventy-eight . . ."

"Hot damn." Ray Don upshifted. "What a haul. Mongoose, you fooled 'em good. And Bobby Lee?" Bobby Lee stopped singing, awaiting his compliment. "You scared the bejeezus out of 'em, brother. Yessir, you done good. Except for these damn colored stocking things. Think you was shopping for some hoor, boy?"

Bobby Lee grinned and broke into song, "Seventy-five . . . ," then fell silent. "Shit fire, boys," he said, "I lost count." He scratched his chin and nibbled his lip, then threw his head back and belted out another line, "Ninety-nine bottles of beer on the wall, ninety-nine . . ."

8

Bernie Bergen spoke into the white tile over the urinal while he shook off Little Bernie below. "Two years you've planned. You're in hock up to your eyeballs. But you *will* pull it off. In ten minutes, the dog and pony show begins, and in thirty, the HydraCorp board will be in love."

He zipped himself up. "Damn. Stuck zipper." He really jerked at the tab, "C'mon, you bugger," only to feel it rip from the treads entirely. "Son of a bitch." He scowled at the two strips of brass teeth, unconnected, and at his watch. "Nine minutes till showtime. Keep a cool head, Bernie." He chewed furiously on his Nicorette gum. "God, I could use a cigar."

Without a moment's thought, he spit the gum into his palm, rolled it into a long, thin snake, pressed it into the zipper treads, and melded them, one side to the other. He smoothed the outside of his fly and, to check his handiwork, stood tippy toes before the washstand mirror—at five foot three, squat Bernie would have seen little more than his face with his feet flat on the floor. "Should'a been a tailor, Bernie," he said to the pink face smiling back at him. "Long as you don't have to pee or sit down in the next hour, no one will know." Then he washed his pudgy, well-manicured hands, retied his orange-red ponytail at the back of his balding head, and straightened the knot in his tie. The conference room, and a significantly more profitable future, awaited thirty steps away.

"All ready, sir," said Baxter, a crisp towheaded Ivy Leaguer, satellite to Bernie's rising star.

"Model's in place, projectors are set," said Baxter's Chinese cohort, Sue Shaw, handsome in the same scrubbed, corporate way as Baxter.

"All right, boys and girls." Bernie clapped his hands. "Break a leg!"

In the conference room, he cast a brittle smile at the eight seated HydraCorp principals, considerably less sure of himself in their presence than he had been in the john. They'd had a week to study his prospectus and all morning to pick it apart.

Otto Grosz, chairman, hefted his corpulent frame from the chair. "Ladies and gentleman, you all know Bernie Bergen, our manager for project development. Bernie has secured a personal option"—he stressed the "personal" with a cocked eyebrow to Bernie, in disapproving acknowledgment of Bernie's failure to act on behalf of HydraCorp rather than himself when the option opportunity arose—"to buy the Pali-uli tract on the island of Hawai'i, cheap, from the financially stressed Ka Pono Foundation."

"Good old Hawiian Pa'a Bank and Fiduciary Trust," said Mr. Tunalufu the Samoan, known as the "Big Tuna" during his football days with the Pittsburgh Steelers.

Laughter rounded the table. They all knew how an incompetent young financial officer had driven the foundation to the brink of insolvency through disastrous speculation in derivatives.

Bernie felt his face flush with a mixture of pride and embarrassment. He alone knew that the financial officer was anything but incompetent—was, in fact, in Bernie's pay, and had delivered the Pali-uli option for a mere two hundred thousand dollars into Bernie's calculating hands exactly as planned.

Mr. Grosz raised a hand to stem the chuckles. "Bernie's option is time limited, so if we are to capitalize on it, and get the Ka Pono Foundation back in the business of feeding and clothing those needy island babies, we must act quickly. You've all seen Bernie's proposal, but in a nutshell, his offer to us is this: The eight of us and Bernie incorporate for the venture. To acquire the land and cover start-up costs, we eight put up twenty-four million; Bernie contributes his option, plus one million dollars, for a one-ninth interest."

Bernie nodded.

"Financing for the development," continued Mr. Grosz, "would come from Stanley Fong's people at Pan-Pacific Insurance. Stanley has, in fact, run the proposal by them and will have more to say later. So"—he turned to Bernie—"let's hear the pitch."

Bernie stepped forward and stood silently for effect. Baxter's fingers played over a control panel to lower the shades and a projection screen, dim the lights, and fill the room with a rhythmic, primitive drumbeat and a low Polynesian chant. "Ladies and gentlemen," Bernie said. He raised his arm to the screen. "Before you is the Hawai'i the first voyagers discovered, a paradise. . . ."

A twelve-projector mosaic of color slides played across a darkened wall. Orchids, flowering ginger, tree ferns, a forested valley, jungle-clad cliffs and incredible waterfalls, all came to life as slides flickered on and off in time to the hypnotic drums. "This," Bernie continued, "is what the ancients called the Pali-uli. A veritable Eden. "My friends, it still exists. Hidden from island visitors. Unknown to all but a few."

Yes. A sideways glance confirmed it—he had their attention, all right.

As the lights came up, Sue Shaw walked to an architectural model, slid the silk cover cloth from it as Bernie announced, ". . . and this, my friends, this is the Pali-uli transformed into—Paradise Valley, Hawai'i's most exclusive, most fantabulous golf resort."

The HydraCorp board members crowded around the miniature world. Sculpted cliffs surrounded a deep valley on three sides. Several crystalline waterfalls dropped to blue Lucite pools. "The forest you saw in the slides?" said Bernie. "Now one of the finest golf courses in the islands. Thirty-six thrilling holes. You can see it fills nearly the entire valley, with no more than a short walk to the course from any of the condominiums—except the row rimming the cliff top, but what a view from there! And when we clear the forest? Valuable wood will be incorporated into the condos and hotel, the rest exported to Japan."

Spidery Mrs. Hamilberg interrupted with a scratchy whine. "Shamefully extravagant. The photography and that model look like something out of a Spielberg movie. No place on earth could live up to the picture you're painting."

Bernie slapped a hand over his heart. "I swear, it's paradise in the flesh, Mrs. Hamilberg. I've never seen anything like the Pali-uli."

In truth, Bernie had never laid eyes on the Pali-uli, but his conversations with the man he'd sent over to hike up there left no doubt in his mind as to the site's beauty.

Nor, in fact, were the photos of the Pali-uli. Baxter had borrowed those from the Hawai'i Visitors Bureau. The longest any slide had shown on the screen was four seconds, and one waterfall flower, Bernie had decided, was pretty much the same as the next. The model *had* been extravagant, it had pained him to write the check for it, but to land the big fish, Bernie knew, you needed fancy bait.

"Ka'u District is dry, isn't it?" asked a scowling Stanley Fong, mid-sixties, tall, slender, immaculate in an ivory silk suit. "You think you can keep a golf course up there green?"

"There's plenty of water," Bernie said, with an expansive wave of his arms. He had assurance from his geological consultant that there were, in fact, waterfalls. "And the altitude, three to four thousand feet, means it's cool. Perfect for golf, Stanley. And a world-class course? How better to snare affluent retirees. You can be sure the hotel will be filled to the brim with moneyed Japanese, too."

"What about birds?" asked tiny Mr. Watanabe the poultry monopolist, known as Grandpa Eggs among Hawaiian grocers.

Bernie had once feigned interest for an hour while Mr. Watanabe discussed his life list, every bird he'd seen, listed in a leather journal. Bernie remembered birds today.

"According to the survey, Mr. Watanabe," Bernie said, "there are authentic Hawaiian birds up there, but they're shy. We'd hoped we could put some in a big cage in the lobby, let the guests feed them, but we were told they wouldn't eat bread, peanuts, sunflower seeds—your normal bird foods—nor would they take to tourists, especially kids. I think we'll have to settle for macaws and parrots, like at Mauka Estates. Much showier, anyway. They say there are local geese, too. Probably fly in, land on our golf course lake."

"Those geese are called *nene,* Bernie," said Mr. Watanabe. "Found only in Hawai'i. However, nene are terrestrial, and prefer lava. They do not enjoy swimming."

"We'll change their minds—wait till they see that lake."

"And impact surveys, zoning, permits, the rest of it?" asked Mr. Gomes. "Any trouble there could be costly. Costly." Round, nearly as large as Otto Grosz, Mr. Gomes appeared sloppy in his baggy suit and unkempt hair, but Mr. Gomes was never sloppy when it came to spending money.

"To begin with, sir," said Bernie, "be assured I have not forgotten to cultivate the friendship of influential members of the zoning commission. I arranged for environmental surveys at the first hints of the foundation's financial troubles. And the results? Clear sailing. Rezoning? In the bag, you may be sure. Not to say there may not be objections from the native groups, the environmentalists, and other obstructionists. But without a documentable reason to block Paradise Valley, they won't have a leg to stand on."

Sue Shaw turned on an overhead projector, and a Geological Survey map appeared on the wall.

"See how Paradise Valley is all but surrounded by forest reserves?" Bernie pointed to shaded areas. "It'd be a bastard—pardon my French—to access ordinarily. But you see this red line nearby? That's the road to the Aeolus II wind farm. Being built by us right now with state and federal financing and county-secured rights-of-way. Earning us gratitude around the state for reducing the island's dependency on oil.

"Now get this, ladies and gentlemen. Not only will Aeolus II provide cheaper electricity for Paradise Valley but its access road will become the entry to our resort. All we need to do is run a short extension from here"—he pointed—"to here, and we're in the valley."

There were murmurs of admiration. But another question was raised by the ancient Mr. Hashimoto, the pachinko parlor magnate. "Mr. Bergen," he said softly in exacting English, "isn't Mauna Loa a volcano?"

Eager to participate, Sue Shaw fielded the question. "Yes sir, Mauna Loa is one of two active volcanoes on Hawai'i. The whole island is a volcano—"

Baxter moved in. "Mauna Loa is a *dormant* volcano, Mr. Hashimoto, a *friendly* volcano, like Mount Fuji."

Fortunately, the projection was fuzzy and the scale not visible, for as Baxter looked at the original, he noted, to his surprise, that a flow as recent as 1950 ended at the very edge of the Pali-uli.

Bernie added, "Mr. Hashimoto, there's a far greater risk living in the city of Hilo than in Paradise Valley. And you won't be running from a tsunami that high on the hill, I guarantee." Laughing, he quickly maneuvered the subject to the board's one common love beyond money: golf.

Mrs. Yum, a pneumatic Venus known to all as Dollie, raised a puffy hand. Dollie had earned her fortune by marrying, when a svelte thirty-year-old, the notable influence peddler Hiram Yum, a terminally ill, dyspeptic skinflint. To her dismay, marriage to the youthful Dollie had extended the old man's life by a seemingly eternal eighteen years. Yet, Dollie endured. Having paid her dues, however, she resented upstarts aspiring to easy riches.

"Mr. Bergen," she said, "after only six years in our business you wish to join us as an equal, to swim with the big fish. . . ."

Big fish indeed, thought the diminutive Bernie as his eyes played over tree-tall Stanley Fong, rotund Dollie, and the heavyweights Grosz, Gomes, and Tunalufu.

"In the ocean," she continued, "there are also sharks. Can you afford to swim with the big fish? Are you comfortable with the risk?"

"I appreciate your concern, Mrs. Yum," said Bernie. "I have accumulated adequate capital. And risk? I thrive on risk. Don't you worry about me."

The board fell silent, and Mr. Grosz concluded, "Bernie, if you would excuse us for a few minutes?"

In the corridor, Bernie popped two Nicorettes in his mouth and paced, followed by Sue Shaw and Baxter. "Damn it, Sue," Bernie said over his shoulder, "you scared the hell out of me with that volcano talk. We were lucky none of them read the morning paper that carefully."

"How so, Mr. B?" asked Baxter.

"A note about an earthquake on Mauna Loa last night. Happens all the time on the Big Island, but the paper said earthquakes like that may signal rising magma. All we need is for the principals to worry their old asses into flubbing this deal."

"Are you concerned, sir?" said Baxter.

"What, me worry? Nah. Too long a shot to fuss over."

Fifteen minutes later, Mr. Grosz summoned them back, Bernie could barely contain himself.

Mr. Grosz spoke. "Three things, Bernie. One: You've done your homework. Paradise Valley is a winner."

Bernie's knees went weak with relief.

"Two: We agree to your terms, your becoming a shareholder in this project, and, if all goes well, perhaps assuming the late Josephus Snyder's seat on the HydraCorp board. Welcome, Bernie Bergen."

Bernie wanted to kiss old Grosz on his jowly cheeks.

"And three," Grosz paused. The principals all looked at Bernie and smiled in anticipation. "We try to conduct these meetings with a certain decorum. Please keep your fly zipped in the future."

Bernie looked down at his parted zipper and blushed. The principals laughed. Joking with him! Bernie was one of the boys.

"In conclusion," continued Mr. Grosz, "we will draw up the necessary documents, and purchase the Pali-uli tract immediately to satisfy your option."

Mr. Grosz noticed Stanley Fong's gesturing. "One other thing, Bernie. Stanley has gone over your figures with his people at Pan-Pacific. They like your data and are eager to finance the project, but they would also like to see us commit to an additional four and a half million, start-up. They're insistent about it, in fact. That's five hundred thousand more for each investor. Considering the projected profit, the rest of us feel we can live with the additional investment. Would that be satisfactory with you, to get this deal moving?"

Bernie's heart dropped to his pin-striped trouser cuffs. Five hundred thousand dollars more? After all this? To come up with the money for the option, the surveys, the payoffs, and the buy-in, he had liquidated his investments, cashed in his savings, remortgaged his house, and borrowed to the hilt. Save for his salary, Bernie was broke.

Dollie squinted at him. Grosz waited. Bernie coughed explosively into his sleeve, blinked twice, and summoned a smile. "Of course, sir," he said. "No problem at all."

9

Look, honey," said Doris. "At the door. That woman in the sun hat, the one looks like she's been sucking lemons. She's giving you the once-over."

"That would be Judith," said Star. "Early. Didn't sound too friendly on the phone."

"I'm sure you'll warm her up." Doris patted him on the head. "She looks like one of those old-time missionaries. Can't be a day older than you, but she dresses like she's at least a hundred and fifty."

Mousy bobbed hair barely reached the collar of Judith's heavy white long-sleeved cotton blouse. Slung over one shoulder, a black canvas tote bag concealed possessions from prying eyes. Below, a shapeless gray skirt covered dark tights.

Star waved her to the table. "Welcome to Papa's. You must be Judith."

Doris poured coffee for Star, set a glass of ice water and a menu on the table for Judith. "Would you care for something to eat or drink, dear?"

"Water will be fine, thank you," said Judith, in a voice cold as the ice water. She studied Star while Doris studied her.

"So, you're Star," she said, stiff-backed, pinching his personals ad like a soiled diaper between forefinger and thumb tips. She shook it once and read, in case he had forgotten who he was: " 'Ladies, Meet Mr. Lucky. Married. Thirties. Good-looking. Fit. Seeking lively companion for discreet fun and games.' " Cold eyes appraised him. "Right," she said. "You look just like I thought you would. A pretty one. You'll do fine. Tell me, what does your wife think of all this?"

He'd used a few: "We have an arrangement. She sees her friends and I see mine," or, "We're estranged, haven't been together for a long time," or, "What the little lady doesn't know won't hurt her, eh?" with a wink, or, "She doesn't like sex anymore and I've always been hot in the sack." He opted for a modified version of the last.

"Of course she doesn't know anything about this, Judith. You know, I love her as much as ever, but over the years she's lost interest in a physical relationship, and I have biological needs I can't deny. I'm looking for a discreet companion who has these needs too." He looked soulful, a bit sad, eyes downcast. "Are you married too? Do you have needs, Judith?"

"Yes, indeed, you'll do fine," she said between pinched lips. "Tell me, young man, how would you like to make five hundred dollars?"

He cocked his head. "Why would you pay for what you might get free?"

Judith sat even straighter. "I am not talking about intercourse, surfer boy."

The offer sank in. Five hundred dollars. A down payment for Mako. He sipped coffee, scanned what he could see of Judith's body. "All right. What exactly would I have to do for the money?"

"Do you know the Reverend Jaycie Pitts and his Church of Heavenly Promise and Earthly Delivery?"

"Jeez. You're pimping for a preacher? Sorry, I'm straight, lady."

Judith glared. "Perhaps you've seen his TV show? The Reverend wears a white suit, uses a jeweled cane?"

"So he's a fancy dresser—still not interested. Wait—with the Cheerleaders for Jesus? Yeah. I saw the Delilahs of the Beach episode." He shook his head. "All those little chickies sitting on his lap and the old guy goes for men."

"Listen to me! I produce the show, arrange the talent. Not that I approve of everything that goes on, mind you"—she looked at her short, buffed nails, and paused—"but the Reverend does have a way with sinners." She looked up again, brighter. "He's immensely popular, and I do believe he saves souls. And no one man has done more to swell the ranks of the Americans for a Family Way than the Reverend Jaycie Pitts. Praise the Lord, our viewers here in Hawai'i are charitable, and the money we send to the Micronesian missions does so much good."

"And you? You're his producer, huh? Tell me, was one of the Delilahs on that last show Sissy Santangelo? That confession about the outrigger crew and the green bananas sounded familiar."

"Privileged information, Mr. Hollie. Just as your identity would remain secret if you wished."

"The preacher kisses and doesn't tell, huh? Lady, I'm not letting your preacher do me, even for five hundred dollars."

"Oh, Lord. Hear me out—I think you would make an excellent sinner on our show. We'll pay you five hundred dollars to appear, discuss your sinning: the ad, your adultery, the women you seduce—none of their names of course, although the more sordid the details, the better. We'll bleep out anything too risqué for broadcast later. Not that we mind. The more we bleep, the higher our ratings, the more generous the contributions."

"You want to pay me five hundred dollars to make an ass of myself on television?"

"It's instructive for good Christians to see the Devil's work firsthand. As to the money, we've found it expedient to pay our guests and thereby better control the show's flow and content. Don't worry about performing. We'll rehearse you. Your identity can remain a secret, too. We can alter your voice, shadow your face."

"I saw a mob informer on TV they did that to. He turned his head and the light hit his face just enough so if you'd known him, you'd have said, 'Hey, that's Sal there!' Good-bye Sal." Star wondered what Cindy, with her murderous jealousy, would do if she saw him on TV, learned he'd been running a personals ad.

"There are other possibilities. You could wear a ski mask, maybe a bandit's kerchief, or a Lone Ranger mask like the ones the men in the pornographic movies once wore." She blushed. "Not that I've ever seen one."

He let it pass. "Five hundred dollars."

"Maybe more."

"How much more?" He thought again of Mako, of broken legs.

"If you let us show your face, mention your name, I could go seven hundred fifty. Or, could you get your wife to appear? A thousand then, I'm sure. Twelve hundred if you both got saved after a tearful confession and reconciliation."

"Let me think about it." If she offered twelve hundred, he knew he could wrangle at least fifteen out of her if he came up with the right woman to play his wife. He'd have to stick with the mask, no names, because if Cindy caught wind of it, he'd be risking his balls. "Hot damn! I might do it."

"Please save your profanity for the show, Mr. Hollie." She handed him a business card. "Call when you're ready."

Miss Prissy Tight-ass, he thought. Be fun to loosen her up. "Judith?" Pleading. "Please don't be judgmental. We're not all as fortunate as you. I can see you're happily married, in control of your life."

"Yes, I am." She straightened the sleeve of her blouse.

"You know, it doesn't come together for everyone. Some people never receive the attention and respect they crave."

"Well, my husband respects *me*."

"I'm sure he does. And I'm sure he appreciates your beauty."

"My beauty?"

"Striking. You have a fine neck, you know. Long. A fashion model's neck. Your short hair sets it off beautifully."

Judith adjusted her hat, smoothed the hair at her temple. "I try to be practical."

"Yes, but you're also obviously attuned to what attracts a man. Covering your body, not revealing it all at once like so many women do. Leave something to the imagination, right? I hope your husband appreciates what a sexually desirable woman he has."

"Sexually desirable?"

"Of course. Such perfect skin. I think you're wise to hide it from the sun, too, with the hat, sleeves, and tights. Keep it protected, soft."

He lowered his voice, leaned forward, looked into her eyes, spoke in a throaty whisper: "Are you aware how incredibly erotic a man finds skin like yours?" Judith had to lean across the table to hear him over the restaurant noise. Their fingertips nearly touched. "A woman's skin is so soft, smooth. The best is rubbing, massaging that skin to release her feminine power. If I were your man, I'd begin by running a finger across your palm—what perfect nails you have—I'd trace it up your arm to that long neck, toy with your ears. Then draw it down to—you know—your breasts."

Judith flushed red, her mouth opened in a silent o.

"Then I'd moved down to those long legs. Spend time, gently stroking, warming. And when you were feeling real loose and dreamy, I'd explore those secret places. . . ."

Silence. Judith, a sparrow in thrall to the serpent, sat rigid, eyes flickering in synch with her heart.

"You know what I thought when I first saw you?"

"No, what?" very softly.

"I thought, here is a strong woman, a woman with rare sexual powers, who enjoys controlling her man, who would, oh so deliberately, bring him right to the brink, then keep him there until *she* was ready. Only when *she* wanted it would she open her thighs, guiding him . . ."

"YEOW!" The bus boy's heel hit a piece of lettuce, slid two feet to send him into a full split. *Crash!* China cups and saucers cascaded to the floor, splintering, bouncing. One rolled into Judith's ankle.

She blinked, twice, as if awakening from a trance. Star had once seen a sleeping crocodile in Arnham Land in northern Australia do exactly that, when, gliding past it in a boat, he had dipped an oar in the water near its head. Motionless, the crocodile opened its outer eyelids, then its inner lids, revealing huge gold-shot eyes with black slits for pupils. In a frenzy, it attacked the offending oar, crushed it to bits with powerful jaws.

Judith stood up, shook her head once. She reached into her black bag, removed a worn Bible, waved it before her, warding off Star's evil. "Exodus Twenty," she screeched. "Do you know the Ten Commandments?"

Star guessed. "The one with Charlton Heston?"

"Thou shalt not commit adultery!" Her eyes darted to the glass on the table. Inspired, she lifted it, pitched ice water in his face. "Cool off, sinner!"

He flopped in the aisle, shaking off water like a fish on the dock.

"Look me in the eyes, creature of Satan."

Ice cubes dropped from his shirt. His eyes stung. Through a painful haze, he watched Judith pull a dark object from her bag—this was no Bible. She pointed it at him. He extended his palms. "No, lady, don't shoot!"

Blam! The flash blinded him. He waved his hands in the air, stumbled against a table, knocked a chair to the floor.

Judith and Doris crossed paths, Judith on her way out, Doris running to Star's aid. "Hold on, honey," Doris called.

"I can't see! I'm blind."

"You'll be all right," she said, and helped him to a chair. "The lady only took your picture. Close your eyes and sit still, you'll be able to see in a minute." She patted him with a towel and stroked his hair. "The woman's business card got wet, but I'm leaving it on the table if you still want it." She blotted it with a napkin.

"By the way, Papa and I were betting on how this one would turn out," she said. "And I won again."

10

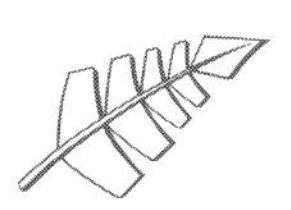

Bernie had been in a foul mood all morning. Pissed off at the world, fuming. "Two years," he mumbled, "I've schemed and planned. Everything comes together exactly like I want—the principals love Paradise Valley, invite me to join their exalted number. And now? All I need is an impossible five hundred thousand dollars more. In three days."

Or he'd lose the option, the deal, a place on the board, his country-club membership, his parking space, his wife. Bernie saw himself on the streets selling chunks of cold pineapple to tourists.

The phone buzzed. "Mr. Bergen?" Kathleen, his secretary, sounded tentative. "I need to tell you—that dreadful man called again, the Reverend Jaycie Pitts. Third time today. Soliciting a contribution to his ministry. It seems certain board members have been relaying his calls to you. I'm afraid they see humor in it."

"I'm not laughing. I recall screening calls falls under your job description, Kathleen."

"I'm sorry, sir, he used Otto Grosz's name as a reference this time. He's persistent. The story around the office is that the late board member, Mr. Snyder, got religion on his deathbed, was 'saved' by this Reverend Pitts, and then willed the man a substantial sum of money. Ever since, Pitts has plagued them all. Of course they won't talk to him, but now they're urging him to 'see our new principal, Bernie Bergen—a religious man—he'll take care of you.' I heard that from Melia, Mr. Grosz's secretary. Pitts said he wants to know what it's worth to you to 'save more good Christian souls like Josephus Snyder's from eternal damnation'—those are his exact words."

"Christian souls? Worth? To me? Jesus, Kathleen, if he calls back, tell him I'm a Jew. Or a Druid. Whatsa difference?"

"Oh, he'll call back, all right, if you don't call him. He left his number, made me promise to give you the soul-saving message."

"You did your duty, Kathleen. Round-file the number."

"I'm sorry to have disturbed you. You'd think with the millions the man makes from that TV show, he wouldn't be pestering businessmen like yourself. If it weren't for Mr. Snyder's bequest—"

"Wait. What was that you said?"

"A weekly TV program. He evangelizes, puts on quite a circus, really. Everyone watches it for the spectacle. His particular angle, as I understand it—"

"I thought I heard the word 'millions.' "

"Yes, it must be immensely profitable. The telephone number for donations flashes on the screen throughout, and they make the giving competitive. He has twelve life-size, cutout apostles on tracks, people donate for one or the other, and the apostles advance toward the finish line: a cutout of Jesus with open arms. Jesus's halo lights up when an apostle reaches him. 'Racing for Jesus,' the Reverend calls it. 'Don't let ol' Judas win again,' he pleads, and the pledges pour in for Peter or James or one of the others. The nonreligious put their money on Judas, of course, but the Reverend wins either way."

"This is a man I'd like to meet, Kathleen. Call him back, invite him up, soon as he'd like."

"You're sure, sir? He's a con man, slick, persistent. You may not get rid of him without writing a check."

"I'll lock my checkbook in the desk, okay?"

Sixty seconds later, she rang back. "He said the Lord was smiling on you both. He had an appointment canceled. He'll be here in fifteen minutes."

Five minutes later, the phone buzzed again. Bernie thought it might be the Reverend, in the office already, but it was his wife.

"Listen to me, Bernie. I'm calling from Muffie's car phone, and I am not happy."

Bernie held the receiver a foot from his ear.

"They just towed my Jag away. The goddamned transmission dropped out at the club. In front of the veranda. Everyone saw it happen, too: the Sandersons, the Cartwrights, Dr. Gordon and his wife, Heather, all of them, sitting under the umbrellas, sipping drinks. And the golfers too. Sounded like a train wreck. Big oily gears rolled all the way across the putting green—tore it to shreds. No more practice putting for a week! How I'll show my face at the club again, I don't know."

"That beautiful car."

"My God, Bernie, I've been driving it for five years. I told you it needed work, but would you spend a dime on it? You can't expect it to last forever. It's old. And it's silver, faded silver. I'm sick of this economizing. I canceled that shopping trip to Hong Kong with the girls, put off retiling the pool, Maria's only coming in once a week now, and I finally told little Jen at Vassar she wouldn't be getting her horse. You'll be wanting me to take in washing next."

"Jenna, it's not like we're eating out of cans. A year from now when the first condos open at Paradise Valley, we'll have money to burn. This is a turning point, you just have to bear with—"

"I've had enough, Bernie. Remember your promise to Daddy? How you would take care of me? Now look at us. Goddamned paupers."

"Jenna, I got to get back to business here, okay? Put the tow and the Jag repair on the Platinum Visa card, hear? Don't write any checks—"

The line went dead. Bernie closed his eyes, massaged his temples until the phone rang again.

Kathleen. "*He's* here," she said. "The Reverend Pitts."

"Great," said Bernie. "Hold him for five minutes, then take him to the boardroom. I'll meet you there."

By the time Kathleen arrived with his guest, Bernie was standing, hands behind his back, before a wall of glass, staring at the panorama of Honolulu Harbor. He turned, and the two men faced off like chessmen, kings of their respective trades, squat Bernie in charcoal pinstripes, the stout, marginally taller Reverend in linen whites. After a brief smiling contest, they walked forward to pump one another's arms like long-separated brothers. Bernie had the stronger grip, but the pain of the Reverend's rings cutting into Bernie's chubby fingers was too much to bear, and Bernie broke eye contact first.

The Reverend was a showman all right, Bernie decided, a real vaudevillian. He could have been a stunt double for Colonel Sanders, down to the glasses, cane, white goatee, and mustache. He had a habit of spinning the cane when he wasn't leaning on it, twirling the diamonds set in its gold head so they flashed like a Fourth of July sparkler. Bernie wondered if the Reverend faked the limp to justify the fancy walking stick.

In contrast to Bernie's sedate wing tips, the Reverend's black alligator cowboy boots sported inlays of turquoise blue crosses and Bible citations on each toe, John 3:3 and 2 Cor 9:7. The left heel read, "Jesus," the right, "Saves."

"Mr. Bergen, Mr. Bergen," said the Reverend. He had a deep, treacly drawl. "When I heard you were taking the place of Josephus Snyder, bless his immortal soul, I knew you and I would get together. Then, this morning, the Lord smiled on me. He said, 'Reverend Jaycie, today's the day. You call up Mr. Bergen, let him know how he can help the Church of the Heavenly Promise and Earthly Delivery with its good works.' "

"Would you like some tea, Reverend?" Bernie asked. Kathleen had been lifting an invisible cup to her lips as a reminder. "Kathleen makes a mean pot."

"Tea would be fine, fine, but I wouldn't say no to something stronger, either, if it was available." He edged toward the well-stocked wet bar.

"Help yourself, Reverend," Bernie said, unnecessarily. The Reverend had already made a selection. Bernie curled a thumb and forefinger in an okay sign to Kathleen.

Kathleen hesitated. Before leaving, she mimed writing a check and shook her head no.

The Reverend poured a tumblerful of ten-year-old bourbon over ice. "Bernie?" He moved to first names with the uncapping of the bottle.

"Brother Bernie?" He took a sip. "You know why we call our ministry the Church of Heavenly Promise and Earthly Delivery?" He didn't wait for an answer. "The Lord promises everlasting ease, milk and honey, heavenly bliss, to the charitable, when they leave this vale of tears."

The Reverend's words assumed a musical cadence. "But it is our experience, our blessed experience, that those who contribute to our church, our blessed church, receive rewards, tangible rewards, right here on earth. We call this the Blessing, the Blessing of Fourfold Rewards. Yessir, brother, Fourfold Rewards. The Lord promises and the Lord's church delivers, right here on earth. For every heartfelt dollar given, the charitable receive four times that back. Four, my friend. Four dollars for one. Give and you shall receive, sayeth the Lord."

Bernie smiled, took it all in.

"You're a good man, brother Bernie, I can see that. A family man, I'd be willing to wager. An honorable man. A man of charity. Yes, brother." Cranked up now, he took a gulp of bourbon, a fast breath, and wiped his forehead with a large, jade green silk kerchief.

"But you are also a businessman, are you not? A man of commerce? A man who enjoys a good return on his money? And why not, brother? Nothing wrong with that. Well, I'll tell you this. I've seen it happen. You give, and give freely, to the Church of Heavenly Promise and Earthly Delivery, and you will receive four times that back. Yea, brother. Your land will appreciate, your ventures prosper, your daughters marry rich, your cattle wax fat, your vines grow heavy . . ." The Reverend had grown red in the face. He sucked air. "Now, brother, let me show you the way—"

"I'm sure you will, Reverend," interrupted Bernie. "But let me show you something first. As a man of the cloth, I'm sure you're familiar with—paradise." He wrapped his arm around the Reverend's linen-clad shoulders and led him to the architectural model of Paradise Valley.

The Reverend hunched over the conference table, tumbler of bourbon beside him, staring at a yellow legal pad and Bernie's notations. Bernie stood behind, his arm still around the Reverend's shoulder.

"Five-hundred-thousand-dollar loan," said the Reverend Pitts, "secured by your interest in Paradise Valley, payable in one year at twenty-three percent per annum."

"Check," said Bernie.

"My choice of the Phase One condos at builder's cost."

"Check."

"A no-cost option on plat number two fifty-six for a Paradise Valley branch of the Church of Heavenly Promise and Earthly Delivery."

"Check. But Reverend, the money must be in my hands in two days. Two days."

"No problem, son," said the Reverend. "No problem at all."

11

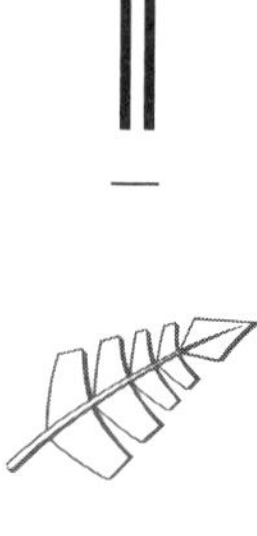

Mai Ling?"

She switched the phone to speaker, thought, Ah, it's Bernie, in his sweet as sugar voice.

Honey filled the room. "Mai Ling, how about you and I meet at our favorite restaurant in Chinatown in forty-five minutes? We'll do some celebrating."

She finished her nails, took a quick shower, and canceled the appointment with her banker to arrive before him. Mai Ling knew Bernie would have preferred the lingerie brunch at Stan's Mr. Meat, All You Can Eat, where men could be boys, drink till they dropped, cough, curse, and belch amid the comforting blue haze of cigar smoke, but oh-so-thoughtful Bernie always took her to the ancient Imperial Dragon on Bishop instead, famous for its dim sum and jasmine tea.

They had their own small dining room, her lucky number 3, as always.

"Order in Chinese, Mai Ling," Bernie urged.

Mai Ling and the waiter went at it like commodities traders, negotiating the freshness, the price, the preparation.

When the waiter left, Bernie chuckled. "I love it when you talk like that, sweetheart. It turns me on to watch a beautiful woman speak such an ugly language."

"Such a naughty boy." She shook her finger and giggled. The movement sent a cascade of light down her waist-length hair. "Cantonese is a delight to the ears. Would so many speak this tongue if it were not? Someday, when you are very good boy, Mai Ling will whisper Mandarin in your ear. Talk of beauty!"

She enjoyed making small talk with him as long as he liked. Besides, the dim sum at the Imperial Dragon was excellent, and Mai Ling enjoyed a leisurely meal. Clearly the day had gone according to Bernie's liking, so it would be rude to turn the conversation to business. All would be revealed in its own time.

"Mai Ling, you and I would make such a hot couple."

"Bernie, Bernie. You had your chance. We came so close, huh? Then Mai Ling finds Bernie has a wife. Such a bad boy."

"What do you say to a hotel room for the afternoon?"

"I say an afternoon of Mai Ling, and maybe Bernie's heart stops."

"Ah, but what a way to go." He slapped both hands over his chest, grimaced, and slumped in his red lacquered chair, immobile, a huge smile on his not quite lifeless face.

Bernie's flirting continued as the food and plum wine arrived.

Mai Ling giggled. Such a delightful man. A master of the small talk. Soon and effortlessly, the conversation will turn to business.

"Well, Mai Ling, if you must leave for Singapore, you must. I'm sure going to miss you." He removed a blank envelope from his jacket pocket and handed it to her. "Here's a little gift to remember me by."

"Thank you, Bernie, but I think that perhaps this gift is something I *earned,* yes?" She slit the edge of the envelope with a long, finely manicured thumbnail, and read the enclosed letter. It confirmed what she had expected: a cashier's check for twenty-five thousand dollars awaited her arrival in Singapore. Mai Ling puckered her lips and blew Bernie a dainty kiss.

"A reward for falling in love," Bernie said.

"I fear I fall in love too easily." She withdrew a manila envelope from her purse and passed it to him. "Here are the photographs of me with Mr. Keoni of the zoning commission, in amour." She passed another envelope. "And, look, more photos, these of Mr. Jamieson, also of the zoning commission, also doing fun-fun with Mai Ling. And Mr. Kamora, wearing only his tie, sitting up like a doggie.

"I will keep the negatives, Bernie, and you see I have marked out Mai Ling's face on these prints, but I think the bare bodies—bare except for Mai Ling's garter belt on Mr. Keoni—should be sufficient for your purposes."

Bernie studied the eight-by-ten glossies wide-eyed. "God, Mai Ling, you are so fine. And to think that wet-behind-the-ears financial officer enjoyed your favors. Doing to you what we encouraged him to do to the Ka Pono Foundation."

"Ah, yes. Martin. Although I concede Martin has been a most appreciative and generous suitor." She held out a hand to show Bernie a stunning star sapphire ring. "Who would guess a minor officer with the bank could do so well?"

"Who indeed?" said Bernie. "Now Martin leaves for Singapore, following his homesick little swallow back to her roost."

"Yes, he plans to follow me. We leave tomorrow, in fact. My arrangement with you will be concluded when Martin leaves Honolulu, Bernie. But who knows how long Martin and I will stay together once we are in Singapore? Who can say? Perhaps neither Singapore nor Martin will please me for long. That is what I am thinking." She winked. "Perhaps a week and I am off to Taipei, alone, to visit my old grandmother."

Bernie leaned forward and touched her hand. "Mai Ling, let me tell you something. You are my kind of woman. Cross my heart, I could really go for you. Look, spend a while in Taipei, see Granny, then come back here. We're building a new golf resort on the Big Island that will knock everyone's socks off. I'll fix you up in one of the A-class condos."

"But Bernie, you are married."

"So were Keoni, Kamora, and Jamieson. And our financial officer? Most certainly not married, but hardly a healthy girl's wet dream. Mai Ling, I'm serious this time. Serious, honey."

Mai Ling held a small white dim sum dumpling, the last, at the tips of her chopsticks. She studied it for a long moment, twisting it as a jeweler might examine a diamond in forceps.

"Thank you, Bernie," she said, "for revealing your heart. Now Mai Ling tells you what she feels inside, too. These others are just . . . men. An assignment, hmmm? I feel nothing for them. But Bernie and Mai Ling? We are alike. Rice from the same paddy, huh? And Bernie, I confess, you are special. Perhaps with you there is a future."

Bernie wiped the perspiration from his forehead with a red cloth napkin.

"What you think I value most about you, Bernie? Your money, you say? No, you would be wrong. Your strong physique?" She giggled. "What Mai Ling likes most about Bernie is, he makes her laugh. So few men have that talent. So, if you are being honest, Bernie, and one seldom knows when you are, let me tell you this: There will be no pillow talk between us as long as you are married. If we are to be true lovers, you must be a free man. And then? Who knows what fate has in store?" She looked up, smiled, and popped the dumpling into her mouth. "Who knows?"

She wrote a few lines along the edge of the paper place mat, tore it off, and handed it to him. "Here. Grandmother's address in Taipei." She kissed him on the forehead and left.

Bernie listened to the clack of her high heels recede across the parquet floor. Sunlight reflected briefly from the red and gold walls as the front door opened and closed. Mai Ling was gone. Bernie wiped a fat tear from his cheek. "Oh, Mai Ling," he said to her empty chair, "I love you so much. You are such a hot tamale."

12

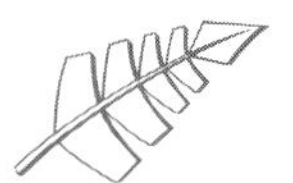

Star watched five noisy teenagers in his favorite booth making mustard, sugar, and spaghetti soup in their water glasses. He cupped his mouth, shouted across jammed tables, "Hey Doris, check out those kids in my booth."

Weaving through tables near the kitchen, a full tray on her shoulder, Doris hadn't checked the booth in ten minutes. "Honey," she called back, eyes on table 6 with the Amvets, "first come, first served. Sanya's got a table open in the corner. You take that. Kids have rights too, you know. Don't be such an old fart."

From the corner of his eye, he watched the one with the half-shaved head press a menu to the top of a full water glass, flip it upside down onto the table, slide the menu out. His pimply-faced buddy, red plastic squeeze bottle in hand, was leaving Doris a tip: EAT A BIG ONE LADY, written in ketchup across the Formica.

"Sure Doris, whatever you say."

Sanya had coffee waiting. Star crossed his arms on the table, rested, chin on forearm, once again weighing Dan's "Can't stand a quitter" comment against the rafting trip to New Guinea and escape from Mako. And then there was his boy, Mr. Lucky. Couldn't take him, couldn't leave him. He had only one more personals interview scheduled, due in ten minutes, and wondered if she would be the last.

When he saw her at the door, he perked up. What a steamer—round, pretty face, pouty smile, a Marilyn Monroe body shoehorned into size 6 slacks.

She didn't need Star's hibiscus shirt to recognize him. "I knew it was you," she squealed, "by the look in your eyes. You are as good looking a man as I've seen in a long time." The six-inch poodle puff of brown curls at the top of her head bobbed as she spoke. "Men who list themselves in the personal ads are usually such liars."

Star squirmed.

"No, don't be modest, you lovely man, you're a real winner. Guess this is my lucky day, huh?" She shook his hand, held on, rubbed the center of his palm with her fingers before she let go. "I'm Melissa."

Melissa set a fat manila envelope on the chair between them, then did a fifteen-second striptease from a silk windbreaker before sitting.

Star eyed the envelope. Advertising, he decided, boudoir photos. Not the first time a woman had brought a portfolio. Way to go, Melissa.

Her crimson lipstick reminded him of the shiny red wax lips the kids used to hold with their teeth, wiggle in front of their mouth before chewing them like gum. Those lips tasted sweet, he remembered, like cherries.

"So, Star, you're a surfer?"

"I catch a wave now and then. Swim, rock climb, run—you know, mix it up, stay in shape."

"As I see. I like a man who takes care of himself. I'm afraid I don't go near the water. But when I'm feeling daring, I'll drive over to Waimea Bay, watch the big waves roll in. Awesome, huh?"

She ordered iced tea and they small-talked about Waikiki. "Sometimes," Star said, "I wonder what Waikiki was like, way back—you know, before Captain Cook discovered Hawai'i."

"Discovered? Tell you what," Melissa winked, "I'll bet the Hawaiians knew it was here all along." Growing serious. "Captain James Cook"—she tapped her forehead, accessing data—"English. 1728 to 1779. One of the finest navigators known to history, crisscrossed the Pacific, Australia to the Northwest Coast. The first to save his crew from the ravages of scurvy by provisioning vegetables high in vitamin

C. Cook was an honorable man, curious, a man of rare accomplishment. A tragedy he was killed."

Star blinked.

Melissa pursed her lips. "Cook's death. Ironic. He sailed into Kealakekua Bay on the Big Island during the Hawaiian Makahiki festival, a celebration of the fertility god Lono. Lono made a ritual circuit of each island every year. He was represented by a polelike structure with a crosspiece and hanging strips of bark cloth, very suggestive of, can you guess?"

"British ships?"

"Exactly. Cook was feted as Lono incarnate, then sailed away at the end of Makahiki, as anticipated. There was a storm, a lost mast, Cook returned. Hawaiian religion said no more Lono for a full year. . . ."

"Uh-oh."

"Indeed. An altercation broke out on shore. The Hawaiians killed Cook, cut up his body, offered it in sacrifice."

"Poor Captain Cook." He raised an eyebrow. "Personally, my kind of sacrifice is tossing virgins in the volcano."

"I'll bet." She smiled. "Point of fact, virgin sacrifice was never part of the Pele cult. So . . ." She cocked her head, fluttered long eyelashes. "I've always felt safe hiking around the rim of Kilauea."

Star settled into his seat, reconsidered this Melissa. Not a word about tanning lotions or happy hours. Hot looking, brains, witty. Well, well, well.

"I know a little about the Pacific, too," he said. "My uncle was a copra trader. I ran away from home as a teenager. Uncle Jack took me with him. Great adventures."

"A Pacific Huck Finn. How romantic."

"Uncle Jack was super. He taught me everything. Gave me his own diving watch." He tapped his wrist. "We sailed a lot between Fiji, Tonga, and Samoa."

"Pivotal islands in Pacific prehistory. I'd love to visit them. Did you ever hear of the Lapita people? They lived in those very islands before, and during, the first millennium B.C. Their culture changed. Over a thousand years or so, they evolved into the people we call Polynesians. The Lapita used pottery, but as Polynesians, in the early centuries A.D., abandoned the technology—fascinating, huh? And as Polynesians, they migrated eastward, settled all the islands between Easter Island, New Zealand, and Hawai'i."

"I found some old pottery on Fiji," he said. "Fragments. Pinkish tan, worn, thick, with markings. Let me think. It was in the Sigatoka sand dunes, high white dunes along the beach. . . ." He also remembered lying there under the moonlight with an inventive, dark-skinned Fijian girl. In the morning, they had walked the dunes, found the pottery. They skipped pieces of it into the surf.

"Wow! That could have been Lapita. Did they have impressed dots, chevrons, whorls?"

I've been there, he thought, but she knows more about the place than I do. His attention was split: half, eager to continue their dialogue about Pacific cultures, half trying to imagine Melissa with her clothes off, inspired as he was by a recollection of the envelope on the chair and the pictures he knew it contained. He could see steam rising from the tan paper.

Melissa looked at her watch. "Sorry, I have to make a call to confirm a business appointment. You know where a phone is?"

"End of the hallway, by the rest rooms."

Melissa disappeared. Then, over the restaurant noise: "Shit!" Doris had discovered the teenagers' table. She slapped a hand over her mouth, looked to see who had heard.

"Kids have rights too," he yelled. "Right, Doris?"

She sidearmed a French fry at him, then spun full circle to see if Papa or anyone else had seen her do it.

Star wiped ketchup from his eyebrow and studied Melissa's envelope on the chair. I wonder if it contains what I think it does? His eyes darted to the empty hallway, back to the envelope calling his name.

One quick peek? He hooked a foot around the chair leg, pulled it closer. He sat tall, tried to keep one eye on the hallway while he cocked the other one down. The envelope had two round cardboard buttons at the top with a red string wrapped one to the other, securing the flap. He glanced at the corridor, down to the envelope.

His fingers seized the moment, unwound the string, opened the flap, and slid the contents out partway.

The item on top wasn't a photograph, but rather a crosshatched pen and ink drawing, technically well executed, whatever it was. Hmmm, anatomical looking. And the subject? He rotated the envelope, still holding it on the chair, and stared for a good three seconds. Jeez, he thought, it looks almost like female—genitalia. Isolated on the page. Hairless. Couldn't be.

Zowie! That's it. Bald as a coffee bean and winking right up at me bigger than life. Had to be, although he'd never really studied one up close in good light. A self-portrait? Shaved? Whew. This Melissa is one hot number.

Eyes wide, he looked again at the hallway. Empty. He shoved the contents back, retied the string, slid his chair from the table, crossed his legs, and leaned back, hands behind neck, a study in nonchalance. But his mind raced.

Melissa rounded the corner, ignored the envelope. "That's strange," she said. "They said Dr. Landau left the country."

"Well," he said, "you never know about people, do you? If you have the time, you want to have something to eat? Stay awhile?"

"Sure, why not?" Their eyes met, and the air between them crackled.

Star cleared his throat, flagged down Sanya. Melissa ordered a salad, Star, a Papa's Mahiwich. But Star and Melissa had more than food on their minds.

"So, what do you do, Melissa? Professionally, I mean."

"Oh, I'm an artist, and I do scientific writing, literature searches. I help people prepare manuscripts for publication."

Bingo. An artist. And a writer, too.

"What sort of things do you draw, Melissa?" Ouch.

"Technical stuff, mostly, but I also have my personal work." She smiled.

Personal work. Zowie. "Like, give me some examples."

"Star, why talk about my work? At the moment, I'm more interested in you. Truth is, I find you very appealing. I mean, here we are with nothing to do this afternoon. Maybe we could, you know, leave and find something *else* to do."

Somewhere below his belt, a tingle blossomed. Then he remembered Cindy's jealous rages and elected to temporize, got Melissa talking about Fijian cannibalism and martyred missionaries. Sanya brought food.

"I see you're wearing a ring," he said as Melissa forked a tomato wedge. "Have you been married long?"

He might as well have slapped her. Melissa stared, wide-eyed. Puppy-brown eyes welled up.

Uh-oh.

"I'm awful," she said. Her voice broke. "I'm no good. I don't know why I'm here." She sniffled. A big tear slid down a pink powdered cheek, leaving a shiny snail track, hung on her upper lip, dangling, then rolled into her mouth. Melissa licked salt from her lip and sniffled.

"Jeez, I'm sorry, Melissa. I didn't know it was a sore subject. I kind of assumed marriage wasn't an issue, with my ad and all. We don't have to talk about it, okay?"

"No, you have a right to know what kind of person I am. I *was* married," blubbering, anxious to tell him all about it, now that he'd opened the wound.

"Melissa, no need to explain." Recently divorced? Reason enough for tears.

"No, I want you to know. Actually, my husband and I were, I guess you might say, physically estranged, even though we were married and lived together. We had an understanding."

Hey, that's my line.

"He was much older than I. He was a scientist, an archaeologist, devoted to his work. Dr. Artemas Bingham Finch. Perhaps you've heard of him?"

Star shook his head.

"Initially, Artemas was a god to me, but as time went by, we became, well, useful to one another. He took care of most of our expenses and I helped with his studies. Gradually we became more like friends. He had, uh, what shall I say? A performance deficit. And I had my, um, needs."

Whoa. My line too. Melissa and I have a lot in common.

"Anyway, Artemas didn't mind my affairs as long as I was discreet and I helped him with his work. Appearances were important. He came from an old, established island family—the Finches go back to the first missionaries. Divorce? Unthinkable. He was happy; I was content and careful about whom I saw." Her hands wrestled one another, plucked a paper hula dancer touting coconut ice cream from the salt and pepper dolly, and began dismembering her. Tiny brown arms, hands, and legs fluttered to the floor.

"Then he was *killed* in an automobile accident. Ten days ago. It was horrible. So unexpected. I've been kind of aimless, went to Maui, holed up, finished some work. Then, when I came back yesterday, I saw your ad and thought, Melissa, you need a *release*. Something to take your mind off it all. So I called you. And I find you're a very appealing man. Simpatico, too, I think. So there you are. I'm being honest. That's what I am."

She looked at him, hopeful.

"Man, I'm sorry about your husband." He backed from the table. Weepy women gave him the heebie-jeebies, and it was creepy, her coming to see him so soon after the old boy kicked off.

Then he looked into her red eyes, watched a tear drop from her chin to the table, and thought, Poor baby, maybe I can make it right for her. What if I was honest, too, shared a secret?

"Melissa, I, uh, haven't been entirely straight either." He cleared his throat. "I have secrets too. I, um, I'm not really married myself."

"Then why . . . ?"

"First, I want to say that I really like you, okay?"

"Me too."

"See, I haven't exactly been looking for a companion. I'm a writer, like you, sort of. I'm working on a story on personal ads for a magazine. I ran the ad to see who responded and why. I've been meeting a lot of women—although none as appealing as you. Really. It's been more like research for me. Maybe like the research you do. In a way."

"You mean you're going to *write* about the women you've met through the ads?" Her voice shrill. "This is a *sham,* our meeting?"

"Well, sort of, but understand, I *like* you. I'd like to know you better. I didn't know anything about you before we met."

"Oh, God! You're going to *tell the world* about what I told you? About *Artemas?* That I answered a personals ad and dated a *surfer?* His family would *die*. I couldn't show my face. . . ." Melissa held her breath. Tears melted mascara, her skin grew splotchy, and her face went red as her lipstick, pupils huge, unfocused.

"No, Melissa. Listen, I wouldn't use real names. I won't mention you or your husband, okay?"

"You son of a bitch!" She backed out of her chair, grabbed her jacket, retreated to the door.

Star threw his bag over his shoulder, chased her, muttering to Papa, "I'll be back." He trailed her out the door, onto the street, grabbed her elbow. "Melissa, stop. Listen. I promise I won't write about you."

She jerked her arm away. *"Liar!"* She sprinted across Kuhio Avenue, dodging traffic. "Liar!" she shouted again from the far curb, then disappeared into a crowd of tourists.

Star leaned against one of the palms outside Papa's. "Tell the truth to a woman," he said to the traffic, "and look where it gets you."

He walked along the beach, dodging the surf, concluding he *was* sneaky, although straight shooting wasn't one of Melissa's fortes either, any more than emotional stability. He told himself there was no way he could have known about her husband's death, that Melissa was the one, after all, who had called *him,* unconcerned whether he was married, and that it was Melissa who had to bear the responsibility of catting around, not him.

But none of it made him feel any better.

13

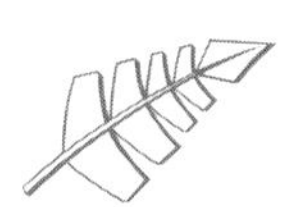

Little Josephine. I still can't believe it," said the Reverend Jaycie Pitts.

"Believe it. Two hundred thousand dollars. Three weeks."

"Lordy." The Reverend ran trembling fingers through his long white hair. "I was set up, Sheldon. Snookered." He twisted the tip of his silver mustache. "I was sure the girl was of age. When she auditioned for the cheerleaders, Judith thought she looked too *old*. And her mother seemed so simpleminded, such a good Christian."

"I had them investigated," said the attorney, consulting a small black notebook. "They're French nationals. The girl was born in Martinique, like she said, but they've been living in Papeete, Tahiti, where they have quite the reputation. The mother gave me copies of the girl's birth certificate and their passport. She's a minor, all right. They're both back in Tahiti now, incommunicado—'Don't call us, we'll call you.' "

"The little slut seduced me, talked me into reading Bible stories to her in their apartment. Her mother went to the movies. Before I knew it, we were playing 'Salome, Salome, where's the head of John the Baptist?' " The Reverend wiped his forehead with a scarlet hankie and closed his eyes, remembering. "I must say, the girl played her part well. Lord, it's true what they say about the French." He opened his eyes, shrugged his shoulders. "How was I to know she was a professional, Sheldon?"

"Irrelevant, I'm afraid. Options? Contact the police. Extortion is a crime, although extradition is unlikely. Even if they were here in Hawai'i and convicted—what, deportation? But if they charge you? I'm afraid our society frowns on sex with a minor. So—not only kiss the show and your ministry good-bye, but"—Sheldon raised his hands, gripped imaginary bars—"court a stretch in the slammer. All I can say, Jaycie," he chuckled, "is, your little cheerleader must have one hell of a set of pom-poms to make you go so hard in one head and so soft in the other."

The Reverend circled, waved his hands in the air. "Enough, Sheldon. I'm mortal, she was French. Okay? I was tempted by Satan, tricked by his strumpet." He looked heavenward for sympathy. "I fear that as a holy man—a damned successful one too, I might add—I succumbed to pride. Pride, Sheldon, one of the seven deadlies. I fell into the trap of the erring Corinthians, who, Paul tells us, believed everything was permissible. Alas, I, too, thought I was above sin."

"Save the sermon for Sunday, Jaycie. The point is, the mother was way ahead of you. She wasn't going to the movies, she was *making* them. Home movies. Digital video, high production values. She showed me thirty seconds of your escapades—you're very agile, by the way, for a man your age. Her audio is impressive, too—you never sounded so good on TV—and the theatrical lighting, pillows, tented bed, robes, veils, the cucumbers, melons . . ."

"And I commended the Jezebel for her imaginative decor."

"The mother maintains the quality of the tape is high enough to market as first-rate pornography. Says she's doing you a favor, selling it back to you so cheap. Claims she could make more than the two hundred thou from Asian sales alone. Hope it's no blow to your ego, but she'd bill you as Colonel Sanders. Worldwide, the Colonel's far better known than the president and not far behind Mickey Mouse. From a marketing perspective, I can see her point."

The Reverend dabbed at his forehead again. "Lordy, Sheldon, you're supposed to be representing *me*."

"I'm sorry, Jaycie. I mention it only to underscore how serious she is. She swears if you don't pay on time, she'll begin duplication and distribution, and send copies to the media here. That's the bottom line. Two hundred thousand. Twenty-one days. Josephine's sixteenth birthday is in three weeks. The mother wants to buy her a nice present."

"I can think of a nice present for both of them."

"Your kind of presents we can do without. One thing in your favor, though, it appears she has a crook's honor. My Tahitian sources tell me if she's paid off, she returns the goods and moves on."

"Lordy, Sheldon." The Reverend twirled his cane, tapped it against his head. "A lot of good that'll do me. I don't have that kind of cash. I never keep money in the Micronesian Mission accounts for long, and I just withdrew five hundred thousand from the mother lode in the Cook Islands to make that personal loan. I can't have more than twenty-five or thirty left there, and twelve here." He spun to face the attorney. "You know my finances. That's about right, isn't it?"

"Close enough, and you need five a week to cover your show expenses. We've got three weeks. That gives you some time to shake the charity tree, put the screws on your people to boost donations—but frankly, I don't see how the TV program can bring in enough by itself. That loan to Bergen seemed like a good deal at the time. Maybe you could get some of it back, offer him a bonus. A quick ten grand for return of two hundred thou. He's a businessman. He'll jump at that."

"Brother Bernie, so good of you to see me."

"Not at all, Reverend. Grab a chair. What's up, my friend?"

"Beautiful office you have here. My, my, what an art collection, all those cartoon characters. Say, you wouldn't happen to have any of that heavenly bourbon around would you?"

Bernie walked to the wet bar and lifted a tall bottle with a black label. "How about Tennessee sippin' whiskey, twelve years old?" He set it on the desk with two cut-crystal tumblers. "Ice?" Bernie poured himself a jiggerful and sat again.

"No, no." The Reverend filled the glass, closed his eyes, and took a long sip. He twirled his cane, fidgeted, swallowed more whiskey, and looked around the office. "Is that a real Woody the Woodpecker painting up there?"

"Original oil. Signed by Walter Lantz. Worth a bundle."

"You know, Woody's topknot and your ponytail look a lot alike."

"Well, what do you know? Old Woody's always been my favorite."

"You have distinguished hair. Nice shade of orange."

"Hair? Hell, Reverend, I'm practically bald."

"Yes, yes, but the ponytail is stylish. And you have healthy hair."

"What is this, Reverend? You selling shampoo? You're not coming on to me, are you? I didn't have you pegged for being light in your boots."

The Reverend stumbled back. "Abomination! Lordy. No. Just making conversation." He removed a powder blue silk kerchief from his pocket and wiped his face. "Uh, Bernie. I have a problem. A serious one. A problem only you can solve."

"Shoot, Reverend."

"I have a bit of a financial crisis." He swirled the amber liquid in his glass. "I was wondering if you might consider returning two hundred thousand dollars of the loan I made to you. I'd be glad to give you ten thousand in appreciation. Cash."

"No can do, Reverend."

"Lordy." He took a mighty swallow. "Look, Bernie. I'm desperate. Return the two hundred thousand, I'll give you the ten and I'll waive the interest on the balance. Three hundred thousand dollars, interest free."

"It's a great deal, Reverend, but the money's gone. Reinvested. Every cent I own or could borrow is in the Paradise Valley project. I'm sorry."

"Lordy, Lordy." He refilled the glass.

"Anything I can help you with, other than money?"

"No, no." He studied the second glass before drinking. "Got myself in some difficulty with a woman. Shouldn't talk about it." His skin had turned lobster red.

Bernie took a drink himself and scooted his chair closer.

"Extortion!" the Reverend blurted. "Young girl. Got it all on film. If I don't pay in three weeks, they go into syndication. I'll be ruined." He ran the cloth over his face. "What kind of woman would do such a thing? Make passionate love before a hidden camera?"

Bernie squeezed his eyes shut, thought of Mai Ling's camera-recorded antics with the planning commissioners. He pressed his palm to his heart. Oh, Mai Ling, my Chinese apple blossom. Are you still in Singapore, or already in Taiwan? Will I ever see you again? He looked back at the Reverend. "Can't imagine such a thing," he said. "Scandalous."

"Can't pay her off. I'll have to skip town. Shave my head and beard. New identity. It's the only way." The silk kerchief wiped, blotted.

"None of my business, Reverend, but why so desperate for cash? I thought you were raking in millions from this TV show of yours."

"Hah! Three years here and I'm lucky to have the five hundred thousand I lent you. Would have twice that if I hadn't had to leave the mainland in such a hurry. A costly exit, that. Oh, sure, the TV show is a hit. Ratings through the roof. But you know what? These people in Hawai'i are too damned content. All the sunshine. The trade winds. Flowers. Ocean. Love to watch our sinners, oh yeah, but it doesn't take. No identification. No guilt. Guilt is what fires the contributions, Bernie. Happy people aren't guilty people. Your best are the ones down in those cold, foggy mountain valleys in Kentucky, the ones who work the mines in West Virginia, the southern farmers poor as dirt. They know their lives are miserable because they're being punished for their sins. And sinful people are guilty people, and guilty people pay the Lord for forgiveness, to buy a shot at happiness.

"Give me another shot of that whiskey."

Bernie poured.

"You think it's easy? Easy to put on a show like I do? Lord, I've worked my ass off, and I'm not getting any younger. I've done it right, too. I have a real divinity degree, you know. Small Bible college, but I earned it. No mail-order certificate for me. No sir. I know my stuff, Bernie."

Bernie nodded.

"And I know what a show can do. These preachers who stand up in their workaday clothes and shout at people? Scares 'em away. People need a role model, Bernie, someone looks like God.

"See this suit?" He plucked at his white sleeve. "Pure bleached linen, tailored. Polyester would give me hives. And these boots?" He tugged at his cuff, raised his leg onto Bernie's desk. "Custom Lucchese. More overlays and underlays than any country-western star—and those people do it right." He lifted his cuff to reveal a thin bluish calf. "These doves flying around the tops? Real sapphire eyes. You think people watch the Grand Ole Opry for the singin'? Hell no, it's to see the gods."

Bernie sipped.

"I'm half in the sauce, brother Bernie. And I'm feelin' down. I've done everything right and it's all goin' to horse poop. You ever have that happen, a successful man like you?"

"Believe me, Reverend. I know the feeling. But don't give up hope. Three weeks?" He drummed his fingers on the desktop. "They're working on the road to Paradise Valley as we speak. Soon as the dozers start clearing the valley, we'll tell the world. Big splash. Land rush. And guess who holds options on most of the land below, along the highway? Yours truly. When the speculators descend on the place, I stand to pick up some quick cash.

"Two hundred thousand? I'd say, yes, Reverend. I'll be able to give you two hundred thousand then. Per the terms you mentioned. And you retain your options on the condo purchase and the lot. You're off the hook and everyone's happy."

"I like the sound of that, but I don't think I followed you."

Bernie poured the Reverend another glass and explained.

"But that could take longer than three weeks, much longer."

"Believe me, Reverend, I'm pushing this thing as fast as humanly possible. Last thing we want is to drag our asses and invite interference. I think you'll be safe with the three weeks. Shall we draw up some paper, do some signing?"

"Yes, yes, of course. But the money's got to be in my hands in nineteen days, tops, or it's no deal. Any later, I'm a dead man."

"Make it twenty."

The Reverend sighed. "Twenty days."

14

Denny's steal your customers, Papa?"

"By eleven, eleven-fifteen," said Papa, "this place'll be jammed. You don't grab your booth quick you'll lose it for the day, miss out on your dollar coffee with the hundred refills." He looked up from the cash drawer, "By the way, your latest girlfriend left a big envelope on the chair yesterday."

Star smiled at the thought of Melissa, afraid to come back to Papa's, afraid to call him, worried he'd publish her dirty pictures in *Pacific Rainbow*. He imagined proposing the idea to Dan, showing him the snatch sketch. "I finally got an angle on that article, Dan—how about a pictorial? Take a look at this. It'd make a great *opener,* don't you think? Maybe a double-page *spread?*"

Star remembered the night before. It had been around eleven. He was sitting before the TV, brushing Mr. Lucky, trying to think of an excuse to call Melissa, when he remembered the envelope. Papa, he knew, would hang on to it.

Be businesslike, he thought, dialing her number, but if she sounds friendly?—see where it goes. If she sounds sleepy, hang up.

The phone rang five times and her machine came on. Damn. Either asleep or out. Hang up? No, leave a message, give her time to reconsider, let her think she'll have to see me to get her pictures.

Beep. "Melissa, it's Star Hollie. Sorry our appointment today wasn't more . . . positive. Listen, you have my word that any sources I use for the magazine article will be anonymous. Okay? Absolutely no names. I wanted to call to let you know that you left that envelope of"—what would be the right word?—"documents with me, and it's safe. Phone, and I'll get it back to you. Hope you're feeling better. Bye."

He hung up.

"Documents"? Why did I mention contents? If she thinks I peeked, I'll never see her again. Although I guess the word's neutral enough. And I've done my duty. Out of my hands now, in Melissa's.

"Star?" Papa clapped.

"Huh? Sorry, I was somewhere else." He remembered, Papa had the envelope. "Hold on to it, okay?"

He thought again about Melissa over his first coffee.

Outside, a large Hawaiian woman with a lion's mane of white hair and a pale yellow, nearly white German shepherd at her heels stopped at the Papa's sign. She pointed to the ground, and the dog sat. He watched her enter, hug Papa. They touched noses—sharing a breath, old Hawaiian style—then broke into an animated conversation in Hawaiian.

Star watched them over the top of his newspaper, saw them look his way, heard them laugh. Papa pointed to him. Jeez, what's this?

The woman walked toward him. Star hid behind a menu.

She stopped at his booth, shadowing the menu with her big-boned body, then dropped onto the seat and stared, as if searching for something in the back of his skull. Seconds passed. "Hello," she said, "I am Walana."

Star blinked. Walana had a huge head and black eyes big as a whale's.

She wore a red muumuu hanging to her ankles—ankles thick as tree trunks, supporting a fleshy, intimidating body like one of the old Hawaiian *ali'i,* chiefs.

He shook his head to break her gaze, and noticed small, dark, geometric tattoos above and below her lips.

"Papa told me what you are doing," she said in a voice soft and buttery, disturbingly hypnotic. "I have an idea I think might appeal to you, something that could do us both good." She smiled.

Aha! An admirer. Star relaxed. "I'm flattered, Walana, and I'd enjoy getting to know you, too." He winked.

"*Auwe!* What you think? I want to bed you, boy?" She belly-laughed. "Look, I know how you deceiving the girls—just what I expect from a pretty boy like you, all sweet as sugarcane. And those girls, they love that fast ride you take them on, don't they? No, Hoku-li'ili'i, my little Star, I'm interested in your writing—not your *ule*."

The laughter died. "My *'ohana* . . . you know the word?"

"Hawaiian society? Extended family?"

"Good boy. My *'ohana* on the Big Island has been working to show young people the old ways, the language, legends, hula. We got a nice wet *kalo* patch growing, rebuilding a chief's fish pond, restoring the traditional life. Understand?"

"Sort of."

"We long on heart, short on money. If people read about us in a big magazine, they might want to help, yes? You write our story. We a lively group. Papa's youngest, Lani, she one of our best. Papa says you know her."

"Little Lani? Sure, I remember. Skinny, long black hair, always playing tricks. She went away to school. Lani's on the Big Island?"

"Lani is a big girl now, degree in forestry, my right hand. When the Hawaiian people get the island of Kaho'olawe back, Lani wants to be the one to make it green again, undo what the navy bombs tore up. We have lot of things going on. What you think?"

"To tell the truth, I'm not exactly on a roll lately. You might talk to the editor. She makes those decisions."

"But if you think it a good idea, she listens, huh?"

"Listen? To me?" He scowled. "Tell you what. I'll mention it to the publisher, Dan Capistrano, okay?"

He glanced outside and saw a car like Mako's drive down Kuhio, reminding him of empty pockets, of a ride in a car trunk, of traction and plaster cast signings. Mako. Twenty-five hundred dollars.

Walana snapped her fingers at his nose. "Where are you, boy?"

"Sorry. I'll talk to Dan, I promise."

She reached across the table and covered Star's hand with hers, dwarfing it.

He flinched at a small but perceptible shock. Walana's black eyes bored through him. "Boy, I see things. You got trouble in your life. I feel it in my bones. I should have listened instead of talking. What is it, going bad with you? Now tell me true."

The hairs at the back of his neck bristled. "Lady, everything is fine. Some uncertainty in my life maybe, but I'm doing great. Great." His hands felt cold, his palms wet. Damn. He wondered if she could feel it, gripping his hand like that.

"Dear," she said, "I mean you no harm. I am trying to help you, understand?"

"Yeah, I guess." He didn't understand at all.

"These feelings of mine are seldom wrong. Things going bad in your life, huh? You having the big dreams? Have you seen signs?"

"No, Walana, no dreams, no signs." He jumped at a sharp rap on the window. A perfectly manicured red fingernail at the end of a long middle finger bounced against the street side of the glass. The finger pointed skyward, but its companions balled into a tight fist. Beyond, a finely tanned bare arm led to a hard athletic body in a black and yellow Lycra workout suit.

Cindy. The Queen of Jealous. Hopping foot to foot like a prize-fighter, while the finger with the message stayed put.

He stared at the fingernail, afraid to look directly at the eyes for fear their venom would shoot through the glass. Jeez. Did she think he was balling Walana? *Walana?* Then he felt his own hand in Walana's and rolled his eyes. All the proof Cindy needed.

"Excuse me for a minute, okay?" A chase down the sidewalk, some shouting and pleading, maybe he could calm her down.

But Walana tightened her grip, ignored the angry wasp buzzing against the glass. "Pay her no mind, boy. She not for you. Can't you see that? You stay put."

It was too late, anyway. Cindy had flown off. Star watched the receding figure, even in his distress admiring the wriggle of her tight rear end. He turned to Walana for direction.

"You poor boy." She released his hand and patted it. "The story can wait. You be careful. I can help." And that was it. She rose, walked to the front, mouthed an aloha to Papa, and left.

He watched Walana and the white dog amble up Kuhio Avenue.

Cindy was long gone. He walked to the register. "Who was that juju woman, Papa?"

"Walana? Walana's kahuna. You know, priest. Big mana. Everybody knows Walana. I don't know what you told her, but let Papa give you some advice: Don't you mess with Walana, pull any of that pretty-boy smooth talk with her. She'll turn you into a toad." Papa laughed, but his eyes said listen up and watch your ass.

Star felt a sudden need for fresh air, a power walk, to take his mind off Walana, Judith, Tammy, Melissa, Cindy—all of them.

An hour and fifteen minutes later, he'd circled Diamond Head, returned through Kapiolani Park, and neared Koki's surfboard stand.

"Hey, Star," Koki waved him over. "Friends of yours were asking for you, maybe half hour ago."

"Who was it? Male, female?"

"Guys. Never saw 'em before."

"Maybe those Canadian rock climbers, huh?"

"No, I'd say these boys were more familiar with breaking rocks than climbing 'em. You know, guns and pussy types—white bellies, red necks, knuckle tattoos. Had on jeans with western boots. Fit right in with the beach crowd. Big fellas, real hard to understand. Bleached hair, twins, could hardly tell 'em apart."

"They know me?"

"So they said. You knock up some biker chick, forget to return her calls?"

Star slapped his forehead. "Mako's boys. What'd you say?"

"Said you'd moved to New Zealand."

"*Mahalo,* brother, I owe you one."

He returned to the coffee shop, found his booth open. He waited for the wiseass crack from Papa about keeping lunch customers away, but Papa kept his eyes to the register, his mouth shut.

Doris set coffee on the table and touched his shoulder. "Honey, have you seen the afternoon paper?" She spread a folded page and stepped back.

He scanned the articles. A photo caught his eye. Melissa. Pretty, weepy Melissa, standing next to an older man. The dead husband? Distinguished, balding, thin, a high-society type. School tie and a dark suit. Melissa, dressed to the nines, showing a nice cleavage. She stood several inches taller than the man—must have been wearing heels. The man's arm circled her shoulders but the stance was awkward, unnatural, because of her height. Apparently a social event and he'd pulled her toward him, posing for the camera. Both Melissa and the man smiled, faces blanched by the flash, the people behind them lost in darkness.

Well now, what had Melissa done to get her picture in the paper?

Then he saw the headline, SUICIDE AT MAKAPU'U BEACH, and choked.

15

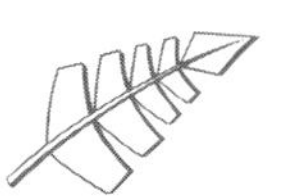

Doris lifted her hand from Star's shoulder and patted his head while he read the article.

> Two young boys walking along Makapu'u Beach early this morning discovered the nude body of a Kailua woman, drowned at the edge of the surf. Identification found in her clothing, neatly folded on rocks near the water's edge, revealed her to be Melissa Finch, wife of the late Dr. Artemas Bingham Finch, notable Hawaiian archaeologist. Dr. Finch died recently in an automobile accident on the Likelike Highway. Authorities believe Mrs. Finch took her own life in a state of depression. . . .

Star rubbed his eyes, stared at the page.

Melissa was survived by a sister in California and parents in the Midwest. The article continued in more detail about her husband. Evidently his death was still bigger news.

But there was no question: Melissa—dead. Drowned. According to the police, she'd done it last night. While he watched TV. Jeez. Was she already dead when he telephoned? If he had called earlier, could he have talked her out of it?

He imagined Melissa stripping, wading into the surf. Then what? Swimming to sea until she was too tired to make it back? Diving into the black bay, fighting her instincts, deliberately sucking salt water into her lungs? He thought of her lying lifeless in the sand, the waves washing her up and back. Oh, Melissa.

The paper said she left no message—must have thought no one cared. The authorities said the death of her husband drove her to it. But Star knew better. He had been with her yesterday and Melissa hadn't been that upset over old Artemas. A little unbalanced, maybe, but definitely not depressed. No. Star knew the real reason she was dead: honesty had killed Melissa Finch.

If only he had shut up and not blurted out the truth, Melissa wouldn't have run out of Papa's, through traffic, with tears streaming down her face, never wanting to see him again. If he'd stuck to his line, they might be having coffee together now, talking about Fiji or French Polynesia, or maybe going back to his place.

Knees to chest, arms around ankles, Star stared out onto Kuhio Avenue. He read the hand-painted lettering on the window, "$2.29 BREAKFAST SPECIAL." The whole damned world was turned around.

He went for a swim, a long one. When the shark fear came on him, way out, he said screw it, and kept swimming, not caring.

He had never met a woman quite like Melissa: brains, witty, a hot number. Yes, he would have seen her again. Although Melissa did have a screw loose. If only he had led her on, not been so stupidly honest, maybe she would be alive today.

Physically wiped, emotionally drained, he walked to his car, hoping he wouldn't run into anyone he knew. But as luck would have it, he saw Scooter, the manager of the apartment where he parked, crouched over a dismantled motorcycle at the edge of the lot, wearing gray coveralls—no skirts for Scooter—and grease from her short tousled hair to her raggedy gym shoes. Although slender and in her mid-twenties, Scooter took no lip from man or woman, or second place in anything.

"New bike," she said. "New for me, anyway." She pushed her

bangs aside, ran the back of a hand across her forehead, leaving a long black streak.

"Harley?" he asked, hoping to leave it at that. He walked by.

"Whaddaya think? I'd own a rice burner? Harley? Hell yes, a 1980 shovel. FXR. Putting in a new cam. Baby'll smoke the tires when I'm finished, but I'm having a bitch of a—"

"Sorry, Scooter," still walking, "kind of in a hurry."

"Star, wait up." She ran after him. "Listen, I'm sorry, really."

How did she know about Melissa? "Yeah, thanks, Scooter. Life's a bitch, huh?"

"I saw her too late. I yelled at her, but she'd already done it. Gave me the finger and walked off."

"What?" Then he saw his car. Four flat tires. Cindy. "Guess this isn't my day." He sat on the ground, tossed his hair back, and stared at a rain cloud scudding across the mountains.

"Keep your cool. Tires are okay—she just let the air out. Old Gruber in 4-E has an electric air pump. I use it all the time. He'll be back in an hour, we'll fill 'em up."

"Yeah, thanks." He blew air from puckered lips in a long sigh. "Listen, I'm kind of out of it. Think I'll walk home." He stood, gave the car a dirty look, and turned his back to it. "I'll deal with this in the morning."

"Take off. I'll fill 'em. Good as new when you get back."

"Hey, you're all right"—he slapped her palm, wiped the grease on his jeans—"for a girl." He jumped back—too late. Scooter caught him in the ribs with a rabbit punch.

He smiled for the better part of a block before the memory of Melissa dragged him down again. On the way home, he picked up pizza and a six-pack.

Mr. Lucky ate most of the pizza. Star put away five of the beers, drifted into a numbing haze before the TV. About eleven, he hit the sack, Mr. Lucky curled by his feet.

Star tossed and turned. Hours passed. He was climbing, far above water, inching sideways along a cliff, arms extended left and right with his feet on a narrow and diminishing ledge. Smooth, fresh basalt, no handholds, cold against his bare flesh. He felt along the ledge with his toes. Narrower and narrower, then sheer rock. End of the world. If he moved, he'd topple, fall forever.

Above, vultures screeched. Below, buzzing. Louder. He lowered his eyes, saw swarming insects. Huge black bees, buzzing so loudly the rock shook. Flying close. Papery wings brushed his skin. Don't move. One landed on the back of his head, burrowed to his scalp. Stiff cold legs chicken-scratched, a barbed tail probed, the stinger plunged deep. Star screamed in agony and reeled into space.

Wide-eyed, he glanced at the clock. Three A.M., sheets wet with perspiration. He lay still, afraid to move, heart pounding, his brain dream-stained. Let me be awake. His diver's mind commanded, Don't move, breathe. There. He was conscious, really awake, but the buzzing kept up, low, by his feet. He raised his head from the pillow, looked down. Mr. Lucky. Not moving. Growling. Low, continuous, unsettling. *Grrrrr.*

Lucky's nose pointed at the window. *Grrrrr.* Then Star heard the alien noise himself. Rattling glass. Jeez! The window, six feet from his bed, ratcheted up. He froze. Curtains fluttered. *Grrrrr.* Oh, no. A hand, an arm. Baseball bat in the closet. Too far. No time to phone. *Grrrrr.* A head. Climbing in, a flashlight in one hand, light beam darting across the far wall. The other hand—gripped a gun. No question, a gun. Shout? Maybe they'll shoot. Run? Never get away. *Grrrrr.*

Indecision. Paralysis.

Fortunately, Mr. Lucky was less introspective. Two strange arms and a head were inside his house already, and there came a leg, and a thing with a light on the end of it, and enough was enough. As soon as the intruder's foot touched the floor, Mr. Lucky leapt from the bed, all the way to the window, and clamped his jaws on the arm with the flashlight, surely as he snagged a Frisbee at Ala Moana Park.

A piercing scream shattered the night, then *Bonk!* and "Uunnk-fuck!" as the intruder's skull slammed the bottom of the window frame. The flashlight clanked to the floor, the arm shook like a fish on a line, up, down, left, right. Lucky held on, snarled like a demon over the burglar's wail.

Then he opened his jaws and the intruder's head hit the window again. *Bonk!* Another "Fuck!" and the head, leg, and arms disappeared into the night, followed by a crash and a third "Fuck!" outside, as the intruder ran into the lawn mower. Finally, in the street, "Get the hey-all out of here!" Squealing tires. Silence.

A mere thirty seconds late, Star sprang into action, ran to the window in time to see Mr. Lucky chasing receding taillights. He dialed 911.

Dingdong. Mr. Lucky stood at the man in blue's feet, tail wagging. A flashlight beam played over the bushes as the cop's partner explored the yard.

Star gave a brief, nervous explanation.

"Nice dog. Does he bite?" A small laugh as Star pointed out the blood on the windowsill. Scrapings of blood. Compliments to Mr. Lucky.

"Thank you, Mr. Felon," sounded outside. The searching partner called through the still-open window, "Guy dropped his gun. Forty-five. Fancy grip, inlaid cobra with ruby eyes. A man with taste."

"What kind of taste would that be, Goosemann?" asked the inside cop.

The outside man ignored him, brought the gun inside, placed it and the burglar's flashlight in plastic bags, and began to poke around the room.

"Okay if I sit down, Mr. Hollie?" said the first cop, Officer Kim, Korean. "Maybe you'd like to sit too, be comfortable, right across from me."

Five empty beer bottles and a pizza box cluttered the coffee table. Dressed in long wavy locks and bright red boxer shorts speckled with green marijuana leaves—a joke Christmas present from Cindy—Star sat on the edge of the sofa, alternately running fingers through his hair and wringing his hands.

Officer Kim opened a spiral-bound notebook. "Now, sir, the spelling of your name, is it like the bush or the woman's name?"

"I don't know how you spell either one."

"I think the bush is H-O-L-Y." He looked at it written. "No, that's 'holy,' like at church. The bush must be H-O-L-L-Y, or is it H-O-L-L-E-

Y? The woman's name, I guess that would be with two L's too, but H-O-L-L-I-E."

"That's it."

"The woman's name?"

"No, my name. You want me to write it for you?"

The Korean cop squinted at him, shielded the notebook.

Kim's crew-cut haole partner, Officer Goosemann, took a long look at Star and his shorts, raised his nose and sniffed the air.

There *was* an odd odor there, like lemons. One of the cops? Aftershave? Star couldn't concentrate. Next, although Star knew he'd explained the burglar never made it through the window, Goosemann began poking around the room for clues. He asked to use the bathroom. Star pointed to the rear of the house.

"Can you describe the intruder, Mr. Hollie?"

"All I saw was his silhouette, but he was a big mother, big as in one of those monster movies."

"They usually are."

"Huh?"

"Never mind," said Kim, writing -ONSTER in the notebook. Kim looked up, asked, "Did he speak?"

"He said 'Fuck.' Three times. Want me to spell that for you? That's F-U- . . ."

Kim narrowed his eyes. "I think I've got that one." He glanced at the window. "I noticed there's no car in the drive. Do you own a car?" Star nodded, explained he'd left it in Waikiki. "So the intruder may have assumed no one was home." Kim paused for effect, watched Star's reaction. "Mr. Hollie, do you have enemies?"

Mako. Of course. "Uh, no. No enemies."

"Burglaries in this neighborhood, especially by armed men, are rare. Perhaps you keep a lot of cash around the house? Cash which business associates may be aware of?"

A joke about being broke. No laughter.

"Do you use drugs, Mr. Hollie?"

"What?"

"Drugs: marijuana, cocaine, heroin?" Eyes running up and down Star's bare arms and legs.

"Coffee."

"Coffee?"

"C-O-F-F- . . ."

"Do you own this house?"

"No, I'm house-sitting for a doctor and his wife in Omaha."

"Oh? And do you have corroborating documentation—as a formality?" He did, somewhere; he'd have to look. A mention of Dan. "So, this Mr. Capistrano—like in the song, huh?—he has a power of attorney with regard to the house and could vouch for your residency, and would it be all right if we call him in the morning, merely to confirm your information?" Yeah, sure. "Mr. Hollie, are you employed?" A writer. "Really?" Talk to Dan.

The second cop, Goosemann, returned from the bathroom—been back there a long time, must have had some trouble, though Star hadn't heard the toilet flush—and flashed a zero sign with his thumb and forefinger to Officer Kim. Kim nodded and closed the notebook.

That seemed to be it. A cautious pat on the head for Mr. Lucky, a warning to keep the doors and windows locked. They'd check hospitals, someone would talk to the neighbors tomorrow, let him know what turned up. They thanked him. He thanked them.

"Mr. Hollie"—Goosemann turned on his way to the street—"this may have been a random break-in, but I doubt it. Could be, somebody's after you—I'd watch my rear end if I was you."

16

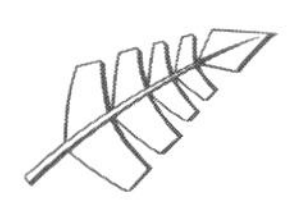

I'd hate to close our island mission on Babelthuap, Judith, but if the offerings don't increase dramatically and soon . . ." The Reverend took another sip of bourbon, leaned back in the crushed-velvet recliner, wiggled his toes in his slippers, spoke again into the phone. "I know, dear, you'll do whatever you can. You always do. But we've got to fire up the donors, give 'em a flashy sinner this week they'll love to hate.

"God bless you." He hung up, rubbed his eyes, and looked over the numbers, the projections he'd been staring at all night. At best, they added up to seventy-five thousand dollars. Added to cash on hand, that totaled barely a hundred thousand.

Reverend Jaycie sighed. Little Josephine had been such a cupcake, but her mother, the blackmailer, was a hard cookie, all right. Two hundred thousand dollars or shameful exposure. Jail. He doubted Brother Bernie could deliver on time. "God helps those who help themselves," he mumbled, scratching his trim white beard. He looked to the picture of Jesus over the mantel for inspiration, but Jesus wasn't talking tonight.

The doorbell rang. "If it's those cursed Jehovah's Witnesses again, pestering me this late . . ."

Reverend Jaycie opened the door and staggered back three steps.

A silhouetted figure filled the doorframe. Its shoulders nearly touched the sides of the jamb.

Two thoughts ran through his mind in quick succession: Angel of Death, and Angry Husband. He stood speechless. Defenseless.

"Forgive me, Father, for I have sinned," said the figure, in a thick Appalachian accent.

"Lordy," said the Reverend, relieved, "whoever you are, you've got the wrong place. I'm no Catholic. Catholic church is two blocks down the street."

"Catholic? Shit fire, me neither," said the man. "I heard 'em say that 'Forgive me, Father' in a movie on the TV." He shook his head. "It's all so strange over here, I never know what to say. Howsoever's the right way, the High-wah-yan way, I need to be saved. Bad."

"It's late, son." He studied the humble giant who had come to his door for succor. "Well, hell." He opened the door wide. "Get yourself in."

The Reverend took in the man's bleached hair, scraggly at the back, the dirty jeans, the cowboy boots. He motioned him to a chair. "Let me guess," he said. "Carolinas or Tennessee. You're a good old mountain boy, aren't you, son?"

"Hail originally from near Jupiter, north of Weaverville."

"Buncombe County," said the Reverend. "I had a ministry in Asheville for nearly a year." Without asking, he got a jelly glass from the cupboard, filled it half full of bourbon, and handed it to the man. With a faraway look in his eyes, he remembered. "I'd still be there if this idea of mine had'na gone foul. Met this fella who had these four monkeys, chimpanzees. Real smart they were. So we worked with 'em. Taught 'em at my sign—I'd raise my right arm like this—to run to my right, jump in the laps of whoever was sitting at that side of the stage. We practiced till we had it down pat. See, I had a wonderful plan."

Wide-eyed, the giant drained a third of the bourbon in one swallow.

"Here's the clever part. For a month I was preaching against the evolutionists. Had everybody fired up. Money was pourin' in, let me tell ya. I declared a 'Monkey Sunday.' Invited in four scientists to debate four fundamentalist preachers. Oh, the words flew. Those scientists spewed out their logic and facts and the preachers read from the Good Book. The congregation—we were televised, too—was roused, shoutin' and hoppin' mad.

"Then I brought out the monkeys, these chimpanzees, all dressed up in corduroys and tweeds, wearing bow ties, carrying evolution books. One had on Coke-bottle-thick spectacles, another carried a magnifyin' glass. They was a hoot, I'll tell ya. So I turn around from my lectern, and I say to the monkeys, so everyone can hear—the monkeys are standing at center stage—I says, 'Monkeys, if you see any of your relatives hereabouts, go to 'em.' An' I raise my right arm like we practiced. Well, the scientists was in a row on foldin' chairs on one side, the preachers on the other—exact same sides as we'd practiced.

"Damned if them monkeys didn't run to the preachers instead of the scientists! Jumped up in their laps, wrapped their hairy arms around those preachers' skinny necks like they was brothers and kissed 'em on the cheeks with those big pink lips of theirs. Damned if they didn't.

"See, when we practiced, I was at the back of the stage, the monkeys was before me. But here on Monkey Sunday they set up my lectern at the front, monkeys behind. I got into my pitch, didn't think nothing about it. But it was bass ackwards,'cause, when I turned around and raised my hand, those monkeys saw that right arm and ran lickety-split thataways, into the preachers' laps. What a hullabaloo. My, my, my. Well, I was out of Asheville by Monday afternoon, and none too soon.

"But I digress. What was it you said you came here for, boy?"

"To be saved. You are a holy man, aren't you, sir? I seen you on the TV."

"Son, you could be saved at home, you know, when I'm televised, or you could get saved on the air, in front of the world."

"No, no. Don't want to be seen on no TV, an' it's not the same watchin'."

"Tell me what you've done, son, that it's so all-fired important you get saved tonight. What's your name, by the by?"

"I'm Bobby Lee."

"I'm the Reverend Jaycie Pitts, Bobby Lee." They shook hands. The Reverend refilled Bobby Lee's glass and got one for himself.

"My brother and me has done bad things, sir, an' I haven't been saved for nigh on two years."

"Where's this brother of yours? Still back in Buncombe County?"

"Ray Don? No, he's right here, sir, in Honolulu. But Ray Don's lost his religion. See, we lived in Harlan County, Kentucky, up Black Mountain ways, for a while and we got into serpent handlin'. You know, to prove our faith? Copperheads, rattlers. We had 'em all over our arms and shoulders during service, in our pockets, everywhere. Never got bit. Except that once. I was wearin' a monster timber rattlesnake round my waist, runnin' through my belt loops. My mind must'a been straying from the Lord, 'cause that old bastard nailed me right on the ass. Felt like a hot poker. I'd'a been a goner if I'd been out in the woods, alone." Bobby Lee rubbed his rear end, winced with the memory.

"Soon's that serpent hit me, though, my dear brother, Ray Don, he does the only thing he can, to save my life. First, he belted me on the jaw to quiet me down. Then he yanked down my jeans an' Fruit of the Looms, flipped me on my stomach, whipped out his penknife, cut X's over the fang marks, dropped to his knees, and . . ."

"Sucked out the poison," said the Reverend. "Lordy, I've heard of such things. What an act of brotherly love."

"Warn't perzactly like that, sir. You see, Ray Don, he couldn't bring himself to suck on my snakebit butt, howsoever bad my butt needed sucking. So he put his knife to the preacher's throat and made him do it. I survived, sir, and I attribute that to my faith, and to my brother's quick thinking." Bobby Lee's face broke into a loving smile.

"The snake preacher, he spit and sputtered, then he pointed to the door of the church and told us to keep a-goin' until we crossed the county line. We never been back since. It was hard on my dear brother. I don't think Ray Don ever forgive hisself. He gave up religion then and there, and his love of preachers and snakes as well. So I'm here alone. Ray Don don't know I came, in fact, and best he stays in the dark about it, too."

Bobby Lee fell silent, groped his posterior, kicked at the carpet. "Sir," he said, looking back at the Reverend, "we killed a man, little ways back. Can't say it was the first, but this one's been weighin' on my mind."

"Lordy! That's a bodacious transgression all right. A bad one. Was it a fight? Argument over a woman? Too much drink?" The Reverend had his kerchief out, worried it with his fingers.

"No, nothin' like that. Well, there was some drinkin'. Guess you could say it was a-cause of our job. It was orders."

"What's your line of work, Bobby Lee, army, marines, police?"

"We're security guards."

"Bobby Lee"—the Reverend placed his hand on the giant's shoulder—"the Good Book tells us 'Thou shalt not kill.' But great men have debated the meaning of that commandment over the ages. Does it mean never-ever? What about the soldier fighting for his homeland? Or the father defending his family? Or the policeman—or the security guard—protecting the innocent? Only the Good Lord knows if there are exceptions. I can't answer for Him, but by men's laws, someone in your profession, following orders, doing what's required of him? Well, Bobby Lee, sometimes a man's gotta do what a man's gotta do. But you're doin' right here, son, shedding your sins and your evil past, getting yourself saved. Kneel down before me."

The Reverend stood. Bobby Lee knelt. "Do you accept the True Lord as your Savior, repent your sins, your evil ways?"

"Oh, I do, I do," said Bobby Lee, his eyes focused on the shag carpet.

Jesus watched it all from above the mantel.

"Verily, verily, I say unto thee." The Reverend's voice rose. "Except a man be born again, he cannot see the Kingdom of God. Are you ready, sinner?"

Bobby Lee nodded, trembled, at the Reverend's feet.

The Reverend set the palm of one hand on the top of Bobby Lee's blond head, made a fist with the other, and thumped it hard onto the back of his open hand.

"Did you feel it, boy? Did you feel the Spirit?"

"I did, sir. I felt its power rock me."

"Then rise up—you're saved, a new man."

Bobby Lee had tears in his eyes. "Thank you, sir. Damn, I feel so clean." Bobby Lee stretched, wiggled his fingers, rolled his head shoulder to shoulder. "What do I owe you, sir?"

The Reverend looked at Bobby Lee's humble clothing. "Bobby

Lee, you keep your hard-earned money, what little of it I imagine you have. The savin's on me tonight."

"My daddy taught me not to take charity, sir. I've got money. How much you want? Fifty? A hundred? Five hundred?"

"Son, where's a security guard get money like that?"

Bobby Lee's eyes fell. "I done other things, sir. Some of it fer money. We hijacked a luau bus not long back, stole their rings an' stuff. Sold the gold an' diamonds for almost eleven thousand. Add the cash, we made close to twelve. I was hopin' the saving took care of the rest of it, too." He looked back up and raised his eyebrows at the Reverend, hopeful, his face full of innocence and light.

The Reverend didn't respond. He was recalling the story of Elijah and the widow. Elijah the prophet was in need. The widow had been a stranger, a foreigner from the land of Jezebel, and Elijah expected nothing of her. Yet she appeared out of the blue, came to his aid. The Reverend had often recounted the story in sermons, to preach the miracle of Providence from unexpected quarters. He looked at Bobby Lee with a growing regard.

"Twelve thousand dollars? How many people were on that luau bus, son?"

"Don't remember, perzactly, sir. Was maybe forty."

The Reverend's eyes closed in silent calculation. When they opened, he was smiling. He turned his back to Jesus over the mantel, spoke to Bobby Lee. "Son—what if you and your brother was to come across, say, three, four, maybe even five hundred captive souls, flush with the Lord's bounty . . ."

17

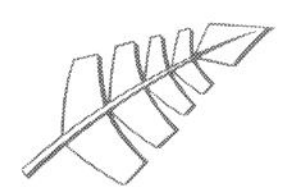

Star fumbled for the receiver.

"Who? What? Dan. I got the morning paper, then fell back asleep on the couch. What time is it?"

"Nine-thirty."

"The cops called you already, huh?"

"Call was waiting when I got in. My God. A gun. Better not mention this to the Townsends." Dan cleared his throat. "I realize this isn't comfortable, son, but do you think there's a chance one of your beach friends may have been hard up for cash and, well—aware you live at the Townsends' house—tried to take advantage of your situation? With your car gone, it would have looked like you were out. Some of those surfing people . . ."

"The police put that idea in your head?"

"Now, now. They have to consider all the possibilities, and you know how naive you can be. We've got to keep our eyes open, okay?"

"Right," said Star. Especially, he reminded himself, when it came to Mako and his men.

He hung up, heard a car door slam. An easygoing police sergeant, plastic foam cup in one hand, glazed doughnut in the other, walked to the porch. At the sight of Mr. Lucky at the open door, he set down the coffee cup, fed Lucky half the doughnut, crammed the rest in his own mouth, and wrestled the dog to the ground.

At sight of Star, he jumped up, brushed white hair from his blue uniform. "Hope you don't mind, sir. I had a border collie myself. Smart, huh? And this guy's got sharp teeth, too, I hear." He retrieved the cup. "I spoke with your neighbors, mostly retirees. Hardly a surprise, they were all asleep until they heard the siren. Haven't been any emergency-room reports of dog bites, but maybe the techs will turn up some good prints on the gun and flashlight."

Star nodded, but he doubted Mako's men would be so careless.

"Your best protection?" The sergeant gave Mr. Lucky a tug on the ears. "Right here. I could suggest an alarm, but truth is, mechanics can't compare with nature's own—hearing, smell, who knows what other senses they have, huh? I saw this TV show, said they can read minds." He squeezed his eyes shut, placed fingertips to his temples.

Woof!

"Me too, boy. There you go. Guess that proves it, huh?" His smile changed to a scowl. "Far as your situation goes, we're stepping up patrols, but I'll tell you what. A man with a gun? I don't like the sound of it. No, I don't. There's something else going on here, all right." He cocked his head and squinted at Star, patted Lucky's head again, and returned to his car.

Star nodded in reluctant agreement as Mr. Lucky's telepathic friend started the engine and waved good-bye. When the car was out of sight, he walked to Waikiki.

True to her word, Scooter had the tires on the Turtle reinflated as well as her Harley reassembled. In the Scooter version of the break-in, Star acted out the swing of his baseball bat that knocked the gun from the thug's hand. "Then I told him to tell Mako I'd shove that bat up his ass if he or any of his men came nosing around my house again."

"Damn straight," she said, and throttled up the Harley. Hog thunder rocked Waikiki.

At Papa's, he nodded off, only to jerk awake with flashbacks of the darkened figure with the gun and Mr. Lucky flying through the air. He lifted the cup. Empty. He looked for Doris.

There—near the register, a gray-haired man whispering in her ear, Doris giggling like a high school girl. Small, wiry, in good shape for his age, the man wore starched khaki trousers tucked into spit-shined black combat boots and an incongruous pink alligator shirt with the collar turned up. Military or ex-military, Star decided, a career man making a bid to look civilian-casual.

She laughed again. Star decided the guy must throw a good line.

The gray-haired man left and Doris came by with the coffeepot.

"Who was that? G.I. Joe's dad?"

"D. L. McWhorter, honey, a new and very charming customer. You're not the only one with admirers, you know."

"I guess. I didn't know you went for military types."

"First time I've seen the man, but D. L.'s a real sweetheart. What a smile."

"You know a military guy like that's probably had a lot of experience with women. You oughta be careful, watch you don't get conned."

"Ho, ho, ho. Look who's talking."

"Yeah. Well, don't you think he looks sneaky with that short hair and the Hitler mustache? And he's barely as tall as you. You're not gonna go out with him, are you?"

"I think his flattop's distinctive, and a Hitler mustache? Hardly. He's tall enough, and I don't know if you noticed, but he's got big hands—and you know what they say about that." She turned and, with a defiant shake of her rear, walked away.

Star left, annoyed, wiped out, eager for easy surfing and a long swim.

On Kuhio Avenue, a block away, he flinched at a familiar, ominous sound: a car horn tooting the first four notes of "Tiny Bubbles."

Mako!

Duck into a doorway? Run! Too late. The car idled along the curb at his speed. Without turning his head, he glanced left. It was Mako's car, all right, a pristine 1987 Chevrolet Monte Carlo SuperSport, lowered to within three inches of the pavement, its ebony metal-flake paint glistening like black snow in the sunlight, covered nose to tail with a delicate tracery of red pinstriping, like veins under flayed skin.

Star shuddered, kept walking.

The blackened driver's window lowered. Star froze. There sat

Mako himself: part Portuguese, part Hawaiian, part Asian, all bad news. He nearly filled the front seat—not that Mako was fat, but rather, uncommonly squat, as if a divine thumb had settled on the top of his head and pushed, to see if vertical compression would do for the human form what it did for the crab.

Mako lifted a comb from his shirt pocket and ran it through a slippery pompadour. "Star, Star," he purred, squinting at the oily pomade gumming the comb's teeth. "You got my present?"

Star stammered.

Mako turned his full-moon face slowly from the comb to Star. Tiny olive-pit eyes blinked at the sunlight. "I asked if you enjoyed my gift."

"I, I got the message. I'll have your money for you, Mako. I swear." Star took a deep breath. "But the loan's not due yet. Why'd your man break into my house last night? With a gun? Jeez. You scared the hell out of me."

Mako's mouth, a three-inch slit, curled into a sinister grin. "Fear is a good motivator, amigo. But a break-in? At night? No. Not my style. Mako knows where you are. When it's time, I'll come for you in the open. And why a gun, when a simple piece of lead pipe would do the trick? I sent the doll in the box as a reminder. This is a re-reminder. A week and a day. Two thousand dollars, plus five hundred interest."

"Mako, listen. I've got the five hundred. . . ."

Mako wiped the comb on his trousers. "Some other time, maybe we could talk about partial payments—but I been having too many people go slack on me. I need an example. And you're it. Nothing personal." He rolled up the window, drove twenty feet down the road, and stopped. The car hopped three feet in the air, "Tiny Bubbles" sounded twice, and Mako was away with a painful squeal of rubber on asphalt.

Star sat on the curb and ran his hands up and down his still-intact legs, then remembered what Mako had said about the break-in.

If the gorilla with the gun hadn't been one of Mako's enforcers, who was he?

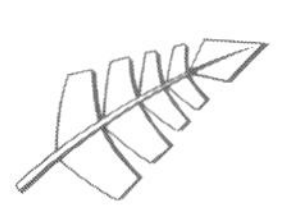

"Think of the good times, Jenna." Bernie pressed the phone to his ear as if it would bring his wife closer.

"If only my memory was that good."

"And what about poor little Jen?"

"Little Jen is back at Vassar where she belongs and wants to be. She's got her own friends, her own life." Three long seconds of silence passed. "Bernie, remember the night before we were married, twenty-three years ago?"

The night before? Bernie thought, God, I can't remember the wedding itself.

"When you and Daddy explained to me how marriage is a contract? That it's a joining of resources, like a corporate merger? My family contributed generously, and I did what was expected. And you? You were going to parlay Daddy's gift into a fortune. I had every expectation you'd follow in his footsteps, surpass him. Now you're headed for a crash."

"Crash? HydraCorp welcomes me, Bernie Bergen, with open arms, and you say 'crash'?"

"I can see the fall coming, Bernie, and I don't want to be around when it happens. This desperate economizing. My God, it's embarrassing."

"Embarrassing? How's this for embarrassing?—me, telling the board my wife's leaving me. It's worse than that, it's emasculating. Did I hear 'poor'? With that castle of ours, the cars, maid, club, daughter at Vassar?Jenna, when Paradise Valley comes through . . ."

"I've heard enough about your precious Paradise Valley to make me barf. You're so wrapped up in your deals—when's the last time we played eighteen holes together, just the two of us?"

"Was only two weeks ago, wasn't it? Sure, I remember, two weeks ago, Saturday."

"Try a year and a half. What we have is separate lives. And now it's time to go our separate ways."

"Jenna, I can't believe you're telling me this. Over the goddamned phone."

"It's easier this way. Face-to-face, you'd talk me out of it, like every other good idea I've ever had. I've talked to Daddy and Mother for hours on end. Walter Carlson's firm will handle the divorce. The Jag—that's the old heap whose transmission wrecked the putting green, in case you've forgotten—the Jag's in the garage and it's all yours. My clothes are boxed and ready to ship. You didn't notice me packing, did you?"

"Sure—thought it was stuff for the Salvation Army, making room for new purchases."

"Good old Bernie. Heather's taking me to the airport. I'll be on Long Island with Daddy and Mommy tomorrow morning."

"Jenna. What will I do without you?"

She hung up.

Bernie closed his eyes to wipe away the tears. Although, when he examined his hand, it was dry. So what? He'd felt like crying, hadn't he? His stomach was still churning, no question of that. Life with Jenna had always been one long upset stomach. He ate a few Mylantas, washed them down with a bourbon and water, popped four Nicorettes in his mouth, and chewed, tried to relax.

He lifted the gold-framed picture of Jenna, little Jen, and himself—taken when, eleven years ago?—and studied it, realizing he couldn't remember the last time he'd noticed it. He slid it into his desk drawer, facedown, near the back, next to the hidden "Wish you were here" postcard he'd received yesterday from Mai Ling in Singapore. Bernie sighed.

One consolation, he thought. Wait until Walter Carlson finds out about the third mortgage on the house, the stripped bank accounts, the promissory notes. The look on old Walter's face will be priceless.

"Mr. Bergen?" Kathleen, on the intercom. "Your new friend, the Reverend Pitts, stopped by. He's asking if he can see you."

"Your new friend." Bernie caught the sarcasm. Kathleen didn't appreciate the good Reverend, but—who'd have guessed?—Bernie enjoyed the old boy's visits more and more. In fact, he realized, the Reverend was the one person he could talk to, straight out. And with Jenna out of the picture—hell, he could never talk to her anyway—he needed a friend. "Send him in, Kathleen. We won't require any tea, thank you." The bottle and one glass were out already. He got a glass for the Reverend from a silver tray on the credenza.

"Reverend?"

"Bernie."

They hugged. That was something new for Bernie. Handshakes, backslaps, arm on the shoulder?—never gave it a thought. But hugging a man? Would have given Bernie the sweats in the old days. But now, the Reverend made it seem, well . . . okay.

"What's up, old buddy?" Bernie asked, pouring a finger for himself and three for the Reverend.

"Due for some rain." The Reverend scratched his chin. "High winds. Storms somewhere off to the north. The temperature may go down to sixty."

"Yeah, this time of year. Watch yourself under those coconut palms, huh?"

The Reverend studied the ceiling. "Bernie. Let me ask you something. Man to man." He glanced at his smiling friend—something was amiss. "Everything hunky-dory with you, brother Bernie?"

Bernie shrugged. "Wife's leaving me. Four of the principals called this morning, worried about the eruption on Mauna Loa. Can't do anything about either one of 'em though. Acts of God, right?"

"Bernie, I'm sorry. Perhaps I could talk to her. You know, as a man of the cloth?"

"Done deal, I'm afraid. Thanks for the offer."

"Eruption?" The word finally registered. "Lordy. Does this mean Paradise Valley . . ."

"Nah. Tell you what I told them. Whole island of Hawai'i is a volcano. Summit of Mauna Loa is thirteen thousand feet up, eruption's at eleven. Paradise Valley's down at three to four thousand, miles away. Lava could stop today or flow down the other slope. If you live on the San Andreas Fault, you don't lie awake worrying about quakes, do you? I'll keep an eye on the sucker and move ahead. They'll be starting the switchbacks down into the valley any day now. Not to worry, Reverend. Not to worry.

"So, Reverend, what brings you by?"

"Bernie." The Reverend pursed his lips. "Have you ever considered doing something that you knew was"—he searched for a word—"contrary, yes, contrary to the laws men are expected to live by? Possibly illegal as well?"

"All the time, Reverend. What's on your mind? Want to rob a bank?"

"Lordy, no. Merely a philosophical inquiry. I'm so worried about this mess I've gotten myself into. Hawai'i needs me. There are strange religions here. There's Mormons. With angels named Moroni. And Hindus, with flesh-eating gods. And Buddhists, who meditate. Even the old Hawaiian religion. Stone worshipers. You ever hear of Pele?"

"The volcano goddess? Sorry to say, I have. Originally, our Aeolus II project was going to be geothermal. Drill into the volcano, pump cold water down, hot water up to drive the turbines—cheap energy, see, no downside. Then the volcano lovers, these Sons of Pele, popped up: 'Break the bones of Mother Pele? Suck Pele's blood? No way.' Protests, the rest of it. Gave us hell. We did our best, but they got the project killed. If I hadn't set up the wind-generator deal, the whole thing would have gone down the tubes. No project, Reverend, no road skirting the Pali-uli, no Paradise Valley. I pulled that one out, but it was a near miss. You want to hear more? About my plan to haul the state's trash to the Big Island, dump it in the volcano? What they said to that?" Bernie shuddered. "Pele. Hope I never hear the word again."

Bernie shook his head fast to erase the distasteful sound, then leaned over his desk to remove a large cigar from a humidor. He rolled it under his nose.

The Reverend's eyebrows rose in appreciation.

"Care for one, Reverend? It's a Corona de la Mofeta. Fidel's favorite, they tell me."

"Thank you, brother. Love a good cee-gar."

"Can't smoke it here, I'm afraid. Sorry, not my rules. Take a handful." He passed the humidor. "Can't smoke myself, so I just smell 'em, suck on 'em. Look here." Bernie leaned over the desk, stuck his tongue out, pulled it further with forefinger and thumb. "Haba prblm widda . . ."—he let his tongue spring back—". . . big red fester on the side of my tongue. I about tossed my cookies when they unloaded the news: the Big C. They cut the damn thing out the same day." He pulled his tongue out again to show a dime-size bite nipped from one side. "Told me if it came back they might have to take the whole thing. Can you imagine a talker like me with no tongue? Doing deals by passing notes?"

The Reverend wrinkled his nose, rolled his tongue in his mouth, then tumbled the cigars from his palm back into the humidor.

"Here, Reverend, try a few of these Nicorettes. Double the dose and they give you a nice buzz."

The Reverend popped two in his mouth. "What was I saying, just before? Oh, yes. It's a theological miasma here, Bernie. Hawai'i needs me. And I do save souls. Point is, I'd hate to pack up and leave again. I need that money or my ministry's down the tubes."

"My friend, I'm doing everything I can to keep Paradise Valley on track, get you your two hundred thousand back in time. But you're covering your ass. Smart. I listened to your program last night, this big revival you're setting up. 'Blessing of the cash.' I like that. Suckers bring their cash for the blessing. And what? You wave your hands over it and it quadruples, right? Great. And while they're under your spell and your tent, you get 'em liquored up on Praise the Lord, and pass the plate, walk away with a bundle. Good business, Reverend."

"I wish you wouldn't paint it in such mercenary terms." The Reverend refilled his glass. "My flock's spiritual needs are real."

"Of course they are. Didn't mean to imply otherwise. You and I,

Reverend, we're two sides of the same coin. You have heavenly intentions, I like the thrill of the chase, but we're both businessmen at heart. We both go for the cash. Right?"

"Yes, I suppose. It's raising the cash that's the problem. Oh Lord. Two hundred thousand dollars."

"I'm doing what I can, friend. The tent I arranged for Omar to lend you—it's big enough? And the land I set up for you to use for this revival—it's all right? Way out in the sugarcane fields, like you wanted. I could get you something closer to the city, you know. No sweat. Hell, I'll fix it for you to pitch your tent smack in the center of Ala Moana Mall if you want. Maybe on the front lawn of Iolani Palace. Can do, Reverend. Call in favors. Fix you up with a sound and light show, too, the Kodak hula dancers—you name it, whatever you want."

"You're a friend in need, you are. Like one of the blessed Israelites under Moses, giving freely for the Tent of Meeting." The Reverend considered the alternate locations and shook his head. "No, those sugarcane fields are perfect. Away from the noise and distractions of the city. Tent, sound system? Perfect."

"You do your thing, then, Reverend. Strip those sinners of their cash, huh? Send 'em home with empty pockets."

"Yes, that's it," said the Reverend. Lord, save my soul, he thought, that's exactly what I'm going to do, too.

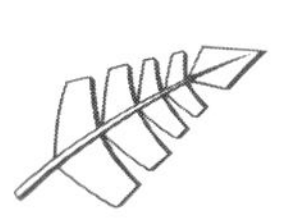

Pull your head out of your ass," said Ray Don. "I swear, I don't know what's got into you, boy. Jobs come along, where's my little brother? If ever the boss found you skipped out like that, he'd shoot you in a city minute. I had to lie, work with that crazy Mongoose. Now you show up, all smiles, like you was a puppy in love." Revelation lit Ray Don's face. "Aha! That's it, ain't it? You got some bird treed, don't you? My little brother's pussy-whipped."

"Shucks," said Bobby Lee. "Ain't nothin' like that." He smiled and rolled one shoulder, then the other, a new angel flexing his wings. Then he blinked, no focus in his eyes, and grinned again.

"Oh no! I shoulda know'd it. That look. Ain't no woman—you done it again. Got your sorry ass saved. Let you outta my sight for two shakes and you go root up the religion like a hog in garbage. Damn it to hell. Only one thing to do for that."

Without warning or windup, Ray Don dropped his brother to his knees with a roundhouse punch to the side of the head.

Had Ray Don thrown his powerful right, Bobby Lee would have been on his back, out for the count, but because of the throbbing dog bite, Ray Don administered the rectifying blow with his weaker, but unimpaired, left. He should have known better.

On his hands and knees, unmoving, Bobby Lee stared at the floor like a stunned opossum. But the moment the aggressor's shadow crossed his back with a poke to the shoulder to see how badly he was hurt, Bobby Lee leapt like a ram in rut, with a punishing head-butt. *Whack!* The sound of crashing foreheads echoed through the empty warehouse.

Ray Don's chin jerked with the impact, dropped to his chest. Although his head saw stars, his lower body reacted independently, reflexively, with a kick to his brother's groin. It was as if, like some antediluvian behemoth, Ray Don possessed a second brain at the base of his spine, doing the thinking for his legs, commanding them to combat.

The heel of Ray Don's size-12 mule-skin Tony Lama barely nicked Bobby Lee's vitals, but it was enough to double him over. He clutched at his crotch, exposing his upper body to a series of stinging jabs.

"Here comes the big one!" yelled Ray Don, with a long, strong right—the hell with the dog bite.

But Bobby Lee blocked it with a swiping fist, unzippering five of Ray Don's stitches.

Ray Don howled, waved his arm. Bobby Lee caught his breath and willed away the gut-wrenching pain from the kick.

Dancing to the side, Ray Don threw a swooping left.

Bobby Lee caught the wrist in midswing, pulled Ray Don's massive hand to his mouth, and bit off the tip of his little finger. Ray Don's scream nearly shattered the windows.

The line had been crossed. Half-blinded by blood and sweat, arteries pumping adrenaline, the brothers traded punches, gouged, and kicked like electronic superheroes. Up and down, down and up, they thrashed, bled, spit, and cursed.

Then Ray Don threw a solid right to Bobby Lee's nose—and connected.

Bobby Lee saw flashing fireworks, felt his arms flop to his side.

Ray Don followed him to the concrete with a flurry—left, right, left, right—then jumped on his brother's stomach and whopped his head from side to side until he saw his eyes roll back. Straddling his chest, Ray Don lifted Bobby Lee's head by the long hair at the nape of his neck and stared, nose to nose, until he saw his eyelids flicker and the light of consciousness return.

Bobby Lee blinked, spit blood from his mouth. "You whipped me," he croaked. "Was a good fight."

"But did I beat the religion out of your thick skull? Did I unsave you, little brother?"

"Shit fire, I guess you did."

"Only way to do it is get your blood boilin'. It's got to be done or you'd go worthless on me." Ray Don sucked on his little finger, popped it from his lips, and scrutinized the bite, satisfied the damage was tolerable. What was the loss of a fingertip to regaining a brother? He lifted Bobby Lee's battered head and cradled it in his lap. "My, my, look at that nose." He stripped off his T-shirt and pressed it to Bobby Lee's upper lip, stanching the rivulets of blood.

Bobby Lee, in turn, sat up, removed his own shirt, and wrapped it around his brother's forearm. Half the stitches had ripped loose. Bobby Lee looped his belt around the dressing, cinched it in place. "You hang in there, Ray Don," he said. "Soon as I find a needle and thread, I'll sew this arm back up. Whatever has you been up to since I been away? I swear, you need me to take care of you."

Ray Don nearly cried. He threw his arms around Bobby Lee's neck and bellowed, "I love you, little brother."

"I love you, too," wailed Bobby Lee.

They squeezed one another for a good two seconds before manly reason parted them.

"Ray Don?" said Bobby Lee. He waggled a front tooth with his thumb. "There's something I got to talk to you about. I met this preacher man, see?"

"Gawd! Here we go again." Ray Don balled his fists.

"No, no. This ain't about religion. Not perzactly, anyways." He looked his brother in the eye, willed away the concussion, free finally of the mystical smoke that had clouded his brain for days. "Ray Don," he said, smirking like the Bobby Lee of old, "this here is about easy money. . . ."

20

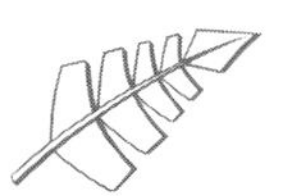

Star answered the phone on the first ring. "Star man here."

"This is Dr. Cassidy MacConnell."

A woman. A doctor. She sounded clinical, detached, as though explaining a suspicious spot on an X ray.

"You've got the wrong number."

"No. I believe you knew my sister, Melissa Finch."

For a moment, Star couldn't breathe. He forced himself to inhale, but couldn't speak.

"Hello?"

He found words. "Melissa's sister? I'm, uh, sorry. A tragedy. Is there a funeral planned?" Thinking, Man, I'll go, but I hate funerals.

"I appreciate your sentiments, Mr. Hollie."

She didn't sound grateful, more businesslike, cool.

"There will be no funeral. Not here, anyway. Melissa's being cremated."

Jeez, burnt up.

"Her remains will be sent back to Michigan. Look, Mr. Hollie, I'd be grateful if we could speak. When would be a good time?"

Accustomed to having her way. Star pictured nurses hovering with syringes and stainless-steel probes, anxious to slap something in her hand. "Dr. MacConnell"—the title made him straighten his back, enunciate—"Melissa and I barely met. I was shocked, really shocked, to hear of her suicide, but I really don't know what I could tell you. Really."

One thing he really didn't care to tell her was how he had sent Melissa running into traffic with tears streaming down her face hours before she killed herself.

"Please, Mr. Hollie, I'll come to your home if you'd like. I assure you I won't take much of your time. What is convenient for you?"

"Hmmm. Where are you now?"

"At the Waikiki Surf."

"Okay. I'll meet you at Papa's Coffee Shop on Kuhio at two. Has a big neon sign out front with three palms, only five or six blocks from your hotel. Everybody on the beach knows Papa's, just ask."

"How will I recognize you?"

"Look for a black aloha shirt with red hibiscuses. I have long, light brown hair, green eyes. They all know me, just ask for Star."

It wasn't until he hung up that he realized his personals-ad shirt, the one he'd worn to see Melissa, might not be the most sensitive choice for meeting the late Melissa's sister.

Papa sent her back. Star saw the resemblance immediately. A year or two older than Melissa. Thinner, good bones, clear skin, could be a head turner if she made half an effort, but no, this wasn't Melissa—this woman was all business. Bookish metal-frame glasses, light brown hair, healthy, but pulled back and pinned behind her head, no makeup, short, clear nails. White shirt like a man's tucked into navy slacks. He imagined her peering over her glasses at an elderly patient missing the cue to leave her office: "Yes? Will there be something further, Mrs. Jones?" And the sick woman hobbling out on her cane, feeling small and apologetic for taking the busy doctor's time.

"Ah, Mr. Hollie." She sat, squinted at him as if examining an equatorial skin fungus. "Thank you for seeing me. You look exactly as I expected. Let me guess. You are a surfer here in Hawai'i?"

"Yeah. More of a swimmer than a surfer, really."

"I see. You and Melissa were close?"

"No. We'd just met."

"Please be frank. I loved my sister and I've always been a great admirer of her abilities. She lived every moment to the fullest and she had rare talents. She was a remarkable artist, you know."

Star raised an eyebrow, said nothing.

"But I also accept Melissa's shortcomings. I'm afraid she was always, well, a bit of a tramp—and you're obviously her type. When I look at you, it doesn't take much imagination to see that you were lovers. Isn't that right?" She leaned toward him. "It's all right. You can tell me."

Not exactly an accusation, he decided, merely a professional solicitation of information, as if asking a young patient: "Jeannie, sexual activity is perfectly normal for a girl of your age. You needn't be embarrassed. However, gonorrhea rarely comes from toilet seats as you suggest, so it's all right, you can tell me the name of . . ."

"We were *not* lovers. I told you, we'd just met. I only saw Melissa once. Once."

"I see. And how did you meet?"

"It, uh, had to do with, with an article I was writing."

"An article? So you're a writer? With one of the beach tabloids, perhaps?"

"No. For *Pacific Rainbow* magazine."

"You're a writer for *Pacific Rainbow?*" She gave him a withering look to see if the liar would lower his eyes. "I know that publication. What was the nature of the article?"

"Umm, I'm afraid that's confidential."

"Confidential. Yes, of course. May I ask when you met—interviewed—Melissa?"

"It was, let's see, five days ago, I think."

"The day she died?"

"I guess."

"The day she died. I see. What were your impressions? Was she despondent? Did you argue?"

Truth had gotten him into trouble with Melissa, he wouldn't let it happen again. "No, she seemed fine, although, uh, yes, I'm sure she was upset over her husband's death. Melissa and I talked a little bit in the afternoon, then we said good-bye and that was the last I saw of her."

"What did the police have to say to you? Did they know you spent time with her the very day she died?"

"The police? Melissa killed herself. Why would the police talk to me?"

"There was some investigation, I understand, although evidently not much of one. So that's it? That's all you care to tell me?"

"That's all I *can* tell you."

"Thank you for your time." She left.

Star realized his shirt was wet, his knuckles white from gripping the table. He decided Dr. MacConnell could give lessons to the cop who had interrogated him after the burglary. It would have served her right if he'd gotten those dirty pictures of Melissa's from Papa and shown her a few: "Here's some of your sister's remarkable art—what do you think of *that?* Right there"—he'd point at the one of her nookie—"that's the most I saw of your sister, Dr. MacConnell."

He took a drink of coffee, held the cup to his nose and inhaled, savored the warm liquid in his mouth to take his mind off Melissa's harpy sister. "Nice to meet you," he said over the cup to the closing door. "So sorry we won't be seeing one another again."

21

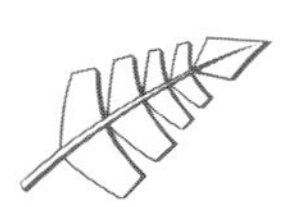

Star cocked his eyebrow, saw the disturbing glint in Papa's eyes, noticed Doris, the other two waitresses, and Charlie, the cook, all smirking. Uh-oh. All of them headed his way, Doris with something behind her back. He edged back, ready to duck.

"Close your eyes, honey," Doris said. "I promise it won't hurt."

His body went rigid, but he squeezed his lids shut.

"Okay, open 'em, you devil."

They laughed and applauded. She had set a cake on the table. No thin iced wafer in pale pinks and blues like the birthday cakes given customers, this one was a real, from-scratch masterpiece, slathered with black frosting and crowned by a thumb-thick black candle. A scarlet sugar devil sporting horns, pointed tail, and pitchfork danced across the top. Red script read, "In appreciation of Papa's Sinner of the Week." Behind the devil lay a field of 666's and pentagrams. Yellow and orange flames leapt around the side.

Star blew out the candle. "Thanks, guys. It's a beauty, and it's nice to know I'm appreciated. But it's not my birthday."

"You don't know what the cake's for?" Sanya asked.

"I know I have a certain reputation, but this is the first time it's been acknowledged so generously."

"Our boy's a TV personality," Papa beamed, "and doesn't know it. You starred on the show with that preacher—the one with the white hair and gold finger rings."

"Huh?"

"The Reverend Jaycie Pitts, Church of the Heavenly Promise and Earthly Delivery," said Sanya. "The one who cries crocodile tears and begs his viewers to 'drown 'ol Lucifer with believers' cash' while he shakes that jeweled white cane of his at the camera."

"With this Holy Staff I smite the horny-hoofed Satan," quoted Rae Jeanne.

"That's *you,* Star," said Doris. "On last night's show, they proclaimed you 'Sinner of the Week.' They zoomed in on that ad you ran in the paper. Trumpets blew, the Cheerleaders for Jesus waved pompoms." Doris swished two napkins in the air. "Give me an S, give me an I, give me an N. And an N-E-R, whattaya got?"

Sanya and Rae Jeanne joined in, "SINNER!"

"Then the Reverend Pitts jumped from behind his golden throne with a huge full-color photograph of you with your name underneath in big red letters."

"My picture?"

"Remember? When that woman threw ice water on you and took your picture?"

"Judith. The bitch."

"It's a great shot—your hands are up waving the camera away, your mouth's open like you're scared to death. Looks like you're trying to escape the Reverend Pitts's Holy Staff, Devil Slayer.

"He set your picture on an easel and shook the cane at it. 'Star Hollie, *you* are Sinner of the Week.' Said he'd challenged you to a wrestling match on the air with 'the Fightin' Apostle of the Lord'—that's him—but claimed when you saw Devil Slayer, you ran off quaking to your sinner's lair—that's here, I guess. Then he cried something awful and offered to save both you and your poor suffering wife on the air."

"Bastard. What am I going to tell my neighbors? All those old folks. What if Cindy saw it? Dan? Melissa's sister? Jeez."

"The Reverend Jaycie Pitts," said Doris, "is better than the Comedy Channel. Everybody watches him."

"Everybody," he repeated.

"Oh yeah," said Doris. "His big revival's about to open. He's pushing it hard—you were the warm-up for the real pitch. Saving of Hawai'i's sinners and blessing of the cash." She laughed. "Go to it, Star. Get yourself saved. Take your 'wife' and your coffee money. The Reverend promises everyone's cash will quadruple 'in a blink of the Lord's eye.' It'll be like four cups for the price of one. How can you lose?"

"Lose?" He thought of his legs. Sure, I'll take the five hundred dollars Dan gave me, get it blessed by the old goat, and make two thousand more. Thank you for the loan, Mr. Mako, here's your cash, paid in full.

"Anyway," said Papa, "the cake—it's devil's food, by the way—is in honor of your celebrity, and for entertainment here at Papa's above and beyond the call." He ruffled Star's hair.

The regulars helped themselves to cake, and every so often one shook a fork at Star like the Reverend Jaycie Pitts did with Devil Slayer, the Holy Staff.

A single a piece of chocolate cake remained on the plate, one covered with 666's and flames, when Melissa's sister, Dr. Cassidy MacConnell, appeared.

She stood beside him and stared at the cake. Star knew with a sinking heart she'd seen the TV show.

She raised her palm. Star flinched, expecting a slap. Instead, she shook his hand, with a mollifying, "Mr. Hollie, I'm afraid I owe you an apology. I spoke with Mr. Capistrano of *Pacific Rainbow*."

"You spoke with Dan?"

She sat across from him. "I did, and he confirmed that you do indeed write for the magazine."

"That's what I told you."

"I confess I was skeptical. Perhaps it was your bohemian appearance or furtive behavior, or Melissa's taste in men. Anyway, Mr. Capistrano and I had a pleasant chat. He thinks highly of you, had no doubt you interviewed Melissa as you said, and that editorial confidentiality would have prevented you from discussing the article, although I assume it had something to do with Melissa's art."

Good old Dan.

"He assured me the timing of your interview and Melissa's death were coincidental. When I expressed my reservations about you with regard to Melissa, he said, and I quote, 'Dr. MacConnell, appearances can be deceiving. Take my word, I'd trust that boy with my life.' "

"Dan said that?"

"He did. And he sounded sincere. I followed with inquiries about him as well, and discovered Mr. Capistrano is well regarded in Hawai'i. So, I accepted his appraisal." She paused, looked outside at the traffic, then back at Star. "Mr. Hollie, I have no friends or acquaintances here, outside of Melissa's husband's family, the Finches, and we seldom see eye to eye. The fact is, I am in desperate need of help. Mr. Capistrano told me you have an inquiring mind, you know Hawai'i, and he suggested you might be willing to assist me. Is that possible? I can pay you for your time."

"I don't know, Dr. MacConnell. What, exactly, is your problem?"

"The fact is"—she looked around the coffee shop, lowered her voice—"Melissa didn't kill herself, she was murdered."

Great, he thought, the sister's screwy, too. The paper said it, right out: Melissa did herself in. Then he realized that if the sister thought Melissa had been murdered, he'd been her number one suspect. Jeez.

"What makes you think Melissa was murdered?"

"I know my sister. First, she loved life too much to take her own life. She had a rare vitality. Surely you perceived that?"

He remembered.

"Second, while Melissa and Artemas respected one another, their relationship was scarcely ardent. Of course she grieved when he died in the automobile accident, but there's no way she would have taken her life over it. An artist, Melissa had her ups and downs—had them all her life, little snits or crying fits one minute, soaring flights of enthusiasm the next."

Star nodded.

"I'm afraid mood swings run in the family—excepting me, of course—I pride myself on my equanimity." She adjusted her glasses, then removed them, closed her eyes, and pinched the bridge of her nose. "But even in times of great stress Melissa's lows never threatened her psyche."

She put the glasses back on. "Third, if Melissa had considered suicide, she would have called me first—they say she didn't even leave a good-bye note, you know. She and I always confided in one another in times of need."

He tried to imagine anyone confiding in Dr. MacConnell.

"And fourth, drown herself? Melissa was terrified of open water ever since college, when she nearly drowned in the ocean during an Easter trip to Fort Lauderdale."

Star raised his eyebrows at that. "When I told Melissa I was a swimmer, she did say something about watching the waves but never going near the water."

"You see? No, there's no doubt in my mind."

"You mentioned the police. What did they say?"

"Open-and-shut. Depressed. Left her clothing in a neat stack on the beach, evidently common in a suicide drowning. Her car parked nearby. No sign of violence, no enemies, no one to benefit from her death, no motives. Hysterical sister from the mainland. Case closed."

"Inheritance? I seem to remember she implied her husband was well-off."

"Old island family, the Finches. They never approved of Melissa, although if it weren't for her, Artemas would never have gone as far as he did. Artemas and Melissa were far less affluent than the rest of the Finch family. No financial incentive. Melissa and I had only each other and our parents. I'm her beneficiary. That leaves only one possibility: a lover."

Star blushed. "I swear. I only met her once, here at the restaurant."

"Uh-huh. But confess—there was an attraction."

"Well, I thought she was nice." He looked away, then back. "The truth is, I did want to see her again. I thought I might."

"You're an attractive man. Melissa would have been drawn to you, I can see that. She had a way of arousing the opposite sex. It's only natural you would have responded. A biological imperative, I suppose."

He frowned.

"Melissa usually told me about her gentlemen. When we spoke, two days before, she didn't mention you or anyone else. So I'm at a loss."

She fiddled with her glasses again. "Although, I *have* considered blackmail. Melissa saw men with disturbing frequency . . ."

Star studied his coffee.

" . . . and I suspect some of them may have been of questionable character. Yes, extortion is a distinct possibility. She would have gone to great lengths to keep her affairs from the Finches, even if Artemas himself closed his eyes to her roving."

Star changed the subject. "So, you got my name from the message I left on her answering machine?"

"Answering machine? No. I found your name and number on a pizza coupon stuck behind a magnet on the refrigerator door. I checked her machine but couldn't find the tape. The house was vandalized after she died, you see. I found the machine on the floor, shattered."

"Vandalized? What did the police say about that?"

"They felt it happened after the newspaper article appeared. As far as I can tell, only the stereo and computer were stolen. It's not uncommon for vandals and thieves to read the obituaries, then prey on the unoccupied houses."

"I had a break-in at my house, too. Happened while I was asleep. My dog chased him away."

"Then you have some sense of my anger, my fears. The chaos of Melissa's house is why I'm at the hotel. I might have stayed with the Finches, but that would be awkward. They've asked the neighbors to keep an eye on Melissa's place until we straighten up. I can stay here for a while if it's productive. I do know I'm not going to run out on Melissa now.

"Mr. Hollie. Will you help me? As I said, I'll pay you for your time."

He looked away, thought, Dr. MacConnell, you are a royal pain in the ass. You may be nuts, besides. On the other hand, I need money in the worst way. He sipped coffee, avoided her eyes.

"Tell you what," he said. "Let me think about it. I'll call you."

She gave him her number and left.

Star, he told himself, don't call. That woman's trouble, and you're in enough hot water already.

22

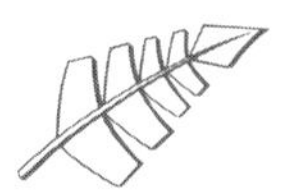

Star had the dream again, as he did now every night: the black cat, the swim through dark hot water, the giant clam, the shell slamming shut to pin him to the bottom. He jerked awake, sat upright, gulping air. Usually it was his struggling, his burning lungs, the surety of drowning that jolted him to consciousness.

But not tonight; the dream hadn't progressed that far. Tonight it was barking.

Star slapped his cheeks to shake the dream from his mind. Yes, Mr. Lucky barking. Not his pretend-to-be-vicious barking reserved for the mailman, but the real thing. And thumping noises outside. Star stumbled to the window, saw a silhouetted figure hovering over his car. He grabbed the baseball bat and ran to the front door, Mr. Lucky at his heels.

Whoever it had been had taken off. He walked outside to the car, and groaned. The Turtle's windshield had been smashed, a brick lay on the seat, and SINNER was spray-painted in red across the hood.

He wiped at the paint with a paper napkin from the car floor, managed to smudge the NER. The SIN was there to stay.

A patrol car slowed while he picked shattered glass from the seat. Officers Kim and Goosemann. They double-parked, walked over.

"Trouble, sir?" asked Goosemann.

"Some jerk threw a brick through the window, and did that." He pointed to the paint, watched Kim open his notebook, write SIN.

"Here's the story," Star said, and explained how he had been proclaimed Sinner of the Week on television the night before.

"Never won a thing myself," said Kim, "although the wife always sends in those sweepstakes letters." He shook his head. "Terrible, isn't it, how jealousy will drive some people to crime?"

"Kim," said Goosemann, "the guy with the brick and the paint wasn't jealous. He was fired up by that preacher, see? He's a vigilante. Could be the same joker who broke and entered with the gun—maybe works for the preacher, was looking for evidence of sinning the first time. I'll bet he did this to get back for the dog bite."

Star hefted the bat. "That damned preacher."

"Settle down, sir," said Goosemann. "You let the law handle this. Okay?"

"Of course, Officer."

He couldn't get back to sleep. At eight A.M. he called Dan.

". . . broke into my house, and then came back and threw a brick through my windshield, painted my hood. It's that bastard preacher. I'm going to find out where he lives. . . ."

"Cool down," Dan said. "Let's go about this like adults. You have no way of proving a connection between this Reverend Pitts and the break-in or the vandalism, although it does sound plausible.

"Tell you what I'll do. Since your ad and our story led to this, I'll pick up the tab for the windshield. You see Palolo Glass, one of our advertisers. Look 'em up in the book. Tell Mr. Sumi I'll work something out with him. That make you happy?"

"That's good. Thanks."

"Back to Pitts. We may have legal recourse, with Pitts putting you on his show. Stand tight. Let me do some checking. I'll call back."

An hour and a half later, the phone rang.

"No easy solution, my boy. You have to understand, getting a prosecutor to move on a religious sect is nearly impossible, unless they sacrifice children in public, or—"

"But we can sue. They used my name, picture. Judith lied to me. . . ."

"Star, I got hold of this Reverend Pitts by phone. Seems a likable old gent."

"Likable?"

"Calm down. First impression, okay? He claims there are always crackpots misconstruing his message, assures me he had nothing to do with the break-in or the car attack, says he's also sorry if the TV 'Sinner' episode embarrassed you. His producer, Judith, was with him. She maintains you were publicity hungry, that you showed her the personals ad, begged her to let you on the show, even offered to bring your wife. Says you posed for the photograph and she thought she was doing you a favor. She also says you propositioned her, offended her Christian sensibilities."

"The bitch."

"A fabrication. So I called our attorney. He points out that you did run the ad, that it and the photo tend to support her story. Looks bad for you. Your word against hers, see?"

"Jeez."

"Proving libel may be impossible. An expensive and potentially embarrassing business in any case."

Star made a sound like Arrghh! and thumped his baseball bat against the floor.

"Cool down, because there is another angle. We have a file on the Reverend Pitts. *Pacific Rainbow* has a correspondent in Babelthuap, Palau, curious about this Pitts's much-publicized contributions to Micronesian charities. The charities won't say a word, but our man suspects the lion's share of Pitts's Hawaiian contributions passes through a series of banks and winds up in the Cook Islands. Unfortunately, that's difficult to prove as well. Your Reverent Pitts is a wily old devil."

The bat thumped twice.

"Wait. It does get better. There are vague references in the dossier to sexual improprieties."

"Now we're getting somewhere."

"When I asked Pitts point-blank about his finances, he went into a coughing fit. When I mentioned the sexual rumor, he hung up."

"Ha!"

"The one thing a man like this fears is public exposure. *Pacific Rainbow* is gathering data. Be patient."

"Patient?"

"Sorry, that's the best I can do.

"By the way, a Cassidy MacConnell called. Bright woman, said she spoke with you briefly about her sister—evidently one of the women you interviewed for the personals article. Sister took her own life."

"Her name was Melissa."

"Yes. Suicide's tough to accept, and Dr. MacConnell got it in her head her sister was murdered. In fact, that you may have had something to do with it. Don't worry—I set her straight. I also took the liberty of suggesting you might help her investigate the death, set her mind at ease. So if she calls again, see what you can do."

"Saw her already. Told her I'd think about it. Dan, she's a pain in the butt."

"She's upset, jet-lagged, grieving. Be patient."

"There's that word again."

"And another matter. A woman named Walana something, long Hawaiian name. Re-creating the old Hawai'i on the Big Island, interested in our doing a story. With Hawaiian sovereignty on everyone's minds, it might be a timely piece. Look into it."

"I spoke with her already. So, Walana phoned you too?"

"She did. Powerful voice, huh? I made some calls. She commands considerable respect in the Hawaiian community, let me tell you—a real force on the Big Island. Something else. She said she was concerned about *you*. Said you were having 'the Dreams,' that 'trouble was stalking you.' I've never been one for superstition, ESP, that sort of thing, but remember that clam dream of yours? And my conversation with her was before the burglary, before this car attack. This is Hawai'i, son. I've heard stories about Hawaiian oracles, priests—kahuna—that would curl your hair. You be doubly careful, okay?"

Star hung up, gave the coffee table a boot, muttered, "Patient? Careful?"

While wiping up the spilled coffee, he thought about Melissa. What if she *had* been murdered?

"What do you think, Lucky? Should I call the good doctor?"

Woof!

"Yeah, I was afraid you'd say that."

He dialed Cassidy MacConnell's hotel.

She answered on the second ring. "Mr. Hollie? Thanks for calling. You'll help?"

"If I can. Look . . ." He swallowed. "I don't want any money, okay? This is for Melissa."

"I appreciate that. Yes. Thanks."

He paused, scratched Mr. Lucky's ears. "You know, Dr. MacConnell, it may be smart to go through Melissa's house, poke around before you and the in-laws put it back in order. If you want, I could pick you up at your hotel."

"I can be ready in ten minutes."

He remembered the broken windshield. "I need a few hours. How about one o'clock?"

"I'll be out front."

23

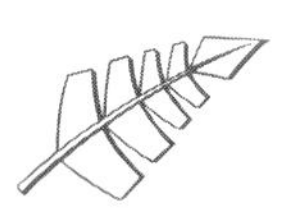

He saw her half a block away through his new windshield, sitting on the edge of a hotel potted palm, tapping her watch.

The doorman, in royal blue trousers and pink aloha shirt, sent a Mercedes limo on its way, walked to the SIN-painted Metro. "One moment, ma'am," he said to Dr. MacConnell, opening the door. He lifted a pale green crystal from the seat, twisted it between his fingers in the sun, leaned down, peered into the car. "Emerald, sir?" he asked Star. "Perhaps it fell from a ring? At least four carats, I'd judge. Worth a bundle, I'll bet."

"Glass," said Star, with a distinct lack of enthusiasm. "Broken windshield." He nodded toward the new one. "Glass people vacuumed most of it up."

"Story of my life," muttered the doorman. He set the crystal on the dashboard. "I attended this tent revival last night and they promised my money would quadruple. Been waiting all morning for my luck to change. Four-carat emerald would carry a nice reward."

"Don't tell me—the Reverend Jaycie Pitts."

"Yes sir. You were there, too? How's your luck been? The preacher didn't exactly put a timeline on the quadruple part, did he?

But they say the old guy's well connected." He pointed skyward. "Puts on a real show, doesn't he?"

"Didn't see the show," said Star, scowling, "but I know the man. Hasn't done much for me." He flicked the glass onto the drive, watched it bounce across concrete into the grass.

"Don't give up yet, sir. Friend of mine, went to the revival with me, took three hundred dollars to be blessed. He walks the beach at dawn every day with a metal detector, see? Today he comes across this place where two people were—you know—intimate last night. Imprint of bodies in the sand, broken high heel from a woman's shoe, coins, a sock, a used—uh, protection. He pokes around—guess what? Finds a woman's diamond tennis bracelet worth twelve hundred dollars, at least. He didn't believe in the preacher and the blessing stuff, but he does now. He's gonna sell the bracelet today, go back to the revival tonight with the proceeds. It quadruples . . . enough said, huh?"

"Hmmmm," said Star.

Dr. MacConnell had been circling the car. She rubbed a finger across the spray-painted SIN.

"Someone attacked my car," he said.

She looked inside at the backseat, at crumpled waxed paper, hamburger cartons, a stiff sweat sock, swim fins, a climbing rope, magazines, specks of glass. "I see they ransacked it, too. Did they get anything valuable?"

He scowled. "No. No ransacking, just attacked the outside, okay?"

She brushed another emerald from the seat before climbing in. "Who did it?"

"Religious terrorists. Tried to frighten me away from an investigatory article I'm doing. I thought I'd leave it like this, as a statement."

"Good for you. You can't give in to those kind of people. Does your writing often put you in danger?"

"I'm learning to live with it." He shifted gears, punched the accelerator, framed a terrorist attack story, then noticed her red-rimmed eyes, and kept it to himself.

She stared out the window as they exited the H-1, drove up the Nuuanu Pali Highway toward the Finch home in Kailua on the other side of the island. Halfway up the mountain, Star spoke: "Ever been to the Nuuanu Pali Lookout?"

"I'm not that familiar with Hawai'i. Melissa and Artemas showed me the sights, but I've never seen, what is it? The Pali Lookout?"

"We're in the Nuuanu Valley now. Up to the right, top of the mountain, see that sawtooth ridge? That was a fort in the old days. Big battle fought there." He pulled onto a long exit ramp canopied by ironwood trees. Near the top, it widened into a looped parking lot.

She followed him from the car toward a clear horizon, onto a raised observation area jammed with tourists. Half the island, rimmed by indigo ocean, opened before them.

It was a brilliant, blustery day. A small historical pamphlet flew from a tourist pocket, somersaulted across the pavement to flatten with a snap against a wall, corners chattering in the wind.

Star peeled it from the concrete. "It's the story of Kamehameha and this place, Nuuanu," he said, pronouncing the words, Kah-MAY-ha-MAY-ha and Nu-u-AH-nu. "It says, 'Kamehameha, an ambitious chief from the Big Island of Hawai'i, was present in 1779 when Captain James Cook, the first European explorer to visit Hawai'i, was feted as the god Lono.' " Melissa, he recalled, knew all about Captain Cook.

He shook the pamphlet, smoothed it with his hand. " 'The chief conquered the eastern islands, Hawai'i, Maui, Lana'i, and Moloka'i. Then, accompanied by his snarling war god Kukailimoku—Ku, eater of islands—he invaded the island of O'ahu, west of Waikiki.' That's not far from your hotel, Dr. MacConnell."

No reaction.

" 'Days of fierce combat forced the defending O'ahu chief and his warriors up the Nuuanu Valley. Foot by foot the fighting advanced toward the mountainous crest of the island. There was no retreat beyond the Nuuanu Pali, a sheer precipice at the top, dropping six hundred feet to lowlands on the other side of the island. With backs to the cliff, the defenders were soon fighting not for the island, but for their lives.

" 'Mercy was neither given, nor taken. Rather than surrender, some three hundred O'ahu chiefs and warriors leapt or were hurled off the Nuuanu Pali to their death on the rocks far below.'

"What do you think of that, Dr. MacConnell? Right here."

"Events like that certainly bring meaning to a place, don't they?" she said, staring at the cliff edge, eyes still red.

"It says, 'The Big Island chief became Kamehameha the Great, first ruler of all Hawai'i.' "

"Hawai'i has a colorful history, no question," she said, face a blank.

Pleased to get at least a few words out of her, he said, "Whoa. Look at that view," swiping a hand across the horizon. A finger traced the far shore. "Trade winds out of the northeast blow up the big waves on the windward side. I surf them. Monsters, believe me. Then the winds shoot across that lowland toward us." He waved to cliffs, left and right. "They climb, accelerate. Here at the top, at this gap, they spill through to the other side—blow like hell."

She leaned on the railing, silent.

"Back here we're protected, but down there?" He pointed at two girls chattering in French. A blast of wind slammed them, they screamed. Skirts flew up, a Parisian hat blew away forever.

A thin smile crossed Dr. MacConnell's lips.

A skinny teenager, nose like a beak, hair shaved short at the sides, long behind, forced his way into the wind. Straining, head bent, he leaned forward at a forty-five-degree angle, hair driven straight back. Chromed, he would have made a nice hood ornament for a thirties cabriolet. Gusts wrenched his mouth and face like the G forces in an old rocket movie as he flung open his windbreaker, held it wide, jumped straight up, and actually flew for a long second. Then, blown backward three feet, he stumbled and rolled, came to rest on his stomach, nose bloody, grinning.

Dr. MacConnell smiled again.

Star grabbed her by the wrist, pulled her toward the pavement bordering the cliff.

Whoomp! Stopped in their tracks. He dropped her wrist. She screamed, slapped a hand to her head as the wind ripped away a barrette, whipped shoulder-length hair around her neck.

Star leapt three feet in the air, lost balance, staggered, landed two feet back.

She laughed at him, then jumped herself. She screeched, jumped again.

They kept it up for ten minutes.

Back at the observation area, out of the wind, she turned her back to him, repinned tangled hair, straightened mussed clothing. Impassive again, she stared at the horizon.

Star thought of comedians who turn their backs to an audience, run hands over hidden faces and reappear as someone else.

He left her to her thoughts, watched a middle-aged couple inch to the cliff edge. Hunkering in the wind shadow of the squat wall, they gripped the pipe rail at the top, leaned over, peered down, then jerked back, no doubt thinking it was a long, long way down. He understood—he'd always wanted to rappel or climb down the Nuuanu Pali, but had never had the nerve.

They walked to the parking lot without speaking. Star slid the key in the ignition. "So, what do you think of the Nuuanu Pali, Dr. MacConnell?"

"Right up there with wing walking." She laughed. Then tears ran down her face and she twisted away, snatched off her glasses, covered her face.

"Hey, sorry." He offered her a wadded Kleenex from the glove compartment.

"No, no. I'm all right. I needed the tears too. I've been keeping too much inside." She rubbed her eyes, then turned and smiled. "You did right, bringing me up here. Thanks. And please, enough of this Dr. MacConnell stuff—call me Caddy."

24

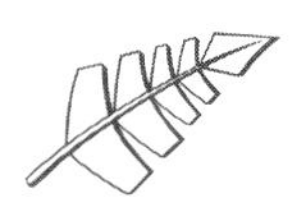

They drove from the lookout down to the highway and through the mountain-crest tunnel. Beyond, cliffs to either side dropped to the windward lowlands like folds of wet green felt.

"It's hard to believe," Caddy MacConnell said, more to herself than to Star, "that this was once a shield volcano with gentle slopes. Amazing what three million years of scouring by wind and water can do. Our lives are so short."

Star nodded, glanced to his right, caught the faraway look.

She sighed. "In a blink of time, humans developed this incredible brain. Yet, we're bound to our animal past, lack the capacity for the long view. Look down at the coast, all those people, the shopping malls, subdivisions, golf course. Spreading over the earth like . . ." Her voice trailed off. "Have you ever watched a bacterial culture fill a petri dish?"

"At Waikiki I often think about how it was, way back when," he said.

"How far back does your mind take you? To when this island was hot lava and bare rock, devoid of life? Do you think about the first birds, bringing the first seeds? How a frail mammal like a bat could cross the ocean? Do you ever wonder how a single pair of birds, landing on a remote island belched from the sea as a volcano, could give birth to a suite of distinct species, given enough time and the right ecological incentives?"

"Practically all the island pigeons are white," he said. "I've wondered about that. Whether one white pair was the first to arrive, got the jump on the rest, like maybe a mama and a papa—see?—part of a nineteenth-century circus traveling the Pacific by sailing ship—flew out of a magician's hat, set up housekeeping in a coconut palm. Or maybe they're all white because of the sun. The white feathers keep them cooler—they live longer than dark birds, have more babies."

"A reasoned observation," she said, studying him. "Then there's the other side of the coin. Extinctions. Particularly with man in the equation. Humans show up and within a few centuries they destroy what it took millions of years to create." Quiet again, then, "Pardon my pessimism. Between the loss of my sister and my profession, I guess I have death on my mind."

"You see a lot of death in your profession?" he asked, hoping she wouldn't provide too many details.

"You bet," face lighting up. "Megadeath! It's really quite exciting."

"Emergency room?" Jeez, he thought, maybe she specializes in plagues. What if she starts talking about pustules and swollen black tongues?

"Emergency room? Oh my, no. Dinosaurs. But, of course, the title confused you. You thought I'm in medicine. No, not me. I'm a Ph.D., a geologist flirting with paleontology. I've become fascinated with dinosaur extinction—good-bye Shell oil, hello UCLA. I'm on sabbatical, finishing up a book. Galleys will be ready any day."

"Wow. A book."

"My first. My specialty is the Cretaceous-Tertiary boundary, sixty-five million years ago—mass extinctions in a geologic heartbeat, land and sea. Suddenly, no dinosaurs anywhere, except for the little guys that became today's birds. The prevailing view now is that a huge meteor struck the earth. Possibly—and this is quite exciting—the event locus has been pinpointed to . . ."

Star tried to follow, drifted, found himself tallying the colors of passing cars.

". . . also a good argument for worldwide ecological disruption from massive lava flows such as the Deccan Traps in India, a cataclysm in either case. Gradualism was once . . ."

Reds led white.

". . . punctuated by catastrophe. Megadeath, my friend." She took a deep breath. "I've been studying the K-T barrier in the geologic record, most recently in Italy, a thin layer, rich in iridium . . ."

Star glanced to his right, saw a manic glint in Caddy's eyes. He imagined a braces-clad, pigtailed teenager in high school, a "brain." Caddy, he decided, was the one kid the chemistry teacher always looked to for the right answer. And the one who sat at home alone on prom night—unless the tuba player in band worked up the nerve to ask her out.

". . . reflecting the Jurassic distributions. Oh, forgive me, I'm lecturing again. A professional weakness."

"No, I love dinosaurs. Who doesn't?" Jeez. A good thing it's dinosaur stuff and not the Ebola virus in Zaire. I was sure she was a doctor. "So, you're a geologist?"

"That's it. Sorry if the title put you off. I confess it's a convenient mask to hide behind."

They reached the coast, stopped for fast food.

Caddy looked at her tray. "Well, isn't this cute? An extinct Hawaiian birds glass—courtesy of the folks who burn off rain forests for pastureland."

Star pointed to a banner above the order counter, "Do your share—collect them all."

"Do you share?" She lifted her glass to look at a silk-screened O'ahu *nukupu'u* honeycreeper, a light green bird with a long, thin curved bill. Star's collectible commemorated the Hawaiian *'o'o,* a black bird with bright yellow feathers sticking from its side like extra wings.

"Wait till Dan sees this," he said. "He just got one-of-a-kind painting of the same bird. Now everyone's gonna have one in their kitchen."

"Like naming subdivisions after what was destroyed." She began to mutter. "Green Meadows, Clear Brook, Forest Glen, Indian Creek, Deer . . ."

Jeez. "You're not gonna start talking about plagues next, are you?"

"What? Plagues?"

"Never mind."

She scowled, went mute again. Back on the road, she directed him with hand signals.

Star stole a glance to his right, caught Caddy looking back at him, nervously.

"I think I owe you an apology," she said.

He waved the air. "No, no. This is a bad time for you. I understand. Forget what I said about plagues."

"That's not it at all. And I want you to know, if I haven't been particularly loquacious or open, it's not you. It's that Melissa and I, and *men* . . ."

He kept his eyes on the road.

"When we were little . . . Our parents were less than fun loving. True Calvinists, I suppose, serious, driven to accomplishment. They drove us, too. Oh, yes. We were worker bees.

"No, not only that." Caddy chewed her lip. "More." She swallowed. "Mother, I later realized, must have been . . . assaulted . . . by a man before she met my father." Barely a whisper. "Maybe as a child. There were oblique references, no more, but I figured it out later. It twisted her perceptions of the outside world. She seldom left the house—doesn't now, not a step outside." She shook her head.

"Anyway, when Melissa and I were growing up, mother told us frightening stories about strangers—men—big, scary ones—and the awful things they did to little girls. The bogeyman to me was a looming sexual monster. Huge, grasping." Eyes closed, she shuddered. "I had recurring nightmares about being attacked. Still do, even though I'm an exceedingly rational woman as an adult. Not that I had any concrete idea of sex then—a word never mentioned in our house, by the way. But it skewed my impressions. Of boys. My first date was to our high school senior prom with a band member. He was all hands, the night a disaster. By college, I was so engrossed in my studies, I had practically no social life. I was happy.

"Melissa, on the other hand." She shook her head again. "Melissa somehow found mother's stories—what can I say? Titillating, or something akin to it. She couldn't wait to find out for herself about boys. 'Oh, Caddy,' she'd say, 'Mother's exaggerating. Old sourpuss, doesn't want us to have fun. No makeup, no short skirts, no dancing, no boys.'

"Melissa found out for herself soon enough, I fear. The boys hovered around her like birds at a feeder. Yes, indeed.

"And now look where it's gotten her. Murdered."

Star studied the double yellow line.

Ten silent minutes later, Caddy pointed to an undistinguished ranch-style house, pale yellow with a low white picket fence around neat flower beds and variegated shrubs. Five tall palms with smooth trunks painted white to chest height grew from a well-trimmed lawn.

"Welcome to Château Finch," she said with a smile, bogeymen back in the cellar of her mind.

Star smiled back. "I never understood why they paint palm trunks like that."

"You had to know Artemas. Very orderly." She retrieved a key from under a potted gardenia. "Prepare yourself. I was so upset the last time I was here, I left without straightening up."

They found pictures ripped from the walls, drawers emptied, cushions torn, books toppled from shelves, furniture tipped. Even the carpets lay in twisted heaps. The only things clearly stolen, however, seemed to be the stereo system—since dust outlined the components' place in the cabinet—and the computer. The monitor sat on the floor, alone, case cracked, screen shattered.

Caddy lifted three five-by-five-foot paintings from the floor and set them against the wall. "Melissa's."

Tropical blossoms in brilliant colors, enlarged nearly to abstraction, filled the canvases.

He walked from one to the next. "I never thought flowers could be so . . ."

"Evocative? Primal? Erotic? Melissa was passionate with everything she did."

They walked to the bedroom. "Oh, my," said Caddy at Melissa's underwear strewn across the floor, most of it brief. Very brief. "This is embarrassing. Perhaps you should wait in another room."

Star stayed put, looked down at a pair of red crotchless panties, at the familiar Teddies of Times Square label, and wondered if Melissa's husband had bought them for her at one of Cindy's lingerie brunches at Stan's Mr. Meat, All You Can Eat.

Jeez.

"Frustrating as well." Caddy scooped the lingerie into a pile and dropped it into an open drawer.

A half hour later, Star said, "I don't see a thing to suggest the cops were off base. It looks like vandalism to me, too."

"I know. Damn!" Caddy kicked a kitchen chair, sent it skidding into the wall. "I'd hoped we'd have found suggestive notes or files, or, well, something."

They righted the furniture and left.

Caddy locked the front door with a muttered "Discouraging."

A thin elderly woman waved from across the street, walked toward them. "You must be Melissa's sister. I'm Ester Kawela. Such a tragedy. First Artemas killed in that automobile accident and now Melissa, poor darling, takes her life. They cut my grass, you know, trimmed the hedges. Wouldn't take a penny, but they loved my coffee cakes. I am quite the baker, if I do say so myself." She turned to the house. "This vandalism . . . all the neighbors are terribly upset. I'm so sorry for your loss, Miss . . . ?"

"MacConnell. That was Melissa's maiden name, and this is Mr. Hollie."

Star squeezed the woman's hand. "Mrs. Kawela, I don't suppose you saw whoever broke in?"

"Dear me, no. I hear the police think it happened the day they found her. If it was kids, they could have gotten in through the back without being seen, I suppose—all the shrubs and tall grass back there by the canal."

"Did you happen to see Melissa the day she died?"

"Ever so briefly, although we didn't speak—I wish we had. Maybe I could have helped. Just talking over one's problems . . ."

He prompted. "You saw her briefly . . ."

"Yes. I saw her come to the door late in the afternoon when the exterminators arrived."

"Exterminators?" Caddy and Star said the word together.

"It's so wet on this side of the island—rains nearly every day this time of year—we have terrible problems with roaches. My, they're big. I swat them with my broom. Smack! They wave their feelers at me and run away. I imagine Artemas and Melissa had the same problem. The treatment was no doubt scheduled long before. You pay an annual fee, and the exterminators come four times a year. Doesn't get rid of them entirely, but it helps."

"The exterminators came to Melissa's house the day she died?" Star asked. "And she let them in?"

"Yes, about six-thirty in the evening—they'll come after people return from work—the better companies are very cooperative. I saw them pull in the drive, carrying those big sheets all bunched up like they use. I guess they started working. Then not too long after, I saw their truck leave. They came back, quite late as I remember, to finish the job."

"Mrs. Kawela, did you tell the police about this?" Caddy asked.

"Oh, no, they didn't talk to me. I was visiting my niece on Maui the day Melissa was found. I think they spoke to Mrs. Tatum next door. Heaven knows why. Patricia Tatum has the curiosity of a snail and she's near as blind. But what could anyone tell them? Poor Melissa . . ."

"Mrs. Kawela," Star said, "try to remember. Can you recall the name of the company, what the men looked like? How many there were?"

"I'm not sure I can remember the name, but the truck was white and had that big smiling roach on the side. You know, the red roach carrying the doctor's satchel with the mirror thing on his head like doctors wear?" She closed her eyes. "Wait, that was it. The Roach Doctor! That's who it was, the Roach Doctor. And there were two of them, wearing those white outfits. One was huge, the other, tiny. I remember thinking about the old films, the comedies, with the piano deliverymen like that—you know, the big one always carries the bench? Understand, I just glanced out my window. But by the end of the eleven o'clock news their truck was gone. I always look out the window before I go to bed, and I'm sure they were finished by then."

Star watched the Finch house and Mrs. Kawela recede in the rearview mirror. "Exterminators?" he said.

"Exterminators!" she repeated, then, "Horrible," a minute later. "Two *men* and Melissa alone in that house. Who knows what happened? Terrible things. Then the brutes threw her body in the ocean to cover their crime." Her voice broke.

"It doesn't look good, but let's not jump to conclusions."

"Get real. Stop at that convenience store. I want to check the phone book."

She came back to the car waving a page of yellow paper. "Look at that, mister," she said, shaking it in his face. "Go ahead, look."

He held her wrist still. In a box ad, boldface letters announced "The Roach Doctor" with a little x on the downstroke of the R in Roach. Below the name, a big red roach with a doctor's kit smiled up at him. A cartoon speech balloon floated over the roach's head. He read it aloud. "Call me day or night—I make house calls."

"You sure do, you son of a bitch," she said. "And I'm going to call you the minute we get back."

"Caddy, that looks like a big company. If two of their employees did murder Melissa—and you don't know that—certainly the company wasn't aware of it. If you call hysterically—"

"HYSTERICALLY?"

"Whoa, listen. *If* those men killed Melissa, you don't want to alert them, do you? They'll catch the next plane out of Hawai'i. The police will listen now. They'll get a statement from Mrs. Kawela, check the company, find who the men are, interrogate them, get confessions."

"Yes, yes, you're right, of course. Call the police first."

"One other thing. You said Melissa was going to be cremated." He shifted in his seat. "Was there an autopsy?" He flinched. Images of a cold room and rubber hoses came to mind. "What I mean is, did Melissa actually drown? Was there evidence she had been hurt or, you know, violated?"

"I insisted on an autopsy as soon as they mentioned suicide. Melissa drowned, they were positive, and no, she hadn't been abused. Another reason the police wouldn't listen. Oh—I see where you're going. Humoring me. You don't really think those men murdered her at all, do you?"

"I didn't say that."

"Damn you. You're no better than the police. Take me to the hotel." She faced her window, tight-lipped.

He tempted her with dinosaur questions—Could a *Tyrannosaurus* eat a caveman in a single gulp? How about that snake King Kong wrestled? Was Godzilla the biggest one ever?—but she wouldn't bite. From time to time her shoulders shook, and once, when the sunlight flashed through the windshield, Star was sure he saw the glint of tears in the reflection of Caddy MacConnell's face in the glass.

25

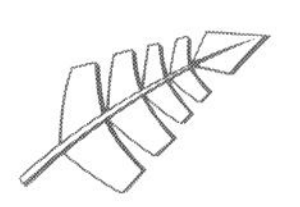

Star rotated his empty cup in the saucer, eyes on Doris's new admirer, D. L., monopolizing her at the counter.

When she came by with the pot five minutes later, he said, "Busy girl," and winked. "You're still up for *our* date tonight?"

"Some date. You'll get us both in trouble. I can't believe I agreed to it." She looked around Papa's to see if anyone was listening, then dropped the afternoon paper on his table. "Check the entertainment section. I circled an ad."

There he was, the Reverend Jaycie Pitts, shaking his diamond-capped staff at the camera. The headline read, "Third and final night of the Reverend Jaycie Pitts' Old Time Revival. Saving of Hawaiian sinners and blessing of cash."

Star crumpled the paper and left. He didn't notice D. L. get up from his stool and follow him to the street.

Maybe I'll go over to Kalakaua Avenue for some yogurt, he thought, check out the chickies. He turned into an alley running toward the International Market Place. About halfway between Kuhio and Kalakaua Avenues, he heard a voice, "Hey asshole!"

"What?" He looked to his right. "You talking to me?" A tall, gaunt, greasy-haired man, late twenties, blocked his path. Aggressive panhandler, Star decided, and walked past.

He heard an ominous snick, looked over his shoulder, saw an open switchblade, and stumbled back. A mugger by the International Market Place? In broad daylight? Half a dozen people walked in full view. "What the hell? Get away from me."

The mugger backed him toward a concrete wall near a hotel loading dock. "Got something for you, Star."

Star's eyes bugged at his name.

"That's right, *Star*." The mugger spit it out, grinned, drew back his elbow, ready to lunge.

Star bumped the wall, nowhere to go. The mugger moved in.

"That's about enough of that, bud," said a firm voice with a slight southern drawl, no more than ten feet away. Star and the tall mugger both turned to see Doris's friend, D. L., standing, hands on hips.

"Look out, he's got a knife!" Star yelled, and edged away.

"Not that big a one, though, is it?" said D. L. "What, a five-inch blade?"

"Get the hell outta here, mister," said the man, "I got no quarrel with you."

Star backed away.

Passing tourists formed a ragged circle, awaiting the show, much as they had the day before at the Battle for the Tahitian Princess at the Polynesian Cultural Center. One woman explained to her husband, "*Knife,* Harold, the skinny one has a *knife* and he's going to cut the *longhaired* one with it. Lookit his *hand* for Chrissakes." A squinting fat woman in thick rhinestone-rimmed glasses gulped air in anticipation and clutched a stuffed monkey to her bosom. In her shadow, a weaselly man in madras shorts rapped on a reluctant camera. A little boy, frightened by the shouting, sniveled behind his father's knees, while his sister—"Gotta go wee-wee, Mama. Now!"—was shushed by her mother. More people gathered, drawn by the promise of spectacle.

D. L. walked slowly toward the knife wielder, who waved the blade in a figure eight. "You want it?" the mugger sneered. "I'll stick you first." He stood half a head taller than D. L.

"Be careful!" Star shouted, eight feet away and still retreating. "He's not fooling around."

"No, don't guess he is," said D. L., less than five feet from the man, his eyes locked onto the mugger's, as if the knife didn't exist.

Star saw it all. Without warning, the man threw the full weight of his legs and shoulders into a thrust. Oh no, thought Star, old D. L. didn't see it coming. He waited for the scream and the red.

But a moment before the knife tip parted the twill of D. L.'s lime green alligator shirt, D. L. and the shirt slipped away. Smooth as Fred Astaire in a foxtrot, D. L. had danced a neat pivot ninety degrees to the left, a move of remarkable grace and economy that left the blade slicing air.

The attacker fell forward, off balance, arm still extended, parallel to D. L.'s stomach. Swish. Like a mantis snaring a grasshopper, D. L. clamped one hand on the man's wrist, another on his elbow, and jerked a knee into the arm from below.

Thwock. Star winced at the muffled sound of breaking bone.

The knife clattered in the gutter. The man moaned, fell to his knees.

D. L. knelt beside him, lifted the arm, and probed the swelling flesh, gentle as a midwife with a newborn baby. Squatting, calmed, the man stared at his arm.

"Feels like a clean break of the ulna," said D. L. in a soft voice, "but the radius isn't broke at all—guess I'm losing my touch. In the business, they call this a nightstick fracture, like when a cop brings his billy club down at some poor schmo's head and the fella holds his arm up to deflect the blow. Bingo—cracked ulna. Couple months in a cast, withered arm for a couple more, and you'll be fine. Nothing to worry about." Then he bent closer and spoke into the man's ear. "What I'd like to know is, why'd you attack the boy here?"

Star, closer now, listened too.

"Screw you," said the man.

"No," said D. L. gently. "Listen up. I'm gonna make this easy. You tell me what I want to know and I let you go—you run away, clean. Cops will be here in a few minutes, and then it'll be too late, so let's make it quick. Here's the other side of it—you don't tell me, I'll break your radius, too." D. L.'s grip tightened on the arm, and the man writhed in pain. "With both bones broke it'll be a bitch to heal. Arms'll be different lengths, too. Clock's a-tickin'—tick tock, tick tock . . ."

"Okay, okay. Guy I met in a bar give me three hundred dollars to stick the longhaired guy in the nuts. Described him real good—green eyes, light brown hair, name of Star—said he hung out at this coffee shop. I waited for him, was just gonna stick him quick, not kill him, like teach him a lesson. The longhaired guy, this Star, poked some fella's little daughter. After I stuck him I was to tell him it was for messing with Tammy, he'd know what I meant. That's it."

"Who's the father?"

"Don't know. Some big shot. Already left Hawai'i. Just wanted it taken care of."

"All right," said D. L., "here's what you do. Keep his money and say you did it. Why not? Doesn't sound like the man's gonna know one way or the other. But either way, you leave the boy here alone. If there's a next time I won't fart around—you know that, don't you?" The man grunted as D. L. helped him to his feet, unbuttoned his dirty shirt halfway, eased the broken arm inside. "Keep your good hand on the wrist, hold it firm against your belly. Shirt'll work like a sling till you get to a doctor. Now hit the trail—and don't let me see your skinny ass again."

Holding the arm, the man looked warily at D. L. and the crowd, drew in on himself like a caged rat, and darted toward the food court and into the warren of stalls and alleys forming the International Market Place.

"Look at him skedaddle," said D. L. "Won't see that old boy again." He turned to Star. "C'mon, let's get a move on. Be gone before the police arrive and embarrass you. Guess you heard what he said. Poked a little girl, did you?"

"I didn't touch the bitch. I can't believe she told her father that. Damn. That scumbag was ready to knife me—you saved my life."

"No big deal. Good thing I was around. I'm D. L. McWhorter, by the way."

"Sure, Doris's friend. Man, you were great."

D. L. glanced at the circle of people, still staring. "Hey, what's this?" he said. "Show's over, folks. Over. Vamoose." He shooed with his hands, scattering the hangers-on like chickens. "Come on, boy, I'll buy you an ice-cream cone. Celebrate your hanging on to the family jewels."

"Jeez, D. L., that guy never knew what hit him. Where'd you learn to do that?"

"Picked it up here and there—profession's security. That sorry nimrod wasn't much of a challenge, though. Overconfident—you notice that? And careless. Should have just walked up beside you and done it. As it was, he had a crowd before he started. And real stupid to underestimate me. Oughta give him something to think about while his arm mends, huh? One of life's lessons."

Ten minutes later, they sat on a wall outside the Baskin-Robbins on Kalakaua. "Never was a real strawberry tasted good as this," said D. L. "What's that yellow guck you have?"

"Guava-berry banana surprise. Not bad."

"Chocolate, vanilla, and strawberry are plenty for me. Stick to the basics, I always say. That's why I like your friend Doris. Good, straightforward woman. Thinks a lot of you, she does. Worried, too. Concerned you're into some trouble with this writing you do and this new woman you met. So, what's the scoop?"

"The woman's sister committed suicide, or so everyone thought. Then we discovered exterminators were in the house the night she died."

"How do you mean that, exterminators?"

"You know, like the kind that kill roaches. They may have had something to do with her death. Dr. MacConnell's turning it over to the police."

"Smart woman." D. L. began to whistle softly.

"What's that?" asked Star. "That song?"

"Didn't realize I was whistling. Bad habit. Let's see." He whistled a bit more. "Not much of a tune, is it?" D. L. laughed. "Got it: Schubert, *Death and the Maiden*. You know it?"

"Can't say I do."

"Lot of life in music, I always say. Never learned stuff like that in school. Picked it up on my own, like everything else worth knowing." He looked down at his cone. "Where were we? Oh, yeah. So, how's your writing tie into all this business?"

"Doesn't really. I'd interviewed Melissa, that's the sister who died, for an article I've been working on. I'm still kind of looking for connections—it always starts out loose."

"Doris seems to think your article's pretty important."

"Only because she likes me. Maybe trying to impress you, too."

"I don't know. Fill me in on that story. I'd like to make up my own mind."

"Not a thing I can tell you." Story? he thought, there's no story at all. I'm spinning my wheels.

"Didn't mean to pry. Just making conversation, you being a friend of Doris."

"Man, I sure was lucky you came by. I thought you were still in Papa's when I left."

"I wanted to catch up with you outside, ask you a question. Doris has a birthday coming up and I was trying to think what to get her. Any ideas?"

"I wouldn't get her anything big, you know, embarrass her. How about giving her a lei?" As soon as the word left his mouth, he regretted it.

"Lay?" said D. L.

Star added quickly, "Flower necklace. Doris loves flowers,"

"Flowers," said D. L. "Just the ticket. Well now, buddy, gotta be on my way. Watch your butt, huh? Never know who's got his eye on you."

They shook hands. Star watched D. L. stroll up Kalakaua Avenue licking his strawberry ice-cream cone. Guy gives me the creeps, he thought, but I'm thankful, no question about it, that old G. I. Joe's dad was behind me back there in that alley.

26

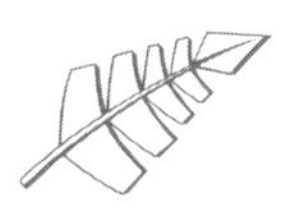

"Got to watch our asses, boy, take care of one another." Mr. Lucky leapt away, crouched low. *Grrrr. Woof!*

The phone rang.

Caddy. "You were right. The police finally took me seriously. They haven't abandoned their suicide scenario, but listen to this: the Roach Doctor never serviced Melissa's house. They keep good records. The day of her death, all but one of their vans were logged back in by five-thirty. The owner's brother-in-law drove the last one—he uses it as a family car."

"Family car?"

"Poor man's Range Rover."

"So they suspect the brother-in-law."

"No. He and the wife and kids went out to dinner—some endorsement for a restaurant, a Roach Doctor van parked out front, huh?—then to a movie. But the next morning, another driver found his van's tank empty, thought one of the other employees had lent it to someone to drive on a 'date'—because of the space in the back—I'm sure you get the idea. They'd run the tank down, left his gear in disarray, and scattered beer bottles and fried-chicken boxes all over the back. The trash is long gone, but this Detective Schott I spoke with is questioning everyone. When he finds who took the van, it looks like we'll have Melissa's murderers."

Star chewed his lip before speaking. "Of course we will," he said, with a good bit more enthusiasm than he felt.

Five minutes later, the phone rang again. He almost answered with a "Caddy?" Fortunately, he did not, because the caller was Cindy.

"Star?" Little voice.

"Cindy? You all right, honey? You don't sound so good."

"Oh, Star." Sniffles. "Last night at Stan's Mr. Meat, All You Can Eat, I was, like, attacked. I'm okay now, but . . ."

"Jeez, Cindy, what do you mean, 'attacked'? Did some pervert at one of your shows grab you?" His heart raced. "You mean like, raped?"

"Almost. I finished a Teddies show, was walking to my car, in the lot behind Mr. Meat's. My Camaro was way back in the corner. This van pulled up, the kind with no windows. A big man jumped out and called my name—it was horrible. He had a pair of *panty hose* pulled over his head. I answered before I saw him. The bastard grabbed me by the arm and dragged me to the rear of the van."

"No!"

"It's true. He opened the door, was about to throw me in the back, do twisted stuff to me, I know, so I screamed real loud—you know how loud I can scream. Stan came to the lounge's back door, yelled at the man to stop, and ran out to save me."

"Loudmouth, lard-ass Stan?"

"That's not fair. Stan was so brave. He would have saved me, too, if the man hadn't punched him in the face. Then another man inside the van yelled for the first one to get a move on and he started to wrestle me into the van."

"Jeez."

"Three businessmen at the show came out the back door. They saw us and yelled at the man, too, then tore off across the lot to help me. I guess they were kind of drunk, because two of them fell down when they tried to run, and the third stopped when he saw how big this ape was. But they confused him. He hung on to me, looked at them and at poor Stan on the ground, holding his jaw, moaning."

"Jeez."

"Then I remembered those defense-aerobics moves from that routine we did with the camouflage undies. I stomped on the guy's toes and kicked him between the legs, real hard in the balls—you know, like I did to you that time? He made this kind of 'Ooof' sound like you did, too, then fell on his knees and almost let me go like he was supposed to. He still had my arm, but I jerked away, grabbed one of the legs of his panty hose, and pulled. By then, more people from Mr. Meat were yelling, and the chef—you know, that big Mongolian, the one they call Wo Fat?—he was almost to us, waving a cleaver. The driver shouted for the other one to get back in the truck, and they squealed out of the lot. I didn't see the man's face, but I got his panty hose. They smelled like Pine Sol. And they were *pink*. Is that sick or what?"

"But you're okay?"

"Yeah, I'm fine, except for a big bruise on my upper arm where he grabbed me. By tomorrow, I'll bet makeup won't cover it, either."

"Cindy, by any chance were they driving one of those Roach Doctor vans?"

"Didn't you hear what I said? An ape with panty hose on his head—a doctor? Get real. It was a van, not a Mercedes. But Wo Fat got the license number."

"Way to go, Wo Fat. Listen." He tried to remember Caddy's police detective. Potts? Scott? Schott. "Cindy, there was some other trouble, serious trouble, with a woman and a van—it had to do with a story I'm working on. A Detective Schott is on the case. You call him, tell him what you told me, describe the man."

"Star, we already talked to the police."

"Yeah, but sometimes they don't talk to each other. Call, ask for this Schott, okay? You want me to come over? Are you still scared?"

"No. Star . . ." Little voice again. "The man broke Stan's jaw. It's wired shut. When he tries to talk he, like, grunts. I can't understand him at all—he has to write notes on one of those Magic Slates. The doctor says he won't be able to chew meat for six months, that he'll have to suck baby food through a straw."

"Stan can't talk or eat meat? That'll be bad for business."

"Star, Stan saved my life."

"I don't know, Cindy, sounds to me like that kick of yours put an end to the trouble."

"No. Stan was so brave. And he was there. And, Star . . . listen, you and me haven't been getting along too well, so, see, I've decided to . . . like move in with Stan for a while. Take care of him. And Stan can protect me, too. Everyone at Mr. Meat thinks it's a good idea. Actually . . . I already did it. I'm sorry, but I think Stan and me . . . like we have more in common. Still, you and me can be friends, can't we, Star? Can't we?"

Star set the phone down, sat back and massaged his temples. He picked it up again, heart in his throat, but guiltily relieved. "Friends? Sure, Cindy. We can still be friends."

27

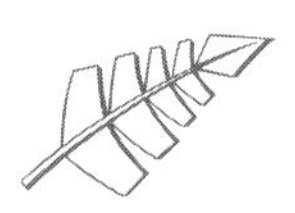

I can't believe we're doing this," Doris whispered. "I feel like such a sneak."

Star dropped the coffee thermos, stooped to pick it up. "Papa didn't mind your taking the night off?"

"I'm taking Sanya's early shift tomorrow." She crossed her arms and shuddered. "It's creepy out here in the middle of this sugarcane. Cold, too."

"Wind's kicking up, all right. Here, wrap the blanket around you."

"I'd have thought after your experience this afternoon with D. L., you'd have learned a lesson. Play with fire, you . . ."

"Doris, a man's gotta do what a man's gotta do." He leaned on his crutch, limped forward.

"We don't belong here."

The line inched forward. "Look at all those friendly faces," he said. "They'll be turning them away soon. Two performances already and tonight's the grand finale."

The tent glowed orange in the blue-black shadows of the tall cane. If insects were singing out there, no one heard them above the drone of the generator and the babel of eager people streaming toward the narrow canvas entrance.

A broad banner snapping in the wind, REVIVAL TONIGHT, nearly obscured the "Omar's Fine Carpets—Liquidation Sale" painted across the front of the red canvas. Painted at each end of the banner were lush tableaux, titled, for those too dim to grasp the message, "Hell" at the left and "Heaven" to the right. (Bernie Bergen had had it painted, gratis, by the woman who had made the murals for HydraCorp's Kaua'i resort.)

In banner hell, devils pitched sinners into seething, fire-spitting island volcanoes, to swim, melt, fry in streams of fluorescent red lava, while the good guys in heaven cavorted on sunny, palm-lined beaches and frolicked in bubbly green 7UP surf.

The crowd murmured at sight of the Reverend Jaycie Pitts's famous automobile, the Leviathan, a lavender Lincoln Town Car, stretched through the wonder of automobile surgery a full five feet, its voluminous chrome gold-plated down to the license-plate bolts. Revivalers ogled at its golden hood ornament, a twelve-inch cross illuminated by tiny hood-mounted spots. They peered at the blackened glass for a glimpse of the holy man. As if on cue, the back window lowered six inches, and a plump pink hand emerged to wave a blessing.

Star clenched his fist. Doris patted his shoulder. "Be a good boy, honey. You'll see him soon enough."

They slid into the last two aisle seats in front of the obscuring center tent pole.

Doris whispered in his ear. "You think they'll ask us questions, like about the Bible or something?"

"Doris, this is a revival, not a quiz show. Kind of like a church with the rev meter cranked up. They'll be flip-flopping and shouting soon enough. Pineapple Eddie came last night, brought thirty bucks to be blessed, left ten for the Reverend, and won seventy-five later in a poker game. Eddie's been telling everyone—stories like that get around."

Twenty minutes later, five hundred whispering, squirming, sweating souls fanned faces, wiped brows, and rubbed cold pop cans on flushed faces as body heat merged with the radiance of a thousand lightbulbs strung like spiderwebs overhead (a favor called in by Bernie from a Honolulu used car lot supplier).

A single organ note sounded from a Casio console near the front.

Backs straightened, conversations trailed away, and a shudder of anticipation rippled through the crowd.

Star craned his neck. “That's *her* at the organ. Judith. The bitch.”

“Behave yourself.”

“For now.”

“What have you got planned, exactly?”

He cupped his hand by her ear, whispered, “This crutch? When the Reverend asks the ones who want to get saved or cured to come forward, I'll hobble up, twist and drag my one leg, make a real show of it. He'll lay his hands on my head and I'll yell real loud for him to save and cure me, so everyone in the tent hears, then I'll throw the crutch down.”

“I can see it coming.”

“I'll manage to stay up, wobble and moan, so everyone sees me. Raise both hands in the air. Then I'll scream that he withered my other leg, too, cursed me, and I'll flop in the dirt. That ought to take the edge off the old goat's revival.”

“Oh, Star.”

“You saw that picture of me on TV, you saw my car. You should see the looks I'm getting from the neighborhood old folks. That man made an ass of me, cost me money I don't have. That bitch Judith lied through her tight lips. And Dan tells me to be patient. Be patient?” he repeated, then shouted it, “BE PATIENT!?”

Left and right, people shushed him, no doubt thinking, The man may be crippled, but damn, can't he shut his mouth and hold on for a few more minutes?

Doris patted his knee, kept her voice low. “Okay, honey, calm down. Look.”

The Reverend Jaycie Pitts, white suit, blue string tie, saintly smile on his lips, stepped onto a low stage at the front, a jeweled white cane in one hand. The TV superstar raised arms and eyes heavenward and froze, statuelike. Surely the holy man saw—what?—a heavenly apparition? An angel?

To either side, the teenage Cheerleaders for Jesus rustled pompoms, *swissssh*. A sustained note sounded, amplified by towering speakers (courtesy of Bernie and the Club Rendezvous, closed, pending appeal of a disputed health permit).

"He looks like that chicken man, the Colonel," said Star.

"Shhhh!" from Doris. "Shhhh!" all around.

Palms touching, the Reverend closed his eyes. His lips moved silently, then mumbled. The crowd fell silent, straining to hear in his words a clue to his vision.

His eyes opened, a loud chord burst from the organ, and the Reverend sang—boomed, "What a friend we have in Jeez-us . . ." The crowd needed no hymnal, no prompting. By the "we have," a dozen voices sprang to life; by "Jeez-us" hundreds joined in.

Star scowled at Doris for singing. Mouth wide, she wagged a finger at him, pointed to his tapping foot.

Another prayer, then "Onward Christian Soldiers." Five hundred heads bobbed, bodies rocked, and the red tent pulsed in the tropical night like a fiery heart.

Reverend Jaycie raised his hands, touched palms, then spread them slowly, like Moses parting the Red Sea. A hush fell over the revivalers.

"Brothers and sisters," he said, "the Kingdom of Heaven is near. Freely have you received, freely giveth, sayeth the Lord."

Yessirs and right-ons rose from the crowd.

"To make it through those pearly gates, each must give a gift in proportion to the way the Lord has blessed you. That means: If you got it, you gotta give it."

"Give it," the revivalers echoed. "Give." "Give."

"Don't squeeze your penny like the miser, for the miser is doomed. Doomed to hell everlasting. Hell: the brimstone pit. And who wants that?"

Heads shook. "No, no way." "Not Satan's Pit."

"Yessir," said the Reverend, "Satan's Pit. Is old Satan knocking? Knocking on your door?" Beads of sweat glistened on his forehead. He wiped them away with a swipe of a linen sleeve, hit a cadence, snatched quick breaths.

Godliness and sin, redemption and damnation, the Reverend made clear through parable, divine quotation, and exhortation, were inextricably bound to money. Nothing wrong with money, mind you, but to grasp is evil, to pass along, blessed. Money freely given generates more money. Aha! an economist might have said, the *multiplier effect,* the old boy knows his stuff, all right. The revivalers, however, didn't need textbook rationalizations. They *expected* to give. And they expected to *receive*. That's what most of them were there for, after all.

"Bless your generous souls!" The Reverend nodded to Judith at the organ and took a deep breath.

"Tell me," he shouted. "Who loves a giver?"

"The Lord!" they answered. They knew what was coming: the Reverend's TV show theme. Back home they had sung along with the studio choir, but to sing it live, here, under this tent, with the Reverend himself? Hallelujah! The revivalers sang as one:

"Oh, how the Lord loves a giver,
With a heart full of char-it-y.
The giver is blessed, above all the rest.
Does heaven, or hell, await thee?

High o'er the clouds is a paradise,
for generous souls, you see.
But it's the pit of hell, where demons dwell,
that's reserved for the miserly.

If it's jewels you hoard, or silver, or gold,
Satan may knock at your door.
Saying, 'Bury your purse, don't share, that's worse,
and never give to the poor.'

Oh, but the Lord loves a giver,
a giver who gives till they're sore.
'If you give it away, it will come back someday,
increased by two times, three times, or four.' "

The Reverend raised his fingers with the words: two fingers, three fingers, four. This was the heavenly promise. "The Lord moves in mysterious ways," he reminded them, "and if you are a giver, He will work for *you*." He spoke again of milk and honey, and fired one more volley of hellfire. There was no middle ground: each and every one had a choice. He fell silent, looked around the assembly to be sure they understood. The revivalers nodded, mumbled. Yes, brother.

He set down the microphone, raised his voice to shout a message too important to trust to mere machinery: "Truly, I say to you, one cannot see the kingdom of God unless he is born again!"

He hefted the mike. "Are there those among you who are blind and wish to see? Sick and need healing? Lame and want to walk? Sinners," he called, "come forward and be saved. The time is now."

Shouts of "Praise the Lord!" rose over falling chairs as sinners, whole and not so whole, rushed the stage, right by Star.

He reached for his crutch.

"What's that in your hand, honey?" Doris asked.

"Crutch, gotta go."

"No, other hand. It's money. You brought money. You're going to mess with the old guy and have your money blessed, too. Shame on you."

"It's not that I believe in this stuff. I just happened to bring some money along." He was clutching ten fifty-dollar bills.

Doris raised an eyebrow.

"Don't look at me like that, Doris. I need money bad. Nothing ventured, nothing gained, right? Figured, long as we were here . . ."

She shook her head, shifted her knees to one side, pretended not to know him as he shuffled past toward the action.

The Reverend set hands on fervent petitioners left and right. A pear-shaped woman in a muumuu and a skinny man in a fishnet T-shirt fainted, taken with the spirit. A Cambodian began speaking in tongues. (Or was it Vietnamese? Who cared? Miracles were afoot.) A tiny lady in her eighties, back to one of the six-foot speakers, shouted, "I can hear! I can hear!"

Star lurched toward the spiritual feeding frenzy, but revivalers blocked the aisle. Instead of starring, he became no more than a sideline supplicant.

Lest the fervor wane, the Revered shifted gears: "And now, brothers and sisters, it is time. Time for the blessing of the cash."

"Yes, yes. Bless the cash. Hallelujah!"

"Hold it in your hands, wave it at me." He waved his fingers in the air as a prompt. Nearly everyone had their money out—handfuls of green paper, thick packets, rolls round as beer cans, grocery bags of crumpled bills.

His first objective thwarted, Star leaned on his crutch, waved his money like the rest of them.

"Close your eyes, children," exhorted the Reverend. "Think of the Heavenly Promise."

Star closed his eyes, held the money out, felt the bills slip from his hand. "What the hell?" He opened his eyes, looked around.

"Thank you," said a diminutive Filipino in an orange aloha shirt two sizes too large, weaving through the crowd. "Thank you, thank you, thank you," he said as he snatched money from people and dropped it into a pillowcase. Confused, angry, they grabbed for him. "Plees." Now he had a bullhorn. "PLEES, EVERYONE. NO TALKING. DON'T MOVE."

Holy cow! The little man had a *gun* in his pillowcase hand, a huge automatic, big as his head. People stumbled, backed away.

"No cause for alarm." He had a friendly tone to his voice, despite the bullhorn and the gun. "Everyone quiet. No moving, plees."

With a better look, people averted their eyes, slapped hands over mouths—the tiny crook with the forty-five was disfigured, his features compressed, his nose all but gone. Leprosy?

No—not leprosy—*panty hose,* the withered legs hidden inside his aloha shirt.

A ten-foot radius cleared around the gunman in seconds. He waved the weapon. "No moving now." Revivalers at the far edges of the tent craned their necks. What's going on up there by the preacher? Did we miss a miracle? Has someone's money quadrupled already?

"Lordy!" said the Reverend into his mike. "Brothers and sisters, there's a small problem here. I'm afraid we're going to have to do what this fella wants us to."

"Thank you, meester," said the Filipino. "See, I have friends by the . . ."—he searched his mind, unsuccessfully, for the correct English word meaning the opening of a tent—". . . doors. Look at my friends, plees." He waved the gun front and rear. Two huge men, intimidating as TV wrestlers, likewise disfigured by panty hose, blocked the exits. One waved a massive hunting knife, the other, a gun like the little man's. Both held pillowcases.

"We not hurting anyone tonight, okay?" said the Filipino into his bullhorn. "All we want is your money, jewels, and gold. A steek-up. Put in the bags plees." He held his pillowcase out.

"Lordy," said the Reverend. "Better do like he says, folks."

Soothed by the Reverend's words and urged along by the little man's gun, people began to throw their bills, then their watches and jewelry, into his bag. "Thank you. See? Ees easy." The big men held out their bags as well, and as frightened people queued up, the same scene played front and back.

One of the big men slashed his knife toward a reluctant revivaler, nicking his nose. A woman screamed at the blood. Like a school of mackerel fleeing a shark, the crowd swarmed away. The big man at the other end waggled his gun in warning. People screamed, stumbled back. Revivalers retreated from both ends toward the center, closed in on the little man. "No, no!" he yelled. "Stay back!" The crowd surged, swirled. He shook the gun. "Wait! We not finished."

Blam! A gunshot shattered the air. The little man fired again, *Blam! Blam!* A horrendous noise. The crowd panicked, reversed direction. People screamed, shoved, ran from the Filipino for the exits and, unavoidably, toward the two big men.

"Lordy, Lordy, Lordy," from the Reverend, his voice an octave higher than it had been during the sermon. "Please, everyone, don't panic."

Pinioned by the crowd, Star saw the Filipino sucked into the melee, fall from sight. One of the big men, towering over the crowd by the entrance, fired his gun as a signal to his counterpart with the knife. He pointed to one of the guy ropes and mimed sawing. In a blur, the tent flaps fluttered, and the men disappeared.

People screamed, panted, pulled, pushed.

The tent shuddered. Strings of lights fell, twisted in the stampede. Bulbs burst underfoot. Helpless, Star watched the center tent pole waver—where was Doris?—then, ever so slowly, fall, bringing with it Omar's red canvas big top.

All agreed the Lord had been watching: no one crushed, no one suffocated. Two short poles at the sides of the tent remained upright, leaving the revivalers in darkness, rolling and tumbling, but with enough air to breathe until rescued.

The fire captain enumerated the injuries to the newswoman from Channel 9: "It looks like three concussions, a broken ankle, four fractured arms, bruised ribs, and lots of sprains, cuts, and scratches. Fortunately, no more than two dozen people were robbed—you're gonna have to talk to the police about that."

A police sergeant took the mike. "The perpetrators? Scuttled off into the cane like cowardly mongooses. My men are chasing them now—we'll have them in custody in no time. As for this man"—he clutched the Reverend's sleeve. The lens zoomed onto the Reverend's dirt-stained face—"your viewers ought to know, we've sorted out what really happened. This Reverend Pitts"—the Reverend struggled, covered his face with his hands, but the sergeant wrestled him into the lights—"this was the real hero. He kept them calm under the fallen big top, encouraged them to sing, kept them from panicking. They say he reunited babies with their mothers."

No doubt embarrassed by the attention, a tearful Reverend blinked at the camera, buried his head in his hands, and prayed.

That moving footage was broadcast on network news two nights running. Still frames of the Reverend, captured from the video, appeared on the front pages of both the morning and afternoon Honolulu papers, and subsequently, with modest electronic embellishment, in the tabloids: HAWAIIAN SAINT SPIES ANGELS IN CANVAS BIG TOP; PREACHER SNATCHES BABIES FROM FACELESS DEVILS; and GIANT SUGARCANE MONGOOSES ATTACK CHURCHGOERS.

28

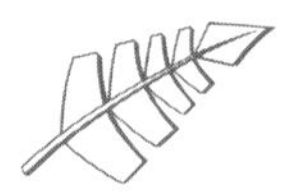

Listen to this, Koki." Star read the morning headline: " 'Panty hose bandits strike again.' Again? Says, 'Armed men disrupt religious meeting, terrify over five hundred.' Paper makes a big deal of how unsuccessful they were. My ass. Says 'only a handful' were robbed.

"Five hundred dollars. All of it. Gone. After I got out of the tent and found Doris, I tried to catch that little bastard with the gun, but he'd sneaked away—probably under some fat lady's muumuu."

"Your five hundred was for Mako?"

"Yeah, loan's due tomorrow. Twenty-five hundred dollars."

"I've got a little over three hundred saved. Yours if you want it."

"I appreciate it, brother." They slapped palms. "But Mako told me it's all or nothing, so even the five hundred wouldn't have done any good. Doris offered to help too—but that was last night. Today she'd turn me over to Mako for the bounty."

"So what's your plan?"

"Hell, I don't know. Dan invited Caddy MacConnell and me to dinner with Angela and him tonight. Only thing I can think of is to hit him up."

"Whoa, that's a lot of money."

"Last thing in the world I want to do is ask. I'll never hear the end of it. He'll make me tell him about the peeing contest, about Mako, everything. The endless lecture." He kicked an arc of sand in the air. "If I don't get the money, though, I'm screwed. Only other thing's to leave the island, hang out somewhere until I can pay off Mako." He kicked sand again, higher this time. "Or sell my diving watch." He covered it with his palm. "My soul's in this watch."

"Here's a picture of your friend, the Reverend," said Koki. "It says, 'Sugarcane saint unites babies with mothers under fallen big top.' "

"The chicken man. 'Quadruple your money,' he promised. One consolation, he didn't get to pass the plate. And his producer, that bitch Judith, got her dress ripped off in the scramble. Crawled out from under the canvas in her undies and bra, sneaky-like. She'd have gotten away, too, if I hadn't wolf-whistled, loud, and pointed her out. You should have seen it—me and thirty firemen, and the news crew with their cameras, and at least a hundred other people got a good look at her."

"Is Doris okay?"

"Was she hurt? Nah. Upset? Oh yeah. Said half a dozen men felt her up in the dark under that tent. I got her home about three A.M. She called, woke me up at nine this morning. She was supposed to open Papa's today, but overslept—first time ever she's been late. Man, Doris has a foul mouth when she's pissed off. Papa had to call her apartment, let the phone ring forever to get her up. So now they're both pissed at *me*. Won't let me in Papa's—I'm banished. Had to get my first coffee at Denny's."

Every two hours, he walked by Papa's, looked longingly in the windows. By four, he was sure they'd forgiven him, but when Papa saw his nose pressed to the glass, he flipped the Open sign to Closed. Above, an overcast sky echoed his gloom.

He grumbled all day over the coming evening. Jeez, with Caddy MacConnell the human Popsicle, and, oh man, hitting Dan up for a loan.

Dan had made reservations at a hot new Thai restaurant. Star picked Caddy up at the hotel, met Dan and Angela at their table. Angela blew Star a kiss and hugged Caddy, then opened with a, "So, dear, are you married?" to Caddy.

Star rolled his eyes at Dan, who returned a You-know-Angela shrug of the shoulders.

"Me, married?" said Caddy. "Trothed to my work, Angela. Dinosaurs are my only love."

"Dinosaurs?"

Caddy explained geology, Shell oil, and UCLA, which led to birds and shoptalk between Dan the Bird Man and Caddy, the Birds Evolved from Dinosaurs Woman.

Star played with his food, rehearsing his "I need money" speech, until Angela asked about Mr. Lucky. Then it was Mr. Lucky stories into dessert.

The women retired to the powder room.

"Fine-looking woman, this Dr. MacConnell," said Dan. "Any interest there, son?"

"Caddy? Not bad looking, I guess, if she let her hair down, took off those glasses, and I had a thing for librarians."

Dan sat, captive, content, with a big meal under his belt. Star mentally rehearsed the loan pitch. He cleared his throat—and found himself asking about Ernest Hemingway's diet. He cleared his throat again later, when he and Dan stood outside in a drizzling rain, huddling under an umbrella, waiting for their valet-parked cars, but somehow never coughed up the plea.

"You dumb ass," he said to himself when he got home. "Why didn't you just ask? He was in a perfect mood with all that bird talk and spicy food. Now what?"

He went to the living room, flopped on the couch, and waited. Nothing. "Lucky? Hey, boy!"

Nothing. Out back? He turned on the yard lights. No Mr. Lucky. "Lucky?" he called again, louder.

Then he saw the open rear gate and the empty red-and-white fried chicken box. Neighborhood kids, little bastards, must have fed him, left the gate open. Chicken bones were a no-no. He walked to the sidewalk, yelled, "Lucky!" up and down the street.

Not like his boy. Lucky wouldn't run away. And he'd fly back when called.

Star's heart pounded as he drove up the street, called, waited, then drove and called again. What if he had been hit? Raining, the roads slick. He grabbed a flashlight, drove every street within half a mile, starting at any object in the road or gutter. What if he was lying in the bushes somewhere?

Come on fella, run out of a yard, tail wagging, okay? He searched a wider circle. Nothing.

Could he have followed the little creeps who fed him? He wore a tag with a phone number, maybe someone called.

He raced home to the answering machine. Yes! Two calls. *Beep*. A male voice, unfamiliar, strong down-home accent, speaking in monotone, like a bad actor reading a script: "Listen up. We got a dog here. White and black. If you want to see this dog alive, do perzactly what I say. If you don't, we'll throw him in the ocean, way out. Hear? Shark food. We want the Finch documents," the last word spoken carefully, as if it were unfamiliar, the syllables enunciated: doc-u-ments. "All of 'em. If'n you copy 'em, tell anyone, tell the police, don't do perzactly what I say—we'll know it. No more dog. And we'll fix you, too. Unnerstand? The Finch doc-u-ments. We'll call at noon tomorrow, tell you where to bring 'em. Noon. No fuckin' around." A pause and then, barely intelligible, a muffled "How was that?" then a "Huh? Oh, yeah," also muffled, and then, aloud, "Here's the dog, so's you know he's still alive. Twist his tail." A squeal, scuffle sounds, the receiver dropped, bounced against something hard. "Shit fire, don't let him get away!" followed by a high-pitched human "Yeooww! Gawdamn!" The phone went dead.

"Mr. Lucky!" Star shook the machine, felt hot tears stream down his face.

The second call was from Caddy MacConnell. "Star, just wanted to thank you for dinner. Angela and Dan are delightful and your Mr. Lucky stories made the evening. It did me good to get out. Talk to you tomorrow. Bye."

Yeah, good time. While I was out, some son of a bitch kidnapped my boy. He thought of Lucky wagging his tail, sitting up, begging for the chicken. Then what? Lure him into a car? Easy. Throw a sack over him?

"I'll get your ass, whoever you are!"

He gulped air, tasted tears, forced himself to breathe. Think. The "Finch documents." Something to do with Melissa's husband? He recalled the man's uneasy pronunciation of "documents" and remembered that was exactly how he had described Melissa's dirty pictures when he left the message on her answering machine. The day she died. He'd said "documents" because he hadn't wanted to admit he'd seen her art. So *there* was the connection. They'd killed Melissa, couldn't find what they wanted in her house, then picked up his message. Caddy said the answering-machine tape was missing.

The man on the phone threatened to throw Mr. Lucky in the ocean. Melissa drowned off Makapu'u Beach. She *had* been murdered.

Why were Melissa's dirty pictures so important? Was someone blackmailing the well-to-do Finch family? What if Judith had him followed, linked him to Melissa, targeted her as a Sinner of the Week? Or what if Melissa had been involved with the Reverend Jaycie Pitts? Dan had said "sexual improprieties."

Did Papa keep Melissa's envelope? No "documents," no Mr. Lucky.

It was after twelve, late to call.

"Mahina?" Papa's wife sounded sleepy. Damn. "Star Hollie. Sorry to call so late, but it's an emergency."

"Star?" Fear in her voice. "Star, my husband, he's all right?"

"Papa? I was calling *for* Papa, Mahina. Why wouldn't he be all right?"

"Thank God! I thought you were going to tell me something had happened to him. He's not here, Star. He's on Moloka'i for his monthly poker game. Third Monday. He flew over after dinner with Harvey Sparks in that little Cessna 150 of Harvey's—it's a real old one. I've always been scared to death of him flying in that plane, but he won't listen. It's the same every month. They fly over, meet friends, go up to that cabin and play poker all night. With this wind blowing, those men are crazy to fly."

"I'm sure they're okay, Mahina. Listen, do you have the number over there? I need to reach Papa. I really do."

"No, honey. There's no phone. No one, not wives, bosses, employees—no one—can reach them."

"Jeez. When's he coming back?"

"Oh, Papa'll be back by six A.M. tomorrow at the coffee shop, same as always. Like he wasn't gone. They stay up all night, drinking beer, playing cards. Harvey, he don't drink any since his liver trouble, and by four, five A.M. they're in his rattletrap Cessna flying back to Honolulu. Papa drives straight to the restaurant. You can call him there first thing—but watch it, honey, Papa'll be in a foul mood. Unless he wins, of course. But Papa, he usually loses."

"Thanks, Mahina."

He called Doris but there was no answer. He realized he didn't know the other waitresses'—Sanya's or Rae Jeanne's—last names, or Charlie the cook's, either. He walked outside. Blue light played over the curtains in Mrs. Hirakawa's window next door. Watching TV. Maybe she had seen something.

He rang the bell. She cracked the front door, clutching a cotton kimono to her chest, then motioned him in when she heard what had happened. "I saw a van in your drive around nine."

"Was it the Roach Doctor?"

"A doctor? In a van? I don't think so. I thought it was you and your beach friends. When I looked again, they were gone. Have you called the police, dear?"

"The kidnapper warned me not to, said they'd know if I did. Anyway, what would the police do?" He worried his hair, picked at the tip of his belt. "I guess they'd sympathize, but kidnapping a pet probably doesn't mean much more to people's law than stealing a bicycle. No, this is something I've got to deal with myself. Tomorrow . . ."

His eyes watered. Mrs. Hirakawa led him by the elbow to her kitchen and insisted on a cup of chamomile tea. Over tea and almond cookies, she told him stories about her wonderful cats, all thirteen of them, and Star explained how he and Mr. Lucky met, how he'd first seen Lucky, a big puppy, five years ago, playing along the side of the H-1, oblivious of the traffic, how Lucky had run away from other good

Samaritans who stopped along the highway, calling him, but how Lucky had run right to Star, jumped in his arms. How Mr. Lucky was the smartest dog he had ever known and what a fantastic friend he was. “The best ever.”

“I know you'll get him back, dear. I just know it,” said Mrs. Hirakawa. She sounded so sincere, Star was nearly convinced he would.

29

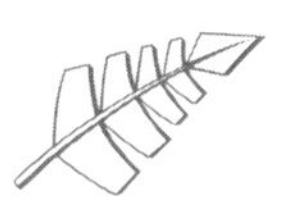

Star had walked through a driving rain from his car to Papa's four hours ago, then had fallen asleep at the edge of the sidewalk, shielded by the peak of the coffee shop roof.

He lurched awake in the predawn twilight, wind howling, and grabbed his wrist. Yes!—still there: his Rolex diving watch. Wallet, too. Five-twenty-five. Papa's opened at six.

He rubbed his eyes, cupped hands on the glass door, peered inside, saw a light. Yes. He rapped on the window with a quarter. Papa appeared, scowling, from the kitchen.

A click and the door cracked, but Star stepped back when it opened, because Papa, as his wife Mahina had predicted, was in a foul mood.

Still pissed from yesterday? Big loser on Moloka'i? Choppy flight from the bad weather? No sleep? So what? Lucky was in trouble.

"Really sorry, Papa . . ."

Papa gripped the door against the wind. "Get your ass in here, boy. I've got a bone to pick with you."

Eyes down, speaking fast, "Jeez, I would have gotten Doris home early. Had no idea we'd be robbed, at a revival, yet. But it's okay, your not letting me in yesterday. I got by all right, ate at—" He almost said the D word. "I wouldn't have called Mahina if it wasn't important. Sorry if you lost last night, Papa. Listen . . ." He stepped inside, looked the big Hawaiian in the eyes. "This is important. Do you remember that envelope I gave you a week or so ago?"

"That's it? An envelope? Shame on you." He turned his back. "Follow me." Papa stomped down the short corridor to his office. "So. Drinking, huh? Fell asleep on the sidewalk. You could have been mugged." He turned, jabbed a finger into Star's chest. A large finger. Poke, poke, poke. "Oughta pay more attention to what's important to you, boy." He turned the knob of the closed office door with one hand, thumped the back of Star's neck with the other, and shoved him through.

Whomp! Mr. Lucky hit Star in the chest. Star bounced off a steel shelf of canned food, rebounded from a stack of corrugated cartons of toilet paper, fell to the floor. Lucky nipped at his nose and ears, licked his face all the way to the concrete.

"Lucky! Lucky! Lucky!"

Papa towered over the squirreling pair, smiling, scowling, pissed, delighted. "So," stern voice, hands on hips, "while you're catting around all night, your dog here runs off, looking for you. Damn good thing I—"

"No, no. Wasn't like that. Mr. Lucky was kidnapped! They wanted that envelope I gave you." Star explained the disappearance, the phone call, the mystery of the envelope, the demand for "documents."

"That explains how I found him," said Papa. He gripped an imaginary steering wheel. "I'm driving in from the airport early, along Ala Moana—I was on Moloka'i last night, flew over with Harvey Sparks—and what do I see?" He did a double take out the imaginary car window. "Trotting alongside of the road, *makai* side by the park, headed this way, looking for you, huh? Mr. Lucky, here. Look at his neck—something else I was gonna ream you out for—I figured if this was some bimbo friend of yours' idea of being cute . . ."

Instead of his collar, a pair of pink panty hose circled Mr. Lucky's neck, the legs triple knotted under his chin, the waist section covering his neck and back like a pink minicape. Tied to the panty hose, a one-foot section of clothesline dragged the floor, the end chewed ragged.

"The kidnappers did that to him, Papa." Star scooped Mr. Lucky in his arms, swung him around. Papa handed him a pair of kitchen shears. Star snipped off the panty hose, ran his hands carefully up and down Mr. Lucky's body, ruffling his coat, looking for damage. "One hundred percent, huh, boy?"

Woof!

Papa put a cup of hot coffee in Star's hand.

"Do you still have it, Papa? The envelope?"

"Let's see." Paper littered the military surplus desk. Papa's big hands flew through the piles of bills, receipts, food service and equipment catalogs, magazines, newspapers, government forms. "I knew you were upset over the woman's death, thought you might have second thoughts, so I don't think I pitched it. But Mahina gets in here, does the books every so often, bitches that I never throw anything away. Man, she cleans house. You know how women are. Neat nest and all that crap.

"Aha!" He pulled an eleven-by-fourteen manila envelope from a lower drawer and waved it. "This look like the one?"

"Yes!" Star took it nervously, unwrapped the string from the clasp. Stopped. "No. Caddy—Melissa's sister—ought to be the first one to see it."

"Star, from what you tell me, these are bad people. Lucky's safe now. Look at me, boy." Star looked up, blinked. "You've got to watch your butt here, and Mr. Lucky's too. He can't go home."

"What can I . . . ?"

"Lucky stays at my house. He knows everyone, the kids, grandkids. Like a vacation. At least two of my big boys and Mahina are there all the time. Our neighborhood's tight, everyone watches out for the rest. No one gonna mess around at Papa's house. Understand?"

"You're right. That's good."

"I'll have one of the boys come by, take Lucky home. You find the sister, call the police, do what you gotta do."

"Thanks, Papa."

"You know you've got friends here." Papa dropped a large hand on Star's shoulder and squeezed. "You need help, you call me or the boys. Doris and the crew at Papa's, too."

"I know, Papa."

"Go, boy. You get 'em."

Star called Caddy, awakened her, explained. Was she free?

She'd be in front, waiting—hurry.

He hunched his shoulders, jogged toward his car, parked behind the apartment near the Ala Wai Canal. High-rises stood black against a pale dawn sky, their tops dabbed deep yellow by a rising sun. The wind still shrieked between the towers, bending palm trees like strung bows. Fronds hissed, slapped straining trunks. Somewhere up north over open water, a hurricane raged.

A half block away, he forgot his mission at sight of a drop-dead blonde with oh-so-long legs, wearing a scarlet miniskirt and four-inch spikes, hands on her head, in a futile attempt to hold her long hair in place. Holy moly, he thought, I never saw *her* here before. Primo posterior. With a face to match? We're headed the same way—I'll see, soon enough.

He watched her swerve, ankles wobbling over the stiletto heels like a teen at her first prom—or a woman with too much booze under her belt. Considering the hour, he decided she'd probably had a rough night. He walked in her footsteps, around the far corner of the apartment, found her leaning against the rear of his car, a shoe off, one hand kneading her bare foot. Get a grip, he told himself, no time for diversions.

"Come here," she called to him. "It's okay, we can't be seen from the street."

Twenty feet away and he could already see far too much makeup for an early stroll. A working girl. With a familiar voice.

"Lady, I'm sorry. I don't have time." Although he allowed several long seconds to check her out, head to toe. Verrry nice. Definitely familiar.

"You'd better *make* time, jerk-off. You don't recognize me?"

"Sorry." But that voice . . .

"I don't believe this. How about now?" She peeled half-inch eyelashes from her lids, wiped makeup and lipstick away with a forearm, stripped a blond wig from her head, shook her own short dark hair in the stiff breeze.

"Holy moly! I don't believe it." The bombshell blonde was no more. Before him stood Scooter, apartment manager.

"Believe. Check this." She spread her fingers, displayed inch-long false red nails. Can you believe anyone putting all this crud on because they *want* to?"

"What the hell's going on?"

"You saw the two trucks out front? The fire-engine red monster pickup with tractor tires next to the yellow tow truck lit up like a UFO? Couldn't miss 'em, right?"

"Pickup?" All he'd seen out front was Scooter's butt.

She rooted through a black vinyl pillbox purse, pulled out a tissue, and began rubbing her face. "I came out early in warm-ups to pick up the palm fronds, coconuts blown down by the storm, and what do I see?" She frowned at the makeup on the wadded tissue, then wiped her lips with a fresh one. "This guy, smaller than me and shifty, he's looking over your car. Asks me about you. Where do I think you've gone, when will you be back?"

With a sinking stomach, Star realized what was going on. No, no, no. Today was M-day. The day to repay Mako the twenty-five hundred. So, he realized, they're after me already.

He looked at his watch, his last resort, the Rolex his uncle Jack had given him years ago. Uncle Jack's own watch. He loved it like a brother, its heft, the heavy gold and chunky stainless steel. He knew at least two people on the beach who would give him three thousand for it, cash. And if he parted with it? Good-bye Mako.

Except it was M-day already. He'd put off selling the watch, and it might be too late. Mako wanted cash or blood, not a wristwatch.

Screw Mako, he thought. Avoid him, at least until I can sell the watch.

"You want to hear about this?"

"Sorry, Scooter." He couldn't quite make eye contact. Nor avoid looking at her long legs, the pink flesh mounding from her tank top. "So, the guy's asking about me?"

"When he turns to walk back to his truck, I see a *gun* stuck in his belt, under his Windbreaker. A forty-five, big mother. I decide I better find out what he's up to."

"Oh, man, a gun."

"I follow him to the street—I'm in my sweats, see?—and I start asking what he wants with you. He tells me, 'Fock off, keed'—guy's got this accent. So I go inside, run into Ellie in the hall—she's the hooker in 3-B, about to turn in for the day. I tell her what's up, the guy with the gun, so Ellie takes me into her place and dresses me up like some doll in this getup. She calls the wig Marilyn, by the way. I'm even wearing one of her bras, one of those push-up things, can you believe it?" Scooter cupped her breasts, waggled her chest. "Check these out."

He nodded nonchalantly.

"So, I go out, walk to his truck again—a new person, right? The little guy's in the cab. How he got up there without a ladder I can't imagine. Soon as he sees me crossing the street, he runs a comb through his hair and wolf-whistles—whole different story now. I can't believe men are such suckers for this froufrou crap—hormones for brains, huh?"

Star nodded again.

"Anyway, he practically faints when I wave, cross the street. He's Filipino, calls himself Mongoose, wants to tell me his life story, how he made his mother proud, how he's making all this money in Hawai'i. What he really wants, of course, is to bang me on the seat of his truck—he flashed a roll of bills thick as your wrist to encourage me. Yuck."

"What happened?"

"I can't get two useful words out of him except he wants to find you. Next, he lights up a doobie the size of your arm. By the third drag, eyes closed, on his way to a fine high, I'm no more than a dream. I duck down, move around the truck, bend his side mirrors up, and watch him from the other side. Another drag, he blinks—where'd that dream go?—rolls up his windows to keep the fresh air out, and cranks Led Zeppelin loud enough to split the windshield. While he's rocking on the seat to the music, I let the air out of his tires. All four of them. Did it real slow so he wouldn't notice—not that he'd have felt an earthquake. That girlfriend of yours, Cindy, gave me the idea. Then I went looking for you."

"Jeez."

"So, now he's out front losing his high, standing next to that big-assed tow truck reinflating what I deflated. And if you're smart, you'll get the hell out of here before he's ready to roll."

"On my way."

Scooter slapped his palm, spalling off two fake nails.

Star drove at idle speed out the driveway, watched Scooter in the rearview mirror, first bending to retrieve the nails, then lifting an ankle nearly to her waist to remove the other shoe, exposing both thighs all the way up.

The Turtle thumped into a croton hedge. Eyes forward now, Star edged the car off the grass, back onto the asphalt. Dead ahead, he saw the little Filipino pacing, making windmill, hurry-up motions at the tow truck operator beside the compressor. Three tires were filled; the last was flat but rising.

Star slowed at the curb, tooted his horn, and waved. The Filipino's face flushed red as his Windbreaker. He clenched his fists, hopped up and down. Star putted away at fifteen miles an hour, hand waving bye-bye out the window all the way down the block. When he rounded the corner, he hit the gas and beat it to Caddy's hotel.

She jumped in the car. "Let me see this envelope."

He cut the engine. "Caddy"—he held the envelope to his left, out of reach—"Melissa opened this when she was with me, didn't show it to me really, but I saw the picture on top. I want you to be prepared. I'm afraid it's . . ." He searched for a word. "Well, hell, pornographic."

"Pornographic? Give me that." She reached across his lap, snatched the envelope. Her fingers unwound the string closure, flipped open the end. Three illustration boards, eight by ten inches, slid out.

Smiling on top sat the infamous drawing of Star's recollection. Caddy stared at it. "I'm not sure what this is."

He rotated it ninety degrees, pointed to her lap.

"Oh, my," she said, and blushed.

"That's what I thought too."

She shuffled it to the bottom of the stack. A second drawing revealed another view of the same delicate subject, and the third, yet another. "Melissa, Melissa," Caddy mumbled. She dropped the drawings to her lap, covered them with the envelope.

"I told you—"

"Enough from you." Reluctantly she lifted one of the drawings, shielded it from Star with her shoulder. "Look here." She held it out, pointed to neat letters at the top left corner; "Addendum, Plate 7, P.U. E21, N24." The others read, "Addendum, Plate 6, P.U. E21, N24" and "Addendum, Plate 8, P.U. E21, N24." "These," she said, "are hardly pornography. They're medical illustrations, intended for publication.

"Hmmm." Her nail tapped a mark beneath each of the drawings. Nearly two inches long, the mark formed a horizontally stretched H. Below it "1 m." "These, my friend, are scientific illustrations, and that mark? It's a scale. Represents one meter."

"A meter? Then the . . . the things must be twelve feet long. Maybe she was drawing an elephant's . . . you know."

"Get real. Twelve feet?" She studied each of the illustrations. "I confess, however, I can't imagine what species she was representing."

"Maybe it's a dinosaur."

"I've seen impressions of skin, scales, footprints, but I'm certain there's never been a fossil record of dinosaur pudenda. In fact, they definitely wouldn't—"

Star interrupted. "What if, get this, Melissa and her husband found a real, living dinosaur?"

Caddy stared at him, shook her head. "A dinosaur? Living? In Hawai'i? Are you out of your mind?"

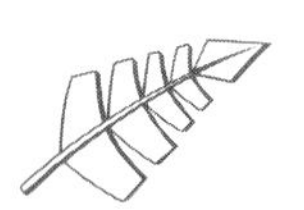

There's more," said Caddy. "An envelope containing Artemas's expense records." She paged through receipts. "Very orderly. They cover a week, ending the day before he died. Artemas had been traveling back and forth to the Big Island. And what's this? Oh, Melissa." She unfolded a newspaper page of personal ads.

Two-thirds of the way down, Star read "Ladies, Meet Mr. Lucky," and coughed.

"You need a pat on the back?"

He saw the ad uncircled, unchecked, un-x'd. "No. Fine. Bug flew in my throat."

She wadded the paper with a scowl, dropped it on the car floor into the fast-food litter. A small polyethylene bag slid from the envelope onto the palm of her hand. "One item more." It contained a single soiled, crushed, and faded yellow feather, labeled on white tape across the top, "*M. nobilis*?? !! c. Landau." "Means nothing to me," she said. "Perhaps one of Melissa's freelance projects, although it looks like Artemas's printing."

"Maybe it's from one of those big macaws. The red, yellow, and blue ones."

"Perhaps. '*M. nobilis*' must be a scientific name. Latin. Easy enough to check."

"Dan would know."

"Of course, his obsession with ornithology. The 'c. Landau'? Could be it's a person whose first name begins with a C, although it's not capitalized here, perhaps the scientist who discovered the species—traditional in taxonomy. Or maybe the abbreviation for *circa*—approximately."

"Or call."

"Possibly."

"Let's check Melissa's house again. Give us something specific to look for."

"By all means."

Star started the car, merged with traffic, thinking about yellow birds and Landaus and the Big Island, failing to notice, for the second time that day, a red pickup truck with monster tires. It pulled from the curb a half block away.

On the Pali Highway the red pickup narrowed the gap. The two lanes on Star's side of the center rail ran along a narrow shoulder. A garbage truck lumbered in the left, barely gaining on a school bus, blocking the right. Star hung behind the truck.

"Idiot back there's tailgating like it's my fault we're not going faster," he said, then, "Uggh!" as the car lurched.

The truck had rammed the Turtle, then fell back ten feet.

Caddy twisted to stare through the rear window. "Oh, no!"

In his side mirror, Star saw the familiar red paint, the huge tires.

Caddy saw the gun, the angry driver tapping it against his windshield.

The tiny Filipino in the bright red Windbreaker who an hour ago had dreamed of romancing Scooter on the pickup's front seat shook the big gun, motioned them to pull over.

"Like hell." Star slowed, searched for a way out.

Caddy peered over the backseat. "A gun! He must be one of those religious terrorists, like the one who vandalized your car. I see a crucifix swinging from his mirror, little statues standing in fur on his dash."

Star had never discussed theology with Mako, but anything was possible. "Yep. That's it," he said, and moved to the right lane, feigning surrender.

Caddy saw it coming and screamed. Mongoose pulled forward to their left, fired two shots over the top of the Turtle, through the pickup's right window—literally *through* the pickup's window, since, in the heat of the chase and dulled by his morning reefer, Mongoose forgot to roll it down.

Shattered glass shotgunned the Turtle with gravelly pops and skitters. Pieces stung Star's cheek and neck.

Neither the bus nor the truck altered course, apparently attributing the banging to one another's backfires. Face red as his truck, Mongoose leaned right, pointed the gun nearly out the passenger window at Star.

"Hold on." Star downshifted, wrenched the wheel to the right, determined to pass on the outside. The Turtle swerved and bumped onto the narrow berm, gained on the bus.

His pickup too wide to follow, Mongoose kept left, tailgated the garbage truck, urged it on with his horn.

The garbageman extended a leathery arm and, with a practiced twist of the wrist, flipped off the little shrimp behind him with the fancy wheels, then moved halfway up the long bus and stayed even with it.

Star rounded the bus, ahead of them all, not speeding—the Turtle earned its name on hills—but accelerating nonetheless. Mongoose, hemmed in by the bus-truck convoy, fell far behind.

Star pumped the accelerator. Caddy pumped the floorboard. "Soon as he clears that bus," he said, "we're done for. We'll never make it through the tunnel, down the mountain. Unless . . ."

Ahead, fast approaching on the right, he saw the entrance to the Pali Lookout. "If I can get off there, loop across the highway on the Lookout overpass without him seeing us, we can take the return ramp back to Honolulu while he drives on to the windward side."

At the last second, he turned right, hit the brakes. Damn. A candy-striped gate blocked the entry road: "Closed—High Winds." The Turtle slid to a stop. "Caddy, try the gate. If you can open it, let me through, close it fast."

She ran ahead, shouted back, "Wasn't locked," and swung open one of the crossbars. Star zipped through and she rechained it. As they sped up the ramp and around a concealing bend, Caddy, knees on the seat, facing backward, gave him the bad news. "He followed us."

"I can't outrun him. It'll be a bitch to hide up here. Grab that climbing rope coiled in the back, put it in my lap. We'll be out of his sight when we round the bend. When I stop, run like hell for the lookout. I'll catch up. I'll leave the car at the side of the mountain. Maybe he'll think we climbed up."

Low wet clouds streaked overhead like a wind-tunnel slipstream. Star ran. Near the observation deck, he glanced back, saw the distant pickup stop next to the Turtle, the small driver jump out, look upslope, then directly at him.

Damn. Spotted.

Mongoose fired a shot from the lot. "No place to go," he yelled. ". . . o . . . lace to . . . oh," his words clipped by the wind.

"Screw you," Star muttered. The drop-off loomed ahead. To right and left, the slopes looked steep, slippery, uncertain, but the original road across the mountains, abandoned for years, still snaked downhill, hugging the cliffs. No. Star knew he could outrun the Filipino, but doubted Caddy, in a pair of stiff sandals, could keep up. And if they lagged within shooting range . . .

"Caddy, run to right of the raised lookout. Stay clear of the wind."

Seconds later, near the drop-off, they halted. If they were lucky, they had ten seconds before Mongoose and his .45 caught up with them. Star looked both ways, settled on misdirection.

He ran to the pipe rail at the cliff edge. A blast of cold air punched him back. He stooped in the wind shadow of the low wall, pushed forward, tied the orange and aqua braided rope around the rail with a figure-eight knot, and threw the coils into the wind, down the cliff, leaving six feet of rope loose at the top, snaking across the pavement. No way to miss it. That done, he ran to Caddy, fighting the wind in a low crouch. He scooped her up and over a low concrete retaining wall at the base of the mountainside.

He shouted over the hissing wind, "Sit. Stay low. He'll be here any second. With luck, he'll think we either climbed down my rope or ran onto the old road. If he thinks we're on the rope, he won't be able to see because of the wind and the overhang. He'll go back down to the highway, try to spot us from below. If he thinks we took the old road, he'll run that way. Either case, soon as he's out of sight, we'll run to our car, drive back to Honolulu."

A peripheral speck of red darted beyond the edge of the raised lookout. Star ducked low, shoved Caddy's head even lower. He crouched, wrapped his arm around her shoulder, held her against him. Unless Mongoose walked right to their concealing wall and looked over, they'd be invisible.

Except for the hiss of the rushing wind and an occasional snap as it changed direction, they heard nothing. Star counted to himself, one thousand one, one thousand two . . . At ten, he peeked over the wall, saw the little bastard tugging at the rope like a fisherman hauling in a lunker. The rope must have snagged a branch, because it wasn't coming up.

Great. He thinks we're rappelling down, weighting the end.

Above, the sky swirled, a dimensionless gray. Thick mist dulled the rock and vegetation, then cleared and re-formed. By contrast, Mongoose was a dancing rainbow. Below his zippered red jacket he wore white bell-bottoms and bright blue patent leather platform shoes. Over his shoulder hung a shiny blue fringed leather bag.

The tiny Filipino raised one foot to the rail, held the unyielding rope with both hands for support, and peered over, unable to see past the bushes and small trees clinging to the cliff. He knelt on the wall, hunched against the wind, an ankle leveraged against the pipe rail for support. Gusts tore at his clothes. The shoulder bag zipped and dipped like an antenna coon-tail.

Some sixth sense told Mongoose to glance over his shoulder. Star ducked. Too late.

"Oho!" shouted the little man over the howling wind, "the rope's a treek, huh? Geeve it up. You come out, I not hurt you."

Star pushed Caddy's head down. In a voice barely loud enough for her to hear, he said, "Stay." He stood.

"Although maybe I doan tell the truth sometime." The Filipino's left hand tightened its grip on the taut rope, but his right hand left it, unzipped his Windbreaker three quarters of the way down, and reached for the .45's pearl handle protruding from his belt. He began to step down. "You make me verrry angry, what you do to my trock. So now, meester longhaired hippie man, I gonna blow you awayyy—"

A sudden *whoomp!* ballooned his Windbreaker open, threw him off balance. Sail-like, the inflated jacket lifted Mongoose up, up, until only the toes of his blue platform shoes tippity-tapped along the rail. Then his feet left it entirely, the gun fell. His right arm beat the air like a hummingbird wing before finding the rope. The shoulder bag slipped from his arm, its strap twisted around his ankle. Both hands clutched the damp rope, his lifeline. Mongoose held on, but inch by inch his hands slid outward as the hungry wind sucked him aloft. A human kite with a shoulder bag for a tail, linked to the railing by two feet of rope, then three feet, then six, Mongoose lofted, bobbed higher, dipped from sight, rose again.

His screams brought up Caddy, hands to mouth. Star ran to the railing, buffeted by the wind. He lay flat, then crawled on his hands and knees to the rope. Crouched low, braced against the wall, he tried to reel in the screaming red and white kite with the bright blue tail, twisting, rising, eight feet away.

Then the wind died, the kite dove, and Star jerked up slack. He peered over at the receding spot of red and drew back. Mongoose the kite sailed into the clouds, toward the golf course far below.

"Gone," Star said.

But not quite. There was the Filipino's blue patent leather bag, tangled in a leafy branch only four feet down, shining like the Star of India. A relic, a trophy, a symbol of failed heroics, whatever, Star had to have it. He wrapped his elbow around the pipe, leaned over, stretched, but was two feet shy.

"Don't be stupid," Caddy yelled. "Whatever it is, leave it alone. All I need is for you to blow away too. God, I'm gonna throw up, I know it."

"It's his bag. I can almost reach it. See how the wind blows real hard, then changes direction, dies for five or six seconds?" He wrapped the rope over his shoulder, down his back, around his rear end, waited for the next lull.

Caddy shouted, "Don't, you idiot!"

The wind died. He popped over the wall, lowered himself two feet, snagged the bag and was almost over the top when a fresh blast slapped him from behind, up over the rail, and onto the pavement. Star rubbed his thigh, wiped a drop of blood from his chin. "See? All in one piece."

He untied the rope, freed now by the wind, hauled it in arm over arm, slung it on his shoulder along with the leather bag. "Done. Let's get the hell out of here before someone comes by."

They ran to the car. He threw the rope and the bag on the rear seat, started the engine. On the ramp from the lookout, headed for Honolulu, he turned to Caddy. "See what's in the bag."

She opened the leather flap reluctantly, glanced inside, wrinkled her nose, poked tentatively, and closed it. "Food," she said. "Ugh. Lots of really foul-smelling food. Something Asian to be sure."

"It's a nice bag anyway, huh?"

"Worth risking your life for?"

"Didn't think about it at the time."

"Men and their trophies. Gonads short-circuit your neurons. Ever hear about Jason and the Golden Fleece? Paris and his trophy wife Helen? Teddy Roosevelt and San Juan Hill? Custer and—"

"I get the idea."

She rubbed her eyes. "Oh. I'll never forget seeing that little man blown . . ."

"He would have shot us. He was reaching for the gun when the wind snagged him."

"Do you think they're more of them, these religious fanatics?"

"I don't know," he lied. Mako had no shortage of hired hands. "I hope not."

She drew her knees to her chest and shivered. "You tried to save him."

And he would have killed me, he thought. For twenty-five hundred dollars. Didn't even ask for the money. Mako had the word out all right. For the moment, however, it was over. They were safe. He laughed.

"You think it's funny?"

"Just thinking. When he was waving around up there in that red jacket, white bell-bottoms, blue shoes and bag—I didn't know whether to recite the Pledge of Allegiance or salute."

She punched him in the arm, hard, then laughed too. Star snickered, and within seconds they were giggling, out of control.

The laughter rippled away, and Caddy broke into sobs. Star looked at his white knuckles on the steering wheel, released his hands one at a time, flexed his fingers. He forced himself to take three long, deep breaths.

They rode in silence back to Waikiki.

31

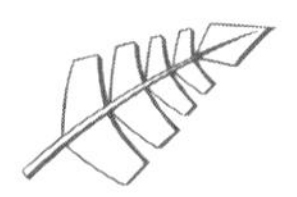

Caddy sat in the car by her hotel, massaging her forehead. "Nearly killed by a religious terrorist," she said for the third time. "I'll never forget seeing that man disappear into the clouds."

"Hey, we're safe now." Star patted her shoulder.

She removed her glasses, rubbed the bridge of her nose. "Let no one say life with Star Hollie is boring—I'd hate to travel with you in the Middle East, mister." She looked at him. "Police. We should call the police."

"Oh? If we do, it'll be tomorrow, at least, before we're back on the trail of Melissa's murderers. They'll question us about the Kite man, take us back to the lookout, have us look at photos . . ."

"Okay, okay. You wait here, I'll run inside and call Dan, see what he can make of our feather and the word 'Landau.' Then we'll check Melissa's house."

"I've got to run by a friend's. I'll meet you here in fifteen minutes."

Watchful, he drove to Scooter's, found her on the apartment's front steps, in jeans and a sweatshirt, no Wonderbra twin peaks, no sign of Marilyn. He explained how Mako's small friend Mongoose had chased Caddy and him up the mountain, sailed off a cliff.

"Man, I wish I'd seen it. *Whoosh!*" Arms outstretched, she airplaned in circles.

"Scooter, listen. We don't say a word to anyone, right? If Mako's people think you were involved . . ."

"Yeah, sure. I never saw him, whoever he was. I hardly know you. I slept late."

"Scooter. Thanks for the warning, slowing him down."

She gave him two quick jabs in the ribs. "That's what friends are for, huh?"

He drove along Ala Wai, turned left onto Nohonani, circling back to Caddy's hotel. A bakery truck backed from a drive with a beep, beep, beep, blocking the road. Star stopped, checked his watch, the watch he would have to sell. Today if possible.

Scuffling at his door. Huh?

The sky went dark as a massive form eclipsed the sun. *Mako*. Not now. Not yet. Star shifted to reverse, his foot shot to the accelerator, but a black road-hog Mercury loomed in the rearview mirror, wedging him in.

Mako motioned to the curb. Nowhere else to go. Star parked. The little car sank three inches as one of Mako's megagoons, a heavy, smelly, woolly-headed Fijian in a dirty muscle shirt, squeezed into the seat next to Star. With one hand, the Fijian snatched the ignition keys; with the other he hefted a two-and-a-half-foot tire iron. A second goon parked the Mercury behind the Turtle.

The car's springs squealed in protest as Mako leaned into the driver's window. A tiny smile sprouted at the center of his long mouth, rippled wider and wider into a shark's leer. "It's time, my friend," his voice somewhere between a growl and a purr. "Pay me back or payback, if you get my drift. A matter of honor between businessmen."

The Fijian to Star's right sat stonefaced, slapping the tire iron on his palm.

"Out of the car," said Mako. "We'll take you for a ride. See some pineapple, how's that sound?"

Star stood, legs loose at the joints. His mouth moved but formed no words.

The Mercury's driver, a stocky, black-toothed Indonesian chewing betel nut, patted Star down with a knowing smile. Scarlet spittle gathered at the corners of the man's mouth, stained bright red from the stimulant.

Mako clapped his thick hands together. "Been waiting for this. Yes I have." He turned to the Fijian, who had slung Star's blue bag and climbing rope over his shoulder. "Check the bag, Caucau," Mako said, "see if our boy brought a weapon. And do bring the rope. We'll think of something imaginative to do with the rope."

The Fijian tied a slip knot in the climbing rope, looped the end over Star's neck.

"Mako," croaked Star. "I have this vintage Rolex. . . ."

"So you *do*, my boy." Mako tapped it with a stubby forefinger. "A fine old one, too. Tell you what. I'll buy it from you. Would you like that? Must be worth thirty-five hundred dollars. I can pay in cash. Cash. Yes, yes, I see that would please you. Why don't we talk about it tomorrow? At the moment, we have other business."

"Boss," said the Fijian. "Some stinky food in the bag. Two Led Zeppelin CDs, and this." He handed Mako a roll of bills bound with a rubber band.

Mako spit, counted the money. "Two thousand eight hundred seventy-four dollars." He peeled off the bulk of it, tossed Star the remainder. "You like the drama, huh, boy? Get Mako all excited, then let him down like this." He spit again. "I admire your moxie though. Caucau might have broken your legs right out. Yes, that took guts." He raised his thick-lidded eyes to Star's, lifted a puffy hand to Star's face, and tweaked his cheek. With a nod, he motioned his men back to the Mercury.

The Fijian dropped the coils of rope around Star's neck, tossed him the blue bag and keys. They drove away.

Star leaned on the roof of the Turtle, chin to metal, heart pounding. There hadn't been a word about the little guy, Mongoose, the human kite. Who was he? Whoever he was, he saved Star's legs.

Star slid behind the wheel, thought of the revival, remembered the Reverend Jaycie Pitts's words: "The Lord moves in mysterious ways."

A mere thirty-six hours before, he had taken nearly every cent he had, five hundred dollars, to the preacher's tent. Lost it. Today, nearly three thousand dollars comes his way, comes very strangely, but comes his way nonetheless. His money more than quadrupled. Who'd have guessed?

He thumped a happy rhythm on the steering wheel with his fingers. "Keep the faith, baby," he said, and fired up the Turtle.

32

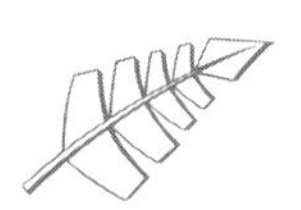

Bernie's mind's eye followed a long drive, sailing straight and high over an emerald green fairway at Paradise Valley. With a tingle in his shorts, he watched the ball drop toward the green and a sure hole in one.

Poof! It disappeared ten feet above the pin as Kathleen's voice over the intercom broke his reverie. "Sir? Sir? He's here."

"Huh?" said Bernie.

"D. L. McWhorter. You asked him to come by."

"Right. Send him in."

No one mentioned tea. Bernie motioned for the small, gray-haired man in khaki shirt and trousers over spit-shined combat boots to take a chair.

McWhorter sat, instead, on the corner of Bernie's desk.

"D. L.," Bernie said, "remember the first time we met?"

"Of course, sir."

"Would you really have put that bomb under my car?"

"Well, that was up to you, wasn't it?"

"Strong measure for a measly thirty-one thousand dollars."

"The casino extended you credit, you ran up a tab, wrote a bad check, left Vegas without a word, then refused to answer their letters, their calls. What did you expect?"

"Tell you the truth, I didn't know. That's why I did it. To see what would happen. And they sent you. I remember when you walked into my office, no appointment. Dropped that thing with the wires and lumpy stuff on my desk. So much for Hydra's security."

"And you offered to write me a check. A check." A thin smile passed McWhorter's lips.

"The bomb or cash," said Bernie. "Thirty-one thou, plus interest, your expenses, and a five-thousand bonus for telling me first—or, blooey!" Bernie's fingers fluttered explosively over the polished mahogany. Papers fluttered, dropped to the floor.

"All the casino wanted was the money, sir, but they would have been satisfied with an example. They do a lot of business with Hawai'i and Japan. A Honolulu welsher blown to bits in his Mercedes? Useful. It was up to me. The five thousand went into my retirement kitty."

"So we walked to the bank, I gave it all to you in cash, offered you a job."

"Chief of security and contingency operations."

"You've been happy?"

"The occasional interrogation, corporate espionage—that holds my attention. But the other crap—overseeing security systems, guards, pilferage, drug testing, the employment stuff, illegal aliens, the rest of it?" He feigned a yawn.

"But it pays well."

"The company is generous. No complaints about the salary. But I'll be happier when Paradise Valley is under way and I have my—you remember the sum, sir? My completion bonus? Payable thirty days after the road is finished on time and construction on the development begins. There'll be no need for me to visit Radio Shack and my old army buddies for supplies, will there, sir?" McWhorter flashed a lively smile, but his eyes didn't move.

Bernie waved away his concerns. "That's our deal. Built into the project budget, listed as paving contingency. Two hundred thousand. Not to worry.

"So, D. L., what are you going to do with all your money? You seem to live modestly. Added to your past bonuses and those salary checks, you must have quite a nest egg. You playing the market? Real estate? Thinking of opening your own business? How about a collection agency?" Bernie laughed at that, but McWhorter simply stared.

"Like I said. Money's feeding my retirement kitty." McWhorter ran his hand over the brush of his flattop, narrowing his eyes at the questions. "Guess you might say real estate, sir. I'm going to run a small country."

Bernie's mouth fell open.

"Plan's finished, all I need are the players. Cold war's yesterday's news. U.S. isn't worried about Communist dominoes anymore, only markets. If some small country, no oil, changes leadership, who gives a damn? Always unrest somewhere. I'll find the right citizen, front man, ambitious, who has the connections, speaks the lingo, but lacks the wherewithal. I'll bring in a small cohort of competent men, and bingo, coup. Front man's the new president, I'm defense minister. I hold the power, the strings."

He scratched his scalp. "Only concern is where? I study the maps, read the *New York Times* every week." McWhorter blinked, looked at Bernie, stone-faced. "This is the last one, sir. After Paradise Valley, I'm afraid it's *sayonara*."

Bernie scowled. "We've had such a good run, D. L. Hey, with me as a real HydraCorp player, who knows the possibilities? Do reconsider."

McWhorter shook his head slowly.

"I see," said Bernie. "Hate to see you go." His face brightened. "We've had our adventures, though. Tell me, where's the thrill for you? I know it's not the money. The risk? That's what turns me on. Sets my old peter to tingling."

"Risk? Need to get the adrenaline up once in a while, keep the ticker thumpin'. But risk? No, sir. For me, it's the thrill of the chase. And the conquest."

"Speaking of which," said Bernie solemnly, "need I remind you that if there's no finished road, no construction—no Paradise Valley—we're both in a world of the smelly stuff. How are we doing, D. L.? Progress report, please."

McWhorter raised his hand, bent his fingers down one by one, enumerating. "Road's back on schedule. Had some problems with volcano lovers and dopers holding up construction." He paused, smiled. "You want the real story, the graphic details, or a sanitized summary?"

Bernie squirmed in his seat at McWhorter's smile. "The, uh, summary should be sufficient."

"I thought so. A corporate man like yourself wouldn't want to clutter his mind with awkward trivia. So, those problems? Small potatoes, took care of 'em. Then there's the volcano itself. Nothing even I can do there."

Bernie pursed his lips. "I check on it every morning. Still flowing. Straight for the Pali-uli, but our consultants tell me it's a minor flow, should play out soon. God, I hope so."

"Our biggest problem"—McWhorter bent his third finger down—"would have been the archaeologist, Finch. We were lucky he was killed in that automobile accident."

"You can say that again," agreed Bernie. "Not that I take pleasure in his death—but when he waltzed in here *after* he'd filed his report, told me to hold the presses, that he'd made this fantastic discovery, that the scientists, the Hawaiians, everyone else would go nuts over it, I about went stroke city. I thought the surveys were in the bag—the biologist, with some incentive, understood our needs, assured me he'd turn up nothing irregular. And I was sure Finch was a dither-head.

"But from what he was hinting at, it was obvious we could kiss Paradise Valley good-bye, or see it derailed for who knows how long. Old fart wouldn't say a word more to me. 'Wait for the press conference tomorrow. You'll be impressed' is all I could get out of him. Then that night, he gets drunk celebrating, runs off the road. A lucky break."

"Lucky," McWhorter repeated. "I've been doing my damnedest since to find out exactly what and where that discovery was. Some kind of shrine, maybe more. I knew something was up even before Finch talked to you. Although Finch didn't say a word to him, his assistant, Kapono, too-big-for-his-pants volcano lover, would have made trouble, too, so I convinced him to drop out of sight." McWhorter chortled, his eyes crinkled with laughter, and he slapped his hand on the desk.

"Care to share the humor, D. L.?"

"Of course, sir. But I thought you wanted the summary. . . ."

Bernie swallowed. "Sorry, didn't mean to interrupt. Go on."

"Finch's wife holed up on another island after his death. She'd worked with him, must have had evidence of whatever it was. I gained access to their computers. Physical access only, I'm afraid. Finch's files were well encrypted. Got the best man in the islands working on it, thirteen-year-old hacker name of Mikey Chang—he's the one cracked the competition's system on Kaua'i for us, you might remember. Mikey got into the marines' mainframe at Kane'ohe by the time he was twelve—had them sending him and his buddies electronics by motorcycle courier, courtesy of Uncle Sam, with zero record of the transfers. Mikey's a good man. But so far he's gotten nowhere with the Finch files.

"Anyway, Finch's wife came back to O'ahu, despondent, killed herself. Another dead end." McWhorter chuckled again, one more finger dropped. "I figured if we could find out whatever this discovery was, this archaeological thing, and keep it to ourselves, we could bulldoze it over. Gone. No one's the wiser. We stay on schedule."

"Great minds think alike, D. L. So where we stand is, we don't know just what this discovery is, but no one else does either? Almost as good. We've got the rezoning, our grading and grubbing permits for the road. They're dozing the switchbacks as we speak. Once the heavy equipment moves in, chances are Finch's discovery will be history, regardless."

"One minor problem, sir."

"Uh-oh." Bernie covered his ears. "I don't like that tone of voice." He took a deep breath, loosened his tie, opened his desk drawer and fumbled with a package of Nicorettes, popped five in his mouth. "Okay. Let's hear it."

"The Finch woman's sister came over from the mainland after the suicide, teamed up with some hippie beach bum in Waikiki. Ladies' man. Maybe had something going with Finch's wife. He'd run an ad in the personals section of the paper. Friend showed it to me—reads, 'Ladies, meet Mr. Lucky.' Appears the Finch woman took him up on it. Our friend Mr. Lucky, real name's Star Hollie, writes for *Pacific Rainbow* magazine. So before she takes the big swim, the wife passes Mr. Lucky information—hard stuff, documents, about Finch's discovery—not the whole shebang, evidently, but enough to get him interested—and now he and the sister are snooping around. They could be a problem."

"Can we buy 'em off? Get something on them? Threaten them?"

"Tried my hand at that. Danger there, you see, is you let them know they're onto something."

"You said they don't know it all? What do you think they do know? Maybe not enough to worry about."

"Could be. But I don't believe in taking chances."

Bernie rubbed his eyes. "Damn, D. L., it was going so smoothly—except for the stinking volcano. Now this."

"Don't you worry, sir. Taking care of problems is what you pay me for. I'm on top of it."

"I know, but . . ." Bernie began to shake his finger at him, but thought better of it. "This is the big one, D. L. For both of us. Stay with it. Do what you need to do: bribes, surveillance, whatever. You need more of Hydra's resources, let me know."

Bernie watched McWhorter leave his office, joke with Kathleen as if he hadn't a care in the world. From the outer office door, the gray-haired man threw Bernie a quick salute, then disappeared down the corridor whistling.

33

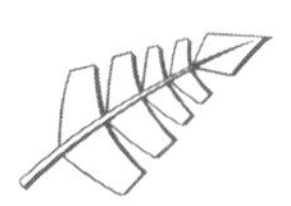

Caddy jumped into the Turtle before it rolled to a stop. "The word 'Landau' meant nothing to Dan. But get this—he says the name on our bird feather is the Hawaiian *'o'o, Moho nobilis*. Big showy bird, a foot long, once common on the island of Hawai'i, hunted to extinction for its feathers. Extinct. Although there's a slim hope it's still hanging on in the forests, up, away from people. As you might imagine, Dan's beside himself, asking how old our feather is, where it came from, who found it.

"He says you know about the bird already. It's the one in the eighteenth-century watercolor he showed you."

"I remember he was worked up over it, but truth is, I didn't pay much attention to what he said. All that bird stuff in his office . . ."

"I promised we'd go straight to the magazine. How far is it from here?"

"Less than fifteen minutes."

"Then get a move on. Chop, chop."

He mouthed the words, "Chop, chop," wondering what she'd say if she knew Mako nearly chop-chopped his legs—would have, if it wasn't for the Kite man's blue bag.

Caddy said, "I called Detective Schott. Guess what? They're finally listing Melissa's death as suspicious. They concluded someone stole the Roach Doctor van, then returned it the same night. Detective Schott thought they had another lead—an assault, two men in a van, someone got the license number—but it turned out that van was stolen, too."

Star decided not to explain. "You didn't tell them about the Kite-man?"

"No. I know I should have."

"No, you *shouldn't* have. Caddy, it's decision time. Do we turn these drawings and the feather over to the police, tell them everything—except about the Kite-man. Tell them about Mr. Lucky's kidnapping? What the kidnappers said to me? The police have resources we don't." He glanced right to see her eyes. "Melissa was your sister. You decide. But understand, they'll tell us to stay out of it. Sit and wait."

"What do you think?"

"Whoever drowned Melissa kidnapped Mr. Lucky. I want the sons of bitches, and we've got leads. But like I said, you make the call."

He drove in silence, waiting.

Caddy wrinkled her face. "I stayed here to find Melissa's murderer. If the police learn anything, they'll let me know. We're onto something." She thumped the dash. "Let's move on it!" She pedaled the floorboard. "Won't this car go any faster? You want me to rent a real car?"

Star rolled his eyes. At the next light, he studied her face. "Caddy, these are bad people. You're sure you're up to it?"

"Me? Of course I am."

He reached over, squeezed her hand.

"Light's changed," she said.

Dan paced the reception desk, waiting. "My office," he said, and led the way.

"BASTARD. SNEAKY. THIEF!" Ernest Hemingway screeched from his cage in the corner.

"That's Star," Dan explained to Caddy. "I hope he doesn't come up with a name for—"

"HOT KNOCKERS!"

"Sorry, Caddy," said Dan. "That's what he called Angela—it got him thrown out of the house. Angela has a low tolerance for profanity."

Caddy moved to the cage, made kissy sounds to Ernest.

"The feather, please." Dan held out his hand.

She returned to the desk, opened the clear plastic envelope, and slid the feather onto Dan's palm. It lay there, shrunken, faded like a wilted petal. "The weight of a soul," he said, and shook his head. "Or so the Egyptians believed. The soul of a species, reduced to this."

"Poor bird," said Star. "Screwed by humans."

"SCREWED!"

"That's right, boys," said Dan. "Crude, but that's the idea." He slipped the feather back into the plastic bag, carried it to his desk lamp. He flexed the polyethylene, held it to the light. "It would have been bright when fresh. This could be a hundred years old, if well preserved, or picked off the ground a month ago—recent but faded." He stared at it. "Do you realize the implications if it's contemporary?"

He walked to a painting hung on the opposite wall. "Caddy"—he rapped on the glass—"this is the Hawaiian *'o'o*. Each of the major islands had a distinct variety, but the Big Island *'o'o* was the most noble. Found nowhere else on earth."

The bird in the painting perched on a cluster of red powder-puff blossoms. Large, bold, iridescent black, it had a long curved beak and impressive black and white wavy tail feathers, with a yellow rump, and two fluffy yellow feathers protruding from its body on each side like butterfly wings.

"Your feather must have been one of these yellow tufts," Dan said. "Assuming it's really a feather from the *'o'o* and not a yellow-dyed chicken feather."

He gripped both sides of the frame. "This is a watercolor by William Ellis, a surgeon on Cook's third voyage to Hawai'i." He ran his fingers along the wood. "Good Lord, it gives me chills to think that this was painted by a man who saw the bird itself. And hanging on my wall!"

"What are the flowers?" asked Caddy.

" *'Ohi'a lehua*. Big, native tree. The *'o'o* fed on its nectar. The Hawaiians hunted the bird nearly to extinction for the feathers. Hawaiian and subsequent European assaults on the environment did the rest. Hawaiian featherwork was extraordinary—leis, chiefs' capes, helmets. There are many in museums, plenty of feathers still around of species now extinct. The last live *'o'o* were spotted around 1900. Although"—he took a deep breath, looked at the single feather in the bag—"there was a report of an *'o'o* song in the thirties, so there's a remote possibility a population still exists somewhere in the *'ohi'a* forests on the Big Island.

"We absolutely must find out more about this. Who found it?"

"Presumably Artemas Finch, my sister's husband," said Caddy, "an archaeologist at Bishop Museum." She spread Melissa's drawings on the desk next to the plastic bag, explained her medical-illustration hypothesis.

"Yes." Dan nodded. "I'd say medical illustrations too, except for the meter scale. Maybe it's an error, a misplaced decimal point."

Star wondered how large a really big dinosaur's snatch might be. Did they have any idea how big a dinosaur penis was? That would be a start. He had never heard so much as a mention of a dinosaur prick. Probably because dinosaurs were so popular with kids. Wouldn't want to frighten them, give them bad dreams, the boys feelings of inadequacy, the girls megadoses of penis envy. Jeez, he thought, I'll bet they were huge. Six feet? Ten feet? Wow.

"The numbers?" Dan speculated, "Some scientific notation. And Landau? A place? A colleague? Dr. Finch was affiliated with Bishop Museum, you said. You've checked there, of course."

Caddy and Star exchanged glances.

"Uh," said Star, "not yet. We were going to, weren't we, Caddy? Wanted to show you the feather first."

"Tell you what," said Dan. "You leave the feather here. Let me run this by an ornithologist I know at the University of Hawai'i. You two check out the museum. Here, call them while I'm still here, it may shed light on the feather. I'll set the phone on speaker."

He checked the number on his computer, began punching buttons. "Caddy, you want to do the honors?"

They were channeled through a recording of coming events, an operator, outreach programs, and two anthropologists. Caddy drummed her fingers on the desk, asked for the chairman.

"Dr. Yamamoto's about to leave for Pago Pago," a harried female voice answered. "He's very busy. Can't possibly speak with you. Who is this?"

Star tapped on the birdcage.

"SCREW YOU!" screamed Ernest Hemingway.

"Excuse me?" said the voice.

Caddy and Dan shot the bird withering glares. Star grinned.

"Must be someone on your line," said Caddy. "They passed us through half a dozen extensions." She was back in Ph.D. mode. "Very wasteful of my time . . ."

Star winced.

"I'm sorry," said the voice, "we have volunteers working—"

"No matter. This is Dr. Cassidy MacConnell of UCLA, here briefly on urgent business. Please put Dr. Yamamoto on the line."

Ten seconds later, "Hello?" The voice nervous, mildly accented. "Yoshi Yamamoto here."

"Dr. Yamamoto, Dr. Cassidy MacConnell, UCLA. Sorry to disturb you."

Star decided she didn't sound sorry, but admitted she got the job done.

". . . was my sister." Voice soft, with a hint of feminine pleading. "It's quite urgent we learn what Artemas was working on before his death. If you could meet with us, even briefly."

"Such a tragedy," said Dr. Yamamoto. "Artemas, then Melissa. Artemas was no longer on staff, you realize. He was a research associate—most of his work was contract archaeology. He did retain an office here. Before his death? A Big Island survey. Artemas was quite excited about it."

Caddy interrupted. "May we come by, speak with you, see Artemas's office?"

"Dr. MacConnell, my plane departs in three hours for Pago Pago. I'm off to four months of fieldwork. I cannot possibly see you. But come by. I'll have my assistant show you the office. And you call Dr. Harmon Fitz, U of H. He and I were both with Artemas the night he died. Dr. Fitz knew Artemas's work as well as I, perhaps better. I'm afraid that's the best I can do."

"Yes, thank you for your time."

Dan covered Ernest Hemingway's cage with a threat he would never see light again if he didn't watch his mouth, and left for the university.

Star and Caddy drove to Bishop Museum, with the drawings and high hopes.

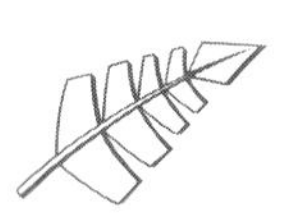

I apologize for the condition of Dr. Finch's office," said Dr. Yamamoto's assistant. "Obviously, the museum custodial staff haven't gotten around to . . ."

Caddy and Star exchanged worried looks over the upturned desk, the ragged stacks of books and papers piled against walls.

"Oh," said the assistant, "you didn't know—vandals. It happened shortly after Dr. Finch's death. Kids, probably. Got away before the guards could catch them. They broke into a drink machine and this office. As far as we can tell, they stole his computer, made this mess, and left."

Star and Caddy sifted through the office rubble, found nothing.

Ten minutes later, Star was punching thumbnail crescents in an empty plastic foam coffee cup in the museum café while Caddy phoned the University of Hawai'i.

She walked behind him, snapped her fingers by his ear. "Got him," she said. "Dr. Harmon Fitz, the man Dr. Yamamoto wanted us to see. He's meeting a vacationing niece in Waikiki this afternoon, said he'd stop by Papa's at four-thirty. Finally, we're getting somewhere."

* * *

Star dropped Caddy at the hotel, motored three times around the block to be sure he wasn't followed, and drove to Papa's house.

Two little girls, grandkids in dirty jumpers, were making Mr. Lucky do tricks on the lawn for French fries. One of Papa's middle boys, Micah, watched over them from the porch, thick arms crossed.

Star and Micah slapped palms, then Star crouched by the girls. "Watch this," he said. He steadied Mr. Lucky's chin with his left hand and balanced a French fry on his snout with his right. "Hold still, boy, don't move." He lowered his hand.

One of the girls giggled. "Oooh, his eyes are crossed. Poor doggie, maybe they'll stick that way. Let him have it. Let him have it."

"Now!" said Star. Mr. Lucky flipped the fry a foot in the air and caught it with a sideways snap. Tiny hands applauded.

Micah pointed to the house on the right, "in-laws," and to the one on the left, "sister's family. I live across the street. The only thing you gotta worry about with your dog here is him getting fat."

He passed his drive at ten miles an hour to check out his house.

Once inside, safe, he collapsed on the couch and fell into a deep and, for once, dreamless sleep. After a cold shower and two cups of instant coffee, he was back in the Turtle, following what was becoming a familiar rear-window-watching routine back to Waikiki. He parked, not in Scooter's apartment lot, but in a hotel garage for peace of mind. Only at the beach did he relax. He hung out with Koki at the surfboard stand, rode some easy waves, took his usual swim, and was at Papa's by four.

"Let me get this straight," said Doris. "You and the sister went kite flying this morning?" She rolled her eyes. "Right. What kind of trouble are you in now?"

"I paid off Mako."

"Congratulations." She patted him on the head. "I won't ask how, but I gather from that whorish blue bag, you came into money. Go on."

"Caddy and I are sure Melissa was murdered—by the same people who kidnapped Mr. Lucky. Melissa left clues. Beyond that?" He shrugged.

Doris hovered, picked at her nail polish, and sighed.

Star took a stab at her problem. "Doris, how's it going with your friend, G.I. Joe's dad?"

"D. L's okay, he's fine."

"Sure."

She slid into the booth opposite him. "I tell you, he's a sweet guy. Great smile, super sense of humor. Likes classical music. Who'd have guessed? Tells me all about opera and fugues and things. And he lets me talk. Enjoys listening to me—there's something new for a man, huh? Even the little, day-to-day things, 'How were tips today?' 'What's your friend Star up to lately?' But"—she fondled a gold-plated porpoise earring, tugged at it—"he—no jokes, okay?—he doesn't seem really interested in *me,* like physically. The man's never held my hand, asked for a kiss. Not that I mind that for a change, but it makes me wonder if I'm losing my, you know, stuff."

"Jeez, Doris. You're the hottest thing around. If we weren't such good friends, I'd . . ."

"You're not putting me on?" Eyes wide. "Not about us, I mean—about my still being appealing to men?"

"Absolutely. Maybe D. L. has a war injury, like something got shot off. Or he's cold inside, all business, like Melissa's sister, Caddy. Or maybe he likes men."

"D. L. does ask about you a lot."

"See? That's it. Listen to this. Last week, after he saved my ass, D. L. bought me an ice-cream cone, just like you would a girl on a date."

"No, no. He does talk about you, but I think it's because he's envious of your being such a free spirit. D. L.'s pretty tight, you know."

Star nodded, swirled coffee around in his cup, then looked her straight in the eyes. "Hear this, Doris: Unless you've really fallen for this guy, forget him. There's plenty of men out there who would give their left nut for a tumble with you." He leaned over the table, squeezed her hand. "Mr. Right's gonna walk through that door and, bingo, you'll know it. Trust me."

She squeezed back, brushed a loose curl from her forehead. "You're the best. You ever get tired of being buddies, just wink. I'm all yours."

He winked.

"Get out of here!" She laughed, slid from the booth, three inches more side-to-side in her wiggle.

Caddy arrived, cocked an eye at Star's Biggah-Burger with fries, and ordered hot tea and whole wheat toast, dry.

"I talked to Dan," she said. "So excited, he could hardly speak. The ornithologist at the U of H says it could be a Hawaiian *'o'o* feather. They want to express it to a woman at the Smithsonian, a world authority, for a thorough analysis. I gave them the okay."

Star nodded to a quick-moving man in his mid-sixties roving the restaurant. "I'll bet that's Dr. Fitz. Looks like a young Santa before he gave up the diet, or a grown-up elf." The man had a friendly face edged with a going-to-gray beard and reddish blond hair hanging to his shoulders.

Caddy twisted to see. "Or a Hawaiian Willie Nelson." She waved, whispered over her shoulder to Star, "That's him for sure. Said he'd be wearing a red shirt. It's red all right. I wonder if he lectures dressed like that."

A scarlet aloha shirt with lavender orchids hung nearly to the bearded man's knees over baggy, wrinkled khaki shorts. He padded back to them in loose white cotton ankle socks and worn leather sandals.

"Dr. Harmon Fitz, I presume?" asked Caddy, cool, academic. "This is Star Hollie. I'm Dr. MacConnell."

The archaeologist's baby-pink face crinkled into a white-toothed smile. "Let's cut the Ph.D. crap," he said. "I'm Digger to my friends: And they call you?" He stuck out his hand.

Star decided he liked Digger Fitz.

"Uh, Caddy." She shook his hand.

"Caddy. Much better." He turned to Star, pumped his hand. "Nice blue bag, kiddo. Had one just like it back at Berkeley, teaching, in the sixties. So, tell me, Caddy, Star, what can I do for you?"

"Dr. Fitz, er, Digger," Caddy began, lowering her voice, "we have reason to believe my sister Melissa was murdered." She began to explain, waited until Doris set her tea and toast on the table and left, ". . . and our only real clues are the feather and the drawings in this envelope. Anything you can tell us about Artemas's work, particularly prior to his death, or what Melissa may have been helping him with, may shed light on what we have here, what these people are after, and why."

"Murder. I can't image Artemas or Melissa being mixed up in anything nefarious." He ran a hand through his long hair. "Let me think back. Yoshi, Artemas, and I had a few drinks the night he died. At Stan's Mr. Meat. I remember I stuffed myself, fell off the vegetarian wagon." Digger patted a small paunch. "Felt like I had a brick in my stomach for three days. Artemas? He stayed on, drank too much, poor fella. Celebrating a discovery he'd made, wouldn't tell us much. Artemas could be secretive." He reached for the envelope. "Let's see what we've got here."

The three drawings spilled onto the table. Digger clapped his hands. "Aha! Artemas, you old dog. You found her, all right."

"Who?" Star and Caddy asked.

Star added, "You said 'she.' Was she a dino—"

Caddy cut him off. "Let the man speak for himself. What is it?"

"I think I should begin at the beginning, hmmm? Give you the whole picture. You up for a short lecture?"

"Of course," said Caddy.

"Couldn't you just tell us if its a dino—ouch!"

Caddy had edged a hot stainless-steel teapot against his arm. "We're all ears, Dr. Fitz."

"Think of this tabletop as the Pacific Ocean," he began. The surface was blue Formica, so that wasn't difficult. "North is up from your side. To your right are the Americas, to the left, Asia." He set the napkin dispenser, Asia, on its side. "The Aborigines were in Australia as early as fifty thousand years ago." A flattened paper tent advertising the Papa's Mahiwich became Australia. "Over the millennia, people migrated eastward out of southern Asia. The Melanesians, dark-skinned, woolly-headed people, settled the big western Pacific islands maybe 10,000 B.C." He spread pieces of napkin, paper islands, north and east of Australia. "Micronesians, smaller, lighter-skinned people, moved from the islands near eastern Asia into the small, low northern islands." He ripped a packet, sprinkled sugar to indicate Micronesia. "Now, um . . ." He glanced up, watched Doris threading the aisle the other way.

You've still got it, Doris, thought Star. Not to worry.

"Uh." Dr. Fitz's fingers ran over the tabletop, the Pacific Ocean, to settle east of Asia, over the torn paper of Melanesia. "Now, a group of people moved out of southeast Asia, into Melanesia and—somewhere around three thousand years ago—beyond. They settled coastal areas, became seafarers, shared cultural traits such as the use of an underground oven, tattooing, and distinctive pottery. They spread eastward, all the way to Fiji, Tonga, and Samoa." He tore an island from an empty sugar packet, set it on the ocean. "We refer to them as—"

"Lapita," said Star.

Take and double take from Caddy.

"You're ahead of me, I see," said Digger Fitz with a cocked eyebrow.

Star remembered Melissa's lecture. She had told him about the Lapita; he had told her about the pottery he'd found in Fiji. He thought again of the dark-skinned Fijian girl, their night on the dunes, their difficulty with the sand.

Star blinked away the memory, turned to Caddy. "The culture of the Lapita, in Fiji, Samoa, and Tonga, gradually changed. They became Polynesians."

"Exactly," said Digger Fitz. "The great voyagers of the first millennium A.D., settling islands throughout this vast area"—his hands moved left and right over the Formica sea—"between New Zealand"—he set the salt shaker to their left—"Easter Island"—the pepper to their right—"and Hawai'i, right here." He pointed to the center of the Pacific, dropped a sugar packet for Hawai'i. "Voilà. The Polynesian triangle.

"The Polynesians share a remarkably similar language, folkways, religion. For example, the principal Hawaiian gods are Ku, Kane, Kanaloa, and Lono. Other Polynesians call them Tu, Tane, Tangaroa, and Rongo, but they're essentially the same, see? Hawai'i also has a volcano goddess."

"Pele," said Star.

"Indeed. While other Hawaiian gods languished, Pele still thrives. Worshiped by some, respected by all. Don't mess with Madame Pele." He jabbed a finger at a startled Caddy, then Star. He leaned close, his voice a low roar. Digger Fitz was quite the storyteller. "Red-eyed, light-haired Pele is capricious, violent. She appears among us even today, sometimes as an old woman with a white dog . . ."

Star remembered Walana, and swallowed.

". . . or a beautiful young woman seducing men who catch her fancy." He laughed, jabbing his finger at Star again, only to be distracted by Doris for the second time.

"Coffee? More tea? Food?" Doris asked, by Star's shoulder. She refilled Star's cup.

"This a fresh pot, Doris?" asked Star.

"You think I'd bring you old coffee, honey?"

"Hmm," said Digger Fitz, "how about some of that coffee for me, too?" When she left, he added, "Haven't been to Papa's in years. I can see I've been missing out. Now, where was I?"

"Warning Star about being seduced by a beautiful woman," said Caddy.

"Yes." Digger's pink face reddened a shade closer to the ketchup on Star's fries. "So, the flaming Pele, according to myth, arrived from Kahiki, the Hawaiian homeland to the south, and looked for a home on the westernmost of the Hawaiian islands. She had a magical digging stick, Pa-oa. Where she struck it, to dig a foundation for her fiery house, a volcano erupted. But the sea goddess pursued Pele, quenched her fires with floods. Fire versus water, you see. Primal. Pele moved from Kaua'i to O'ahu, same story. She moved further east and south, gaining strength, to Maui and the peak of Haleakala. . . ."

"Dormant today," added Caddy.

"Yes. Pele was happy there. Then another battle, she was chased out, moved to the southernmost island of Hawai'i, where she lives today in the fire pit of Halema'uma'u in Kilauea volcano. The Pele myth echoes geologic fact—you see Caddy?—all the islands are volcanic, the oldest to the northwest, the most recent, volcanically alive, where she lives today."

"Fascinating," said Caddy. "But what about the drawings?"

"Hold on, there's more. Pele wasn't alone on the Big Island. Do you know her rival, Poliahu, the snow goddess who lives on the high peak of Mauna Kea?"

"The drawings?" asked Star.

"The drawings," said Digger Fitz. "Sure." He cleared the tabletop of Pacific islands, arranged Melissa's drawings in a fan, flanked them with open palms. "I would have preferred to explain more thoroughly about Pele's family. . . ."

"Get on with it," said Caddy.

"Very well." Digger's finger tapped the center illustration. "What you see before you, kiddos, is—you're ready for this?"

"Is it what I think?" asked Star.

"C'mon, c'mon," from Caddy.

"The Flying Vagina of Kapo," said Digger Fitz, with a very straight face.

35

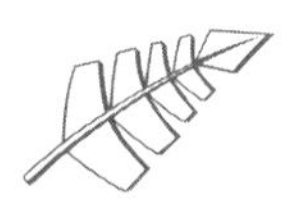

Digger Fitz linked thumbs, fluttered his fingers. His hands flew over the table. "The Flying Vagina of Kapo," he repeated.

"Is Kapo a *Pteranodon*?" asked Star.

"A *what?*" asked Digger.

"You know, a flying dinosaur," said Star.

"A *Pteranodon* is not a dinosaur," said Caddy.

"What?" repeated Digger Fitz. "What?"

"He thinks Artemas and Melissa discovered a dinosaur on the Big Island," Caddy explained, inadequately.

Digger scowled. "A dinosaur? Living? In Hawai'i?"

"My words exactly," said Caddy. "Now please explain this Kapo. Is it a bird? We found that feather too, you know."

"No, not a bird, definitely not a dinosaur. I was explaining, before you interrupted, about the Pele clan. Prominent is dear sister Hi'iaka, ever suffering at the hands of capricious Pele. We have Laka, patroness of hula. And—here you go—sister Kapo, a sorcery goddess who can change shape at will, also associated with hula. Kapo and Laka are Hawaiian Aphrodites, both manifestations of reproductive energy. Then there's the dark side, the counter to fertility and growth. Death. The goddess Nuikapo.

"Most germane to our story are Kapo's magical powers. She possessed a flying vagina—more precisely, vulva—her *kohe-lele*, that she could detach and send on magical errands, distracting, befuddling men."

"I should think so," said Caddy.

"Wow," Star said, trying to imagine a twelve-foot vagina sailing through the air. "I don't know if I'd run for it or from it."

Caddy glared.

Digger snorted.

Encouraged, Star cupped his hands, palm to palm. Hinged at the wrist, they clacked open and closed like a mouth. "Snap, snap," he said, biting the air by Caddy's nose.

She huffed, slapped them away.

"Ah-hmmm," Digger cleared his throat. "This is serious business, kiddos. Okay? Let me tell you about Kamapuaʻa from Oʻahu, the hog god, but also god of the forest, of rain, who took a fancy to Pele. Kamapuaʻa sometimes appeared as a brutal monster, sometimes as a handsome young man. An archetypal duality, eh? Kamapuaʻa visited Pele's fire-pit home, where he watched the beautiful volcano goddess dancing in a plume of fire, her sisters twirling in vapor and sparks, surrounded by a sea of bubbling red lava. He was overwhelmed, or, as the Victorians, and no doubt the Hawaiians, would have said, his 'loins burned with desire.' "

"Sounds to me," said Star, "if he got Pele in the sack, his loins would burn with more than desire."

"Don't interrupt," said Caddy.

"So," Digger went on, "Pele's sisters saw the beautiful young man at the edge of Kilauea and urged Pele to allow him to visit and whatnot—they were a lusty bunch, unburdened by Judeo-Christian concepts of sexual sin and guilt, you see. But, Pele, fickle as some women are wont to be . . ." Digger Fitz smiled innocently at Caddy. "Pele not only rejected Kamapuaʻa, but insulted him. Chanting insults was a high art among the ancient Hawaiians. She called him a son of a hog, filthy, malodorous—stronger, more colorful words in Hawaiian, I'm sure. Kamapuaʻa insulted her right back, threatened her. They carried on a stormy courtship, but perhaps not that unusual when a spirited boy and girl are attracted to one another, eh?"

He sipped coffee. "Pele burned, Kamapuaʻa flooded. Fire against water—that old duality—and a metaphor for the continuous battle on Hawai'i between destructive new lava flows and the weathering of old ones. The countryside was devastated. Kamapua'a got the upper hand, was about to vanquish Pele when sister Kapo distracted him with, can you guess what? Waved it under his nose, led him all the way back to O'ahu with it, then ditched him."

Stars hands snapped the air, flitted across the table.

"Melissa's drawings," asked Caddy, "represent Kapo's vagina? But that's a legend. These are so exact."

"Twelve feet long," added Star.

"Artemas," replied Digger Fitz, "claimed he had discovered the thing itself, Kapo's *kohe,* remarkably lifelike. Sculpted? A natural formation? Artemas didn't say. Or, if you are a devotee of Pele, it's lying there fossilized, dormant, awaiting another magical journey, an incarnation of the most essential themes—sex, reproduction, death. Artemas also said he found not only the *kohe,* but very old religious and other cultural features as well, possibly linked to traceable Hawaiian genealogies. Do you see the implications? It would mean the legend has a basis in fact."

"So, is that a big deal?" asked Star.

"Many archaeologists," said Digger, "tend to view myths as fairy tales: worthy of recording, useful insights into a culture's worldview, but objectively suspect. Artemas was inspired by Heinrich Schliemann's analysis of Homer's *Odyssey,* Schliemann's discovery that Troy was a real city, not a figment of some ancient's imagination. Artemas spoke enviously of Hiram Bingham looking for the 'Lost City' of the Incas and finding Machu Picchu, and Kathleen Kenyon's excavations in the Jordan River valley that proved biblical Jericho existed in fact, that its walls had indeed 'tumbled down,' even if not blown over by Joshua's trumpet."

Star tooted through a paper straw. Caddy slapped it from his fingers.

"Artemas," continued Digger, "hoped to make similar associations in Hawai'i. But fanciful speculation invites criticism. Any archaeologist who starts talking about UFOs landing at Nazca, Peru, or who goes off searching for Noah's Ark or the Holy Grail better watch his academic butt. Artemas, however, was convinced he had a defensible correlation of the Kapo *kohe* myth with a specific site, perhaps with real events. That's why he was so excited the night we met at the restaurant."

"Where *is* this thing, then?" asked Caddy.

"And what's Kapo doing without it?" added Star.

Digger ignored him. "On the Big Island," he said. "District of Ka'u. Artemas told Yoshi and me that much. But he was secretive, a bit paranoid, some might say. He kept nearly everything in his head or in his computer. He destroyed his notes frequently."

"Computers," Star said. "Someone stole their computers."

"I doubt if it did them any good," said Digger. "Artemas's files were well encrypted, you may be sure."

"Who else knew about his work?" asked Caddy. "And why would anyone go to the trouble to rob his office, their home, to murder Melissa, to kidnap Star's dog, threaten Star? How valuable is this . . . this thing?"

"Monetary value? None. No treasure to be found in Hawai'i, kiddo. No gold, no rubies."

"What about a rival archaeologist?" asked Star.

"Artemas's discovery would have garnered accolades, particularly if there were associated structures, datable, tying the legend to particular genealogies, events. After so many years of dead ends, that would have meant a lot to him. Jealousies? Perhaps. But theft, violence? Over an academic find? I can't imagine."

"Who else knew about his work?" Star asked.

"He'd told only Yoshi and me that night. Melissa knew, of course. And Marcel Landau."

"Landau!" Caddy and Star said the word together.

" 'Landau' is written on the bag with the feather," Caddy explained. "The feather which we believe belongs to the extinct, or allegedly extinct, *'o'o*."

"A living *'o'o,*" said Digger. "Wouldn't that be something! Well, if Artemas thought your feather was significant, he would have asked Landau, because Landau is a biologist. Sometimes the two of them pooled resources if they were conducting parallel surveys, and I recall him saying they both had been working on the Big Island for the same client, and that both had filed surveys with the state. However, he also said that having turned in his report, Landau was about to leave the country for the Philippines on a new project—Landau would have been gone before your sister died."

"Damn."

"Artemas also had an assistant—Kapono. Hmmm. Kapono headed a radical Pele cult, the Sons of Pele. They were instrumental in blocking one Big Island geothermal project, delaying another—a violation of Pele, they maintained, piercing her sacred body. Artemas liked Kapono because the boy was as driven as he was to find evidence of Pele. Kapono was sharp, an industrious worker, but theirs was an uneasy alliance. Kapono would have opposed making such a discovery public, opening what he would have seen as a sacred shrine to public, particularly non-Hawaiian, scrutiny."

"So where can we find this Kapono?" Caddy leaned over the table, excited.

"Sorry. Kapono's dead, too. Fell into Halema'uma'u fire pit in Kilauea volcano, Pele's home. Ironic, huh? The media had a field day with it—'Son of Pele falls into mother's volcano'—they love that sort of thing. I went up there once with both of them, Artemas and Kapono. The boy had no fear, dancing around the rim. Artemas told me Kapono spent all his free time there, making offerings, incantations. Evidently he miscalculated, lost his balance. Horrible death. He died before Artemas, and Artemas made it clear to Yoshi and me that he had kept Kapono in the dark about his discovery."

"Then who's left?" asked Caddy, voice rising with a desperate edge.

"Beats me," said Digger. "Artemas said his find came out of his and Landau's surveys of a large tract of Big Island land fenced off as a nature preserve, owned for a century by the nonprofit Ka Pono Foundation—beyond reproach. Perhaps rumors arose about the Kapo site, or the bird, and the foundation had hopes of finding them. Or maybe they planned to run a new fence line, maybe an access road, either of which would have required surveys for the necessary permits. Or possibly they simply wanted to find out what cultural and biological features the land held—although, in that case, I don't know why the surveys would have been filed with the state."

Digger scratched his beard. "Safe to say, if Landau had found a living *'o'o,* we would all know about it by now. But maybe Artemas saw the bird and recovered the feather after Landau finished and hadn't had a chance to report it, or maybe the feather's not from an *'o'o* at all, or . . ." He shrugged his shoulders. "Hell, I don't know. It's all speculation, isn't it?"

"What's the chance of pinpointing this Kapo site?" Star asked.

"Let me see those drawings again." He studied them. "Here, this notation, 'Addendum, Plate 7, P.U. E21, N24.' This is a supplement to Artemas's report. 'P.U.'? He called the tract the Pali-uli. Hawaiian name, in the district of Ka'u I'm sure, but no, I can't pinpoint it offhand. The 'E21, N24'? A grid reference, east and north, standard procedure. Arbitrary, but certain, once you know where he set his datum point to establish each axis.

"If I were you"—he looked at Caddy, then Star—"I'd check with the foundation to see why his and Landau's surveys were commissioned, then check with the state, look up the file copies, check Artemas's grid references. Bingo, your questions answered."

"Good advice," said Caddy. "We'll do it."

"Keep me informed," he added. "Artemas was not only a colleague, but a friend. And this site would be of significant interest. And the bird, if it exists? Incredible."

Digger sat tall, swiveled his head to scan the restaurant. "Now, I'd like some more of that good coffee. Where is Doris? You did say her name was Doris, didn't you, kiddo?"

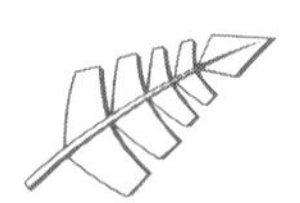

Two security guards unlocked the chained gate, slipped through, relocked it from the inside, and strolled across the warehouse yard. One chewed gum. The other scratched his rear end. The scratcher stopped, jigged on one leg, hiked his trousers to root at the source of that infernal itching, then double-stepped to catch up with his partner.

It wasn't much in the way of duty. The warehouse sat empty as a backcountry church on Monday morning. No hissing trucks, no beeping tow motors playing chicken on the ramps, no anxious clerks tapping clipboards, no shouting supervisors.

It wouldn't be long, though, before the off-island project came on-line. Once the forest had been cleared, the land recontoured for the golf course, and construction begun on the hotel and condos, this warehouse would hop, crammed with everything from Italian marble to French bidets and gilded whale sculpture, all awaiting transshipment from O'ahu to the Big Island of Hawai'i.

One of the guards punched buttons on the keypad by the heavy loading-dock door. He cocked his head at a muffled sound on the other side, cracked the door to hear better, then opened it wide and jumped back at the rumbling that filled the empty building, reverberated from its bare walls like thunder from hell.

"Holy shit," said the second man, "what is that?"

"Don't know, but it's damned loud," said the scratcher. "Scared the bejeezus out of me." He edged inside. "Sound is all jumbled, bouncin' around, but it's comin' from upstairs. We got company, all right."

They climbed the stairs two at a time, unconcerned with the clanging of shoe leather on bare metal, more likely unaware of it, given the intensity of the ominous, bone-rattling noise. The first man opened the door at the head of the stairwell. With comprehension, the fear on his face turned to anger. "Gawd, Bobby Lee," he said over his shoulder, loud enough to be heard over the noise, "it's gotta be Sarge playin' his elevator music on *our* new stereo."

"Like to bust my eardrums," said Bobby Lee. "Owee, what caterwaulin'."

"I heard that," said D. L. McWhorter, seated, arms clutching his knees, on the worn oak desk no more than twenty feet away,

"Oops," said Bobby Lee.

"Oh, oh," said Ray Don.

"Caterwaulin'?"

"I'm sorry, Sarge," said Ray Don, "It's real purty. You can use our stereo anytime you—"

"Elevator music? You blockhead. That's Verdi's *Requiem*. Give me ten quick ones."

Bobby Lee stepped forward. "Sarge, with them dog bites on that arm a'his, Ray Don can't do no push-ups. It ain't fair. Let me do 'em for him."

"Brotherly love—ain't it sweet? Do 'em one-handed then, Ray Don. I'll match you, two of mine for one of yours. That sound fair?"

"Shit fire, Sarge," whined Ray Don, nose to the sickly green asphalt floor tile, doing his best to balance on one arm, let alone raise his bulk. "This ain't gonna work." He began doing them with both hands, grunting.

D. L. counted. ". . . five, six . . ." He turned to a worried Bobby Lee. "Those stitches in his arm won't bust loose from a few pushups. ". . . nine, ten." To Ray Don, "Son, I hope you don't expect me to match those sissy two-handers." To both: "All right, take a seat."

"Cain't hardly hear," said Bobby Lee.

"Criminy. Go turn it down then, but not off. There's a message in that music. Food for the soul." He closed his eyes, lifted his chin, head back. "Don't it just make your hair stand on end?"

"Yeah, sure," said Ray Don, seated in one of the sweep-arm school chairs, ruffling the stiff loose ends of his sutures.

HydraCorp used the big room for instruction, briefing O'ahu security staff, drivers, and supply clerks. D. L. had set the brothers up, not only with legitimate jobs, but with a room in the back for an apartment. He stopped by without warning to be sure they were making their beds, keeping the latrine clean, behaving themselves on company property. And to give them special assignments.

Bobby Lee settled into the chair beside his brother. D. L. stood at parade rest two feet from their faces. "Elevator music?" He slapped both their heads with a single swipe. "It is a nice stereo, though. Must have cost you a bundle."

"No, Sarge," said Bobby Lee, "Ray Don got it from the Fin—ouch!"

Ray Don kicked his ankle.

"There's a reason for the music, boys," said D. L. "It's a memorial. Sorry to be the bearer of bad news, but, your friend and mine, little Mongoose, has bit the dust."

"Dead?" asked Ray Don.

"Little Mongoose?" said Bobby Lee.

"Friggin' longhaired hippie beach bum calls himself Mr. Lucky, the one who owns the dog you let get away, the one who owns the house you were supposed to burgle—that one. He killed Mongoose. Threw him off the top of a mountain. I sent Mongoose to follow the guy after you nabbed the dog, to see where he had the Finch documents stashed."

Bobby Lee and Ray Don eyed one another. With the dog gone, Sarge wouldn't be getting those doc-u-ments he wanted so all-fired bad.

"This Mr. Lucky must have spotted the tail, lured Mongoose up the mountain, then threw him over a cliff to make it look like an accident—that's what the police are calling it, an accident. Found his body on the green of the seventh hole of that golf course, other side of the island, lying belly down over the cup, pole sticking out of his back. He must have dropped onto the pin and the flag skewered him like a shish kebab.

"At first they thought some golfer speared him. Figured he was a caddie, had pissed off one of the members, given him the wrong club, blabbed about his cheating, or maybe poked the guy's wife in the parking lot.

"Then the cops found his truck up by the cliff, at the lookout. There were high winds yesterday, the road blocked, no one supposed to be there. They decided he'd been blown off. He had his Hydra security ID on him, so they called me.

"Boys, let us pray." D. L. swatted the twins' heads down, bowed himself. "Mongoose was a good boy, Lord, bit of a loud dresser, had a bitchin' temper, lousy taste in music, and was an intemperate toker, but under it all, a good boy. We laughed at him a lot, didn't we, boys?" Heads still bowed, they nodded. "He took his work seriously. Died on a mission. No better way to go. Sent money home to his mama, too. So, Lord, you watch over little Mongoose up there. Don't let him fall off any clouds, hear?"

D. L. laughed. "Sorry, Lord, that just kind of slipped out. Amen."

He began to pace. "You can raise your heads now, boys," he said. "I got some good news, and I got more bad news. Which do you want first?"

"Good news," said Bobby Lee.

"Bad news," said Ray Don.

D. L. flipped a quarter. "Bad news it is."

The brothers got small in their seats, stared at the plywood writing arms of their worn student chairs. Neither the dirty rhymes, nor the ballooning breasts, nor the badly drawn and grossly exaggerated genitalia scratched in the varnish over the years by bored and remarkably inartistic students brought sniggers or smiles today, because Sarge had a burr up his ass and was about to toss it the twins' way.

"Look up at me, boys." McWhorter snapped his fingers. "I swear, if your dear old daddy hadn't of saved my life down there in Biloxi, and if I hadn't promised to watch over you two ten years later, when the old bird was dying in my arms, his life's blood ruining my new pair of khakis there on the filthy floor of that redneck bar, knifed as he was by that toothless little cracker hoor with the one leg because of what he done to her . . ." He sighed. "But I promised, and D. L. McWhorter is a man of his word. You boys, though, are screwups of the first order."

He walked back to the desk, began unwrapping a soft burgundy cloth.

Bobby Lee and Ray Don exchanged worried looks. They knew what it was. "You ain't gonna shoot us, are you, Sarge?" wailed Bobby Lee.

D. L. held his pistol in the air, sighted along the barrel. "Army issue. Colt forty-five automatic. Custom pearl handles with cobra inlay. Real ruby eyes. Whooee, this gun and me have seen some times." He squinted at the twins, "No, I'm not going to shoot you. Not yet, anyways. Go get *your* guns, boys, the ones identical to this, the ones I had customized for you, gave you as presents. Go on, get 'em."

The brothers shuffled back to their room. McWhorter waited, at least five minutes. "Time enough, boys," he shouted, "come out and face the music."

Bobby Lee had the twin of McWhorter's .45 in his hand. "Sarge," said Ray Don, "I got this problem, see?"

"Yeah. And the problem is, no gun," said D. L. "Mr. Lucky's probably got little Mongoose's now, and he could have had yours too, if he'd wanted it." He nodded at the surprise on their faces. "That's right, boys, I know all about it. The boys in blue have it. Fortunately, they don't have your fingerprints along with it."

McWhorter leaned onto the arms of the desks, looked each of them in the eyes. "How does old D. L. know this? I called a buddy on the force to inquire about a friend of a friend who I said was having bad dreams over a break-in at his house. Poor kid. Did they have any information on the felons? No—and that's damn lucky, too, because maybe I'd have to shoot your asses if they did. Cops had the felon's *gun* though. Description fit this one to a tee." He set the gun gently on the cloth, then slammed his fist on the desk. "Why the hell did you take your gun with you for a pissant searchin' party? And then *leave* it there?

"Lesson time, boys. Sit back down. Now, what did I tell you when I gave those guns to you?"

"Not to shoot no pigeons or tourists with 'em, Sarge," said Bobby Lee.

"And?"

"Told us to fill out those forms," said Ray Don.

D. L. rolled his eyes. The forms. The NRA applications. He had thought if the boys signed up, joined comrades in arms, it would help socialize them. The first problem was Ray Don's worrying the government would know where to find them if they wrote down their names and addresses. "NRA's not likely to share their lists with the Feds, boys," D. L. had said. "Besides, the government's already got your names, Social Security numbers, and the rest of it from HydraCorp's personnel files." That had really worried them. Then there had been the applications themselves, the boys' difficulty with writing. Of course they didn't have checking accounts either, so D. L. had had to write a personal check for their memberships. It had been a bad idea, one of his worst.

"Forget the friggin' forms. What else?"

"Never to lose your gun," said Ray Don in a very small voice for such a large man.

"Congratulations, Ray Don. Go to the head of the class. Right about here." He pointed at the floor. "And give me fifty."

Ray Don grew red in the face, puffing, barely able to lift his body from the floor by push-up twenty-seven. D. L. kicked him in the ribs a few times, managed to get five more out of him, but that was it. "All right, you pussy," he said, "let that be a lesson to you. And don't be asking me for another gun, because you're not gonna get one. Not for a long time."

Ray Don sat back in the chair, rubbing his side, breathing still labored.

"And Bobby Lee," said D. L., "you hold on to that gun of yours like it was your mama's wedding band. Hear?"

"Yes, Sarge. Uh, Sarge?"

"Bobby Lee?"

"You said *good news,* too."

"So I did." He reached behind the desk, pulled a long canvas bag from the floor, and set it on the desktop. "How would you boys like to settle a score? Pay back our friend Mr. Lucky for doing in little Mongoose? Time to close that chapter before his snooping puts the kibosh on Hydra's Paradise Valley."

The twins' faces brightened.

"What we have here"—D. L. lifted a cruel-looking weapon—"is a Seabear AK-72 pneumatic speargun." McWhorter held it at chest height, rotated it. "Russian. Titanium. Laser sight. Admirable range and accuracy. Some piece of work."

James Bond would have lusted for it, but no more than the twins. Afraid to get up without permission, yet oh so anxious to see Sarge's marvelous toy, the brothers rocked their chairs forward, slid them closer and closer with their heels. *Chunk-squeak. Chunk-squeak. Chunk-squeak.*

"Criminy, boys, get your butts up here. I want you to study this thing."

Ray Don got tangled in the arm of his chair, knocked it over, but was at McWhorter's side no more than a second behind Bobby Lee. They took turns stroking the shiny gray metal, touching the needle-sharp barb at the spear tip.

"Now," said McWhorter, "our Mr. Lucky takes a long swim off Waikiki Beach every afternoon. Far enough offshore that a small boat could drop a diver within a couple hundred feet of him and no one would notice. You with me, boys?"

"Ray Don did scuba on the oil rigs offa Corpus," said Bobby Lee, happy as a puppy.

"Know all about it," said D. L. "You still remember your stuff, son?"

"Tell him about the mermaid, Ray Don," clucked Bobby Lee.

"Mermaid?" asked D. L. "That's a new one. Do tell."

"I saw her, I did," said Ray Don. "Don't care what they said."

"Who's they?" asked D. L. "What did they say?"

"Said it was something called the rupture of the deep, that what I saw was a big grouper. Shit fire, a fish! That mermaid flipped her tail at me, smiled, pleaded with me to stay down with her. Oh, I wanted to. She made me feel so dreamy. Shouldn't have gone back up. No sir. But I did, and when I told them about her, how I wanted to go back down, they made me talk to the wacko doctor, like something was wrong with *me*. Hell, I was the one who seen her. What did they know? Wouldn't let me dive after that."

"No," said Bobby Lee, "not perzactly. Warn't the mermaid kept you from divin', it was accounta the crew chief you pitched off the drillin' platform for laughin'."

"Ray Don," said D. L. "Listen up. Do you remember your training? If I get you the gear, drop you offshore, show you Mr. Lucky swimming out there, give you this fancy speargun, can you do the job?"

Ray Don fingered his stitches, thought of his lost .45 with the pearl-handle grips and the inlaid cobra with the sparkling red eyes. He remembered the pain of the first dog bite, and cracking his shins on that damned lawn mower when he ran from the hippie's house. He thought of the second dog bite when the dog got away, the fun times with little Mongoose, of getting back in the good graces of Sarge, and the prospect of spearing a man to death. Especially the prospect of spearing a man to death.

"Shit fire," he said. "I'm your man. How soon can we do it?"

McWhorter held the speargun to his shoulder, aimed it at a smiling lifeguard in a safety poster on the far wall. "You boys got a line open on your dance cards for tomorrow afternoon?"

37

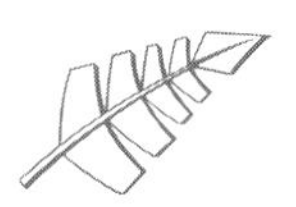

More tea, Caddy?" Dan tilted the Mother Goose teapot.

"Thanks." She held out her Franklin Mint *Beloved Birds of America* loggerhead shrike mug.

Dan set down the teapot and began to pace the office.

Star swirled the remaining half inch of dark Kona in his mockingbird mug, held it up. "How about more coffee over here, Dan?"

Dan waved air in the direction of the carafe on the sideboard. "Help yourself, boy." He walked once more around the desk, digesting their news, hands locked behind him. He stopped, rocked from one foot to the other. "You two had a productive afternoon yesterday, no question. Finding this archaeologist, Harmon Fitz, was serendipity. I've set my staff to work, put my best investigative reporter on the case." He thumped his barrel chest. "Me."

Star poured himself another cup, began to poke through the bars of Ernest Hemingway's big cage. "Hello, dumb bird."

"First thing this morning," Dan said, "I called the Ka Pono Foundation, since they'd contracted the surveys. I asked for their director, Willis Cottingham. Willis and I have met socially. I knew he'd recognize my name."

"Polly want a cracker?" Star wiggled his finger.

"Soon as I mentioned *Pacific Rainbow,* the receptionist put me on hold, returned to inform me Mr. Cottingham was ill, would I mind calling one of their directors? An attorney, as it turned out."

"Stupid bird. Cat got your tongue?"

Dan scowled at Star. "I called, mentioned as a door opener I was publisher of *Pacific Rainbow*, looking for information about a foundation matter. Could he help? 'No comment,' the man says. Excuse me? 'Sorry, no comment.' That was it.

"So"—Dan raised his shoulders, palms open—"I ask myself, what the hell's going on with this foundation? I decide to come at the matter obliquely. I have a business acquaintance with the Hawaiian Pa'a Bank and Fiduciary Trust, which, I recall, handles the foundation's finances. Old institution, like the foundation. Dusty, crusty, fusty."

"Can't you even say hello?" from Star. The bird cocked its head, silently sidestepped toward him.

"So," said Dan, "I get the man on the line, ask, What's going on with the foundation? Long pause. 'Sorry,' he says, 'Can't talk to the media. No comment.' What the hell? Neither of them gives me a chance to say word one about the surveys."

"SHIT!" from Star, finger in his mouth, dancing away from the big brass birdcage.

"SHIT!" from Ernest Hemingway, bobbing on his perch.

"Please, Star," said Dan, "don't encourage him. He has a foul enough mouth as it is."

"He bit me!"

Dan shook his head. "I've warned you, boy. Ernest Hemingway doesn't like to be teased. Why don't you sit, behave yourself?" He scratched his temple with a thick forefinger. "Now where was I? Ah, yes." The finger dropped to his bulbous Mediterranean nose, traced its length. "This sniffer of mine says there's a juicy story here."

Star stopped sucking his finger, rotated it six inches from his face, assessing the damage. Without looking up, he asked, "So, what about the surveys?"

"That's the question, all right. The surveys. Next I called the Hawai'i Department of Land and Natural Resources, half expecting another 'no comment,' but the state folks came through. Yes sir, surveys were filed. Would I like to see them? I hotfooted it downtown myself. Matter of public record, they said. Gave me copies." He motioned to the desk. "That set's for you two, but don't get your hopes up.

"One of their archaeologists paged through Artemas Finch's report for me, explained the archaeological features—rock carvings, minor foundations, trails, and so forth. Then I saw something that got this old nose a-sniffing."

"Was it Kapo's snatch?" asked Star.

Dan hissed, "Watch your mouth, boy," from the side of his mouth. "A lady is present." He turned his back to Star, smiled apologetically at Caddy. "My interest was piqued because of what was *missing*: three pages in the Finch report appendix, the pages with maps."

"Aha!" said Caddy.

"SNATCH!" yelled Ernest Hemingway.

Dan glowered at Star, put a finger to his lips, then pointed to the bird. He turned back to Caddy. "They couldn't explain it."

"The maps," said Caddy, "had Artemas's coordinates for his grid. With those, and the notations on Melissa's drawings, we could have pinpointed the Kapo feature."

"Yes," said Dan, "so we're still in the dark. But presumably, so are your adversaries, because if they couldn't crack Finch's computers and don't have these drawings . . ."

"Doc-u-ments," mumbled Star, recalling the phrasing of the dognappers.

"Damn," said Caddy. "So, do we know where Artemas or Landau did their work?"

"You bet," said Dan. "Your man Harmon Fitz mentioned the Pali-uli. It's an old Hawaiian name appearing in both reports. The state archaeologist said it's a large land tract, been under care of the Ka Pono Foundation for over a hundred years." He went to the desk, unrolled a U.S. Geological Survey map, pointed to a squarish area highlighted in fluorescent turquoise. "The Pali-uli."

"Looks big," said Star.

"Over six square miles. Remote."

"South of Volcanoes National Park," said Caddy, tracing a finger over the map. "On the slope of Mauna Loa volcano, nearly surrounded by state and federal land. It's a big upslope valley, thirty-two hundred to over four thousand feet in elevation, formed, no doubt, by faulting modified by erosion and volcanism. Steep cliffs on three sides. The open end drops in another cliff toward the coast.

"It's forested. Has water, too. See?" She pointed to pale blue squiggles. "Flowing here, intermittent there. Three waterfalls. These marks indicate faulting, and these, old volcanic features, so I wouldn't be surprised if there are steam vents and hot springs." She traced beige speckles tracking down the mountain. "A major lava flow came close in 1950."

"I read the biological survey carefully," said Dan. "There's no mention of the *'o'o*. In fact, the flora and fauna are identical to Volcanoes National Park." His voice lowered. "Guess what I was told, off the record?"

"That there's a possibility of dinosaurs in the Pali-uli?"

Caddy jabbed a finger at Star to end that line of inquiry. To Dan: "What?"

"That this Marcel Landau who conducted the biological survey may have been milking his clients. Did less work than he reported. He was qualified, but under suspicion of not doing the legwork himself, of borrowing data from preexisting studies of similar areas."

"Such as Volcanoes National Park," said Caddy. She pointed to the neighboring park.

"Yes. The park is well documented. It's possible he spent little time in the Pali-uli itself."

"May not have seen the *'o'o* bird, if it's there," said Star.

"You bet," said Dan. "From what I've read, the *'o'o* lived high in the treetops, wasn't easy to spot by even a conscientious observer. I can't wait until we hear back about that feather."

"Dan?" asked Caddy. "Why the surveys?"

"The big question. I asked the state archaeologist. He suggested I contact the zoning commission in Hilo to see if any applications were filed there."

"The purpose of which," said Caddy, "as I recall from my old days with the oil company, would be permits for alteration of the land or rezoning for development."

"Trouble," said Star, "if you're a rare bird or a twelve-foot vagina, exposed in the middle of a virgin valley."

"Indeed," said Dan. "Makes no sense, however, considering the history of the place and its ownership. But then there's this 'no comment' business. I have a man checking in Hilo. Since we have no hard evidence of the bird or the Kapo shrine, I said nothing to the state about our discoveries. Meanwhile, I have one more lead." He rubbed his hands together, reached for the telephone. "A surprise guest."

"Who is it?" asked Star.

"Dr. Finch called the state archaeologist the day before he died, requesting they hold up the reports. Artemas told him he had additional information, said he was going to inform his benefactor and then the public of his discovery."

"The doc-u-ments," said Star.

"We have fragments of that information," added Caddy. "The Finches' computers undoubtedly held much more." She paused. "You said 'benefactor.' The foundation?"

"Perhaps someone else," said Dan. "My archaeologist recalled HydraCorp here in Honolulu underwrote Artemas's survey. Artemas was grateful for their generosity, planned to dedicate his discovery to them. Couldn't wait to tell them. And my man remembered the name of Artemas's contact."

"Who is this mystery guest?" asked Caddy.

"A man named Bergen," said Dan. "Bernie Bergen." He dialed the phone. "Here, I'll put it on speaker so we can all hear."

Dan introduced himself to Bernie Bergen's secretary as publisher of *Pacific Rainbow*. After a long pause, a cheery voice filled the office.

"Bernie Bergen here, how may I help you?"

"This is Dan Capistrano, Mr. Bergen, of *Pacific Rainbow* magazine. One of our writers, Star Hollie, has uncovered some information on the Ka Pono Foundation that perplexes us. I wonder if you might answer a few questions."

"Love to, but I'm a businessman, not in the charity game. Ka Pono Foundation? Yes, heard of them. Feed and clothe little brown babies around the Pacific, right?"

"Do the names Artemas Finch and Marcel Landau mean anything to you?"

"Entertainers? Magicians, maybe. Play at the Hilton Hawaiian Village?"

"No. Scientists. I understand you underwrote a research project of Dr. Finch's."

There was a long pause. "Oh, Finch. Yes, I remember. We do our share of philanthropy. The islands are good to HydraCorp, HydraCorp is good to the islands. We gave Finch a grant, maybe the other fellow too. Yes. Can't remember the specifics."

"Dr. Finch was killed in an automobile accident."

"Coming back to me. Yes. Tragedy."

"We determined Finch and Landau surveyed a tract of land called the Pali-uli on the Big Island, owned by the Ka Pono Foundation. We were wondering, why the surveys?"

"Have you asked the foundation?"

"This is the odd thing. They refuse to speak with us. In our business, when someone goes mum, we wonder what's going on."

"Hmmm." Paper-shuffling sounds in the background, a chair squeaking, drumming sounds, like fingers tapping wood. "All right. Can I speak off the record?"

"If you feel that's necessary."

"I spoke with Willis Cottingham of the foundation a way back. They're planning a surprise for the islands. Mr. Cottingham asked me not to talk about it until they were ready to release the good news. A confidence I respect, as a businessman, hmmm?"

Another pause. "Here it is. The foundation is planning to open an interactive nature center on the edge of this land. Harmonious architecture, as I recall, with exhibits, guides, trails, endangered species petting zoo, all of that. They plan to bring up youngsters from around the islands, poor kids, especially, and Hawaiians who live in the city, have never known the beauty of the wilderness. Show 'em what it's all about."

"Sounds like bullshit to me," Star muttered, barely audible.

"BULLSHIT!" screeched Ernest Hemingway.

"No, no! It's true. I swear," said Bernie Bergen.

"I'm sorry," said Dan, glowering at Star and Ernest Hemingway, "that was someone else in the room. Another conversation."

"Oh. Yeah. Okay. So, we're running a road nearby for a wind farm. Clean, cheap energy for Hawai'i. The foundation wanted to run a branch from our road to their nature center. We thought, Why not help them out? So we underwrote Finch's and Landau's surveys so they could get the necessary permits, whatever. That's it. I would have been up front with you about it, but I promised Willis I wouldn't jump the gun on the foundation's press release. So, please, Mr. Cappuccino, you didn't hear it from me. Okay? Wait till they're ready. Four or five weeks, I'm sure they'll be glad to fill you in on the details."

"I appreciate your candor," said Dan.

"No problem." The line went dead.

"Sounds plausible," said Dan, "except for the adamant 'no comments' from the foundation and the bank."

"The guy sounds about as sincere as that TV preacher," said Star.

"My man's checking it out in Hilo," said Dan. "In a day or two, we'll know more about the feather and this foundation business. You kids take off. Call if you hear anything I should know."

Nearing Waikiki, Star said, "Caddy, if you don't mind, I'll drop you off. I need to clear my mind, spend some time alone with the fishes."

38

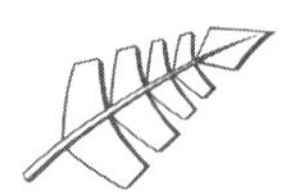

The boat's exhaust sounded, *thruppita, thruppita, thruppita,* the engine barely alive. They puttered again toward Diamond Head, idling parallel to Waikiki Beach for what seemed the thousandth time.

Waves slapped the sides of the rocking boat, echoed through the fiberglass hull with a dull and predictable thump. Above, gulls circled, screeching for handouts. Fifteen hundred feet of intervening surf muffled the beach noise, though occasionally a laugh or shout skipped across the water with surprising clarity. Between the boat's course and the shore, a hundred heads—surfers awaiting the perfect wave—bobbed like floating coconuts.

D. L. McWhorter wore his usual khakis and combat boots, but from the waist up was disguised in tourist mufti, a loud aloha shirt, floppy Panama hat, and sunglasses with red plastic frames.

He kicked at a wad of dried fish scales, let go of the wheel, stretched, and filled his lungs with the tangy salt air. "Ah!" he said. "A day at sea. Ain't it grand?"

He spoke over his shoulder: "Smells heavenly, don't it, boys?" Then added, "Except for the boat's dead-fish stink, the gasoline, your greasy fried chicken, and that hospital pine and lemon perfume you two wear."

The boat rocked in a big swell.

"Gawd, this is awwwful," moaned Bobby Lee. "Uurp." He ran for the side, leaned over, and emptied his stomach to pay the ocean back for his misery.

"Hotter'n hades," said Ray Don, seated on the cooler. "And we're nearly out of beer and chicken." He dumped the last three pieces of extra crispy onto his hairy thigh, swiped his palm around the inside of the paper tub, and licked salty crumbs from his hand. "How long we gotta stay out here, Sarge?"

"Until he shows. Criminy, boys, haven't you ever been hunting before? What happened to patience? Imagine you're crouched in the daisies back in Buncombe County, half snoozing, listening to the birdies, waiting for some big twenty-point buck to traipse over the ridge. Think of that *k'zing* of the arrow or *k'pow* of your rifle. Heart-shot. That old buck dropping in his tracks, the big talk back at the bar, you in venison for months, that rack of his over your mantel."

"Shit fire, no ridge I ever been on rocked and rolled like this son of a bitch," groaned Bobby Lee.

"Tripod!" yelled D. L. Ray Don crouched by the side of the boat. D. L. rested a spotting scope on his shoulder, peered through it. "Mr. Lucky won't let us down, boys," he said. "Any minute he's gonna show up at that surfboard stand like he does every day. He'll swim out to us, chest first, like that Buncombe County buck. You got your scuba equipment together, Ray Don? When I give you the suit-up order, I don't want to hear you're missing a flipper."

Ray Don sat back on the cooler and drained the dregs of the second to last beer. "All here, Sarge. You done good with the gear." He waved a handful of fried chicken forward to D. L., then back at Bobby Lee wallowing in the stern, dying a horrible death. "Two scrawny wings and a dinky leg is the end of it," he said. "Mostly gristle and skin. Who wants what?"

It was enough to send Bobby Lee to the side again.

D. L. turned the boat. "Here's how it's gonna play. I'll get you within a couple hundred feet of him, point him out real clear. Ray Don, you're up and over the side. My able-bodied seaman here and me will beat it back to the marina. Soon as you do your business, you swim for the shore, but wide, not straight in. You ditch your gear on the bottom, a good piece away, stroll onto the beach like you're some slow-witted Okie on honeymoon—that shouldn't be difficult—find a phone—be sure you take change with you—and call us with the good news. We'll pick you up by the police station on Kalakaua. How's that for a rendezvous?"

"Can't I wait to watch the fun from the beach, Sarge?"

"Yeah, I guess you deserve that. But you stay back in the crowd, don't go telling anyone it was your work, hear?"

"Golly, Sarge, you think I'm stupid?"

D. L. patted him on the head with a fatherly smile. "Dear me, son, how could you ask such a question?"

He lifted a big set of navy binoculars to his eyes and scanned the shore. Thirty seconds later, his body stiffened. "Here we go—Mr. Lucky off the starboard bow!"

Ray Don scrambled into his diving gear and sat on the deck, Russian Seabear AK-72 titanium speargun at his side.

D. L. handed him the binoculars, aimed Ray Don's head. "Get a good look," D. L. said. "I've watched him before. He'll come out five or six hundred more feet and tread water for a while before he sets off to do laps. While he's floating there, you surface near him. Be sure it's him. Keep your speargun under the water, out of sight. Then drop down, swim underneath, and, zippo!"

"I see him, Sarge." Ray Don watched the approaching swimmer for nearly a minute before he set the binoculars down.

"He's coming in a straight line," said D. L. "Get ready." He nosed the boat closer to their victim, pointed the bow to the beach to hide Ray Don's dive. Ray Don leaned over the stern, spit in his mask, slurried seawater in it, and awaited the order.

"Go, boy!"

Ray Don raised one hand to his mouthpiece and goggles, held the speargun to his chest with the other, and flipped over backward. *Kersplash*.

The excitement of the hunt brought Bobby Lee to life. He raised his chest from the deck, rested his chin on the gunwale, and stared at the water. A minute passed. Then he watched a trail of bubbles head for the approaching swimmer like a sleepy World War II torpedo.

D. L. throttled the engine, somersaulting Bobby Lee into the cooler. The boat arced to sea.

Star left his bag and clothes with Koki and ran across the burning sand, eager for the smack of cool salt water on hot skin. He splashed through two waves, dove into another, and swam an easy crawl past screaming children and bobbing potbellies toward the surfers, then beyond most of them.

He paddled, zoned out. To his right, across the pale, jade green shallows, rose the volcanic cone of Diamond Head. He thought of the diamonds discovered there by nineteenth-century British sailors—diamonds that turned out to be worthless calcite crystals. He back-floated, spoke to his toes: "I'm no better than those sailors. If I hadn't thought I'd get rich from the peeing contest, I wouldn't be in all this trouble.

"Although I'd be bored stiff now. Never would have met Melissa or the rest of them. Or Caddy, that pain in the ass."

His mind wandered again. Without warning, the old shark fear seized him. He flipped onto his belly, breaststroked in a circle to scan the horizon.

No fins.

He forced himself to tread water, scull in place, settle down.

Ray Don sank like an anchor. Must be that tub of fried chicken I ate, he decided as his butt and the tank bounced across the bottom. Then he remembered his buoyancy control vest. He let a little air into it, enough to allow him to hover at, what? Fifteen feet? Shit fire, he thought, it's shallow here. I thought it would be forty, fifty feet deep.

He floated near the bottom like a waterlogged stump, listened to the metallic hiss of his own breath. In, out. In, out. Been a long time, he thought, breathing a little too fast. Hope I remember this stuff. He looked up. There was Sarge's boat, bobbing above him on the silvery surface. *Swoosh*. A surge tipped him over. Damn. Way out here, still feel the swells. Then he remembered all the surfers and realized it had to be shallow for the waves to break so far from shore. Had to be no more than six feet deep where the waves rose.

He prodded the light sandy bottom with a swim fin, saw rounded coral heads, dark, long dead. Ray Don realized he was alone.

Where the hell am I? He wanted to surface, get his bearings, but knew Sarge would see him, maybe throw a beer bottle at him, or kick poor Bobby Lee instead, because he, Ray Don, was supposed to know what he was doing—swim straight as a shot for Mr. Lucky.

Aha! Compass. Almost forgot. Shit fire, why'd I drink all that beer myself? He answered his own question: 'Cause Sarge don't drink when he drives, 'cause Bobby Lee has been puking his guts out since we hit the water, and 'cause I was dry, that's why.

Think, Ray Don. Which way? North. That's the beach, other way's the ocean. Head for the beach, not the ocean.

He flippered for the shore, bubbles trailing behind. Overhead, he heard the boat's engine whine, saw the bullet-shaped silhouette whip away in a feathery white crescent.

How far? He tried to remember Mr. Lucky's speed. If they were swimming at one another, they'd meet. Simple. Ray Don, he told himself, don't miss your target or your ass is in a sling.

Water's kinda cloudy with all the current. Need to take a look topside, get my bearings. Sarge has got to be long gone.

So he kicked off the bottom, waggled his swim fins to send him straight up. Up, up—into the clutches of some *animal!* Its rubbery legs wrapped around his neck. It kicked, clawed at his skin, screamed, loud and high. Ray Don screamed back, a muffled "Yeaowwr!" He shook his head and the animal flew off, landed six feet away. Ray Don spun around to see it splashing on the surface.

Little Oriental kid.

Shit fire, what's that pissant slant-eye buzzard doing way out here? He shuddered, dropped below the surface again, watched the tiny form scramble away, a pale yellow cloud blooming in its wake.

Back to the bottom to settle his nerves. Don't screw up, Ray Don. Damn surge. Back and forth, back and forth. He counted his fingers and his toes, slowly, in his mind, to calm himself. Not being able to see his toes inside the fins helped, made him concentrate.

. . . twenty. Got to go up again.

He broke the surface. There. It's him, maybe seventy feet away. Coming right at me. Ray Don's skin prickled, his heart pounded. He floated at the surface, got the creepy feeling he was being watched. He spun around. Sarge was back there, wasn't he?

"Yeaowwr!" Ray Don screamed for the second time.

He backpedaled, dropped the speargun. This, this thing, coming for him, had a hairless soccer-ball head, brown, horny beak, huge yellow eyes, blinking, blinking. Ray Don knew it from his dreams, heart-thumping ones, the ones he didn't tell even Bobby Lee about. It was the Evil Mermaid, come to punish him.

He shut his eyes. Like in the nightmare, it would laugh its devilish laugh and drag him out to sea, rip him to shreds.

He sank to the bottom, eyes squeezed shut, awaiting that awful laughter.

The rasp of his breathing filled his brain. Not so much as a chuckle from the mermaid. Then he thought, Maybe it's not the Evil One, maybe this mermaid is just ugly, like some women. Hell, they can't all be pretty as the one I seen in Texas.

Eyes still closed, he huddled, hoping. He opened one eye, looked up.

Shit fire! It's a *turtle*. Get a grip, Ray Don.

He watched the turtle slap a winglike flipper and soar to sea.

He hunkered on the bottom, nine feet down. Remember what you're here for: Mr. Lucky. Where's the speargun? Lying in the sand. Didn't fire. That's a break. He retrieved it, regained control of his breathing. Long ridges ran across the sandy bottom. They would be parallel with the shore, which meant Mr. Lucky would cross them, swimming out to sea. Ray Don looked up at the rippling mirror that marked the end of ocean, beginning of sky. The surface. That's where Mr. Lucky will be.

Butt to the bottom, Ray Don looked up. And there he was. Paddling toward him. Pale legs kicking. Treading water.

Ray Don checked the speargun, the laser sight, the trigger. He used his swim fins to keep his back to the bottom. The surge made it tricky. It wrestled him forward, then back. Side to side. But Mr. Lucky was swimming his way now. He would be over him in seconds. Ray

Don watched the ruby laser dot streak across the surface, settle on the kicking legs. Higher, to the stomach. Zigzagging across the body. Wait for a clean shot.

Zwisshh! The spear streaked nearly straight up.

Ray Don saw the legs jerk, the froth of bubbles as Mr. Lucky thrashed. The spear in him, no question of that. A rust red cloud spread with the bubbles. On the surface, he knew, it would be brilliant scarlet. From below, he heard the muffled scream. He'd bet they could hear it from shore. Maybe even Sarge could hear it from wherever he was.

Shee-it! You done it, boy. Now get the hell out of here.

He swam at least three hundred feet, surfaced once to check his position, then dropped to the bottom, shed the tank, regulator, the buoyancy control vest, weight belt, mask, and, reluctantly, Sarge's wonderful toy, the beautiful Russian speargun.

He walked out of the water. Not much of a beachgoer, Ray Don was annoyed at the difficulty of walking in loose sand. He shot the sand a wicked look. Uh-oh. Swim fins.

He flip-flopped back to the ocean. Ditch the damn things. Walk out again.

No one noticed. They were all pointing to sea.

"Someone's drowning," a bikini-clad coed screeched to college mates, lying tummies to beach towels, hurriedly retying tops, anxious to see.

"No, it's a surfer, got hit by a board," said a male hanger-on.

Two cops spoke anxiously into radios.

"Shark attack," said a pear-shaped man in striped Bermuda shorts. "God, like on the TV."

"No sharks here at Waikiki," said a dark Japanese local. "Must be epilepsy. You know—someone threw a fit. Lifeguard's on the way."

"Did someone say *shark?*"

"Ate some guy. Look, lifeguard's almost to him."

"I see a fin!"

"Shark?" "Shark." "Shark!" The contagious S-word reverberated across water and sand.

Panic in the surf. Scrambling, shoving, splashing. Mothers screamed for children. Sunbathers rolled, stumbled, collided. It was bedlam on the beach.

Ray Don grinned. Hot damn, he thought, won't Sarge be proud of what I done this day?

39

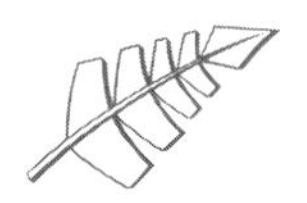

Scooter rapped on the counter. "Papa—you have any idea where Star is?"

"Coupon says buy one meal, the second's free," said the man with the white hair. "We're still within the deadline."

"Yes, but this is *Papa's,*" said Papa, ignoring Scooter. He spelled it for them, "P-A-P-A apostrophe S."

"Tell him we belong to the AARP," said his wife. "Don't let him cheat us, Harold."

"Let me see the owner," said the man. "Denny himself. Go on, get him."

"I'm the owner," said Papa. He swiped a napkin across his forehead. "Look at your coupon, our menu. See? The names are different."

"This is the last meal we eat at Denny's," said the man, scattering bills and change across the counter. They stomped out.

"Why didn't I keep up with the ukulele?" muttered Papa, chasing coins. "Now, what's your problem, Scooter?"

"Star," she said. "I haven't seen his car or him for two days."

Papa jerked a thumb to the back.

Star sat in the far corner. "Damned kids had my booth again."

He motioned Scooter to sit, nodded at her baggy warm-ups. "Glad to see you dressing like yourself again."

"You and me both. Hey, I was worried about you. Haven't seen you around."

"Sorry. After the Kite-man trouble, I've been parking in hotel garages, different one every day." He frowned. "Scooter, tell me something. Do I look weird? Something odd about me today?" He flashed a Hollywood smile, left profile, right.

"Same pretty face."

"Doris's friend D. L. came by this morning. When he saw me, he went so red I thought he'd explode."

Scooter shrugged.

"Maybe," said Star, "it was because Digger Fitz was talking with Doris at the counter. D. L. saw them all right, although they didn't see him. Digger's been hanging around here—around Doris—like a bee on a can of Coke. But D. L. seemed pissed off at *me*—he left the second he saw me."

He spread a newspaper on the table, tapped at an article. "Speaking of weird, look at this."

> SWIMMER SPEARED OFF WAIKIKI BEACH. Alarmed beachgoers yesterday witnessed the emergency rescue of a badly bleeding man from the surf off Kuhio Beach Park.
>
> Initial reports of a shark attack led to panic and numerous minor injuries. Police soon determined, however, that the victim, Jesus San Sebastiano of Los Angeles, had been stabbed by a marine speargun dart. Attempts to trace the weapon and the perpetrator are in progress.
>
> Several items of scuba gear washed ashore within hours of the incident, leading police to theorize that a scuba diver, perhaps a Russian tourist, mistook Mr. San Sebastiano for a large fish, probably a shark, and speared him. The assailant, according to this scenario, realized his tragic error, abandoned the diving gear, and fled.
>
> Subsequently, however, authorities discovered that

> Mr. San Sebastiano is wanted in Los Angeles for a string of gang-inspired drive-by shootings.
>
> Is the Waikiki spearing a reprisal?
>
> Police refuse to speculate. They acknowledge only that representatives of the Los Angeles Police Department are enroute to Honolulu, and that Mr. San Sebastiano remains in "guarded" condition at the Queen's Medical Center.
>
> Mr. San Sebastiano's distraught companion, Miss Patata Caliente, sunbathing during the attack, made a brief and tearful statement to the press. "Jesus and me, we come here for fun, the relaxation, and look what happen. First the luau bus is hijack, and now this. Is no one safe in this horrible place?"
>
> Has gang violence come to Hawaii? Is Waikiki to suffer further swim-by spearings?
>
> "An isolated and regrettable incident," said the Governor, who promised to swim along Waikiki Beach himself this noon in a dramatic demonstration of "the tranquillity of our breezy, sun-kissed shores."

"I was swimming there yesterday," said Star. "Must have zoned out, missed the whole thing. And I didn't see the paper until after lunch, so I missed the governor, too."

"Sorry to call you away from Papa's, son, but this couldn't wait." Dan squeezed Star's shoulder, shook Caddy's hand. "Thanks for coming by on such short notice." He rubbed his palms together so fast they nearly ignited. "How's this? The Ka Pono Foundation is rumored to be in financial trouble. The Hawaiian Pa'a Bank and Fiduciary Trust, so my sources say, gave them disastrous financial advice. Litigation is possible. No details yet, but"—Dan tapped his nose—"there's a certain story for *Pacific Rainbow* here. Yessir.

"And someone said the foundation owned the Pali-uli, didn't they?"

He answered himself. "Yes, that's what they said, and no, they certainly do not." He slapped his hands together. "The foundation *sold* it to HydraCorp, the resort people. Quaint little nature center? Ha! HydraCorp, get this, is planning to build a *golf resort* there, call it Paradise Valley."

"Holy cow!" said Star.

"HOLY COW!" echoed Ernest Hemingway from the top of his cage.

"Then this Bernie Bergen . . . ," said Caddy.

"Lied through his teeth," said Dan. "I confronted him with it, and he said, guess what?"

"No comment."

"Exactly. Bergen must have one hell of a sway with the planning people, because they've rezoned the land, have issued grubbing and grading permits for the entry road. All on the rush-rush-hush-hush.

"As for the elusive Marcel Landau, I got hold of a colleague of his who says as soon as Landau filed his report on the Pali-uli, he left for a lengthy personal project in a remote area of Palawan in the Philippines, under a generous grant from—are you ready?—HydraCorp of Honolulu.

"I had my man in Hilo fly over the Pali-uli tract, and he says earthmoving equipment constructing a road to a wind farm is cutting a branch into the valley as we speak."

"But surely," said Caddy, "if there's an important archaeological feature . . ."

"The features in the survey, the official ones? Oh, yes. HydraCorp plans to preserve, incorporate them into their development—decoration for the swimming pool, golf course roughs. The Kapo site? Officially, it doesn't exist. Nor, of course, does an *'o'o* bird in that valley. Proper surveys were conducted, submitted, accepted."

"What about our feather?" asked Star.

"The biggest news of all. We have an answer from the ornithologist at the Smithsonian." He read, mouthed details from a report, " '. . . with microslides of comparative material . . . microstructures of barbs and barbules . . .' Here we go, 'does appear to be from *Moho nobilis,* the Hawaiian *'o'o.'* But, 'given the poor condition and lack of data regarding the specimen's provenance . . .' " Dan slammed a fist into his palm. "The bottom line is, we have no proof that feather came from a live bird in the Pali-uli."

"So, what now?" asked Caddy.

"We go there ourselves," Dan said. "See if we can find the bird and the site. We'll stay no more than three days. If we're successful, we'll be able to delay the construction, make our case. If we're not? Come back and see what influence, if any, we can wield before they destroy the forest."

"Lord," said Caddy. "Melissa was *murdered* for *golf*."

"MURDERED!" shouted Ernest Hemingway. "GOLF!"

"That's how it looks to me," said Dan. "Millions are involved here. Fast profits for a lot of people. HydraCorp has the most to gain or lose, but your murderer could also be someone in Big Island construction or real estate. Or someone with the foundation, afraid their secret deal with HydraCorp could be jeopardized."

"What about Bergen?" asked Caddy.

"I've asked around about him," Dan said. "Smart. A dealmaker, a business gypsy, not beyond skirting the law if it's to his advantage, but he's hardly the violent type."

"We *will* find who's responsible," said Caddy. "And when I get my hands on them . . ."

"If we begin shaking the bushes," said Dan, "you may get your chance. So be careful. I've been planning. We'll leave the day after tomorrow. Me—I know birds—you two, your friend Harmon Fitz the archaeologist if he can go, and someone from the Hawaiian community who knows the land and the goddess Pele. Star, I called your friend Walana."

"Walana gave me the creeps."

"CREEPS!"

"And what about Ernest Hemingway?" asked Dan. "You want to go along, buddy? Keep us entertained?" He walked to the birdcage, put a peanut between his teeth, bared his lips, and leaned toward the alert macaw.

"Watch out," said Star, "that bastard bites."

Ernest plucked the peanut gently from Dan's mouth with his

beak, transferred it to his right foot, cocked his head at Star, and screeched, "BASTARD!" Then he lifted Dan's gift and began silent surgery on the shell.

Dan turned to the map on the desk. "Gather round, troops," he said. "Let's work on a battle plan."

40

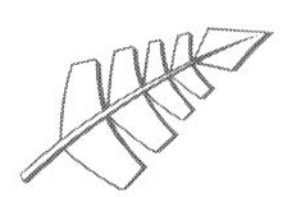

But you're a hero, Reverend," said Bernie. "I saw those articles. *People, Time*. Tabloids are saying you performed miracles, saved dozens of babies when the tent collapsed. When you make the *National Enquirer,* Reverend, you know you've arrived. You can turn this into big bucks, believe me. Lecture circuit, a book, made-for-TV movie. All you need is a good agent. I'll make a few calls, set you up."

"No, Bernie, I don't deserve it. I'm a sinner, a worthless sinner. Although"—the Reverend's face, up to now a portrait of torment, softened—"I did save those little babies. One, at least. Still"—the worried look returned—"it was all my fault for luring them there in the first place."

"Nonsense, Reverend."

"Bernie, I'm going to share a secret with you." He looked up, eyes focused beyond the acoustic ceiling tile, past the scudding clouds in the forever blue Hawaiian sky, farther even than heaven's Pearly Gates. Reverend Jaycie gazed upon the Golden Throne itself. "From beneath the gloom of that fallen canvas I saw a wondrous light. An angel? I suspect it was. I know it was a sign from the Lord. A voice sweeter than any on this dismal planet whispered to me, 'Brother Jaycie, you have sinned. But your work is good. Carry on.' "

"However"—he frowned, suddenly saw no farther than the four walls of Bernie's office—"standing in the way of this divine directive is that damnable, blackmailing harridan in Tahiti and her trollop of a daughter, little Josephine." For a moment, a mere moment, a lascivious gleam of fond recollection twinkled in Reverend Jaycie's eye; then alarm tightened his face. "If I don't get that two hundred thousand dollars to her soon, it's curtains. Curtains for doing the Lord's work in Hawai'i."

He turned to Bernie. "Do tell me your project is on schedule. That I can count on your repaying me the two hundred thousand soon. Any returns on those options yet?"

Bernie bit his lip, played with his ponytail, tinkered with his dancing-whales music box. He tapped the larger whale and it began to sing. "Three Little Fishies" tinkled through the office. Bernie tried, unsuccessfully, to shut it off, finally spoke over the music. "Reverend, I'm afraid we've got a small problem."

"Lordy. No. The volcano?"

"Well, that too."

"There's more? Noooo."

"Busybody snoopers, Reverend, poking into my business. Sand in the wheels of progress. There's a possibility, a slim chance, they could grind our grand project, Hawai'i's most spectacular golf resort, to a halt."

"Lordy." The Reverend held his head, fingers ruffling silvery locks. Eyes closed, he rocked, keened softly.

"Nicorettes, Reverend?" Bernie popped half a dozen in his mouth, passed the candy dish to the Reverend, who grabbed a handful and began chewing. "All's not lost. I've got a good man on it, a real can-do sort of fellow."

The Reverend moved to the familiar bar, poured familiar bourbon into a tall glass.

"Busybodies," muttered Bernie. His lips curled into a conspiratorial leer. "My man, though, has been watching them. He bugged the ringleader's office yesterday, has a tape, knows who they are." He lifted a file from the desk, scanned the contents.

"He says they plan to go to the Big Island, to the Pali-uli to snoop around, look for irregularities in our zoning applications, hold us up.

Zoning was all approved, permits . . . hell, everything's on track, but . . ." His voice trailed off.

Rubbing his temples, Bernie walked with the file to the model of Paradise Valley, now occupying the corner of his office, and looked with paternal pride at the rolling green deal of his dreams, nestled in the cozy mountain valley. "Barring interference from these busybodies, the earthmovers will be clearing that valley soon. They're dozing the switchbacks as we speak. When they get to the bottom, I'll make the big announcement—and that's when I begin selling options on the surrounding land. Maybe only four or five days from now the money starts rolling in. I repay your loan, everyone's happy."

The Reverend began to smile—until he saw Bernie's chubby pink hands curl into fists.

Bernie pounded his desk. "But I can't help worrying about these damned thorns in our side." He lifted the surveillance report. "Maybe you know them. Do I have your ear, Reverend?"

Reverend Jaycie set down his nearly empty tumbler, leaned against the wall, soothed his forehead with a pale tangerine hankie. "Read away, brother."

" 'Star (Mr. Lucky) Hollie, hippie surfer and reporter. Cassidy (Caddy) MacConnell, geologist. Danielo (Dan) Capistrano, publisher of *Pacific Rainbow* magazine. Harmon (Digger) Fitz, archaeologist. Walana—last name unknown, volcano lover. And Ernest Hemingway, foul mouthed *Pacific Rainbow* employee.'

"Do you know any of these people, these thorns?"

"I think the Capistrano fellow called me once," said the Reverend, "about one of our TV shows. Can't remember the details. The names Star Hollie and Ernest Hemingway have a familiar ring, but I can't place them. The others? Nothing. But what I don't get is, what do they have against golf?"

Bernie decided to spare the Reverend the ugly details, the bird and shrine business. "Against golf, Reverend? Maybe they're bitter, been turned down for country-club memberships. A surfer? A woman? Enough said there. The old prof probably can't afford greens fees, let alone dues, and maybe the publisher got a membership revoked for not replacing divots, or farting in the locker room, or who knows? Word gets around fast in the golfing world. The point is, they've got it in for golf and Paradise Valley."

Bernie took an imaginary swing, watched his imaginary ball sail high and far. "Golf," he said fondly. "Anyway, my man is sending two of his people over today. He's going himself tomorrow to observe these thorns, see if their spying will give us trouble. He doesn't know it yet, but I'm going with him. I want a firsthand look. My future. Yours. The HydraCorp board's. All those eager golfers', too."

"I'm going with you," said the Reverend.

Bernie scowled.

"I know, brother Bernie. You think my old bones and this limp will slow you down in the wilderness. Don't worry, I'll keep out of the bush, out of your hair. I'll stay behind, in civilization, close as I can. I'll give you spiritual support, pray for you morning, noon, and night. Remember, as the Eighteenth Psalm tells us, he who calls to the Lord is saved from his enemies."

The Reverend wobbled to Bernie's side, drained the last of his bourbon, swirled ice cubes in the empty glass, and set it on a Paradise Valley fairway. "No need to worry, brother." He looped an arm around his friend's small shoulders. "The Lord is just. You'll see."

41

"Gawd, I ache. I never done so many push-ups in my life. A hundred. Sarge standin' over me, slammin' his boot in my ribs ever time I caught a breath. I've got hurts, Bobby Lee, where I never knew it could hurt."

"You took your punishment like a man, brother. I was proud of you. Now you rest in the shotgun seat here, and I'll do the cartin' and packin' myself."

Bobby Lee nestled the crate of hand grenades in the trunk of the rented Ford, next to D. L.'s camouflage rifle case, and returned for more gear.

D. L. had sent the brothers to the Big Island in the HydraCorp company plane to avoid the embarrassment of their carrying ordnance past Honolulu airport security. The flight had been a memorable experience for the twins.

"Can you believe that airplane?" said Bobby Lee, chipper as a schoolgirl on amphetamines. "Whatever we wanted. All we could drink." He arranged the next load on the rear seat. "Man, I must have ate thirty bags of peanuts. That pretty little chicken in the skirt, waitin' on us? She almost said yes when I asked her for a hump in the back of the plane. I know she would of, wasn't for you and the pilots around. Hardly said nothing when I grabbed her butt, even. That's a sure sign they like you. My, my, what a sweetheart. Sarge, he's forgive us, Ray Don, now that he punished you, or he would of sent us by boat instead of plane. *Brrrrr*! I hate boats. And look at our car. Brand-new, and legal, too. Rent one, don't steal it, says Sarge. The company's paying for it all. Hotel room, yet, up at the volcano. Hot damn, we're gonna have a good time before Sarge gets here. Company's payin' for the food. . . ."

"Bobby Lee, I ache nearly to death and I drunk too much on the way over. My head hurts something awful. Keep the talk down, huh?" Ray Don slouched in the seat, rested his Tony Lamas on the dash, set his hat over his eyes, and tried to sleep.

Forty minutes later, they were on Highway 11, twenty-five miles from Hilo, not far now from the town of Volcano and Volcano House Hotel, in Volcanoes National Park, situated, as the names imply, by the volcano.

"Golly, I never drove up a hill this long in my life," said Bobby Lee. "Not a down in the road. Up, up, and more up."

"This old mountain is still boilin' and puffin' at the top, little brother," said Ray Don, reasonably refreshed from a much-needed nap. "Man, I can't wait to see it."

"This is like a vacation, ain't it? Think they got women up there? Beer?"

"I suspect they got both, but we is under orders to behave our asses, and I, for one, don't want never to see another push-up. We'll just check it out, eat a bite or two, rest up, and wait for Sarge to get here tomorrow. Okay, little brother?"

"Whatever you say, Ray Don." Bobby Lee knew they'd find something fun to do, regardless.

Ten minutes later, they stood before the Volcano House reception desk. The clerk, a proper, pale, bespectacled young man, was doing his best to be hospitable to these disturbingly large and speech-impaired men in western attire. "Yes, sirs. We have your reservation. Two, to be charged to the HydraCorp account."

"I see a bar over there?" asked Bobby Lee.

"Yes, sir. Bar. Restaurant, too. All-you-can-eat buffet. Whatever you wish. Simply charge it to your room."

"You hear that?" Bobby Lee opened the door to their room.

"Charge it, the guy with the bow tie says. All we can eat, all we can drink. Was gonna ask him about women, but he was such a homely Jethro, I figured, what's he know? He probably don't get none." Bobby Lee heaved one of the packs onto the bed.

"Do your business if you got to, brother," said Ray Don. "I want to get outside, see this volcano. You sure you closed the trunk?"

Bobby Lee rolled his eyes. "Ain't me what fucks up all the time, big brother."

Ray Don stared though the window at an incredible vista. The hotel perched on the very edge of the vast caldera of Kilauea volcano, round, cliff-rimmed, three miles across. Inside, the crater loomed: black, steaming, foreboding. In contrast, the hotel grounds and the caldera rim nearly glowed with sun-dazzling green vegetation.

"Mama! It's cold out here," said Bobby Lee, five minutes later.

"It's high, Bobby Lee, high as Black Mountain. Look, tourist people. Let's check 'em out."

A group of nine, standing near the edge of the cliff, faced a uniformed guide.

"Uh-oh," said Bobby Lee. "Cop."

"No, brother," said Ray Don. "It's a park ranger fella, like at the Great Smoky Mountains. See the stupid hat? C'mon. I want to hear what he's tellin' 'em."

"Oh yes," said the ranger, hardly a fella, but, rather, a robust female, large and solid, the kind of ranger suited for arduous hikes, difficult rescues, and motivating recalcitrant mules. A thick blond braid hung halfway down her back. "Kilauea is dormant now," she was saying, "but there is an eruption in the vicinity nearly every year. The southwestern rift of Mauna Loa"—she pointed to a distant, cloud-shrouded hump, far higher than Kilauea—"is active as we speak. When Kilauea erupts, there are fountains of fire, red-hot pools of magma. It's an incredible sight, and safe—from here. Fortunately for us, Hawaiian volcanoes are rarely explosive."

The twins joined the party. "Ranger's a girl," said a surprised Bobby Lee.

"No, brother, that's a woman," answered Ray Don. "And she's got some real meat on her, too. Check out that ass and those melons." He made chest-high squeezing motions with his fingers.

"Children here!" whispered a slender man in pressed khakis and a raspberry red L. L. Bean windbreaker, holding his hands over the ears of his daughter while twisting her head away from the twins, toward the ranger.

"Shhhh!" shushed several of the others.

"The berries?" the ranger was saying. "Hawaiians call them *'ohelo*. Can you all say that? O-heh-low."

O-heh-lows sounded around the group.

"No, they're not poisonous, and yes, they are edible. They are also sacred to Pele the volcano goddess." She turned her back to the group, pointed to the caldera. "Pele reigns over Mauna Loa and Kilauea volcanoes. She is often referred to, respectfully, as *Tutu* Pele, or Grandmother Pele. Some call her Madame or Mother Pele—apt, considering she is, literally, the mother of this island. Madame Pele may walk the earth as an old white-haired woman, or as a ravishing beauty, seducing young men who catch her fancy. Her home is there, in the fire pit of Halema'uma'u. Can you say that? Hall-lay-ma-u, ma-u."

She waited for the echoes. "Pele is respected, even worshiped in Hawai'i, and with good reason. We see evidence of her everywhere. She is willful, violent. When angry, she spouts lava, burns the land. Don't mess with Madame Pele." The ranger waggled her finger.

Uncertain laughter chirruped left and right.

"Back to *'ohelo*." She bent to pluck a sprig of bright red berries from a low shrub. "We always throw the first to Madame Pele as an offering, so she won't be offended." She tossed berries over the edge of the chasm, ate the remaining two. "Not that I want to encourage people to pick these," she explained, "because we must conserve what is here for others. Yes? But I wanted to demonstrate our respect for the volcano goddess."

Nods all around.

"And please, don't take even the smallest of stones with you as souvenirs. Over at the interpretive center we have many letters on display, written by people who removed pieces of lava from Pele's home and suffered bad luck. Every week the postman brings packages with pieces of stone people removed and are returning to us, with apologies to Madame Pele."

"How about me takin' a piece of *you?*" asked Bobby Lee with a hee-haw.

A hush fell over the group. The ranger squinted at him, silent, then slipped off her Windbreaker, let it drop to the ground, revealing a short-sleeved shirt. She rolled a sleeve high up her shoulder, slowly raised a bare right elbow, formed a fist, and flexed a biceps large and hard as a boccie ball. "How would you," she asked in a voice cold enough to freeze hot lava, "like a bust in the chops, plowboy?"

"Uh," said Bobby Lee. He took three steps back, developed an interest in the toe of his boot.

"That's better," she said, the music back in her voice. "And are there any other questions?" She slipped the jacket back on.

"What's with that stink-hole?" asked Ray Don. He pointed to an open crack in the earth, two feet wide, six long, puffing foul-smelling steam.

"A legitimate question from the candid and, so far, well-behaved twin in the back," said the ranger. "Dr. Jekyll, I presume?"

"Say what?"

"Far below," she continued, "the rock is molten. Closer to the surface, it is still hot. Very, very hot. Hot enough to turn sinking groundwater into steam. See the fringing ferns growing around the top of that crevice? We call them *uluhe*. They like the steam, the warmth. Frequent rainfall here, so there's plenty of water dropping onto the hot rock. You might compare the mountain to a Crock-Pot, a pressure cooker. Now—" she shook her finger—"I want you all to be extra careful up here. Stay on the paths, away from orifices like this. They can be very deep. All too often, we have people wading through the vegetation, dropping into crevasses. . . ."

"Splat! Hiss," said a little boy. "Eeeuuu," squealed his sister.

"And please," continued the ranger, "no dropping litter or pop cans into these holes. Madame Pele is down there, and she doesn't like garbage dropping onto her head any more than you would. Respect, hmmmm? Now, let me tell you a bit about the history of Volcano House. In 1877 . . ."

"Old stuff makes me puke," said Bobby Lee, quietly enough so the ranger with the big arms couldn't hear him. "Let's get the hell out of here."

On the way back to the hotel, Ray Don said, "Bobby Lee, I been thinking. That ranger gave me an idea."

"Those melons of hers gave me two ideas," answered Bobby Lee, more confident with thirty yards between himself and the dangerous female. He made feelie gestures and sucking sounds.

"No, brother. About them holes in the ground. You ever put a M-80 in a mailbox? Or a cherry bomb down a chipmunk hole? You followin' me, Bobby Lee?"

Comprehension lit Bobby Lee's face. "Shit fire," he said. "We got hand grenades!"

That night over dinner, and later in the bar, before the fireplace, people spoke of the spectacular view, of sore feet and the joys of grandkids, of basketball and football, of the blizzards back home, of shopping in Waikiki, of sunburn and suntan lotion, but, invariably, conversation returned to the mysterious and frightening booming noises heard around the park that afternoon. Military planes breaking the sound barrier? An ominous swarm of bizarre earthquakes? No one knew. Not even the rangers, who seemed to know everything.

Ray Don and Bobby Lee drank beer, and listened, and snickered.

42

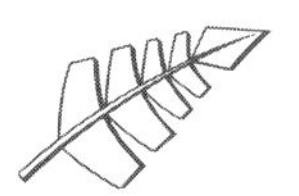

High noon at Volcano House. Lunchtime, and the all-you-can-eat buffet was jammed. Hungry tourists bumped shoulders, clutched trays of food, jostled one another for tables—although no one seemed to covet the nearly empty table for six, the one by the window with a panoramic view of the volcano, the table with the two giants in denim, napkins at their necks, dawdling, one with his boots on the tablecloth, the other snoozing, a western hat shielding his eyes.

Ray Don and Bobby Lee had staked it out forty-five minutes ago. Sarge had said to hold lunch until he arrived, so the boys were holding.

Bobby Lee's Tony Lamas slid to the floor with a thump. "There he is! There he is!"

Ray Don raised his hat. "Who the hell's that with him? Two men. Can't hardly see 'em from here." He craned his neck. "Sarge wouldn't bring someone else to do our jobs, would he?"

D. L. left his companions at the restaurant entrance and walked to the twins' table. "I want good behavior, boys," he said, a hand on each of their shoulders. "It's the friggin' boss and a friend of his. Wasn't my idea, believe me. I don't want to hear any bragging lunch talk about how you pushed Finch's car over the cliff or drowned his wife, understand? And not a word about our dismal dealings with Mr. Lucky, hear? You two are just hardworking security guards, helping carry supplies, right? *Supplies*. No mention of the ordnance, got it? Nod your heads if you follow me."

They nodded.

"All right, then, let's get some food." He set his fatigue hat and a map case on the table to post it off-limits, and walked toward his traveling companions with the brothers in tow. "Mr. Bergen, Reverend Pitts," said D. L., "these are Hydra security guards, two of our best, Ray Don and Bobby Lee. Say hello, boys."

At sight of the Reverend, Bobby Lee stepped back, got tangled with Ray Don, who stumbled sideways into a gaggle of Japanese tourists elbowing their way to the head of the line. Two of them fell to the floor.

D. L. lifted the slight men in navy slacks and white shirts by their elbows, spoke a mollifying phrase of Japanese, bowed apologetically, and turned with an angry "wait till later" look for the boys.

The twins, however, stared straight past D. L. at their come-from-out-of-the-blue, silver-haired collaborator in the revival tent fiasco. The Reverend, speechless himself, and obviously equally dumbfounded to find *them here,* was subtly but vehemently shaking his head side to side. No, no, you never saw me before.

"Uh, hello," said Ray Don. "Hi," said Bobby Lee. "Sorry," they both said to Sarge.

"I think it was your title that scared them, Reverend," muttered D. L. "I doubt these boys have been inside a church since their mommy and daddy got hitched."

"I understand, brother," said the Reverend, and with a flourish he motioned D. L. and Bernie, then the boys, ahead of him into the food line. At the silverware station he tugged at Ray Don's red flannel sleeve and whispered, "The revival robbery never happened. We never met."

Ray Don nodded—"Don't I wish?"—then pointed to the stack of eight-inch salad plates. "Here's a free tip for you, preacher. Don't let 'em cheat you with these puny suckers. They's got bigger ones down the line." He grabbed a quarter loaf of white bread, tucked it under his arm, and advanced to the greens.

Bobby Lee let his brother pass, lingered for the Reverend's ear. When the others had moved ahead, he spoke over his shoulder. "Please, sir. It was wonnerful you saving me, but I missed two important jobs with my brother a-cause of it, so let's not talk about the saving around these folks. Okay?"

"And not a word about the revival robbery, right, son?"

"Especially not to Sarge, sir. Sarge, he's our boss, D. L. McWhorter."

"My lips are sealed."

Bobby Lee reached for the rolls. "These are the best ones, sir, real soft. If you squeeze 'em tight in your fist like this"—he demonstrated—"they get small as a walnut, taste just like dough balls. And you can get a lot more on your plate that way, too."

"What a clever boy you are," said the Reverend.

Bobby Lee left the Reverend experimenting with crushing rolls and hurried down the line to catch up with his brother. He lifted the clear plastic sneeze guard as Ray Don leaned over a bowl of multicolored pasta salad, past a tray of lime Jell-O flecked with shredded carrots, to spear cherry tomatoes on an aluminum-foil-lined vegetable platter.

"Thank you, brother," said Ray Don. "Damned thing kept banging me in the forehead. Most fun of the lunch line is to sneak up on these little red buggers—look at 'em, layin' down there like that, fat as porkers, unsuspecting—and stab 'em fast to make their guts squirt out." He jabbed with his fork. "Splot! That was a good one. Didn't know what hit him."

"Brother," whispered Bobby Lee, head near his brother's under the sneeze guard, "I know you hate preachers, and especially the Reverend after that tent job gone bad like it did, but he's a nice old guy and a friend of Sarge's boss, an' . . ."

"I know, I know," mumbled Ray Don. "Good behavior. I been real gentlemanly to him already. Tipped him off about the small-ass cheat-you plates, even."

"Bug!" Bobby Lee plucked the hair at the back of Ray Don's neck with the salad tongs.

"Old trick, brother. Didn't fool me one bit. Better get your ass in gear, I smell chicken ahead."

Standing behind Bernie, D. L. shoveled a square of anonymous breaded fish onto his plate, bent over to sniff it. With his head low, he checked to confirm that the boys and the Reverend were still back by the salads, out of earshot.

Earlier that morning in Honolulu, Bernie had shown up at the company plane to drop the bomb on D. L. that not only he, but the Reverend Jaycie Pitts as well, would be joining D. L.'s expedition to the Big Island. This was D. L.'s first chance to speak with Bernie alone.

"Sir," said D. L., "it would be a good idea not to mention my completion bonus around the boys, particularly the dollar amount. Wage earners that they are, they may get the wrong idea. . . ."

"Give me some credit, D. L. I know better than to discuss finances in front of employees." Bernie looked back at the fish, wrinkled his nose. "Think I'll stay with the shrimp and crabmeat. How fresh do you suppose they are way up here?" He flipped a few shrimp over with the tongs to check the color of the ones underneath. "Uh, D. L., the Reverend's a good man, but a bit naive. Just as well we don't speak of surveillance, hush money, and that sort of thing in the open, huh? He's interested in building a church by the links, thinks you're a prospective golf pro."

"Me? A golf pro?"

"You have that look of authority, the kind of man who would choose the right iron every time. Anyway, I let the Reverend know there may be golf spies out there, sneaking around the valley. People who have it in for golf, see? And we're checking them out."

"Whatever you say, sir. Just be sure he stays here at the hotel, like you promised. Your coming was a bad enough idea. I don't want to baby-sit some preacher, too."

D. L. moved to the table, joined in short order by the boys. Each had three plates heaped with ten-inch pyramids of mostly fried chicken.

"Criminy, boys," said D. L. "Let's watch our manners around the old gent and the boss. All you can eat means you can go back for seconds, you know."

"Never can be sure when they're goin' to run out, Sarge," explained Bobby Lee.

Back on the food line, Bernie whispered, "Reverend, it might be best we don't speak to D. L. about our monetary dealings, especially your loan to me. I don't want him thinking I have chinks in my financial armor. I'm his Rock of Gibraltar, see? That okeydokey with you?"

"Certainly, brother Bernie. And, brother," the Reverend whispered back, "this shameful business about my being blackmailed over little Josephine, that's a personal confidence. Don't want my dirty laundry paraded before strangers."

"Not to worry, Reverend. My lips are sealed."

"There's the empty tray," said the Reverend, "but, shoot, where's the fried chicken? The desk clerk said the cook did it up right at this place. I had such a hankering for chicken, and it's gone already. Guess I'll have to make do with this unnamed fish and the succotash."

Eventually they all took seats, but poked at their food in silence, uncertain who should eat first, reluctant to begin a conversation lest it lead to a spilling of verbal beans onto the wrong man's plate.

The Reverend made the first move, but instead of plying a fork, he stood and bowed his head. "Let us say grace."

Bobby Lee kicked Ray Don under the table, glared at him to go along with it. "Sayin' grace is nothing like being saved, big brother," he whispered. "It's hardly religion at all."

"The Lord," began the Reverend, "has safeguarded our journey to this idyllic rest house, provided wholesome bounty to ease our hunger, given us this marvelous view and the warm company of friends. Let us join hands, form a ring of fellowship."

Huh? Say what? No one moved.

"Let us not be shy, brothers. Grasp the hands of your neighbors, hold them high."

Eyes stared at the table, the seconds ticked off, hands clutched their owner's knees, beads of perspiration formed, dripped here and there down embarrassed, increasingly angry faces.

"Reverend," said Bernie after an interminable silence, "I don't think this is a hand-holding crowd. Why not just finish the prayer, and we can eat."

"Thank you, sir," D. L. muttered to his superior, grateful for the first time that day to have Bernie by his side.

The resilient Reverend continued, undaunted, on a new tack. "Brother Bernie tells me you gentlemen face adversaries, thorns as he calls them, those who would thwart your plans for this magnificent golf resort. Keep in mind Psalm 138, when David says, 'Though I walk in the midst of trouble, thou wilt revive me; thou shalt stretch forth thine hand against the wrath of mine enemies, and thy right hand shall save me.'

"May the Lord be with you, brothers, in your trials to come. And, may your own right hand deliver you a hole in one on your very first drive on Brother Bernie's magnificent new golf course. As they say on the links, *fore!*" He followed with a soft, "Amen. You may raise your heads."

"Reverend," said D. L., "that was a mighty fine prayer. Short and to the point. Go ahead boys, chow down."

"Four what?" mumbled Bobby Lee between bites.

"Four of us," said Ray Don. "Preacher's staying here, see? You, me, Sarge, and his boss is going to the valley. That's four."

"Boys," said D. L., "from the way he's staring at your plates, I can see the Reverend would like a piece of that fried chicken. You share it with him, hear?"

Bobby Lee scowled, shoved one of his plates to the Reverend, who, with a "Bless you, son," speared a fine breast with his fork.

Most of the diners left for an afternoon at the volcano. D. L. scanned the empty tables, squinted at the remaining Japanese twenty feet away, tour flag at their center, then at four guffawing Germans at the other end of the room, and decided he could speak freely. "Initial briefing, men," he said, sweeping aside coffee cups and the boys' second-helping dessert plates. He unrolled a map and a satellite blowup of the Pali-uli. "The Reverend here's going to stay at the hotel, give us moral support. Right, sir?"

"Indeed I am."

"Mr. Bergen's thorns," said D. L., "as a little birdie told me, are going to arrive in Hilo by scheduled air at two o'clock today. Four of them."

"Four," said Ray Don to his brother. "Just like us."

"Four thorns," said D. L. "All but this Ernest Hemingway, who evidently stayed back in Honolulu to watch the shop. They'll be meeting a fifth, name of Walana, somewhere on the Hilo side of the island. They'll pick this Walana up, drive through here—maybe you'll see them, Reverend, this being the only road between Hilo and the Paliuli. We'll be ready."

D. L. tapped the map. "Here's our valley. Being trespassers, our thorns won't come up the wind farm road on the southwest like we will, so that means they'll hike in, probably from the northeast."

At the other side of the table, below it, Bobby Lee held open a pillowcase while Ray Don tipped in a plate of surplus fried chicken he had secreted on his lap.

"Our thorns," continued D. L., "will be in the valley, looking for whatever it is they hope to find, and we'll to be up on top, watching them. If they don't find anything after three days—that's their deadline—and they give up, then we've got nothing to worry about. If they do find something, start taking a lot of pictures, whatever, and leave early, then it's decision time. I imagine Mr. Bergen here will try to negotiate some kind of deal with them.

"That's it in a nutshell, troops. Boys, finish that extra cobbler if you still want it, and let's get crackin'. Reverend, you keep the car we came up in. We'll take Ray Don's and Bobby Lee's, since it's already packed with our gear. Anyone need to use the little boys' room, now's the time—you won't see an indoor john again for three days."

Fifteen minutes later, the Reverend waved a pink silk kerchief at the receding Ford. He had pressed a miniature Bible and two gift-wrapped boxes of Nicorettes into Bernie's hands as a parting gift, and felt lonely already.

Psalms were on Reverend Jaycie's mind. The words of the powerful Twenty-third spoke to him, "Yea, though I walk through the valley of the shadow of death . . ." He shook his head. Surely, he thought, Brother Bernie can take care of himself. Brother Bernie, he reflected, who not that long ago had been a financial adversary, but who had since become, next to Jesus, the best friend he knew.

He tried to imagine little Bernie in his Bermuda shorts, golf shirt, and fancy loafers crashing through the bush in the wake of this disturbing gray-haired man in camouflage fatigues and combat boots, flanked by his barbarian minions, and sighed.

It's never too early for prayer, the Reverend decided, and retreated to his room for a talk with the Lord.

43

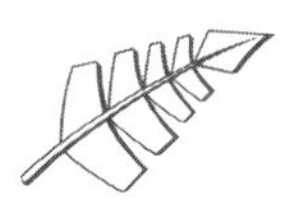

"This is it," said Star. "On the right, the mailbox by the stone cairn." He sounded nervous. The house belonged to Walana.

Dan drove onto a black crushed-lava drive that ran a hundred feet through dense brush, then petered out in low, wiry grass. Fifty yards farther, an aging one-story frame house peered through a sparse forest of tall gray-barked trees and ten-foot tree ferns. A ragged line of parked cars and trucks filled the front yard.

Dan squeezed the car between a pristine white Toyota Camry and a brush-painted green Volkswagen van. A sticker on the Camry's bumper read "My Kids Are Honor Students at Hilo High." Taped to the VW's rear window, a hand-lettered banner proclaimed "The Independent and Sovereign Nation of Hawai'i." Above it, a six-by-twelve-inch card said "Free Bumpy."

"Evidently an eclectic crowd," observed Dan.

Caddy read the signs. "I wonder what Bumpy is."

"Bumpy is that new Baskin-Robbins peanut brittle flavor," Star said. "I hear they're giving it away free to Hawaiians—the ice-cream people doing their part for the sovereignty movement."

"Bumpy is a jailed political activist, Caddy," explained Dan with a roll of his eyes.

Caddy shook her head. "Star—my font of misinformation." She noticed the house. "Cute cottage."

No more than thirty feet long, the body of the house sat under a low-pitched overhanging roof of corrugated sheet metal, once silver, now rust-stained orange. One broad, windowless gable faced the highway. A raised veranda ran around all four sides.

"Cute?" said Star. "It's painted black."

"Yes, but what a cheery door."

"Bloodred. It reminds me of the witch's house in Hansel and Gretel. Dark, hiding in those trees like the witch's oven."

They skirted the building, passed plantings of red and green ti and stands of banana and papaya to reach the rear, where over fifty men, women, children, babies, and dogs milled noisily.

"I feel we're intruding," Caddy said. "Do you think it's a family reunion?"

"Spooky, isn't it?" said Star. "Maybe they're sacrificing something. Or somebody."

"What's gotten into you, boy?" Dan said. "It's some kind of party. Walana said to make ourselves at home, she'd find us later."

Star repeated the name. "Walana."

The four newcomers stood on the sidelines, uncertain, ignored, until a Frisbee bounced off the back of Digger's head, followed, four long seconds later, by "Duck!" and cackling laughter. Digger flipped it back at a sixty-year-old, deeply tanned, bandy-legged Hawaiian in baggy shorts, and chased him into the woods.

"Uh-oh," said Dan, panic in his voice. "Mynah bird in a cage. Kids with sticks." With Caddy at his heels, he trotted toward a chicken-wire box in a grove of bamboo, waving his arms.

"Hey, Star!"

Star turned to see a former beach buddy, Billy, and another man, both in their thirties, dark, vaguely Asian.

"Bruddah," said Billy, "what you doing on the Big Island, way the hell up here?" Before waiting for an answer, he followed with, "Star, Kekoa. Kekoa, Star." The three slapped palms. "You bring your father, sister, and grandaddy along?" Laughter, then a recounting of the peeing contest for friend Kekoa, and more laughter. "Hey, man," Billy added, "I didn't know you were Hawaiian."

"Hawaiian?" Star said. "Not me, Billy. Some kind of Celt, I guess. Maybe a Gaul. Who knows?"

"Then what you doing here?" asked Billy's friend Kekoa with a squint. "This here's for Hawaiians."

"Really?" said Star. "I know Billy's granddaddy was Hawaiian. Hard to tell with you. Bunch of these people"—he looked around—"are, sure, Hawaiian, but it looks to me like you've also got haole, Japanese, Chinese—lots of folks."

"All Hawaiian," said Kekoa. "Except you."

"Chill, Kekoa," Billy said.

"You say all Hawaiian, you mean a hundred percent Hawaiian, part Hawaiian, or what?" asked Star.

"Same difference. Any Hawaiian in your family in the old days, you're Hawaiian now."

"So," said Star, "if that guy over there, the Japanese-looking one, is fifteen-sixteenths Japanese and one-sixteenth Hawaiian, then he's not really Japanese he's . . ."

"Hawaiian," said Kekoa. "And you and your haole friends are not, and you got no business here. This is a Hawaiian gathering. *'Ohana.*"

"Is there some difficulty here?" asked a short, plump woman with rounded Hawaiian features, hair in a bun, neatly dressed in a Lilly Pulitzer blue skirt and floral-print blouse.

"This smart-ass," said Kekoa, "and his haole friends aren't Hawaiian. I was asking him to leave."

"Shame on you, Kekoa," she said. "What must he think of our hospitality? These folks are our guests."

"Yeah? Who invited them?"

"Walana."

"Oh." He cast a furtive glance at the black house. "Don't know why she'd invite haoles."

"She's inside. Shall I call her out here? Tell her Kekoa has a problem?"

"Nah," he muttered. With a shrug he kicked at the grass. "No big deal. Billy and me was gonna get a beer, anyway. Right, Billy?"

"Sure," said Billy. He hesitated, took Star's elbow, whispered, "Sorry about that. Kekoa was out of line. But you cool your jets if you meet Walana. She's kahuna. Big mana. You show her plenty respect, huh? For your own good."

"I'm Mary Thompson," said the woman in the blue skirt. "I teach history at the Hilo campus of the U of H. I apologize for Kekoa. I fear he and his Sons of Pele friends are a bit too spirited.

"As you can see"—Mary waved across the yard at the people—"other than our ancestry, it's hard to pigeonhole us. We're like the flowers of the forest."

"Some of your flowers have bees in them." Star swatted the air.

"Touché," Mary said with a slight bow. "But for most of us, being Hawaiian means fellowship, tradition, *aloha 'aina*—a love of the land." She scowled. "Walana says there's trouble in the Pali-uli?"

"Trouble all right . . ."

Mary raised her palm. "No need to explain. You wait, talk it over with Walana. She'll know what to do." She smiled past Star's shoulder. "And these would be your friends?"

Digger, Caddy, and Dan, beers in hand, had filtered back. They waved, walked over. Star introduced them.

"I was pleased to see you rescue that poor bird," Mary said to Dan and Caddy. "I shooed those kids twice already. They were lucky Walana didn't catch them." She turned to Digger. "I know you," she said. "My cousin, Henry Poai, the fisherman, told me how the two of you went down to Ka Lae, tip of South Point, to look at those petroglyphs carved under the surf, the ones like swimming fish."

She wagged her finger. "Henry also told me how you had a cooler of beer and a pizza, and he brought some, how do you say, Kona Gold?" She winked. "Not that I ever heard the term, being a schoolmarm and raised a good Christian. Henry also told me how you met those German tourist women, convinced them Henry was the chief of Puna and you were the mayor of Hilo—hah!—took them out in Henry's boat, got them high and . . ."

Digger was grinning; Caddy, Star, and Dan were attentive.

Mary stopped in midsentence. "Pardon me," she said. "Luke has arrived. Please, help yourself to the food." She walked toward a small pickup truck trailing dust, weaving its way into the center of the group. In the bed sat an immense man—considerably too large for the cab—in his mid-thirties, unquestionably Hawaiian, with mahogany brown skin, a pockmarked face, and long black hair.

"Get a load of the big boy in the Hawaiian limousine," Star whispered to Caddy. "He must tip the scales at five hundred pounds."

Caddy jabbed him in the ribs with her elbow, hard. "Not funny," she said. "I'll bet the poor man can barely walk. It was thoughtful of them to bring him."

One man lowered the tailgate; three others helped the big man down from the truck bed. He stood, leaned on a thick wooden cane hand-carved with vines and flowers. Barefoot, he wore dusty black trousers and a tent-sized T-shirt. Several people stepped forward to touch his hand, mouth greetings. A young woman hung a thick yellow and green lei around his neck. Children tugged at his trousers, ran fingers over his walking stick. He ruffled their hair, patted them on the cheeks.

The big man waddled to a large stump, still rooted, sculpted into a chair, its back carved into floral and geometric bas-reliefs. Children crowded his feet; adults settled onto the grass, pulled up lawn chairs, or stood around him in twos and threes.

Mary Thompson gestured to Star's party. Come on, hurry. She held a grassy spot clear.

"Look," Star said to Caddy. "On the back porch, the woman in red, in the shadows. That's *her*. Walana." He whispered, as if Walana could hear him.

Walana saw him, nodded, but remained on the porch, unsmiling. An aura of electric white hair rimmed her large dark head.

"Best seats in the house," said Mary, patting the ground. Conversations dwindled to whispers. "Luke," Mary explained in a low voice, "is a *haku mele,* chant master, and *ha'i mo'olelo,* storyteller. We're very fortunate to have him with us today." She took Star's chin between her forefinger and thumb and shook it. "You listen, young man. And behave yourself."

Luke placed a hand on the edge of the stump, the other around his walking stick, and struggled to his feet. He closed his eyes, took a long, deep breath, paused for at least thirty seconds, long enough for his audience to settle in, get the feel of the place: the sun, the sky, the swish of the breeze soughing through the grass and trees. A car whooshed by on the highway. Near the edge of the woods, two irreverent dogs wrestled over a bone. Above, an *'apapane* twittered.

Then he opened his mouth and chanted, in Hawaiian. Rhythmic consonant-vowel and vowel-vowel syllables rolled from his lips, chilling, mesmerizing, directed, it seemed, not at the people around him but to *'aumakua,* ancestral spirits, or *akua,* gods, listening from the cool shadows of the fringing forest.

Star shut his eyes, felt the hairs at the back of his neck rise.

The chant stopped. Luke sat, regained his breath. *"Mai Kahiki ka wahine, 'o Pele . . ."*

"It's the story of Pele," whispered Mary, "how she originated in the ancestral homeland, Kahiki. How she came to Hawai'i."

Luke continued in baritone Hawaiian for ten or fifteen seconds, then shifted to English, speaking now not to gods, not to spirits, but to the people at his feet. Like all master storytellers, he drew them in, commanded their attention by pitch, pace, and body language, subtle one moment, theatrical the next. When he paused, closed his eyes, lowered his voice, they leaned forward; when he shouted, waved his massive arms, they jerked back. He played them like hooked fish.

". . . and so, now deep in her volcano home, Pele dreamed. In a spirit journey she dreamt to the west, to the green isle of Kaua'i, drawn by the irresistible music of a handsome young chief, Lohi'au. They became lovers, Pele in her spirit body, Lohi'au in the flesh. . . ."

Pele awoke, Luke explained, determined to have Lohi'au at her side. Unable to leave her volcano home, she called for a messenger to fetch the young chief. Aware of Pele's unpredictable furies, the uncertainties and dangers of such a mission, no one dared accept, until Pele's little sister Hi'iaka stepped forward. While reluctant to leave her sacred forests of *'ohi'a lehua,* where she danced with a beautiful companion, Hopoe, Hi'iaka agreed to undertake the journey—on condition that Pele respect the trees in her absence.

Luke's deep voice rose an octave, became Pele's at her most saccharine: " 'Of course, little sister,' said Pele, 'your trees will be safe with me, but you must also promise to resist the charms of handsome Lohi'au.' "

Hi'iaka journeyed to Kaua'i, battled dragons, only to find Lohi'au dead, heartbroken that Pele had left him. Hi'iaka battled for Lohi'au's ghost, recovered it, and magically brought the young chief to life. She carried him to the island of Hawai'i in an odyssey full of peril, teeming with monsters. Hi'iaka and Lohi'au fell in love—yet Hi'iaka honored her vow, kept her distance from the chief.

Time had passed, far more than the forty days Pele had allowed for their return. No Hi'iaka, no Lohi'au. Pele fumed, sparked, rocked the ground with earthquakes, and in a fit of temper, not only destroyed Hi'iaka's treasured *'ohi'a lehua* trees, but consumed Hi'iaka's companion, Hopoe, as well.

When faithful Hi'iaka finally arrived, Lohi'au by her side, at the rim of Kilauea, Pele's volcano home, and saw her *'ohi'a* groves devastated, her friend Hopoe dead—she placed leis around Lohi'au's neck and embraced him in full sight of Pele.

Furious, Pele spouted fire, surrounded the pair with a flood of hot lava. Divine, Hi'iaka survived, but the lava incinerated Lohi'au, turned him to stone.

Hi'iaka attacked Pele, nearly vanquished her before their fearful sisters intervened.

"Meanwhile, Lohi'au's ghost departed the islands, flew across the great southern sea toward ancestral Kahiki. A voyaging brother of Pele, however, ashamed of Pele's rash anger, caught the spirit, returned home and restored charred Lohi'au to life. Lohi'au joined his love Hi'iaka, and they moved to green Kaua'i, the gentle land of sunsets, and there lived happily the rest of Lohi'au's mortal days."

"Beautiful," said Caddy, and dabbed an eye.

Star swiped his own eyes, said, "Don't mess with volcano women, that's the moral."

"What a storyteller," said Digger.

"This Luke's gonna make a hell of a feature for *Pacific Rainbow,*" said Dan.

"So, you were impressed?" said a deep, disturbingly familiar voice near Star's ear. A heavy hand squeezed his shoulder, snatched at his soul.

He whipped around. Walana! Blocking the sky with her mountainous bulk.

"Please," she said to the others, eyes on Star. "Why don't the four of you come up to the house? Join me for some *mamaki* tea?"

Dan, Digger, and Caddy walked abreast of her, chatting, Star lagged behind, sweating already, worrying about hexes and spells, wondering what it would be like to hop on all fours, eat bugs.

From the porch eaves, swaying in the breeze, hung bundles of grass, dried leaves, feathers, bits of wire and glass, bound with string, fishing line, and faded strips of bark cloth. Star ducked to avoid touching them.

Walana motioned to a rusting iron porch swing and two low, worn wooden benches. "Have a seat," she said to Caddy, Dan, and Digger. "Enjoy the shade. Star can help me with the tea inside. Star?" She crooked a finger for him to follow.

Like the spider to the fly, he thought, and froze. He looked to Caddy, Digger, and Dan for support. They sat, smiled at him like simpletons.

Walana took him by the wrist, led him in.

The screen door banged shut. Walana closed the red wooden door, too, and shuffled across the darkened room. Her dog, the white German shepherd, lay in one dim corner.

I can barely see, he thought. Hell to pay if I trip over something and break it. He made out a bare wooden floor and shiny, hazy, wrapped forms, looking like—jeez—gigantic insect carcasses sheathed in spider's silk.

But as his eyes grew accustomed to the low light, he realized the mysterious forms were, in fact, a sofa and two armchairs wrapped in clear plastic slipcovers. Place is still creepy, he decided. One big room except for a bathroom in the corner. I wonder where she sleeps? On the couch, on that plastic? On the floor? Maybe she hangs upside down from the rafters. Or doesn't sleep at all.

"I sleep on the lanai," Walana said, "—the porch. I have a bed on the west side. It's cooler out there." She motioned to the dining corner of the large room and a chrome and vinyl chair mended with duct tape, tucked under a worn kitchenette table. "Please," she said. "Sit."

He sat, noticed jars, of, what, herbs? Bits of forest stuff. Bowls of *kukui* nuts, white coral, surf-rounded lava rock, a bleached sea turtle shell. Man, he thought, if I see a skull, I'm outta here. Moss, flower petals, colored earth, red- and black-stained *kapa* bark cloth. No skulls.

Walana heated water. "You're still having the dream?" she asked. "Where the monsters chase you? *Kaimoni* gonna get you, huh?"

"My dream about the giant clam? How do you know that? Did Dan tell . . ."

Walana raised a palm, waved it back and forth as if to erase the thought from his mind. "You and me," she said, "got a sticky string between us—fates joined, huh? I know the dream, but you, boy, you got it wrong." She smiled. "A giant clam? I like that. Very good!" She clapped her hands and laughed again, a deep rumble. "No, no. This is Kapo's *kohe* you see, calling you, drawing you to it.

"Let me tell you this: When you truly see it, when it calls? Resist. Kapo and her *kohe* have strong mana. They eat you up, you not careful."

He nodded, unsure what to say.

"Don't worry," she said. "I have faith in you."

She patted his knee, then popped the lids of two tins of chocolate chip macadamia nut cookies with a long, horny thumbnail and arranged them on a heavy Fiestaware plate. "You heard Luke today, felt his power, the force of Tutu Pele in your own bones, yes? You're on *her* island now. Pele's up there, waiting." She tipped her head to the side, up-mountain. "This is more than *he'e nalu*—surfing—no mere adventure you're on. You know that, boy? Plenty danger ahead. You must do the right thing, watch your step. Trust your heart, hear?"

Star sat, uncomfortable, unsure what to say. Danger? Did she know about Melissa? About Mr. Lucky being kidnapped? About the bird feather?

"Ah, yes, the bird," said Walana. "The *'o'o*. If this poor thing still exists, it's like my nene, our wonderful mountain goose. Here on the island all that time, happy, innocent, then threatened by intruders. The birds, the *kohe,* all in danger. You got to save 'em."

"Me? Jeez. Why me? How?"

She shrugged. "Makes no sense to me either. A silly haole boy like you, *le'ale'a* all the time." She laughed. "Who'd have guessed? You, having the big dreams." The smile dropped from her face. "You the one, *Hoku-li'ili'i*." She walked from the stove toward him.

He watched her thick arms rise, reach for his neck. Holy moly, he thought, she's going to strangle me. Sacrifice me. Jeez. Right here in her kitchen. She'll tell them I fell or something. Run! Now. But he couldn't move.

Walana rested her hands on his shoulders. "What's this? I believe you're trembling. Look me in the eyes. Don't be afraid of me, boy, I'm here to help. Don't you understand that by now?"

"I know," he said. "You're going with us into the Pali-uli."

"Me? No, no. I'm staying here, will pray for you. I'm sending my right hand. Lani. My messenger. You know Lani. Papa's youngest? Here." She pressed a hand-drawn map in his hand. "Soon as you leave here, you pick up Lani. She's waiting for you at the Mauna Loa Nene Preserve. Lani knows her way around the backcountry."

She set the teapot, a jar of lehua honey, plastic spoons, paper napkins, and five unmatched ceramic mugs on a black tray with a decal hula dancer at each corner. "Now," she said, "you can help me serve the tea and cookies to your friends." She handed him the large plate, carried the tray herself. "One more thing. A little secret."

Star's fingers tightened on the china.

"No need to mention the cookies are store-bought, hmmm?"

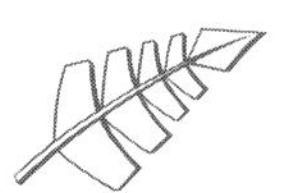

Digger shouted at Dan from the backseat, "You drive like a maniac—serve you right when one of us throws up." The car lurched. "Oof! The way we stuffed ourselves at Volcano House, it won't be pretty, either."

Bumping over rough forestry roads for nearly an hour hadn't done much for their humor.

Dan ignored the threat, hunched over the wheel, whipped it to the left.

"Right," said Star, navigator. "Right. I told you to turn *right*."

"Yes," said Dan, "you did. And that's why I turned left. You want to know why? Because you couldn't read a map to save your life. That's why."

"The reason I said right," said Star, "was because I *wanted* you to turn left. Left was right. So you did the right thing." He patted Dan's head.

"With Abbott and Costello up there," said Digger, "we'll be lucky if we ever find the place."

Caddy jammed her palm to the roof to save her head from another rap. When the car settled, she said, for about the hundredth time, "I loved Big Luke."

"Maybe Walana can fix you up with him," Star said over his shoulder.

"He spun a great tale, all right," Dan said, then, "Ugh!" as the car bottomed out.

"Not just a tale," said Digger. "The Pele myth is a Hawaiian epic. Touches the soul of the islands. Think of our visiting Walana's house as a rite of passage, warriors girding for spiritual battle and all that. Be sure, she honored us with the invitation. Yikes! Slow down. Umpff!" He rolled into Caddy's chest.

"Do that again," said Caddy, "and you get an elbow in the bread-basket."

Digger righted himself and grinned. "It'll be well worth it, too." The road leveled out, and he looked through the window at the forest swishing by. "Walana, you know, is reputed to be a woman of big mana, a kahuna." He craned his neck to look at the rising horizon off to their right, the crest of Mauna Loa. "The farther you get from the city," he said, almost to himself, "the easier it is to imagine the old ways."

"I know she's praying for us back there," said Star, "or whatever she does, but she still spooks the hell out of me."

"She makes a hell of a chocolate chip macadamia nut cookie, I'll tell you that," said Dan. "I should have gotten the recipe for Angela."

"Oh," said Caddy. "I forgot to tell you. This is great. On the way up from Hilo, at Volcano House, when I visited the ladies' room before dessert? Guess who I saw in the hallway?"

"Can't wait for this one," said Star. "Elvis Presley's ghost, singing 'Blue Hawaii'?"

"Colonel Sanders! The fried-chicken man."

"Caddy," said Dan, "I'm pretty sure Colonel Sanders has gone on to greener pastures."

"I don't know where he is now, but I saw him there at dinner."

"What I meant," said Dan, "is that the Colonel is deceased."

"You're wrong there," she said. "I stood no further from him than you are to me now—it was the Colonel all right. You know, you see pictures so many times of someone famous, when you see them in the flesh, you don't know what to say."

"So, what *did* you say?" asked Star.

"I just looked at him, kind of dumbfounded—there I was, a Ph.D., acting like a silly freshman. I blurted out, 'I really like fried chicken!' Pretty lame, I know. He spoke to me—invited me to his room to read Bible stories. Cute, huh? Then he said I was lucky to be there early for dinner, because at noon they'd run out of fried chicken. Isn't that funny? To run out of chicken with the Colonel as a guest? Colonel Sanders. Imagine."

The car and everyone's teeth rattled. "That was the third cattle guard," Star said. "Entrance should be around the next bend."

"With your directions, we may wind up back in Hilo," said Dan.

"What do you know?" said Caddy. "Mauna Loa Nene Reserve."

"It's after six. They work late," said Digger.

A navy pickup and a white sedan, both with federal stickers, and a Jeep Cherokee stood in front of the modest frame building. Behind it, a confusing array of fences and enclosures ran for a hundred yards.

Car doors slammed, and they walked toward the office. Fifty feet away, four men in dark slacks and white short-sleeved shirts trailed a young Hawaiian woman in a khaki blouse and hiking shorts, and enough camping paraphernalia hanging from a wide belt at her waist to outfit a covey of Cub Scouts.

Star's eyes met hers. He stopped in midstride, nailed to the ground by her looks—a Gauguin princess, solid, muscular, no more than five foot five, with black waist-length hair, large, wide-spaced dark eyes, and soft Hawaiian features. He jumped to catch up with Caddy, Digger, and Dan, four paces ahead, and tripped over his own feet. Great. The Hawaiian girl saw him stumble. He felt his face burn. He grinned, raised his palms—How in the world did that happen?—and winked.

She not only winked back, but ran toward him. What? He looked over his shoulder to see who was behind him. Bushes. She flew through a gate, jumped onto his chest from three feet away, nearly knocking him over. Arms around his neck, she gripped his hair with one hand, curled the other around his head, and pulled it down to plant a wet kiss on his mouth.

"Well!" said Caddy.

"Indeed," said Dan.

"My kind of welcome," said Digger.

"I'm sorry," the girl said, giggling, "but I've wanted to do that since I was thirteen years old. You do recognize me, don't you, Star?"

"Lani?" He stood back, wiped his mouth with the back of his hand, looked her over head to toe. "Can't be. Last time I saw you . . ."

"I know. *Wiwi,* like a stick of bamboo." She turned to Caddy, Dan, Digger. "I'm Lani Kanikele." She shook their hands with a wrestler's grip. "Walana told me all about you. Wait here—let me say good-bye to our other guests, Department of the Interior types—and I'll give you a quick tour." She ran back to the four men, flashed a smile, and led them to the lodge. Five minutes later, she came through the front door.

"Turned 'em over to the boss. I give the warm touch, he feeds them numbers. I told them Star was my brother, by the way. Give them something to think about on the flight home. C'mon." She moved fast, walked behind the building, opened a gate, talking all the way. "It's late. Soon as I show you around, we'll take off. I'll want to go over your camping gear first. Got all my stuff in my Cherokee. If you need anything else, I'll try to rustle it up. Leave your car, we'll take mine."

Star let the others move ahead, shifting his eyes from Lani to Caddy and back. Lani had a swimmer's body, he decided, softly contoured, but with lots of muscle. Under the librarian exterior, Caddy was the track type, slender, taller, wiry. Caddy had a narrow nose, well-defined cheekbones, while Lani's face was rounder, with plump Polynesian lips. Hmmm.

Hold it. Caddy's in Hawai'i for one thing: to find her sister's murderer. She's a Ph.D., all business. And Lani is Walana's protégée, Papa's daughter.

Whew! Traveling, he remembered, always made him horny.

". . . really cute, aren't they, Star?" from Caddy.

He jumped. "What?"

"The baby geese. Don't you see them?" She took his wrist and pointed his hand to a grass hillock forty feet away. A large goose nudged three goslings with its bill. The bird, black across the top of its head, with yellow buff on the cheeks, had small radial stripes streaking its chin and lower neck.

Caddy held on to the arm.

"Wonderful, wonderful," said Dan, zapping the goose family with a motorized Nikon and telezoom.

"That mama's an ex-patient," said Lani. "Hit by a car—can't fly, but she's safe here. Nene are tame, evolved without fear of predators. They mate for life. Real sweethearts—and that's their problem. They're too trusting. Other Hawaiian birds didn't last long with humans on the scene. We're doing our best for these guys.

"They were hunted nearly to extinction, first by our people—there were still around twenty-five thousand nene when Captain Cook arrived—then by the Europeans. You can imagine what firearms did to friendly birds."

She cocked an eyebrow at Caddy, who tightened her grip on Star's arm. Lani frowned. "By the 1950s, there were fewer than thirty wild nene. Today, maybe four hundred. It's amazing there are any left. Feral cats attack the young. Mongooses eat their eggs. Then there are rats and grazing goats and, especially, pigs. Pigs root, rip up the boles of tree ferns for the starchy interior, then the rotting trunks gather water, provide a breeding ground for avian malaria."

"Pigs," she spit the word out, "are the reason for the cattle guards and fences you passed on the road—they're not to contain geese, but to keep pigs out. We wage a constant war against pigs."

She repeated the foul word. "Pigs." In one sudden, continuous, sinuous move, she crouched, unsheathed a fifteen-inch Bowie knife hanging from her belt, wheeled, and slashed the air with it no more than eighteen inches from Caddy's nose. Caddy stumbled into Star's chest. Digger and Dan bumped shoulders.

"Didn't mean to frighten you." With a wicked grin, Lani slipped the knife into its sheath, smooth as a samurai, and continued walking. "They call me Lani the pig sticker," she said over her shoulder.

"You mean you've actually killed pigs with that knife?" asked a shaken Caddy.

"Dogs corner them, I jump on their backs, slit their throats."

Dan and Digger exchanged looks.

Jeez.

Chins lifted to a faint beeping high overhead. A tiny speck grew into a goose, circling widely, then closer and lower. Half a minute later, it sluiced through tall grass for a landing twenty feet away and waddled toward them. *Honk, honk.*

"Hi, baby," said Lani. "This is Gertrude, folks. Some bastard shot her last year. But you're fine now, aren't you, sweetie? The nene is the Hawaiian state bird—absolutely no hunting permitted—but there are always crazies out there." Lani fingered the hilt of her knife. "See the way the feathers grew in white on her right wing? No mistaking Gertrude. And she's real vocal. Honks for attention. We fixed her up and sent her on her way, but she likes us so much, she keeps coming back."

Gertrude walked toward Star. *Honk.*

"I think she wants me to pet her." He looked to Lani for permission.

"Go ahead," she said.

He walked slowly toward the bird, palm out. Gertrude bobbed from one leg to the other, anxious, facing him, making gurgling sounds. She waited until he was five feet away, raised her wings, wheeled 180 degrees, ran ten feet fast, and turned to face him. *Honk.* Star edged toward her again. He got to within six feet of her and she danced away. *Honk, honk*. Once more. The fourth time, he gave up.

Click, whirr, click, whirr, click, whirr, from Dan and his Nikon. He rolled from his belly to his knees, reloaded.

Lani laughed. "It's Gertrude's little game. She'd keep it up all afternoon. We don't like to hand feed them, but I did this for the Interior suits to give them a close look. . . ." Lani pulled a handful of food from a pocket. "Purina Nene Chow." She winked. "Gertrude's favorite." Lani made a low clucking sound, held her hand out. Gertrude flapped her wings and bobbled to her, ate the pellets from her hand.

"Perfect, perfect," said Dan. "Wait, give her more. I need a vertical."

"Check her feet," Lani said. "Reduced webbing. Nene hang out on rugged *a'a* lava instead of water."

"Close-up. Yes. Yes." Dan focused, zoomed.

"You have enough yet? I counted somewhere around fifty frames." At Dan's nod, Lani clapped her hands. "Gertrude, GO!"

Gertrude ran, flapped her wings, fluffed air with each step. Twenty feet away, her feet left the ground and she went airborne. *Honk, honk,* from two hundred feet up, still rising.

Dan switched to a 500mm mirror telephoto, *click, whirr, click, whirr*. "These'll all be fuzzy," he mumbled. "Damn lens is a bastard to focus."

"With luck you may get another chance in the Pali-uli," Lani said. She glanced at her watch, a man's stainless diving model. "Speaking of which, it's late. If we're going to get anywhere near the Pali-uli and make camp by nightfall, we'd better move out. We'll camp at the eastern side at the top, climb down tomorrow morning. See what the five of us can turn up."

Caddy, Dan, and Digger walked to the car. Star lingered. Lani caught his eye and said to the group, "I *am* anxious to check out that equipment of yours."

She cast an oh-so-brief glance at Star's crotch, and chuckled.

45

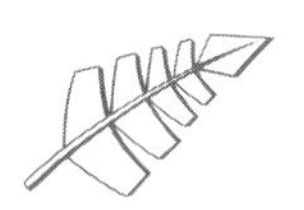

It does look like a snake," Bernie said. "The goddamned king of all blacksnakes."

A ribbon of lava ran down the mountain. At the bottom, it bulged, then split into an upside-down Y, like the forked tips of a snake's tongue, each prong less than a hundred feet wide. It was actually wider toward the top; perspective created the illusion of uniform width as the flow twisted downslope, scaly black here, silvery gray there, eventually to disappear in the clouds shrouding the summit of its mother, Mauna Loa.

"I thought lava was red," Bernie said. "Or yellow, or orange."

"That's right, sir," said Frank, HydraCorp construction chief, "when it's fresh. What you see is crust, cooled down, gone black. Take my word for it, it's hot as hell inside. When it's on the move, it looks like molten iron."

"So if it's black, it's stopped flowing? Just in time. Can't be more than quarter mile above our access road."

Frank cast an uneasy glance up-mountain. "The geologist we hired flew over the vent on the southwest rift—he tells us it may have stopped at the top. The lava followed the 1950 track for a while, then took a new path, way up there." He pointed. "You can see the stream's gotten thinner farther down the mountain—less lava and the slope's steeper. Is it over? We thought so yesterday when it was a thousand feet above where it is now. Then—wham! Who knows why?—it let loose again, almost caught one of my men kicking at it. You think it's still, see, but it's sneaky, always shifting, creeping. It talks, too, when you're close to it. Makes sounds like running fingernails down a blackboard."

"Look at the bastard," said Bernie. "Damned snake, flicking its tongue at us. Can't you throw a dam around it, or maybe blow the hell out of it?"

"Curious story," said D. L. "In 1935, again in '42, the U.S. of A. Army got their best minds together, decided to bomb a flow headed hot and fast for Hilo. Fun for the flyboys, I imagine, but a waste of ordnance. The lava kept coming, then stopped on its own accord before it reached the city. Quite the tactical challenge—see, you can't kill lava."

"That's right," said Frank. "It's like those horror movies where the slime monster won't die. Plus, if you puncture that black skin, the red stuff pours out, even if the eruption's finished at the top. It's liquid, see? All it wants to do is flow down. And down is where we're at. Sometimes it creeps like a snail, but when it wants to, it can outrun a man, even a Jeep. I've got a lookout with an air horn. You hear that sound, you'd better run your ass off—no disrespect, sir, but I'm afraid it'll be every man for himself."

Frank cast a wary look upslope. "Far as a dam goes, we're ahead of you. We sent earthmovers up there, built a thirty-foot-high berm below the bottom of the flow three days ago. When the lava got pissed off yesterday, decided to move again, it ran into our dam and pooled behind it—formed the snake's fat head there—then spilled over, split by a ridge into that Y."

Bernie searched desperately for a golden lining. "Except for the paving, the road to the valley looks nearly finished. You're ahead of schedule, right?"

"Yessir, you bet," said Frank. "The switchbacks into the valley are cut. We're nearly ready to move the big dozers down, start clearing the forest—although for the moment, I'd feel safer taking the men and equipment back to the wind farm road. That's on a ridge, two miles away, so there's no threat from the lava. And Paradise Valley depends on our finishing that road first, so there's really no loss of time if we work there for a while."

"That's a good idea, sir," D. L. said to Bernie with a wink. He lowered his voice. "We don't need everyone over here while we reconnoiter, if you know what I mean."

Bernie winked back. "Sure, Frank. Have your men work on the main road for a few days."

Frank, visibly relieved, left to issue the retreat orders.

"What are your boys doing over there, D. L.?" Bernie asked.

"Chucking rocks at each other at the moment," said D. L. "They got the gear loaded already. They'll be carrying most of the weight, so they may as well have fun before we leave."

"I assume you've got food, canteens, sleeping bags, toilet paper—all that camping stuff."

"Survival's my business, sir. I also liberated a jacket, a hat, and some long pants from one of the road crew for you to wear—if you're really going with us. Between the sun and the brush, your shorts and that golf shirt won't give you much protection."

"I brought extra socks and underwear, a pair of tennis shoes, toothbrush, deodorant, plenty of sunblock."

"With that fair skin of yours, you'll need it. Sir—" D. L. removed his fatigue cap, screwed up his face. "It's time you and me had a talk. I told you at the plane your coming was a bad idea. We dumped the preacher, so he's no longer a problem, but this could get awkward. Dangerous."

"What? Poison ivy? Poisonous snakes? We're going to be above the valley, you said, no climbing. Surely those people pose no threat. They're on our land, after all."

"Different kind of danger. Look, there's no poisonous snakes up here—no snakes in Hawai'i, no poison ivy." D. L. frowned, slapped the cap against his thigh. "The real danger is: you'll screw up the mission. Sorry to be so blunt, but in Honolulu, you're the boss. As it should be. But in the bush? D. L. McWhorter is lord and master." He slapped his leg again. "No one's gonna get in the way of this project and my completion bonus. You wanna come along, those are the terms. Nonnegotiable, as you say to your business cronies."

"D. L., my ass is on the line. Every penny I have is invested in

Paradise Valley. The last thing I want is to stand in your way. Don't ask me to twiddle my thumbs away from the action, wondering whether these thorns are going to hold us up. I don't know anything about woods stuff like you. So, sure, you're the boss. I swear I won't slow you down." Bernie stuck out a small pink hand. "Deal?"

D. L. looked at the pudgy freckled fingers, the shiny manicured nails, the delicate gold watch with the diamonds for numbers, and already regretted his offer to take the man. I ought to wring your lily-white neck, he thought. But what he said was, "Very well, sir. Long as it's on my terms. Deal."

He squeezed the tiny hand enough to make Bernie's eyes water, to let him know who was boss from here on in. Then he put two fingers in his mouth and whistled. "Put down your projectiles, boys," he yelled, "and rustle those packs up here. Time to move out."

It wasn't that long a hike, less than two miles as the nene flies, three by foot, but the vegetation and terrain were rugged. Two-thirds of the way, despite heroic efforts to keep up, Bernie's short legs gave out. Ray Don had to carry him the final stretch piggyback. Even with Bernie clinging to his neck, Ray Don carried a fully packed duffel bag strapped over his shoulder. Bobby Lee carried another, plus both twins' backpacks.

They made camp well before nightfall. D. L. chose a site at the head of the valley, at the top of a four-hundred-foot cliff spouting three waterfalls. Scanning the clear sky, he declared the tents could wait for the next day.

Bernie had hoped for the fireside ghost stories of his youth, but the day had been long and conversation grew thin. Bernie had little interest in classical music or firearms, D. L. knew nothing of finance or golf, and the twins lived in a small, hard world of their own.

Ray Don and Bobby Lee toasted fried chicken on sticks over the fire—they had a pillowcase full of it, courtesy of the Volcano House buffet—while Bernie and D. L. picked silently at army field rations.

The twins unpacked surveillance equipment, a spotting scope on a tripod and powerful navy binoculars, and set them alongside two boxes of hand grenades, brought to destroy whatever the thorns were seeking, should it materialize. Bernie watched D. L. remove a long fiberglass case from one of the duffel bags. He hoped fervently for a musical instrument, but suspected contents more sinister.

"That's right," confirmed D. L., reading his mind. "It's a rifle. For protection. So are these." He hefted two large automatic pistols with garish snakes on the handles. "One for me, one for Bobby Lee. Ray Don's got to make do with his huntin' knife."

D. L. shot the twin a cold stare, then turned to Bernie. "See, there's pigs up here that'll go straight for your balls if they get hold of you. And grizzly bears that'll take your head off, too. The construction crew's seen their big-assed footprints all over."

D. L. and the twins laughed at that. They laughed again when Bernie asked if pigs or grizzly bears came out at night. They laughed even harder at his Woody the Woodpecker boxer shorts when he disrobed.

Driven more by fear than fellowship, Bernie set his sleeping bag between D. L. and the twins. He shut his eyes tight. How could they be so fearless? He wriggled and oonched for hours, staring at stars he never knew existed, wishing D. L. had mentioned wild animals earlier in the day, knowing full well, of course, he'd have come anyway, driven by the need to know if the last impediment to Paradise Valley, those damnable thorns, would have their way and ruin his life.

46

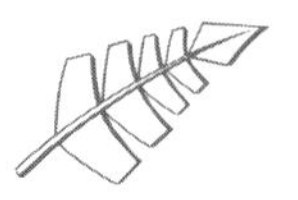

"Four-wheeling's better than sex." Lani pumped the accelerator to jump a fallen log.

"My God," said Dan.

"Forgive me, Dan, for whatever I said about your driving." Digger bounced off the seat onto the floor.

"Urm da mupft . . ."

"Star can't talk," Caddy said. "I think he bit off the tip of his tongue."

Ten minutes later, the Cherokee lurched to a stop. "That's as far as rubber'll take us," said Lani. "End of the road."

"You mean we've been on a road?" Caddy asked.

"You bet. They ran it years ago to upgrade the pig fence around the valley." Lani opened the door, leapt to the ground. "The only way I'd drive off-road out here would be with someone walking in front to check for crevasses. You roll into one of those, or drop into a lava tube cave, it's aloha to you, my friend, good-bye, good-bye."

The group disembarked, stretched, checked for cuts and bruises.

For the next half hour, it was hard breathing, tromping boots, and swishing brush. The column halted at a fallen tree, tipped to thirty degrees and leaning over an old but sturdy fence. To shouts of

"Yes you can" and "No way" and "Push his butt," they tightroped up the trunk and dropped onto the far side.

Minutes before sunset, they reached the valley's eastern rim and made camp. At their backs, the sky grew bluer than lapis, while ahead, it glowed an incandescent orange. Packs slid to the ground. Shoulder to shoulder, silent, they watched the sun drop to the far horizon. Below, impenetrable shadow cloaked their destination, the Pali-uli.

"I imagine," said Caddy later, around the campfire, "that Kapo's *kohe* is a natural formation in *pahoehoe* lava."

Lani laughed. "Only stone, you think? Hah!"

Ph.D. voice: "As a geologist, that's my considered opinion. *Pahoehoe*—frozen syrup, puddles of melted stone."

"Wouldn't matter. Tutu Pele *makes pahoehoe*."

Digger raised a palm. "Now, now. You two aren't going to settle this by arguing. The composition is irrelevant to its significance, anyway. Stone or whatever, recognizing it shouldn't be a problem. The *kohe* is big—it should jump out at you."

"If a twelve-foot vagina jumps out at me, they'll hear me back in Hilo," said Star.

Caddy punched him on the arm. He punched her back, and they began to arm-wrestle.

"Listen up," said Lani. "Kapo's *kohe* isn't funny. It's *kapu,* hallowed ground, big *mana*, dangerous. If you do find it, stay clear. Call *me*." She tapped her chest. "You seem more concerned with where the *kohe* is and what it's made of than what it means. This is a sacred shrine. We're here to guarantee its protection for the Hawaiian people."

"And for science," added Digger. "For posterity."

"Yes," said Caddy, "and to save the bird, and . . ." Her voice cracked. She cleared her throat, pointed at each of them. "We're here because the site and the bird and this valley are connected with my sister's death. *I* want Melissa's murderer."

Dan touched Caddy's shoulder. "Different facets of the same problem," he said. "We're a team, right?"

Star motioned thumbs up, Digger and Lani nodded. Gradually,

they drifted into small talk. Star told stories about the canine wonder, Mr. Lucky. How Mr. Lucky chewed up the arm of the burglar and saved Star's life, the time his neighbor's championship poodle Juliette gave birth to an unexpected litter of border collies, and how he taught Mr. Lucky to snatch loose bikini tops from sunbathing girls at Ala Moana Park.

Eventually storied out, Star lay on his back in the flickering shadows, head against his pack, while the others talked on. Lani's voice jolted him awake.

"Do I *what?*" she said to Dan.

"I merely asked," he said, "if you really believe in things like *kapu,* mana, and the old Hawaiian religion? I'm Catholic myself. Not that I don't respect tradition, but Pele as anything more than a legendary figure? A god? I'm sorry, dear, that's sacrilege."

"Dear?"

"Meant nothing by it," said Dan. "Point I was trying to make is—"

"The point you made is that Christianity is a patriarchy. God's a man, right? Pele, a goddess, with a small *g.* Women in their place, huh?"

"Actually," said Digger, "old Hawai'i had many *kapu* restricting women's activities—"

"You keep out of it."

Digger shut up.

"Father knows best," Dan said with a sly smile.

Star rolled his eyes, waited for the lightning.

Lani stomped her foot. "I was raised a Christian like all my people," she said. "I know the drill. You men are supposed to be the decision makers, right? Women stay at home, pop out the babies. Let me ask you something. The Bible is thousands of years old. How do you know any of that stuff happened at all?"

"I have my faith. . . ."

"Faith, huh? You believe in oceans parting? Virgin birth? Walking on water? Impressed by burning bushes, are you? Welcome to Hawai'i."

Lani slid her knife from its sheath, pointed the blade at Dan's large nose. "Palestine is halfway around the world, mister, but Pele is *here, now,* under our feet. She's alive—in Kilauea, Mauna Loa—

Hawai'i is her island. If you don't believe in Pele, you damned well better respect her, or she'll fry your ass."

Buddha-like, Dan sat calmly, hands folded over his small pot-belly, smiling. "False gods . . ."

"False, huh?"

She's like Pele herself, thought Star, full of fire. Dangerous. A hot ticket. Wonder what she'd be like to . . . Whoa. Walana's kahuna-in-training? Papa's daughter? Back off. He pinched himself.

Eventually the campfire died and conversation with it. With clear skies above, no one pitched tents. They unrolled sleeping bags, arranged them around the fire.

Bone-tired, Star fell asleep within seconds, but tossed fitfully. Sometime during the night, he began swimming. Down, deeper, hotter, with demons at the edge of his field of vision, clawing at him, the familiar giant clam his objective, dead ahead. He swam deeper, reached into it. The clam shifted shape, became Walana. She wrapped mammoth thighs around him, squeezed. . . .

He awoke screaming.

"What the hell?" from Digger.

"Holy Mother of . . . ," from Dan.

Caddy held Star's right arm, Lani gripped his left.

"It was the big dream," explained Lani. "Kapo's *kohe* is nearby."

Star awakened the next morning to the smell of brewing coffee, the dream forgotten. Dawn sunlight burned through trees rimming the valley, speckling the shadows with red confetti.

What's this? He ran a hand through his sleeping bag and retrieved half a handful of tiny, shiny black stones, like seed pearls, some large as raisins, strewn in the bottom and along the edges. No wonder I had trouble sleeping, he thought. He wrestled into his jeans inside the bag. The stones seemed too pretty to pitch, so he slipped them into a pocket.

"Star," Caddy called to him. She and the others stood on a ledge overlooking the Pali-uli. To their right, at the valley's origin, a waterfall plumed from a hole near the top of the perimeter cliff. Two others slinked down the nearly vertical face to either side. Below, shrouded in mist and the purple shadows of early morning, thick forest alternated with low, open bush.

"Virgin growth," said Dan. "If the *'o'o* lives, it's down there."

"Like the Lost World," said Digger.

"Walana calls this Pele's valley," said Lani.

"I still can't help wondering if there's any chance of dino—"

A knuckle in the ribs cut him off. "Don't you ever give up?"

"Look," Lani said, pain in her voice. "Through the mist, at the other side." Switchbacks, gouged from the green valley wall, zigzagged to the bottom.

"The construction crew's retreated," said Dan. "Because of the lava, I guess. But they'll be back soon enough, begin clearing the valley."

"Soon enough," Lani repeated.

"Look, higher," said Caddy. "Lava. That smoke is from burning vegetation, so it's still flowing below, although the last report I saw said the eruption had stopped at the vent."

"At the top, *pau,*" said Lani. "Finished."

"A shame," said Dan. "I hoped it would shut them down for a long time."

"Way back," said Lani, "lava threatened Hilo. Princess Ruth Ke'elikolani threw a lock of her hair into the flow, prayed to Tutu Pele, and it stopped. I'm gonna pray to Pele to do it the other way around."

"Fine. You do that," said Caddy. "It can't hurt."

"You watch your sarcasm," Lani said, "or Pele'll burn you up." She turned from Caddy to the others, clapped her hands for attention. "Let's get breakfast under our belts, move out. No time to spare."

Following Walana's directions, she led them to a slippery, overgrown trail near the valley mouth, descending along a deep, eroded crack in the cliff face tracing an ancient fault.

Near the bottom, they stopped to rest. "Shhh," said Dan. "Hear it? Trilling? Sounds like a whistle?" He fumbled for a his binoculars. "There. An *'oma'o*. Hawai'i thrush."

"I see it," said Star. "Brown bird. Doesn't look like much."

"Hawaiian endemic," Dan mumbled, hurt. "You want colorful,

look up there. *'Apapane,* top of that tree." A crimson bird flitted through the branches, making buzzing sounds. "See? They're all over. Other red bird, there, that's an *'i'iwi*. Honeycreepers."

"Not big, but bright," said Star. "Small. Fast."

Lani pointed. "And that tiny bird over there, with the white on it? That's a native flycatcher, *'elepaio*."

"I see it—should say, I saw it," Star said. "They're all so fast. I don't know how you tell 'em apart. The only one I'd know for sure is the nene."

"You'll learn," Lani said. "It won't be long before you pick up the clues—the way they fly, tail length, color, song. Right, Dan?" Dan was scowling, staring into the treetops. "Dan?"

"That's right," he muttered; then, half to himself, "If only we could find a living *'o'o*. If only."

Lani removed her knife, began cleaning her fingernails. "Those highest trees?" She waved the blade at the treetops. "Over eighty feet. They're koa. You'd never see trees like that if there had been cattle grazing here. Nor all those tree ferns, *hapu'u,* twenty to thirty feet high. Those, and the smaller *'ama'u,* are undisturbed—no pigs here either." She slid the knife into its scabbard. "Most of the other high trees, the ones with lighter, grayish green leaves, are *'ohi'a lehua,* like the small ones here."

Caddy reached for one of the feathery red blossoms.

"Wait," Lani said. "Those flowers are sacred to Pele. It's bad luck to pick them on the way in—okay on the way out, though."

Caddy shielded her face from Lani with the palm of her hand and made bug eyes at Star.

"You know why the tree and flower have those names?" Lani asked.

"I'm sure you'll tell us," said Caddy.

Lani ignored her. " 'Ohi'a was a young chief, handsome. He spurned Pele because of his love for a beautiful wahine, Lehua. So Pele burnt 'em up. Later, she felt sorry for what she had done, so she turned 'Ohi'a into a tree." Lani pointed at Dan. "See? You mess with Tutu Pele, if you don't get fried, you'll be growing bark soon enough—all the birds you want, making nests in your branches." She stuck her arms up, wiggled her fingers like leaves. "And Lehua? Pele transformed her into a flower on 'Ohi'a's tree. Now the two are together, forever. *'Ohi'a lehua.*"

"A story with a happy ending," Caddy said. "I wish I felt more confident about bringing Melissa's murderers to justice."

"Have faith," said Dan.

"Faith," Lani said. "We each have our own." She glanced at her watch. "Meanwhile, we're not helping the *kohe,* the bird, or Caddy's sister by sitting on our butts. Let's get a move on."

At the bottom, the air seemed heavier, scented with growth and decay. They hiked toward the waterfalls at the head of the valley, wading through thickets of fern and mixed shrubs. Tree ferns with shaggy red trunks towered over their heads. Higher, trunks of *'ohi'a* and, here and there, koa rose from the understory, along with an occasional fan palm and lower-growing trees such as *'olapa,* with bright yellow-green leaves that fluttered and snapped in the breeze. Small orchids waved on long stems, spidery epiphytes clung to branches, and blankets of tiny ferns, mosses, and liverworts cloaked every trunk.

Birds darted through the treetops, pinpoint silhouettes. Below, small, iridescent green and larger, orange and black butterflies dipped and bounced like flames around their heads.

"Those butterflies?" said Lani. "Found only in Hawai'i. Not just native birds endangered. There's a tiny bat, *'ope'ape'a*. And spiders, crickets, damselflies, snails, lots more. And plants—big trees, shrubs, herbs, vines, grasses, tiny things you'd pass right over without looking."

"It's Eden," said Dan. "And we're interlopers."

"We're guests," said Lani, "here by the grace of Pele. Not like those." She nodded to the far side of the valley, then looked long and hard up the flank of Mauna Loa.

"Walana says the gods sometimes choose humans to do their work," she added. "It's on our shoulders now."

They left the forest and crossed ancient flows of *pahoehoe* and stretches of sparse growth. Twice they huddled under ponchos while rain showers swept the valley, followed within minutes by intense sunshine and rainbows. By noon they had set up camp in a clearing near a pool formed by the largest waterfall, eager to begin the quest for Kapo's *kohe* and the bird that might or might not be.

47

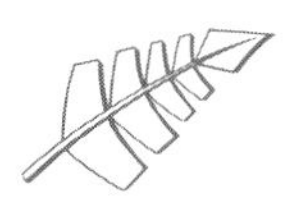

With Artemas's survey tucked under one arm, Digger pointed to an eight-foot boulder riddled with cracks and holes. "Right here—evidence of the valley's mana. The ancients called this a *piko* stone. People would have traveled from far outside the valley to place newborns' umbilical cords in its crevices, to assure a long life in harmony with the gods and the earth. And there"—he pointed to a slight rise in the vegetation by one of the waterfalls—"a *heiau* where hula was performed. In those cliffs"—he waved a hand around the valley walls—"there are no doubt chiefly burials.

"Even in this report, Artemas had become convinced the features he found in this valley were linked, making it a powerful focus of reproductive energy, centered on worship of the Pele clan. But the key, the Kapo site, eluded him. Then, just before I saw him for the last time, the old fellow found the final piece to the puzzle."

"Only to die before revealing it to the world," Caddy said. "How tragic."

"Indeed," said Digger. "So, kiddos—it's up to us."

But by evening, they had checked off nearly a third of the major archaeological features listed in Artemas's survey, and none led to the *kohe*. Caddy's search for suggestive *pahoehoe* was equally fruitless, and although Dan had added two new birds to his life list, neither was an *ʻoʻo*.

After a far less hopeful dinner than breakfast, Lani disappeared into the forest. Star sat in the shadows, missing Mr. Lucky. The other three relaxed around the campfire, talking about birds, dinosaurs, and rocks.

"Pssst. Star, come here." Lani, from beyond the firelight. "I want to show you something."

He followed her into the shadows.

"It's about eighty yards away, by one of the other pools."

"I can't see a thing."

"Take my hand."

Star's face burned with her touch. He could barely see her as they walked between stands of tree ferns, but she smelled great.

"Are you wearing perfume?"

"A lei of maile. Made it after dinner. Look."

They entered a clearing. A half moon was rising to the east over the silhouetted crest of the valley wall.

Lani's long hair shimmered in the yellow moonlight. It was easy to imagine her as Lehua, ʻOhʻa's lover.

"Thought you might like a swim," she said. "The air down here's still warm and the rocks are hot. The pool's nice and deep. I took a dip after dinner." She motioned to her boots and socks by the water. She was barefoot.

Far above, the three waterfalls glistened against the dark rock like silvery tinsel. The rim of the matte black cliff gave way to a field of shimmering stars, magnitudes brighter than he had ever seen in the city. Fifty yards away, falling water hissed.

"Lani, I didn't bring a swimsuit."

"You have a problem with skinny-dipping?" She was already loosening her belt, unbuttoning her blouse. With her back to him, she dropped her blouse, stepped from her shorts, and walked to the water's edge. She faced him, forearm across her breasts, laughed, dropped the arm with a twist of her body, and dove into the pool.

Star stripped and followed. Unsure of the dark water, he jumped feet first. "Yeow! Cold! Cold! Cold!" He flopped back onto shore.

Lani bobbed in the pool, giggled behind him, then followed him onto the rocks. She placed a hand on his shoulder and turned him to face her, stepping back to give him a leisurely once-over.

He squirmed. Fascinated as he had been by the contents of Lani's khaki blouse, now that the objects of his curiosity were at arm's length, jiggling in full view in the moonlight, he had a hard time looking at them. Not looking at them. Looking at them again.

"All those stories I hear," she said. "And what a disappointing little peanut I find. Poor *keiki* didn't like the cold water, huh?"

Star crossed his hands at his crotch.

"Shy? Star, of the many stories, shy? I am studying to become a kahuna, you know. I have the power to make things grow." Her hands touched his.

"Lani," he said, "I don't know . . ."

She giggled, rolled her shoulders, brushed his chest with her nipples, then slid her hands between his legs and squeezed. "You see? Growing already." She laughed, dropped to her knees.

Star shivered, twined his fingers in her hair. The shiver turned to a shudder, and he grabbed a thick hank, lifted her to her feet. They kissed.

Lani's smooch at the nene reserve was unexpected, fun. But this one, fueled by a day and a half of rising speculation and raging hormones—doubled, squared, cubed—was a real head-popper. Round and round they twirled, then sank to the ground, dizzy, to wrestle on the rocks, mouths, arms, hands full of one another.

Five minutes later, Star parted her knees.

Lani laughed. "A missionary man. I should have known. You may not care about your knees, but I take good care of my back. Come with me." She took his hand, led him to a bed of leaves she had prepared earlier, padded beneath with soft tree fern *pulu* fuzz. There, in Lani's little Hawaiian gorilla nest, they made love under the stars. Made love again. And again.

Three times.

Jeez.

"It's Kapo's *kohe,*" Lani explained. "It's close."

Star's lips moved, but too weak to speak, he cradled Lani in his arms, woozy, sated, unsure what to say should he regain the power of speech.

As consciousness and conscience returned, however, he began to worry. What if Dan or Digger or, worse, Caddy had walked over here? How loud were we? How long have we been gone? What if they come looking for us? Holy moly.

Lani untangled herself from his arms, traced his cheek with a fingertip, and kissed him lightly on the forehead. She stretched and slipped back into her clothes. "Give me ten minutes," she said, "then return to camp. I know the way in the dark. Here's my flashlight. Through there, not far, you'll see the campfire."

Alone, Star stood on rubbery legs, swiped his shirt over his hair in a futile attempt to dry it, then realized the shirt was now wet, too. He struggled into his clothes, counted the minutes on his diving watch, rechecked his buttons, his zipper.

He returned to the clearing, expecting, *knowing,* Caddy, Dan, and Digger would be waiting, standing, hands on hips.

But he found all three sitting by the fire discussing the same rocks, dinosaurs, and birds. Lani too, laughing, telling Dan a nene story—didn't even look up when Star sneaked from the shadows like a thief in the night to slip into his sleeping bag.

It'll be all over tomorrow, he decided. She'll hold my hand. Roll moony-eyes at me, give it all away. She'll tell me she loves me, tell *them* she loves me. What will Caddy say about *that?*

No. Lani's tough. She'll try to hide it. But they'll figure it out soon enough from the look on her face. I was her fantasy all these years, and I took advantage of it. Oh, man, I hope she's on the pill. I can't believe I screwed little Lani. Walana's Lani. Papa's daughter. Lani with the big knife.

Jeez.

48

"No reason to sulk, boys."

Ray Don and Bobby Lee lay bellies to earth, watching the thorns in their valley camp. Ray Don had the big set of military binoculars, Bobby Lee, the spotting scope on the tripod. Both twins wore tiny earphones, wires running to cassette players at their belts. They refused to turn around, pretended they didn't know D. L. stood behind them.

"I know you can hear me," he said. "I made you bury your fried chicken because it was smelling up the camp, and on account of the flies. Worse, I was afraid the thorns down there might get wind of it and turn tail on us. You wouldn't want that, would you?"

Bobby Lee kept his head to the scope, but spoke. "What difference would it make? We ain't doin' nothing but watching, anyways. What good did it do to bring the rifle, the grenades, the forty-fives?"

"Patience, my young hostile," said D. L. "The thorns are looking for something hidden. Like they're on an Easter egg hunt. This egg could cause the boss and me trouble. So when they find it, we'll blow it up, see?"

"Who gets to do it?" asked Ray Don behind the binoculars.

"Why, you do, boys. What do you think those grenades are for?"

The twins exchanged glances.

"And what if they don't find it?" asked Bobby Lee. "We been up here for two days now with nothin' to do but eat. And now our fried chicken's gone, and we got to eat from cans like you and the boss. And no TV."

"You're getting to the heart of it, son," said D. L. "Not the food or the TV part, but the 'what if they don't find it?' part. Where *is* that little man?" D. L. looked both ways.

"Doin' his business in the woods," said Ray Don. "Made me scout for bears an' pigs for him first, like he does every time."

"I'm afraid the boss lacks our courage, son. But he does hold the purse strings, so we've got to humor him. At least until this deal is over. Listen boys, gather close." He motioned them over. "No fartin' around, now. I'll let you in on a real secret. Good news."

The twins scooted to his side.

"Keep an eye out for the boss, because this is for your ears only. Hear? Take them damn earphones off, too. I want your full attention."

Headsets disappeared into pockets. Ray Don watched to the left, Bobby Lee to the right.

"Tomorrow is it, the third day. If they don't find this Easter egg, it's good-bye thorns. We do 'em in. And if they do find it, it's good-bye thorns, too. Then we blow up whatever they found. Afterwards, we cart their bodies over to the road, punch a hole in that lava on the hill, and dump them in it. *Zzsssst*. What thorns? So, tell me boys, how's that grab you?"

The brothers smiled. "Who gets to do it?" asked Bobby Lee. "How?" asked Ray Don.

"Be easy to pick 'em off up here with my sniper rifle," said D. L.

"No fun." Ray Don scowled, then grinned. "No need to shoot 'em at all. We could sneak down there with knives, take 'em out one by one."

"I want the women," said Bobby Lee.

"Me too," Ray Don said.

"Tell you what, boys. You've been behaving yourselves real good since we got here. Polite to the boss, no noise, surrendered your fried chicken without a fuss. I want Mr. Lucky for myself, all the friggin' trouble he's caused us, but you can have the rest. Each of you can take out one of the old guys and one of the women."

"Now you're talkin'," said Ray Don. It was in Ray Don's heart, if not his brain, to hug old D. L. on the spot. "Can we do 'em, the women? You know, have fun with 'em first?"

"Boys will be boys, eh? You know I don't approve of that sort of thing, but—just this one time—let's pretend we didn't talk about it. Long as there's a happy ending, I'm satisfied."

"I want the black-haired one," said Bobby Lee.

"I want the brown-haired one," said his brother. "I never done sisters before."

D. L. raised an eyebrow. "You're referring to the Finch woman? The sister? I told you boys not to lay a hand on her before you drowned her. If I . . ."

"No, no, Sarge," said Ray Don, hunching back. "I swear, I didn't touch her that way. I stripped her, like you told me—I may have looked, I mean, shit fire, I ain't no sissy—but I pitched her in the water without doin' anything friendly to her. Cross my heart. What I meant to say was, I never did *in* sisters before."

D. L. squinted at him. "There's a forty-five slug with your name on it if I find you ever disobey me, boy." Then he patted Ray Don on the head. "I saw the police report, son. I know you behaved yourself with the Finch woman, just drowned her neat like I told you. So it's settled. You can divvy the ladies up however you want. Tomorrow's the day."

"Hello there," from the bushes, nervous. "Where is everybody?"

"Here, by the edge." D. L. put a finger to his lips for the boys to keep their secret. "Mr. Bergen, keep back, like I told you. We wouldn't want the thorns to look up here and see us, would we?"

At the sight of Bernie, Bernie with the orange hair, looking shrunken in his borrowed, oversize hat, trousers, and shirt, cuffs rolled at his ankles and wrists, Bernie with a roll of toilet paper clutched like a baby to his chest, diminutive Bernie, who knew nothing of their wonderful secret, the boys got a fit of the giggles.

D. L. gave them a friendly cuffing on the heads to shush them.

"Sir," Bobby Lee said to Bernie, wiping the tears from his eyes, "my turn." He took the roll of paper and walked into the bush.

A minute later, his objective forgotten, bowels tight, he was back in camp, beside himself. "Sarge, Sarge," he said, breathless, "there's a big bird out there. A fat-assed goose. Just standin' there. He's dinner, Sarge. Give me my gun."

"Your gun?" said D. L. "Have you lost your mind?"

"You took our chicken, I found a goose. Only fair."

"No way in the friggin' world anyone here's gonna fire a gun and alert the thorns, unless I choose to waste two bullets and put an end to your sorry lives. You want the goose? Take the machete over there. Do it like the Indians did it, boy. Let's see what kind of a stalker you are."

Bobby Lee grabbed the long knife and disappeared into the brush. Where was that fat bird, anyway? He circled. Fifty feet away, a hundred feet, finally, three hundred feet from camp, he saw it.

Honk, honk, said the goose.

You are a sassy one, Bobby Lee said to himself. And look at those old-bird feathers on one side. Think I'll call you White Wing, keep that wing for a trophy. "Here bird," he called, the machete behind his back.

Honk, honk. The goose bobbed from its left leg to its right, didn't move.

Bobby Lee edged closer. The goose stayed in place. *Honk.*

Another three feet. You are one dumb goose. Shit.

The goose turned tail, flew ten feet, cleared a small tree fern, landed, faced Bobby Lee. *Honk.*

Bobby Lee scuttled around the tree fern. Eight feet, six, five. He raised the machete. Damn!

Honk, honk.

He got close enough the next time to begin his swing before the bird ran. It didn't fly, merely ran, fast. Bobby Lee closed the gap. Gonna get your ass, goose, he mumbled. Big brother and the boss and even Sarge are gonna be proud of me, too, when I walk into camp with that long neck in one hand, that fat goose body in the other. C'mon, you sombitch, stay still. "Here goosie," he called, friendly as could be. He held out one hand. "Got some fried chicken in this hand for you. That's it, don't move. Hold it right there. Damn."

Honk.

Bobby Lee sat on his haunches, fuming. He contemplated throwing the machete. But if he missed, his magnificent goose might fly away forever. Had to have that bird. Couldn't go back empty-handed. He imagined the aroma of roasting goose and drooled.

The goose stood in place, butt feathers wriggling, head bobbing. *Honk, honk.*

Here we go again. Bobby Lee crept forward. Seven feet, five feet. He raised the machete.

The goose flapped its wings, lifted three feet off the ground, and flew over a low hedge of dense green ferns, steam wisping from between the fronds. Four feet on the other side, the bird stopped, faced Bobby Lee, fluttered its wings. *Honk, honk, honk.*

There we go, baby. You hold still. Think I can't see you behind those ferns? You got another think coming. Bobby Lee crouched low, fooled the goose into believing he didn't know where it was by turning his head, looking one way and then the other like the Indians used to do, avoiding its eyes. He scooted closer. Oh, baby, I've got your ass now. Five feet between me and roasted goose for dinner. He raised the machete. Stupid goose. One more step.

It was a big one. Bobby Lee's right foot plunged through the ferns into—nothing. Space. Momentum snatched his body forward, down. He yelped, thrashed, dropped the knife, clutched an armful of forest plants, then plummeted head over heels into a steaming crevasse, caroming off the scalding walls like a crazed pinball on a hot roll. By the time he came to rest, stunned, on a sizzling shelf thirty feet below, Bobby Lee was dreaming his last dream, a dream of frying chicken.

High above, a final *honk* sounded over flapping wings as the playful goose rose into the wide Hawaiian sky.

49

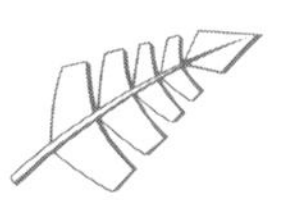

It was day two in the Pali-uli, nearly dinnertime, with no hint of a stone vagina, no sign of an *'o'o*. Lani sat on a boulder across the water by the base of the falls, sharpening her knife, Digger and Caddy prepared food near the tents, while Dan prowled for birds. Star feigned interest in Artemas's archaeological survey, avoided Lani.

Hands closed over his eyes.

"Surprise!"

Lani. Sneaked up behind me.

She took his hand. "Come with me, mister." She led him toward the forest to her love nest.

No way, José, he said to himself. But he followed, knowing when she popped her top, he'd go along with anything. How could he say no? Did he want to? And if he declined? How would Lani with the big knife handle rejection?

"Dan's out there," he said.

"No, Dan went the other way. I've been watching."

She'd been a good actress so far, he had to admit. Tight mouth. The others didn't have a clue. A hundred, a thousand times he had imagined permanent banishment from Papa's, worried what Caddy would think and the others say, what a hex would feel like, whether

Lani would go for his throat or his balls with that big knife if he crossed her.

They arrived at the pool beside her wilting bed of leaves.

"Sit," she said.

He sat.

"Star, that was wonderful last night, wasn't it?"

"Yeah."

"Yeah? That's all you have to say?"

"I mean . . ."

"You're having a problem with it aren't you? Look me in the eyes."

He looked at his feet. She expects me to talk about it. About how I feel. In broad daylight. Do nothing, see what happens—only way to handle a situation like this.

"Well?"

She wants me to tell her I love her. All these years, she's created this romance in her head, I'm Lohi'au, she's Pele's little sister Hi'iaka. We'll live happily ever after. And I jumped her bones, encouraged her. If I tell her what she wants to hear, that I love her—jeez—there'll be no end to it. She'll blab to the others, to Papa. If I tell her I don't, there'll be worse hell to pay. Maybe if I tell her I *like* her a lot, she'll be satisfied. He tried to form the words in his mouth, made a sound, "Imma-likah . . ."

"What? You're babbling. Hah! Star, with all the lines. Unbelievable." She shook her head. "Okay, I'll do the talking." She grabbed his chin. "Look at me when I speak. You were always my hero, you know."

Here we go.

"You're quite a man in the sack—or in the bushes." She laughed. "I wasn't disappointed."

He managed a weak smile.

"You're behaving like a schoolboy. I thought you'd be more mature."

"Imma-likah . . ."

"Eyes up here. That's it. Can't have you mooning around like this, so I'll say it straight out."

The three deadly words.

"Star, um, the truth is, last night, well, it was just sex for me."

"Huh?"

"From the minute we set eyes on one another, the sexual tension was thick enough to slice with my Bowie knife. It made me edgy, got in the way of what we're doing here, jeopardized the harmony of our group. Caddy saw it. She and I were practically at one another's throats. Couldn't you see how jealous she was?"

"What? What?"

"I thought the best way to deal with it would be to get it over with. Have at one another. Bang, bang. Tension gone. Nice memory. Friends. That was the plan, anyway. What do you say? I'm really sorry if I let you think there was more to it than that. . . ."

He hugged her. "I love you," he said. "I really do." He pushed her an arm's length away, looked her in the eyes. "Well, not *really,* but like buddies do, you know? Jeez. I thought . . ."

"What *did* you think?"

"Uh, I think you were right. Absolutely right." He shook her hand. "Friends?"

"Friends."

Desperate for the written word, Bernie reread the tent assembly instructions for the fiftieth time. He shook his head at the translated English, nearly as unintelligible as that of the demon twins: "Final, you putting stick A into hore B, then electing tent over head. . . ."

If only he had his overnight bag. But oh no-ooo, they left that behind when his legs gave out. D. L. ignored his pleas to retrieve it. "Didn't want to bring you in the first place, sir," he said. "Remember?" and then, "Boys can't carry you and your luggage, too. All's you need in the woods is a clear head, a good weapon, and the shirt on your back. I already stole those clothes for you, and I got weapons enough for all of us, so cut the whining. Think of this as a learning experience, like one of those Outward Bound field trips they arrange for you sit-on-your-ass executives."

If I had that bag now, Bernie thought, I'd have two *Wall Street Journals* and a *Forbes* to read—even the Reverend's Bible would be a step up from this moronic tent brochure. I'd have my shaving kit with the sunblock, deodorant, toothbrush, and the rest of it, clean underwear, tennis shoes instead of these tattered Cole-Haans, and above all—God, I'm a twitching wreck—the two boxes of Nicorettes the Reverend gave me as a parting gift. A learning experience? Just wait until we get back to civilization, D. L., you son of a bitch.

"It's been an hour, Sarge," said Ray Don, a worried edge to his voice.

"I know, boy. Let's take another look for him. I can't believe a mountain man like your brother could get lost, and he's not the type to turn tail."

Ray Don's fists balled. "Sarge, don't you ever . . ."

"I said *not* the type, hear? If he twisted an ankle, broke a leg or whatever, we'd hear his bellowing. One possibility keeps eatin' at me, and I don't like the implication of it." D. L. moved to the spotting scope.

Bernie, huddled by the tents, knew the answer. Pigs. Or grizzly bears. He shuddered.

"What is it, Sarge?" asked Ray Don.

D. L. squinted through the eyepiece at the valley. "He's down there now, but he was away the last time I looked. He's had plenty of time to get back if he knows a way up and down this friggin' cliff."

"Sa-arge," Ray Don whined. "Who? What?"

"Mr. Lucky. I can't help wondering if he didn't catch sight of us. He could have climbed up here and ambushed Bobby Lee when he went looking for that goose. We underestimated that hippie bastard before, let him throw little Mongoose over the cliff. Worst mistake you can make, underestimating an enemy."

"No! Can't be, Sarge. Not Bobby Lee." Ray Don wheeled in circles, pawing the air in frustration. He picked up a stone the size of a basketball and heaved it over Bernie's tent.

Bernie watched the rock fly eight feet above his head, listened to it crash in the forest. It's finally come, he realized. Every waking and sleeping—what little there had been of that—moment since he'd entered the wilderness with these frightening men, he'd awaited the violence, wondering whether it would come from a slavering animal running from a thicket, from that horrific, stinking lava, or from one of his barbaric companions themselves, wielding a hammer fist, a firearm, a knife, or a hand grenade.

"Don't start your grieving yet, son," D. L. said. "I'm only running over scenarios."

Haven't they thought of the obvious, Bernie wondered, these hot-shot woodsmen? He was reluctant to bring it to their attention, for fear their rising anger would redirect at him. "It could be—" he said aloud, but his voice failed.

"What? What's that?" asked D. L. "Did you see him? Mr. Lucky?"

"Grizzly bears," said Bernie. "Pigs, going for his—you know." There. He'd spit it out.

D. L. shook his head, said nothing. He looked again at the valley, lifted the ever-present fatigue cap from his head, and spoke, not to Bernie, but to the brother.

"Let's reconnoiter, do a thorough search this time, keep our ears open, our senses sharp. I'll go left, you go right. And keep your voice down, boy."

"Gimme Bobby Lee's forty-five," said Ray Don.

"No way. Mr. Lucky's back at his camp now. I *don't,* repeat, *don't* want to scare them off with gunshots. You find your brother, one way or the other, you bring him back here, and we'll decide what to do next."

My God, Bernie realized, they're abandoning me. "Don't leave me alone," he pleaded. If they were too thick to see the obvious, that a wild animal had gotten the man, he was not. And he didn't want to sit in camp, helpless, his back to a cliff, if the beast, now that it had a taste for human blood, returned for more.

"I don't want you following me," said D. L., in an increasingly foul and dangerous mood. "Stay in your tent, or go with Ray Don if you want."

No sunblock. Even at this late hour, Bernie knew the sun would fry him. His nose was peeling already, strips of skin sloughing off like bark from a lightning-struck tree. He climbed into the big construction worker's trousers and shirt, the ones D. L. had appropriated for him, and put on the worker's Skoal Bandits baseball cap.

Snuff. Bernie's mouth watered. He prayed silently: My Lexus for a can of snuff. Or a pack of cigarettes, or, oh God, a cigar. A juicy Corona de la Mofeta.

He scooted from the tent, ran to catch up with Ray Don, then followed him at a safe ten paces, heart pounding, ears alert for growls or grunts.

Modern tourists and the Hawaiians of centuries past share a common experience. Today people say *luau*. Once, they said *'aha'aina*. Both employ the underground oven, *imu,* to cook *kalua* pig. In the old days, upon priestly behest, it was *imu kalua loa,* for baking human sacrifice.

To prepare an *imu,* dig a pit in the earth, line it with lava rock, and set wood afire on the stones. When the rock glows red, cover with banana, ti leaves, or grass, set the carcass onto the steaming vegetation, cover with more leaves, then earth, and allow to simmer in its own juices.

Bobby Lee had not gone meekly. He had kicked, snatched, and dragged an armful of vegetation with him into the steaming crevasse. A cascade of ti and other leaves had preceded him, then showered behind, to cover his body. Baking along with him, on the sizzling six-hundred-degree shelf of rock thirty feet down, lay the starchy bole of a *hapu'u* tree fern, sugary ti root and rhizomes of ginger, a half dozen mountain apples, a branch of *'ohelo* berries, and a handful of spicy *kukui* nuts—in other words, a reasonably well-balanced *'aina ahiahi* of meat, carbohydrates, fruits, and vegetables.

The scent of *kalua* Bobby Lee, roasting in his volcanic *imu,* rose, drifted, permeated the air.

"Shit fire," said Ray Don, "I smell cooked goose."

"I smell it too," said Bernie, nose twitching. "Ummmm."

"Where are you, brother?" Ray Don paraded back and forth, sniffing the humid air for the source of the mouthwatering aroma. "You're cookin', ain't you, Bobby Lee? Cain't hide, cain't keep it to yourself. Goddamn, show yourself, brother."

But Bobby Lee remained mute.

They searched until sunset, but search as they might, they failed to find the fire, the goose on a spit, or the missing twin.

"I caught a whiff of cooked goose myself," said D. L., "but not a sign of Bobby Lee. Son"—he placed his hand on the big twin's shoulder—"sit down on this log." Ray Don sat. "I think I figured this out, and I don't like it one whit. This is bad news."

Ray Don covered his eyes.

"I think your brother did catch that goose. I think he built a fire, began to roast it. Planned to sidle back into camp with that cooked bird on a stick to surprise us. But what I think happened is, old Bobby Lee got surprised himself. By Mr. Lucky. Mr. Lucky snuck up here somehow, done him in, hid his body good or threw him over the cliff like he did little Mongoose, then skedaddled back to the thorns' camp with the goose. I'm sorry, son, but it's the only scenario that plays out."

"Noooo!" moaned Ray Don. "Not my little brother!"

Before he could bellow, D. L. slapped him hard on the side of the head. "Sorry, son, but you needed that. No noise, huh? Hear me out. You smelled cooked goose. Would Bobby Lee roast a bird and eat it all himself, not share it with us? Keep it from you, his brother? Would he hide out there for hours, knowing you were worried about him? Listening to you call for him?"

"No," said Ray Don in a small voice. A guttural roar rose from his throat, he ground his teeth, picked up a three-inch-thick log from the fire, cracked it in two over his thigh.

Bernie backed into the shadows, watched Ray Don wrap his arms around a tree fern thick as Bernie's thigh, wrest it from the ground, and hurl it ten feet into the forest.

"Son," said D. L., "keep it down, and save your strength. There'll be retribution on the morrow, I promise."

"Re-tri-bu-tion," said Ray Don, with hate in his eyes.

D. L. reached high to place an arm around Ray Don's massive shoulders. "It hurts to lose one you love, a comrade in arms. Revenge is sweet, but it don't pay to run amok, neither.

"It's nearly dark. If we go after them now, Mr. Lucky may escape. They're going nowhere. We'll wait, let them eat goose tonight, but there'll be hell to pay for it tomorrow."

"Cross your heart?" asked a watery-eyed Ray Don.

"Have I ever lied to you, son?"

"Forty-five? Sniper rifle? Grenades? Knives? Bare hands?"

"All of the above. Why not?"

Bernie stepped toward the fire. "D. L.? How do you know it wasn't wild animals? Surely there's no need to resort to violence. . . ."

D. L. marched toward him, stopped ten inches from Bernie's face, glaring at him with icy, unblinking eyes. "I didn't want you along," he said in a voice cold as gunmetal, "but you came. I expected trouble, and it happened. I'm going to deal with that trouble. I let my guard down and I fault myself for that, but no one's going to fuck D. L. McWhorter again on this mountain. That's my promise."

"Yes, but . . ."

"No buts. No back talk."

Without warning, D. L. reached behind Bernie's head, grabbed his ponytail with one hand, sliced it off with a knife Bernie didn't know existed with the other, and slapped the sorry, squashed spider of orange hair onto Bernie's palm.

"You get your lily-white ass back to that tent," D. L. said, "and keep your yap shut. Ray Don and me'll spell each other at guard. You can sleep, or play with yourself, or do whatever you want to in that tent, but if I hear so much as a peep out of you, so help me, I'll cut your tongue out."

Bernie flew to the tent, closed the flap behind him, burrowed into his sleeping bag, trembling, hoping, fervently, for the first time, that his friend the Reverend, snug in the bosom of civilization, was praying for him this awful night.

50

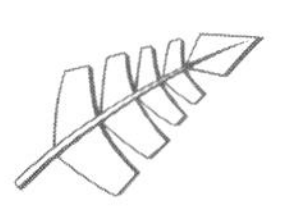

So, you had a nightmare last night, too?" Star said, lingering over his morning coffee. "The bogeyman you told me about? The one your mother used to scare you with?"

"None other," Caddy said. "The monster laughed about murdering Melissa and then came for me. Horrible." She closed her eyes and shuddered. "And yours?"

"Same one I've been having. I'm swimming, trapped underwater."

"Bad dreams. Something we have in common, huh?" She laughed.

"We both drink coffee, too." He winked.

"You know, I swim. Climb a bit as well."

"Really?"

"I stay out of the ocean at home," she said. "Too cold. But I swim laps—half a mile, three times a week. I swam competitively in college. Been putting in some real mileage in the ocean here." She noticed his cocked head. "That surprises you? You think because I wear glasses, have a Ph.D., I'm not athletic? I'm a Miss Peepers?"

Star waved a no and cocked his head again. "You climb?"

"I am a geologist, you know. I've had some pretty rare opportunities, foothills of the Himalayas, for instance, the Apennines, Rockies. I'm not that great, but I give it my best. Aha! Women don't do that sort of thing, huh? Unless, maybe, they carry big knives?"

"I didn't mean that. Back at the *pali,* though, when we ran into the human kite and you saw my rope, why didn't you mention it?"

"You seemed to have matters under control. More coffee?"

"Thanks. Coffee, even this stuff, is about my favorite thing in the world."

"A man who's easily satisfied, hmm?"

Unsure what she meant by that, he looked away, sipped the bitter brew, watched the surrounding bush.

Caddy lifted the pot from the camp stove, refilled his aluminum cup, said, matter of factly, "Ladies, meet Mr. Lucky."

Star splashed hot coffee down the front of his shirt, into his lap. He jumped to his feet, slapped at the scalding liquid. "What? What did you say?"

"You heard me. Got a rise out of you, didn't I?"

She was laughing at him. Laughing. "Where did you hear that?"

"Where do you think? Dan showed me the ad, explained everything last night."

"Damn that Dan."

"Dan's a sweetheart. He'd tell me anything."

"Then you know . . ."

"How you met Melissa? I had it about half figured out myself already. I know Melissa. I know enough about you. You didn't exactly lie to me, but it was obvious you weren't telling the whole truth, either. Boy meets girl, huh? But who was using whom?"

"What do you mean by that?"

She laughed again.

"You're not angry?"

"When I first met you? I would have skinned you alive. But you and your boyish charms have a way of growing on a girl. And you cared about Melissa. That was genuine. You offered to help. And you have helped—endangered yourself to do so. I appreciate that."

She stood, ruffled the hair at his forehead with her fingers, then bent to lift her daypack and swung it to her shoulder. "I'm on my way to check out that lava flow. We can't see it from down here, and I'm burning with curiosity. It's been years since I've seen Hawaiian lava up close. I'll climb up the new road. If I don't make it back by lunch, tell the others to eat without me." She turned, walked toward the tall trees.

Star watched her calf and thigh muscles flex, nicely visible below khaki shorts. He imagined her hopping from rock to rock through a stream bed, keeping her balance, laughing, doing her best to stay ahead of him—and concluded she may have been a step or two ahead of him from the start.

He drank more coffee, tried to get his ass in gear. They'd had no luck so far. Dan wanted to stay another day. Why not? Maybe he'd take a look at the lava himself.

Ten minutes later, Lani ran into camp, breathless. "Dan and Digger found something, want you to come right away. Where's Caddy?"

"Checking out the lava. Back by lunch."

She pulled him by the wrist. "Drink the coffee or dump it. C'mon."

"The bird? Did they find the *kohe?*"

"I think the bird, but Digger's discovered something, too. They're both excited, sent me back for you two."

Ray Don, hand grenades hanging from his belt, crouched beside D. L. at the spotting scope. "Re-tri-bu-tion, Sarge?"

"In spades, son. The two old guys and the Hawaiian girl must have left before daybreak. It looks like the brunette's hiking to the entry road. Damn. She's in the woods already. I wanted them all together, although four out of five's not bad. The Hawaiian girl just picked up Mr. Lucky. Bet she's taking him to the old guys. They're way down there." He pointed. "Still well within range of Sweet Honeybun, my M-21. Go get her, boy."

Ray Don retrieved the ominous fiberglass case, the one Bernie had hoped so fervently contained a musical instrument. The twin opened it, gently lifted a rifle, and handed it to D. L.

D. L. cradled the long gun to his chest, planted an affectionate kiss on the stock. "Sweet Honeybun," he said. "I love you, baby."

Bernie watched in horror as Ray Don assembled a small tripod for the rifle like the one holding the spotting scope. "C'mon over," D. L. said to Bernie. "You may enjoy this. A new experience."

Bernie crawled from his tent on hands and bare knees, wearing only his Bermuda shorts and polo shirt, by now dirtier than the mud caked to his shredded Cole-Haans. "My God, D. L., tell me you're only going to scare them away."

"Okay. I'm only going to scare them away," D. L. said with a chuckle and a wink. "Just kidding, of course, sir." He clapped his hands. "Gather round, folks, it's shooooww time."

Bernie slapped a hand over his mouth, sat on his haunches eight feet away, speechless.

"What we have here," D. L. said in a calm voice, "is an M-21 accurized sniper rifle with a precalibrated M-1D adjustable ranging telescope, which we're about to fine-tune." He turned to Ray Don. "Cartridges, please, son." He opened a small case. "Hand loaded," he explained to Bernie. "I anticipated shooting closer than this, but I'm a fair shot, if I do say so myself. Our targets are close to nine hundred yards away, close to five hundred feet lower in elevation. We'll set the scope for . . ."

Bernie shivered. Listen to him. Like an appliance salesman ticking off features on a washer-dryer to some housewife. "D. L.," he pleaded. "Surely you're not going to *shoot* those people. There's no evidence they've found anything. They'll go away, our men will come back soon, begin clearing the valley."

"The hippie took down one of my boys. *Him,* I'm saving for something special. He's a nobody, far as your project's concerned, but look what else you've got here: a magazine publisher, two university profs, a damned volcano lover. You think they won't go back and get the archaeologists in an uproar? The volcano lovers? The friggin' Audubon Society? All the old ladies in Hawai'i? Oh, they'll hold up Paradise Valley, all right. Let 'em go?"

D. L. cocked an eyebrow. "But the alternative? They wandered into this valley, they don't return, see? Sorry, sorry, everyone's sad. Search parties? Why not? Our men will look for them too, while they're clearing the valley. Maybe the lava got 'em—that'll be the tragic conclusion. The geologist woman got them fooling around with it. A real Pandora, that one. You know what? I saw 'em myself, poking sticks into that lava. I warned them it was dangerous. Ordered them away, but they ignored me. Awful. Ate up by lava. Who's to say any different? The construction crew's miles away. There won't be any bodies."

"No, no, no . . ."

"You hired me to do a job, I'm doing it, like you knew I would. It would have been easier for you to stay back in that plush office, let me get on with it. But no, you had to come along. And what were our terms?"

"I never thought you'd . . ."

"You spineless fat cats in suits make me puke. I'm in command out here, and our deal, in case you forgot, is that my bonus comes through thirty days after construction on your golf park begins. You've got two minutes to make up your mind. Hit the road, or sit and watch the show."

D. L. turned to Ray Don. "Son, when the four of them get together, I'll pick off the two old guys and the Hawaiian girl, then I'm gonna stalk Mr. Lucky, have some fun with him. Soon as I'm finished shooting here, you take off, do in the brunette, however you want, but be quick about it. If you follow the top of the cliff, you ought to reach the road about the same time she does. Leave her body near the lava where you can find it. I can carry the Hawaiian girl, but you'll have to cart the others back over there when we're finished. You understand that?"

"Perzactly," said Ray Don.

"Exercise will be good for you, boy, burn off some of that fried-chicken fat." D. L. smiled. "Tell you what. I'll leave Mr. Lucky alive, let you finish him, tear off pieces of him like you do to bugs. Would you like that, son?"

"Re-tri-bu-tion," said Ray Don.

"Oh God," Bernie said. He edged away, stumbled into the forest, wanting only to be far, far away when the shots rang out.

"The boss skedaddled," said Ray Don.

"Just as well. He won't go far. In about thirty seconds he'll decide he's more afraid of pigs and grizzlies than a man's work, and he'll creep back. We'll find him whimpering in his tent when we're finished. You'll have to haul him out on your shoulders again, I guess, along with the bodies. He's still the man who signs the checks, so we don't want nothing happening to him."

D. L. pointed to the valley, passed a pair of binoculars to Ray Don. "You see where they are?"

"Yessir." Ray Don checked the hand grenades at his waist, fondled his hunting knife. "Promise you'll leave Mr. Lucky alive enough for me to pull apart?"

"Criminy, I promise."

"Forty-five?"

"Hell. Take the damned thing." D. L. fished it from his pack.

Ray Don slipped the automatic—Bobby Lee's gun—from its holster, smiled at the inlaid cobra with the red jeweled eyes. He slung the gun belt over his shoulder, bandolier fashion, slid the pistol back in.

"I've got my range, here," said D. L., lying prone. He swiveled the rifle forty-five degrees from his targets, aimed it at a rock the same distance away. "Don't like to alert them, but I want at least one shot to zero in."

Ray Don lay on his stomach behind the spotting scope, trained it on the two men, soon to be three men and a woman.

Crack!

"Not half bad," D. L. said. He made a fine adjustment to the sight, swung the barrel back to his targets. "How far away are Mr. Lucky and the girl?"

"Almost there."

"What did they do when they heard the shot?"

"Looked around, confused."

"Men, too," D. L. said. "Got 'em in my scope now. They haven't a clue where it came from. One's got binoculars, but he's not looking up here. They'll settle down soon, get back to whatever it is they were doing."

"Mr. Lucky and the black-haired girl is on their way again, sir."

D. L. kept the scope trained on Star. "I love this part," he said. "Kind of like the end of a movie."

Minutes passed. D. L. wriggled his body, listened to Ray Don's play-by-play.

"They's all together now, sir. Talkin', pointing up at a tree, down at the ground. One with the binoculars is all excited, has a camera."

"Make that snapshot a good one, old man," said D. L. "It's your last." He took a deep breath, exhaled. Inhaled again, slowly, stopped in midbreath, touched his finger lightly to the trigger, and squeezed.

51

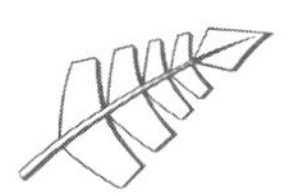

Star, Lani, just in time," Dan said. "I saw an *'o'o!* No more than a silhouette in the top of that *'o'hia* tree, but, damn, I feel it in my gut."

"Way to go!" Star saw only trees.

Dan frowned. "Then that shot, or whatever it was, scared it away." His binoculars scanned left, right, up, down.

"Could have been a hunter," said Lani. "Maybe one of the construction workers."

"Hunters are our least concern at the moment," Dan said. His eyes swept the forest canopy. He set down the binoculars, lifted his Nikon with a long telephoto lens to his chest, at the ready, should the bird reappear.

"What's in the hole, Digger?" Star asked.

Digger crouched in a depression of weathered *pahoehoe* lava on the rim of a fifteen-foot-long, four-foot-wide crack in the thick crust. "An old lava tube cave," he said. "Its ceiling collapsed or you wouldn't know it was under us. Way back, molten lava poured down a trough, the top cooled, solidified. But underneath, it still ran, like water through a straw. When the flow stopped above, the liquid rock emptied from below, leaving the tube intact. Some tubes extend for miles, unseen." Digger shielded his eyes with a saluting hand. "I thought I saw petroglyphs—carvings—and was getting up nerve to jump in. No mention of this in Artemas's report. But if he wasn't right on top of the entrance, he would have missed it."

"I'll check it out." Star jumped into the open roof of the cave onto a fern-covered pyramid of soil, forest litter, and broken stone fallen from the ceiling. The cone rose from the floor to within five feet of the surface. He slid into dim light and a passage twenty feet in diameter, ran his fingers over the stone, called to Digger above. "It's cool down here. The surface is smooth, looks like frozen gray syrup, has the feel of sandblasted glass. Thirty or forty carvings, eight to twelve inches high, pecked into the wall. They're stick figures, each one standing on the shoulders of the next. Three lines of ten to twenty."

Digger cupped his hands, called into the dark. "That's a real find."

"Digger, this is spooky. Like, I'm standing in the tracks of whoever made these carvings—what, hundreds of years ago? It's as if the carver just left, and we're—it's hard to say what I mean—linked in some way."

"Star, my boy, you're beginning to see why I'm in archaeology. It's not the facts and figures, it's about tuning in to people's lives. There, but for two centuries, go I—right kiddo?"

"Yeah, I think that's it. These carvings must have been important, huh?"

"Indeed. Not for a second were those graffiti. If they were, you'd see them all over the island, instead of in clusters in special places. Those probably represent lineages, your carver's ancestors, perhaps fecundity. Remember the *piko* stone, where Hawaiians placed their babies' umbilical cords, to bond them with the earth? The hula *heiau,* the other petroglyphs? All echoes of Kapo's reproductive energy. Someone chose that spot for a reason. Caves are mystical ground, the earth's womb.

"Now, look a little higher and tell me if you see what I think I see."

"It's a much larger figure, full body. Wavy lines over its head like hair, or fire. I guess female, cause there's a deep hole where the legs come together."

"Aha! And do you think that hole signifies the *kohe* is *present?*" asked Digger, "or *missing?*"

"Could this be Kapo?"

"It sure as hell could. We're close, all right."

Star explored. "Digger, forty feet either way, the passage is blocked, collapsed."

He heard shouts above, from Dan.

"There. *There*. Do you see it? The *'o'o!*" Dan raised the camera and lens.

Crack! in the distance.

"Uummph."

Shouts from Lani and Digger.

Star hoisted his body waist-even with the surface. Three feet away, he saw Dan writhing like a flipped turtle, blood splattered on his shirt.

Crack!

"Ungh!" from Digger. He stumbled, fell into the pit at Star's right.

Lani crouched to help Dan. *Crack!* A *thwok* sounded from a tree trunk, three feet behind the space her head had occupied half a second earlier. "Dan's bleeding!" she shouted. "What happened to him?"

Crack!

Lani stood, looked for the source of the noise.

Pock! Rock disintegrated ten inches from her foot, cut her calf. She stared at her own blood, uncomprehending.

"Shooting! Someone's shooting at us!" Star yelled, "Get down!"

Crack!

Lani's arms flew straight out. Like a skater in a spin, she wheeled toward the hole, and tumbled in.

Star stretched over the rim, grabbed Dan's pant legs, and tugged. *Crack! Crack!* Bullets exploded to either side. A bee sting on his cheek, another on his forearm. With both Dan's cuffs firmly in hand, he dropped into the cave, let gravity pull Dan behind him.

"Three out of three, Sarge," Ray Don said at the spotting scope. "The one old guy and the girl got knocked into that hole Mr. Lucky climbed in. The other one had a chest full of blood. Mr. Lucky dragged him inside, but he's a goner. Hot damn! That's some shootin'. The girl spun like a top when you hit her. Hair whirlin'. Must have caught it in the shoulder. Shit fire, it was purty."

"Sweet Honeybun never disappoints," D. L. said, running his fingers along the barrel. "And Mr. Lucky's cornered in that pit. Couldn't be better. Here's what we'll do. You go, take care of the geologist woman, pronto. Follow the top of the cliff to reach the new road. Wait for her at the head of the switchbacks. Be quick about it, then hustle your ass down to that hole Mr. Lucky's in."

D. L.'s voice had a manic edge. "Damn, I love to shoot. I wanted to take care of that hippie bastard myself, but this is too easy. I'll keep him pinned down until you get there. Then, Ray Don, son, Mr. Lucky's all yours. Pay him back for your brother. All I ask is that you throw him onto the surface before you do him, so's I can watch. Got my opera glasses here—it'll be like having a box seat at the thee-ay-tah. La-dee-dah. All's I lack is popcorn."

Ray Don had but four words to say to Sarge's levity: "Re-tri-bu-tion."

52

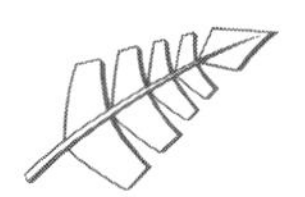

Caddy climbed the switchbacks, alone for the first time in—how long since she had been this alone? Her mind soared, sank.

Oh, how she missed Melissa. Pretty, talented, foolish Melissa. Would they ever find her killer?

Their adventure would be over soon. She would return home. What about Star? Damned if she didn't miss him already. Star, and his smart-assed mouth. Hell, she'd miss them all. Dan and Digger were such sweethearts, and even the pain in the butt, Miss Big Ego Hawaiian Princess, had a spunky charm about her.

Was there something going on between Lani and Star? At first she'd have put money on it, but last night they acted like brother and sister. People in the islands could be so, well, insular, quirky, how could one tell?

Caddy said his name aloud, "Star Hollie," thought, For the first time, this morning, Star and I actually talked of common interests. Swimming, and rock climbing. Right. And nightmares. And we both drink coffee, and breathe air, too. How's that? Caddy MacConnell, could you be interested in a *surfer?* Oh my, I hope not. She laughed at the thought.

Does this surfer have a brain? He can be such a simpleton. Dinosaurs in Hawai'i? Too much! Then, when I least expect it, a surprising pearl of wisdom passes those shell-white teeth of his. Dan has hope for him, says all he needs is culturing, whatever the hell that means.

What would I have done without him, though, alone, trying to track Melissa's murderers? He cheered me up. Wouldn't take a cent—as if he doesn't need it, with that pitiful car. And at the Nuuanu Pali? He risked his life. A real Lancelot. And such a hunk. That long, wavy hair, those green eyes. Nice body, nice buns. She laughed, spoke aloud, "Caddy, Caddy. You're not Melissa. All your life you've been careful around men, especially men like Star Hollie. Watch yourself, woman."

A lowering cloud bathed her in moisture. She turned up her collar, sniffed the air. Hydrogen sulfide, sulfur dioxide, that tarnished-spoon taste in her mouth. Beloved lava, not far away. Her heart ka-thump-thumped with anticipation. She had it in her blood, all right.

The new road was desolation itself. She walked through the fog, listened to the scrape of her boots on crushed rock, felt the ominous silence, recalled the valley's bird chatter, missed its leafy security.

The sun burnt through a misty rain over the valley, and a rainbow arced from the top of the waterfalls down to the forest where Star and the others were searching for the bird and Kapo's *kohe*. Caddy thought of the butterflies, the plants—living in harmony, in isolation, undisturbed. She looked to either side of the road, at the green cliffs softened by centuries, millennia, of wind and water. Where the bulldozers had slashed the ancient ash fall, it glistened red from the cloud-mist. Yes, she could see how the Hawaiians might look at an assault like that and speak of ripping Pele's flesh.

She stopped, gazed at the valley, still lush, full of life, and saw its future: captains of commerce, transistor samurais, generals of take-over wars—wearing clown suits, driving Shriner cars over sterile grass, chasing tiny white balls.

Melissa, Melissa. Killed for golf.

Caddy sighed and trudged on.

At the top, her spirits rose. There it was—lava. Alive. At least five hundred feet lower than when they arrived, and a short five hundred feet above the road. Trees, brush, and grass smoldered at the flow's edges, here and there burst into flames.

She glanced at the road by her feet, stooped to pick up several shiny, pale yellow tufts and strands, fine as thread, nearly as long as her palm. The first I've seen this trip, she thought, and smiled—Pele's hair, finespun glass, drifting on the wind from the eruption. She blew the fibers from her hand, curtsied the mountain in acknowledgment.

She climbed, saw the high earthen wall thrown across the lava's path by the construction crew, the twin branches of lava overflowing the rim. Caddy smiled at the futility of damming a determined lava flow.

"Hello, missy."

She spun, lost balance, fell to her knees, righted herself. A huge man in filthy jeans, T-shirt, and dusty western boots grinned at her from thirty feet away, downslope.

"I didn't see any equipment," she said, alert. "I assumed you had all left."

"Oh, they's gone. You can be sure of that, missy. Two miles away." He had short, bleached hair at the top. Matted dreadlocks swayed like dead snakes at the back of his neck.

"Who are you, what do you want?" Caddy saw the gun belt over his shoulder, the—could it be?—hand grenades dangling at his waist. She looked past him, at the empty road. No car, no one else in sight. A hunter? The shots she'd heard earlier? No, men didn't hunt with guns like his, and certainly not with hand grenades. Only police in Hawai'i carried handguns. But this was no policeman. This was trouble.

Oh shit.

53

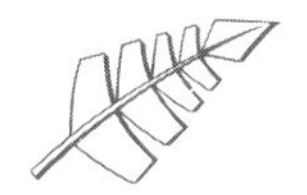

Star bit his lip at sight of the blood. "Dan? Can you hear me?"

"Yeah . . . hear you." He sounded weak, far away.

"Where does it hurt?"

"Where doesn't it?" He tried to laugh, coughed instead. "Chest, side, shoulder."

"How does he look?" from Lani, on the other side of the cone of broken rock, fallen from the collapsed cave roof.

"Lani? You're all right?"

"Sore butt, from when I landed. A good thing for the *uluhe* thicket I fell into. The bullet ripped through my daypack, through every page of the field guide Dan gave me, and then broke the handle of the camp shovel strapped to the pack. Digger? I'm checking on Digger."

"I'm bleeding. Son of a bitch! It hurts, burns," said Digger. "I'm going to take off my shirt, see what—it's my arm, chest. Ow! Need some help here, Lani."

"You're lucky, you old goat," she said a minute later. "The bullet cut your chest, passed through the back of your arm." Another minute passed. "I'm flushing the wound, wadding cloth against it. Here, hold your arm to your chest, I'll bind it there."

Digger moaned.

"Let me work some pressure points."

"Hurts where you're pressing," said Digger. He winced. "But my chest and arm?—feel better. Yes, less pain."

"Now lie back. I'll check on Dan."

Dan's head lay on Star's lap. "He's pale, Lani. Skin's cold, sweaty."

Lani and Star exchanged worried looks at the blood.

"Star, cut his camera strap. I'll open his shirt." She handed him her knife.

"Nylon webbing, won't cut." He began to work the strap off Dan's shoulder, down his arm.

Lani had the bloody shirt open, ran hands across Dan's chest, touching, probing. "Not bleeding from his mouth," she whispered. "That's good, anyway."

"Jeez. Look at the lens," said Star. "The bullet ripped hell out of the barrel."

"That explains the injuries. He must have been holding the camera and lens in front of his chest, the impact drove them back." She leaned close to his face. "Dan, you were shot. The barrel of the lens broke your collarbone. You may have some cracked ribs. Dan? Dan, do you hear me?"

"Uh-huh," weakly. "I can feel the ends of bone rubbing against one another. Hurts when I breathe."

"Hang in there." She held her water bottle, still intact, to Dan's lips, and whispered in Star's ear. "There's no way of telling how bad he's hurt inside, where the bullet went. Keep him warm. Reach in my pack, get my jacket." She gave Dan another sip. "Dan." She spoke softly. "I'm cutting your shirt, improvising a splint. I don't want you moving if you don't have to."

He moaned.

Lani looked at Star and shook her head.

"I'd like to get my hands on whoever did this," Star said.

"Bastard." Lani gripped her knife.

"Caddy's sister," said Star. "Murdered over Artemas's discovery. Mr. Lucky kidnapped. They threatened me. And now this. And while we're talking, they could be moving in to finish us off." He raised his voice. "Did anyone see where the shots came from?"

"Sounded far away," said Lani. "Hard to tell. But to clear the trees, they'd have to be high, top of the cliff. We may be safe for a while, considering they'd have to climb down to get to us. On the other hand, they've got a clear view of the entrance."

Star placed his shirt and Digger's hat on a stick, jiggled it along the edge of the cave mouth.

Crack! A bullet slammed into the lip of the entrance, sent rock fragments into the cave. One cut Star's arm, and he swiped blood. "Damn! Get back. I don't think they can shoot into the cave from that angle, but ricochets could play hell with us. The ferns and that rock pile at the center ought to shield us from most of it if we move back there." He pointed. "From where that bullet hit, it means the bastard with the gun is somewhere in a line between here and the waterfalls. The high angle makes sense. That puts the gun on the cliff, near the falls."

Lani turned to him. "One of us will have to stay with Digger and Dan, the other run for help. I know first aid, healing, so it's better I stay, you go."

They moved the wounded as far away as possible. Star crept to the center.

"Lani, I've got an idea. Take these rocks, climb on my shoulders. Keep down, but ease them onto the ledge at the top. We'll build a little wall, be able to look through the cracks without them seeing us."

Five minutes later, they had also built a cairn on the cave floor. Star stood on it, peered through their wall while Lani waved the hat near the far side of the entrance.

Crack! They heard chips of rock skitter across the surface.

"Yes!" said Star. "I saw a glint, at the top of the cliff, over the falls. There's our shooter."

"So how do you get out? Any movement, they shoot," said Lani.

"There's dead wood here," Digger called from the dark. "Pile it on the rocks under the entrance, start a fire, throw green ferns on it. You'll have plenty of white smoke to cover your escape."

"Yes!" said Lani, then added, "Matches, lighters? Damn. I left them in camp."

No one had either.

Star snapped his fingers. "Dan's lens."

"Brains against bullets," Lani said. "Good for us."

They piled wood on the center cone of fallen rock, out of sight of the sniper. Star worked a shard of convex glass from the shattered camera lens while Lani prepared a small pile of fern fuzz and shreds of paper below a shaft of sunlight.

"Star," she said. "There are four ways out of this valley. Back the way we came, which will take forever. Down the valley to the coast road—but that way, you'll have to climb down another cliff with no trails that I know of, so that's not much better. Or across the valley to the new road. You follow that, you'll find people, construction workers with radios."

"Caddy!" he said. "That shot we heard. What if . . . ?"

"You can't think that," she said. "No. If Caddy was headed for the switchbacks from camp, she would have gone into the forest right off, would have been hidden from the top."

"Jeez, I hope you're right. If she's all right, she must be near the lava. If she comes back, that bastard will shoot her. I've got to find her."

"If you head that way from here, you'll cross open ground, be an easy target. And you may miss her. There's a fourth way: a trail up the cliff, near the waterfalls. It runs along cracks like the trail we followed into the valley. It's overgrown, out of sight. If you're careful, you could skirt the shooter and hike to the new road across the top, along the cliff rim, see Caddy, warn her."

"Lani, how do you know these things?"

"Walana knows everything about the Pali-uli."

"Walana."

Lani explained the route, made him repeat her directions. The lens, focusing the sun, lit the tinder, and within minutes a lively fire burned near the top of the rock pile.

Crack! Crack! Angry shots rang from above to no effect, except for the disturbing ricochets into the unoccupied recesses of the cave.

Star squeezed Dan's hand, promised Digger he'd run like the wind, and hugged Lani. They threw green fronds on the flames, watched the smoke grow white, opaque, spiral around the mouth of the cave, and drift out.

The shooter must have realized their plan, because he fired in quick succession, randomly, furiously, back and forth across the entrance.

Star hoisted himself onto the ledge in the thickest smoke, rolled outside, and dashed for the high grass.

54

Don't be afraid," the giant said. He stepped toward her.

"Who are you? What do you want?" Caddy backed away.

"Name's Ray Don. Come here, missy."

"Get away," she said. "I have friends. They're nearby."

"No. Your friends are hurt, see? That's why I'm here. To take you to them."

"What? Hurt. How?" She could barely understand the man.

"Fell in a hole, all of them."

"Fell in a hole? Who are you?"

"Security guard. Yore trespassing, missy. Dangerous here. You don't want to get hurt, too, do you? Please, you come with me." He held his hand out, curled his fingers for her to approach.

"You, a security guard? I don't think so. Let me see identification."

The man fished in his hip pocket, retrieved a wallet chained to his belt. He flipped it open, flashed a silver badge, flicked it shut. "See?" Twelve feet and closing.

"Right. Get the hell away from me."

"I tried to be nice, tell you easy." Ten feet. "Fact is, missy, your friends are dead."

"DEAD?" She staggered back.

"Like your sister. The purty one, what drowned."

"What do you know about Melissa?"

"I know she was built like a brick shit house. I know, because I ran my hands over every inch of that pussycat-soft body before I pitched her in the ocean. I know she couldn't swim, just flapped like a shot duck before she sank. What else you want to know?"

"YOU BASTARD!"

"That may be, but I'm goin' to be a happy bastard soon enough, 'cause you and me is about to party. What do you say to that, missy?" Eight feet away.

Trapped by her nightmare bogeyman, Caddy backpedaled. He would snag her if she ran left or right, and behind lay the earthen dam and the lava pool. She felt heat at her back already.

She turned, stumbled to the top of the berm. A raised crust of *a'a*, clinkery cinders, in some places eight feet high, rimmed the dam. Behind, a lake of silvery, shimmering tar—viscous, congealing *pahoehoe*—stretched a hundred and fifty feet. She heard it, the *a'a*, shifting, the *pahoehoe* swelling, like a thousand panes of breaking glass, a painful sound, stressed, angry, a trapped animal seeking escape.

"Nowhere to go, missy." The bogeyman loped up the slope, stretched his arms wide, a spider's embrace nearly seven feet across. "C'mon, baby, give old Ray Don some lovin'." He opened his mouth, wiggled his tongue.

Caddy gagged, felt a stab of vertigo, realized this must have been how Melissa felt when he came for her. Oh, Melissa.

No, she thought, don't let the son of a bitch get you, too. He's a man. Only a man. You know what he looks like, now. Escape. Get Star.

He had to have lied about Star and the others. Had to.

She glanced over her shoulder at the lava. Would the crust support her? She staggered, slapped by an invisible, suffocating blanket of heat.

Caddy knew lava, had investigated fresh flows, dashed over them to take samples. In. Out. It might be possible. But a hundred and fifty feet of unstable surface? This pool was still being fed from above; the crust was swollen, ready to rip apart.

Domes of pillowy *pahoehoe* appeared dark, deceptively solid, but crevices glowed cherry red, and here and there, where the crust had torn, molten stone glowed at two thousand degrees, a fierce yellow-white.

The giant with the gun and hand grenades lunged forward, snatched at her arm. Caddy danced to the side. Ray Don sidestepped with her, laughing.

He's toying with me, like a cat with a baby rabbit.

Assailed by an unholy smell of lemons, sweat, and sulfur, Caddy breathed through her mouth.

No options. She turned, took three quick steps onto a heap of *a'a,* cool but treacherous. It would slice her to ribbons if it shifted and she fell. She looked at the flow, felt the man's fingers crease her blouse, brush her breast. She stepped onto the hot *pahoehoe*. Without conscious thought, she charted a course and ran for her life.

Take light steps, she told herself, don't stop. Blasting heat. Two-thirds of the way across she saw a tiny *kipuka,* an island of earth with singed grass and a few trees that might survive if the flow rose no higher. Like bouldering—running across a field of rounded rocks, one to the other—she kept moving, stepped onto the highest, darkest, most solid *pahoehoe* pillows. And then she was there, on the island, standing in smoldering grass, coughing, the soles of her hiking boots smoking.

"Bitch!" yelled Ray Don. "Yore mine." He had the gun in his hand now, waved it. "I'll do you one way or the other."

If he shoots, I'll die. She considered running from the island, across the remaining lava, then thought, No. That's *him*. Melissa's *murderer*. Fear evaporated. She no longer wanted to escape. Caddy MacConnell wanted the bastard dead.

"You chicken-shit coward!" she yelled. "I made it across. What's wrong with you? Come and get me if you want me." She unbuttoned her blouse, reached behind her back, unsnapped her bra, stripped to the waist. "Come on, big talker," she taunted. "This is what you wanted, isn't it? To party? Here I am!"

Ray Don stared at her bare breasts, blinked, swiveled his head side to side, glared at the plain of lava before him.

Caddy stepped from her shorts, stood naked except for her bikini panties and hiking boots. "What's wrong, can't get it up? Never seen a real woman before?" She shed the panties, threw her arms wide. "Come on, Bubba, I'm waiting."

"Goddamn bitch!" he yelled, and stepped onto the *a'a*. He set one foot onto the *pahoehoe*. It supported him. Ray Don charged.

While Caddy had glided, Ray Don stomped. Twenty-five feet from the dam, he rocked, waved his hands in the air, lost balance.

"Shit fire!" he yelled, and turned to retrace his steps. A pillow of lava shifted, twisted beneath his feet. Orange cracks surrounded him. One foot sank. Ray Don yowled, lifted a thickened, glowing red boot, then fell to his hands and knees, screaming.

Caddy pressed her palms to her ears, tried to look away, but stood transfixed as the giant fell flat on his belly, smoke curling from his burning clothes and charring flesh. He lay there, immobile, silent, flaming.

She looked away, then back, as a resurrected Ray Don screamed a last, furious bellow. He pressed his palms to the surface, no more than a silhouette against the glowing sludge, and struggled to rise. He lifted his shoulders, his chest, in one terminal, fiery, demonic push-up. Then he collapsed, and the pillow of lava he lay on tipped and slid into the molten pool below with a puff of acrid smoke.

Tears streamed down Caddy's face. She dressed, prepared for the final dash to safety. At her feet, she saw a bush with scarlet berries. *'Ohelo*. She stripped off a handful, threw them onto the lava lake with a glance to the mountaintop. Then, without further thought, she ran, skittered across the remaining *pahoehoe* to a ridge of cool earth fifty feet away.

She sat on a ledge, wiped her eyes, then cried again, not for the man, but for Melissa.

Whoomp! The lava pool by the construction crew's dam bubbled. Red magma splattered over the dark crust. An eruption, this far from the summit? Impossible.

Thoomp! Thoomp! Mushrooms of lava belched into the air.

What the hell? Caddy backed up the slope, then realized what was happening. The hand grenades. The swollen black crust cracked, opened, orange lava upwelled, surged like slow-motion surf against the dam.

Whoomp! The pool lowered perceptibly where the giant had met his end. How could that be? She moved closer. The dam. The lava had broached the dam, was spilling over.

Thoomp! Whoomp! Two more orange bubbles blossomed as cascading lava carried the final grenades over the top of the earthwork. A ten-foot notch appeared in the berm. Above, the crust buckled, sagged, broke apart. Molten stone surged through the gap, melted, consumed the rock beneath and widened the channel, then raced down the mountain, liberated.

Red and yellow, dotted with floating chunks of black, the lava slithered downhill like one, then two angry coral snakes, coursing along the twin channels of earlier flow, toward, then across the Pali-uli access road, severing it, not once, but twice.

55

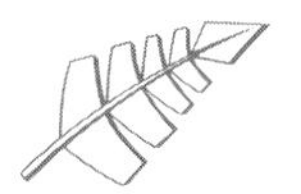

Star crouched, ran low inside the cloud of smoke to a fern thicket, crawled through it on his stomach to higher cover, then sat with his back to a tree trunk, heart racing, listening to rifle fire pelt the cave.

"I made it."

Lani answered from the cave, "Then get the hell out of there."

He circled wide, stayed to the densest growth, aware that from above, the slightest movement would be detectable. Only when he reached the base of the shaggy green cliff did he feel safe. Staggered shots rang out every few minutes, telling him, one, that the shooter was unsure who remained in the cave, and two, that the sniper hadn't moved from his position.

He found the trail where Lani said it would be, on the far side of a large boulder near the smallest waterfall. While nearly invisible on the valley floor, as the ground rose, chiseled steps and handholds appeared, long overgrown with moss and roots. The climb was rough and slippery, nearly straight up.

Forty minutes later, he scrambled onto the top.

Crack! Another shot sounded from the same position.

Star jogged wide of the shooter, but curiosity got the better of him, and he found himself edging closer to the cliff and the gunfire.

He slowed, crept in during a lull in the shooting, and crouched behind a tree fern. He parted vines to see.

From his back: "Well, well, look who's here."

He tripped, arms tangled in vines. "Jeez! D. L.! What are you doing here? Get down, there's somebody with a . . ." He saw D. L.'s rifle, the holstered pistol at his waist. "You? I don't . . ."

"You took out my man, you did, disappeared him, real smooth-like. Then you dropped back down and ate the man's goose, strutted around your camp in plain view without a care in the world. Some balls. You did it to rub it in, right? To let me know what a bumbler I was—careless, to let my man get taken so easy."

"What?"

"Today, one minute you're in my sights, the next you're up to Indian tricks with the smoke, and—poof—here's Mr. Lucky at my side, slipped up the same secret trail he used last night. You're slick, boy, I'll give you that. And look at you, unarmed. How were you gonna do me? Garrote? Neck chop? Broken spine? Or just boot me over the cliff like you did poor Mongoose? Yessir, you've got guts. *Mano a pistolas,* huh?"

"That's crazy. What the hell are you talking about? You wounded two people. Dan's hurt real bad."

"Only two? I counted three, son. And wounded? No. Three, either tryin' out their heaven's wings already or bein' fitted for 'em as we speak. More of your psychological tricks, eh, Mr. Lucky? Let old D. L. think he's slipping, missing his marks? Yessir. Slick.

"Damn, I underestimated you, boy. That time at the International Market Place, you were fartin' with me, weren't you? You could've taken out that nimrod with the knife easy, but no, let old D. L. show off, think you were some harmless beach pansy. Maybe I am slipping. Nearly snuck up on me, too. D. L., D. L., you're growin' old and feeble, outsmarted and nearly outflanked."

"I don't get it. I . . ."

"What you're gonna get is dead. Tell you what I'll do, though, sport that I am. You've been playin' with me, right? Now I'm gonnna play with you. A game of tag, how's that sound? Forty-five tag. And you're *it*. I'll give you fifteen seconds." D. L. lifted the .45 to chest height and cocked it. *Kchik—snick.*

"What? You really . . ."

"One thousand fifteen, one thousand fourteen . . ."

Star ran.

He must have put fifty yards between himself and D. L. when he heard D. L.'s voice, half that distance behind him. ". . . four—three—two—one," shouted fast. "That's right," D. L. yelled, "I cheat."

Kbang! Star heard the bullet flick through the leaves to his right. He picked up the pace, caught his toe on a root, and tumbled into a flying somersault. Suddenly on his back, he shook his head, blinked, remembered where he was and why he was running.

Kbang! Flit, flit, flit. Another shot. Low scrub all around. D. L. would see him if he stood to run—game over.

Then ahead, partially hidden by the brush, Star saw refuge: the irregular aperture of a lava tube cave, open at the top like Digger's.

"Mr. Lucky? Where are you, boy?" Sweet voice, concerned, not far behind.

Star crept to the entrance, saw a mat of ferns and moss lining the bottom, and rolled in. Ten feet down, a cushioned landing. He scrambled into the darkness, huddled against the wall.

"Oh, Mr. Lucky? Come out, come out, wherever you are."

Star's eyes adjusted to the dim light. Past the entrance, this floor, like Digger's cave, was flat and free of debris. Only this one ran long and clear as a subway tunnel.

D. L. yelled from the surface, "Left a trail like an elephant, you did. A blind Indian could track you, boy. Goin' spelunking, are you?"

Kbang! The ear-shattering noise boomed, reverberated the length of the cave. Star's hands flew to his ears. No option but to keep running.

Behind, D. L. dropped into the cave with an ominous thump.

Unlike Lot's wife, Star kept his eyes forward, preserving dark-adapted eyes from the shaft of sunlight stabbing through the cave roof. He trotted down a dim, descending stone corridor into the bowels of the mountain.

"Hello, up ahead. Floyd Collins? Is that you?"

Star remembered the name. A renowned caver in the 1920s, Collins was famous for solo explorations of Kentucky caves, until he was trapped by fallen rock in a newly discovered passage. For two weeks, an aboveground media circus followed his decline and eventual death from injuries and exposure.

"Oh Floyd? Mr. Not-So-Lucky? Let me tell you something. I've been spelunking myself the last few days, and you took the wrong path. Goes nowhere fast. Have you hit the water yet?"

Kbang! The bullet rattled along the smooth walls, skittered past Star into the stone tube. Fragments of rock, broken loose by the bullet, rattled the walls and floor. Two stung his back.

"If you want to give it up now, I'll make it quick when we get outside. But if I'm gonna have to haul you out, I guarantee it'll take a painful half day before you kiss this good earth good-bye. A fair offer. What do you say?" *Kbang!*

The shot echoed, amplified. Star heard it as loud in front as behind, and sensed that D. L. was right, the cave led nowhere.

Splash. His right foot hit water. Then his left. *Splash*. Ahead, a weak doubling of the ceiling reflected in receding ripples. He ran to both walls, felt the stone, turned around, realized the cave sloped downhill and disappeared into a pool of water.

"Splishity, splash, are you takin' a bath? Yep. I heard it, all right, Floyd. Can you make out the ceiling yet? How it tilts down? Yoo-hoo, Mr. Unlucky. I'm not far behind you now."

Star looked over his shoulder, saw D. L. forty feet away, silhouetted against the distant light.

"So," said D. L., "Floyd here's wondering, If I run at old D. L. fast, can I catch him unawares? Maybe D. L. exhausted his clip, has no ammo left? Maybe he's had a change of heart, was only funnin', huh? That right, Floyd?" D. L. answered himself: "Wrong! Wrong! Wrong!"

Star saw the shadowy arm rise, distant light glint on gunmetal. He twisted away, sucked air, and dove.

Two sensations registered as his body plunged below the inky surface: the muffled roar of the gunshot and an odd sensation of warmth.

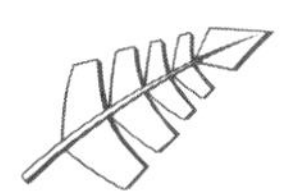

Star swam through water dark as black coffee and nearly as hot.

His mind raced. In a frightening flash, he realized he was living his plaguing nightmare. The details, skewed, but the sensations? Identical. The shock of the black cat clawing him, the desperate race, the underwater swim, the heat. He swam. Deeper and deeper.

Think. If the cave angles up, I might find a pocket of air along the ceiling, outwait the bastard, make him think I've drowned.

He floated higher, one hand before him. Right. And if it goes nowhere? I *will* drown. If I turn around now, I can make it back. Back? A snapshot image rose through the void of G.I. Joe's dad, gloating over his bullet-ridden body.

Star jerked as his fingers touched stone, the cave roof. He frog-kicked along it, one hand brushing rock.

He swam, lungs and skin burning, like a shrimp in a boiling pot. Hot water? He thought of Pele, magma, groundwater percolating through heated rock.

How long now? Twenty seconds, thirty, sixty? Hypoxia sucked at his consciousness. White light sparked at the edges of his vision. The dream demons.

Then ahead: pale twilight. And above, an undulating mirror. He broke the surface, gasped—gasped again, filled his lungs with air—flopped onto hard stone, eyes closed, body trembling.

The air felt wet, warm, dank, with the musty smell of a stone-walled root cellar. He blinked at the hiss of falling water, and sat up, saw a continuation of the lava tube, dimly lit as if by moonlight. He stood, turned full circle. Water gushed down one wall from a long narrow crack in the ceiling, pooled to fill the submerged section he had swum through, flowed past him for forty feet, then disappeared in a gurgling whirlpool.

The passage rose, continued, curved to the right. Star followed. Around a bend, he saw the light source: a beam shining from high in the roof, an ancient gas vent from the cave's youth, when frenzied lava coursed down Mauna Loa, through the tube, over the cliff, and into the valley. The vent ran at least thirty feet to the surface, but was no wider than his leg.

He trotted into the passage, nearly retched from disappointment when he saw the dead end, fifty feet ahead. The roof had collapsed long ago, sealing the chamber with rubble, floor to ceiling. He climbed the fallen rock, probed every crevice. No way through.

He backtracked to look again at the ceiling vent. Too high, too narrow. He sat on his heels, shut his eyes, and blew a long bitter breath through his lips. Seconds passed. He brushed idly at the dusty cave floor and saw . . . not frozen lava, but cut stone.

Cut stone?

Heart racing, he followed the pavement to a narrow, darkened, tunnel-like side chamber, dropped to his hands and knees, and worm-crawled into it. Twenty feet ahead, he saw a shoulder-wide opening and twilight. He slithered through, flopped into a dead-end, fifty-foot bubble, a blind probe by the original lava stream. Pale light lit it from two more narrow vents winding skyward.

High above, a passing cloud glided from the sun, and the dim chamber glowed as if electrified, revealing, ten paces away, the object of Star's quest: the flying vagina of Kapo.

He fell to his knees, head spinning in a dizzying bout of déjà vu. From a crouch, he stared at the giant clam of his nightmares, Melissa's drawing come to life, every nook and cranny of it, blended into a surreal hologram aglow in the cavelight: twelve feet of moist stone flushed with red ochers, rippling in long, parallel, crescent-like ridges to either side of a central rift. The surrounding flow of fossilized, blue-gray lava lay smooth; the *kohe* stood in high relief.

A surge of vertigo rocked him sideways. He righted himself, palms flat on the pavement. Be rational, he told himself. It's stone. Caddy was right. See? It's only ropy swirls of *pahoehoe* lava.

No. Not stone—flesh. It's alive!

He shuddered. There, near the far end of the central depression, rose the pearl his fingers had nearly touched so many times but never felt: the rounded, swollen, glossy tip of a reddish lava stalagmite.

He blinked, and the *kohe* became a seductive mouth, inviting him to leap into it, to claim the pearl glistening like rose gold in the cave light.

Compelled to wrap his hands around the glistening red nodule of his dreams, he lurched forward, then rocked back, woozy, six feet away. In the shadows of his consciousness, he remembered Lani's caution of *kapu*, forbidden ground, and Walana's warning of dangerous mana, spiritual power. He shook his head, tried to retreat, but desire overwhelmed him. He crawled closer.

Suddenly the *kohe* transformed into a monstrous flayed moth. If he stepped inside, he knew it would flap wet stone wings around his body, smother and swallow him. Run, he told himself. But his legs wouldn't move.

Outside, a dense cloud, pregnant with rain, shielded the sun. The cave went dark. Star closed his eyes, struggled to escape the *kohe*'s spell.

Light returned. He tore his eyes from the *kohe*, and a chill ran up his spine, set the hairs at the back of his head on end, as he saw no less than ten of the same shrouded, pupalike forms he'd thought he'd seen at Walana's, lurking in the shadows at both sides of the chamber, lying on low, raised stone platforms. These were real: rotting wicker caskets and bound bundles of age-tattered, melted bark cloth—ancient burials, no doubt placed near the *kohe* for its spiritual power. Among them, he made out crumbling wooden bowls, remnants of gourds, stone tools, shells, disintegrating feathers, bones. Offerings.

The back of his right hand tingled, itched. Star glanced down, saw a white spider crawling up his wrist. He shook it away and shivered. Once more he tried to run, but his feet were rooted in place. He looked again at his wrist, then at his pocket. Pocket? A freeze-frame of black spheres drifted through his mind, escaped into the ether. He closed his eyes, and the image returned. He remembered the mysterious seed pearls he had discovered in his sleeping bag their first night at the edge of the valley. Still in his pocket? Yes. He rolled the shiny obsidian teardrops across his palm and, on impulse, tossed them into Kapo's eager vagina.

The psychic tether binding him to the *kohe* snapped. He fell backward, rubbed his eyes, looked at the *kohe* again, and saw *pahoehoe*. Cold stone.

He drove back into the entry tunnel, wriggled through, and ran all the way to the end of the cave.

How long had he been there? With renewed panic he remembered D. L. and his guns, Lani and the others trapped, Caddy unaware, a walking target. He had to escape, save them. How?

Wait. Whoever carried in the burials had entered and left. He frowned with the answer: they must have arrived before the tube collapsed.

Then what about Artemas Finch?

He climbed the rubble again, examined it. Near the top he saw fresh stone, fallen from the ceiling. It lacked the aged patina of the rest, must have collapsed since Artemas discovered the site, no doubt dislodged by earthquakes following the Mauna Loa eruption. He strained, couldn't budge the tightly wedged chunks.

The other way, the submerged passage? D. L. could still be waiting, his gun ready. Star remembered the falling water, ran back, confirmed there was no way through the narrow crack at the top, even if he could reach it; but the hole in the floor, below the whirlpool of exiting water? That might be wide enough to slip through.

He lay on the floor, lowered an arm into the turbulence, felt stone as far as he could reach. The hole seemed to widen as it dropped. Star listened, heard only a watery roar, then held his breath, lowered his head and upper body into the flow. Hot water pummeled him, tugged at his clothing.

He opened his eyes. Ink.

He reversed, lowered his legs, down to his armpits. Water sucked at his body. His feet kicked freely at the bottom. Think it through, he told himself. It could be an endless chimney, or another, lower cave, which meant a hell of a fall. Into water? Onto rock? He could suffocate, or drown. Or break a leg. In the dark.

The all too familiar shark fear nibbled at his brain. At the thought of razor-sharp teeth shredding his legs, he panicked, scrambled to raise himself. Then he remembered D. L. shooting Dan and Digger, hunting Caddy, murdering Melissa, hurting Mr. Lucky. He shut his eyes, took a deep breath, raised his arms straight over his head, and cast his fate with the falling water.

57

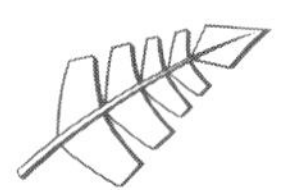

Star rebounded through the narrow rock chimney in a blinding wipeout, swallowing hot water, choking. After a long second of free fall, he cannonballed into waist-high water, cold, flowing from another source.

He bobbed to the surface, coughed, tried to stand, slipped, then floated like a cork in a log flume, awash in a stiff current. He had dropped into another lava tube, velvet black upstream, but downstream? Brilliant daylight, a hundred feet away.

Way to go! He slapped the water at his good luck.

The tunnel, twenty feet wide where he entered, narrowed toward the light, channeling the current faster and higher. He tried to swim to the side to find a handhold, but the stream swept him eight feet downstream for every two he gained sideways. A swirling gyre spun him in a complete circle, dragged him under.

He bounced up, hacking and sputtering, and in a disturbing insight saw, in its entirety, the geography of the valley, the cliffs and caves. Two of the three waterfalls spilled from grooves high above the valley, the third from a hole in the cliff face. From a lava tube. The one he was in.

Uh-oh.

The exit, forty feet ahead, had to be four hundred feet above the valley floor. Within seconds he'd be swept into space with the water, like a man in a barrel, without the barrel.

He swam for his life to the side, bounced along the wall, a mere twenty, now fifteen feet from the opening, hands slapping the wet rock for a handhold. One hand felt a protrusion, slipped. He stuffed three fingers into a pocked recess, jammed his feet to the cave floor against the current, and braced himself between the lower ceiling at the side and the floor, eight feet from the exit. Water swirled chest-high around his body. He pushed against the roof with his head and shoulder, shifted his grip on the wall, shuffled toward the exit.

The tunnel mouth spanned twelve feet. White water gushed around two coffin-size chunks of long-ago-fallen lava crust, one wedged at a rising angle from the bottom, the other upended along a side.

He winced as the current slammed his shin into the lower rock, but managed to wrap his arms and legs around it and climb above the water in a wedging crouch. He hugged the second rock at the side and leaned out, watched the water below him spout fifteen feet before curving into a hundred-foot free fall to splash the cliff face and continue its descent in a widening white cascade.

Could he get out, climb up or down? Near the exit, mossy rock glistened. Slippery. Beyond? Still smooth, but here and there he saw enticing fractures, pockmarks, crevices. Possible? Yes. Dangerous? Definitely. Did he have a choice?

Star looked up at slick overhanging cliff; although forty feet away, the rock rose sixty feet straight to the top. His mind reeled at the thought of climbing down four hundred feet. He considered a sideways crab-crawl past the overhanging ledge, and a climb to the top. Then he remembered Lani's secret trail from the valley. A protrusion of cliff hid it from view, but the trail couldn't be more than a hundred and thirty feet away. And a horizontal climb would conserve strength.

He needed full range of motion, so he stripped from binding jeans to T-shirt and briefs. He removed his boots, tied the laces together, and pitched them into space, watched them spin like a bola, diminish to specks before they dropped through the leaves of the valley vegetation. Socks and trousers, rolled and tied by his shirt, followed.

He massaged stiff, water-soaked feet, and charted a course. Without a glance at the ground, hundreds of feet below, he reached out, gripped a crevice, and then, nose to the rock, extended his leg until his foot rested on a small ledge.

He cleared the exit, moved with a dancer's rhythm. Grip, shift, reach. Stretch, slide a foot, pause. He kept his center of gravity as close to the rock as possible, pulled or pushed straight down or up rather than out with each grip, to avoid dislodging weak rock.

He pinched small extrusions or jammed crevices with a hand, arm, or foot for support. Sometimes his fingers found a low, upside-down ledge and pulled up, wedging him hand to foot. Toes worked like fingers, probing round, bubble-shaped holes formed by gas when the lava was fresh, or catching barely felt ledges. He avoided shrubs or roots which might pull loose, send him caroming to the bottom.

Occasionally, he angled up or down. Up was easier because he could see ahead, but more often, his hands and feet did the charting by feel: a sweep over the rock, a tentative touch, a firm grasp. He kept arms low to keep them blood-fresh, and avoided prolonged grips or too many of the same moves.

Keep the rhythm, he told himself, don't freeze, don't look down.

Twice, he encountered slick rock and had to backtrack, set on a new course. His goal, now thirty feet away, was a continuous six-inch ledge, an ancient fault, that extended around the convex cliff. Halfway there, he wedged his body into a shallow, three-and-a-half-foot-wide crack in an easy crouch, back to the rock, knees to chest, feet flat to the other side, to rest, regain his strength.

He left the crack, stretched into a long X, less than ten feet from the ledge, the ledge that would give him easy travel to the trail. His mind soared in a climber's high, the fear dissipated. He had the touch.

Then, from sixty feet above: *Kbang!* Twelve feet away: *Cachick!* A palm-sized chunk of rock exploded, bounced into space.

Star's left hand stung, bled, lost its grip. His right foot slipped. Only his right index finger and the toes of his left foot saved him from falling.

Above: "Yoo-hoo, Mr. Lucky? Mr. Fly on the Wall? If you let go now, I won't shoot you. How's that for a great deal?"

Star looked to the right, to the left, saw no way clear of the gunfire.

"Best deal you'll get today. What's that? Sorry, son, my sales manager tells me the deal's expired. Like you, Mr. Lucky. All gone." *Kbang!*

Rock flew, twenty feet away. Star realized D. L. was firing the .45. If the gray-haired bastard had his rifle up there, he wouldn't be so sloppy.

Kbang! The bullet struck fifteen feet to his left.

"My, my," from above. "What *is* wrong with my aim today?"

Kbang! Ten feet to the right. He wasn't missing—he was clowning.

D. L. called again, chipper-voiced, "When you didn't swim back, I figured you'd drowned. No way to the surface, I knew that. But wait, I thought, that cave pointed to the cliff. What if Mr. Lucky swam past the water, got out some hole in the rock? And whadaya know? That's just what the clever boy did."

Kbang! A wide miss.

Star remembered the crack, eight feet back. He retraced his moves, scuttled toward momentary safety. Three shots hit left, right, left. He rounded the curve of the cliff, wriggled back into the recess, no more than a foot and a half deep. He could crab-crawl up or down a foot or two, but that was it. He scrunched into as small a ball as possible, but his right shoulder and hip still protruded beyond the crack, out of the line of fire by grace of a small overhang and the curving cliff.

"Mr. Lucky. Where'd you go, boy? Are you in trouble? Hold on, son, I'll help you out."

Silence. Star crouched in the tiny space. What now? D. L. must be walking along the top, past the curve of the cliff, to regain a line's-eye view. He wondered if Lani had heard the shots, if she had slipped out of the cave while D. L.'s mind was on a more immediate murder, if she was on her way to warn Caddy. Jeez.

A peaceful breeze blew, the waterfalls hissed, a small red bird flew by.

'I'iwi, he thought automatically, and realized how easily he could tell them from *'apapane* now.

Rock dug into his back. He shifted the pressure from his lower hip to the back of his shoulders, then leaned out.

There! A diagonal crack twelve feet away, leading toward another ledge, lower, dipping beneath protruding rock. If he could reach that, he'd be clear of D. L.

He edged out, extended a foot.

"Helloooo . . ."

D. L. Not above, but beyond the curve in the cliff, at Star's level.

What the hell? D. L.: sailing in space, ten feet past the curve, less than twenty feet away, wearing a harness, rappelling on a bright blue climbing rope.

Star scooted back to the concealing recess.

"Yessir," said D. L., out of sight. "That's about the right length, wouldn't you say, Mr. Lucky?" He appeared again, at Star's level, bobbing like a pendulum, kicking from the hidden rock face, riding the rope past the curve of the cliff, into full view. Star saw carabiners, ascenders. The man came equipped.

"Whoa! This is fun." D. L. appeared again, farther from the cliff face, big gun in one hand.

Next time out, five seconds later, D. L. sang, "Da-da-da-*dumm*." He dropped from sight.

Another five seconds, in view: "Know that tune, Mr. Lucky? Beethoven's Fifth. That's death knockin.' Da, da, da, *dummm*."

Star scrunched back in the crack, considered racing for the ledge he'd seen, knew he'd never make it. He forgot the pain, the perspiration, his pounding heart, and waited for the end.

D. L. could shoot him any time he wanted. In the shoulder, in the thigh, ricochet into the crack. Murderer's choice.

Star watched with one eye out of the crack. D. L. way out this time. "Growing tired of this game, Mr. Lucky. Gettin' dizzy from all this swinging. Let's get it over with, next time out. What do you say?" He pointed the gun at Star's face, but didn't fire.

Star jerked his head back, managed to make himself an inch or two smaller, but still felt the breeze on his shoulder and hip. Four seconds to live. He thought of Mr. Lucky, of Caddy, of the times they might have had. All over. He shut his eyes.

"Wheeee!" D. L. cleared the curve. "Aloha, Mr. Lucky!"

Kbang!

Star flinched. But felt no pain. The noise, in fact, wasn't where it should have been, but lower. Had D. L. screwed up, dropped ten feet? Star poked his head from the crevice, saw, not D. L., but a length of loose, snaking blue rope. He looked down, saw the man, thirty feet below and dropping fast.

Oblivious of his free fall, D. L. kept the gun pointed at Star, firing as he fell. *Kbang! Kbang! Kbang!*

A bullet struck within a foot of Star's hip. Fragments of basalt slashed his skin, cut deep. He winced at the pain, but kept his eyes on the falling, shooting man. He watched D. L. drop, disappear into the trees hugging the cliff.

Only then did he look at his leg, an eight-inch gash bleeding freely, but fortunately, not spurting bright arterial red. He managed to remove his T-shirt, tie it around his thigh, then took a deep breath, and climbed from the crack. Don't look down. Forget the pain. Get to the ledge, to the trail.

He regained his climber's rhythm, considered for the first time how D. L. could have fallen. Had D. L.'s rappelling torn loose a bad anchor at the top?

As he rounded the bend, reached the ledge, nearly clear of the overhang, it dawned on him. D. L. wouldn't have made such a stupid mistake. It was Lani. Lani and her big knife. When the rifle shots stopped, she'd gotten out, climbed the cliff trail, gotten behind D. L., cut the rope. Jeez. Lani.

Beyond the overhang, he had a clear view up. He raised his eyes, scanned the top. There! Arms raised.

Not Lani. Caddy! Waving something in her hand.

"Swiss Army knife," she called down. "Never leave home without one."

58

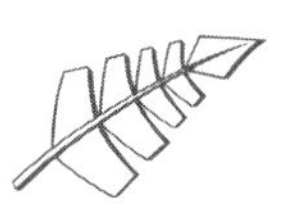

Reverend Jaycie zapped the sound on the TV and cocked his head to the door. Was that the maid in the hall? The cute Filipina with the long orange fingernails with the smiley faces on them? The one with the big black eyes and the slender legs who, he was certain, oh yes, longed for his acquaintance? He stood clutching an ice bucket of fried chicken, wearing only an armless white undershirt, his boxers with "The Lord Moves in Mysterious Ways" embroidered in royal blue over the fly, and his fancy cowboy boots with the biblical inlays. Should he slip on his robe before letting her in?

No, he decided, let's see how she reacts to the shorts. If she giggles? I'll offer her a piece of chicken, a tumbler of Jack and Coke (he was pouring the second glass already), read her a few verses of Solomon's Song of Songs to get her in the mood, and see where the afternoon takes us.

He opened his lavender, leather-bound Bible on the pillow, arranged it just so, tucked in his undershirt, rearranged the elastic band of his shorts above, rather than below, the roll of his belly, and waited for the knock. There we go. He opened the door wide and flashed his best Howdy Neighbor smile.

Lordy! He stumbled back, spilled two thighs and a breast on the Volcano House carpet. There in the hall was . . . what was it? A cinder. A small black and red cinder, glowing like a charcoal briquette, swaying, mumbling.

Good Lord. A *man*. Blistered, peeling, filthy, stinking, dressed in muddy Bermuda shorts and a polo shirt that might once have been baby blue, wearing shredded shoes on feet so swollen they looked like half salamis. Reverend Jaycie wondered if the cinder could speak through those puffed lips. And if it could, did he want to hear what it had to say?

A Hilo hobo this high on the mountain? How did he get past the front desk? Was he dangerous? The Reverend thought fast: I'll throw some chicken in the hall to occupy him, slam the door, call security.

A sparkle of gold at the man's blackened wrist caught Reverend Jaycie's eye. I'd know that diamond-studded watch anywhere. Lordy—it's Brother Bernie!

The Reverend dropped the bucket of chicken barely in time to catch Bernie as he collapsed. On the way down, three words escaped from Bernie's parched and blistered lips: "Disaster," "Bourbon," and "Nicorettes."

Walana patted the familiar kitchen chair. Star sat, still wearing his valley clothes, retrieved by Lani from below the cliff: pants, shirt, shoes, wallet, keys and all. One trouser leg had been cut off at the hip, revealing a bandage-swathed thigh.

"How's the leg?" she asked.

"A hundred and five stitches. They say the muscle is okay—no running or swimming for a while. The crutch is for sympathy. I'm fine, really." Walana's white German shepherd rested her head on his good leg. He scratched her behind the ears.

"Your friends?"

"They flew us to the hospital by helicopter. Digger can leave today." He scowled. "Dan's still in intensive care."

"Poor man. Lani and I will pray for him, go the hospital, do what we can. I'm so sorry. And your lady friend?"

"Flying to Honolulu tonight and Los Angeles tomorrow to proofread her book and catch up on work. Says she'll be back for a day or two to finish with her sister's estate."

"Don't look so glum. You'll see her again." Walana poured him a cup of *mamaki* tea. "Your dog? He's with Papa?"

"I called soon as they stitched me up. Lucky's doing great. I can't wait to see him."

She patted his knee. *"Hoku-li'ili'i,* my little Star, I sensed there would be violence. I prayed for you and your friends, against your enemies. The big dreams have their way, but Lani and I did what we could to influence fate's aim."

She placed a finger under his chin, lifted it to look into his eyes. "Lani said you wanted to see me, alone. Well?"

"Wa . . . I, uh . . . see, I . . ."

"Have some tea, a cookie. Take your time. You can relax now, hmmm?" She ruffled his hair, tapped his nose, passed the platter.

Star sipped, nibbled. His lips moved but said nothing. Finally he spit out the words he needed to say. "Walana, I saw it."

"It?"

"Yes, *it*. Kapo's *kohe*."

"Of course you did."

"You knew?"

"Our dreams, eh? Like I said, you were the one." She pursed her lips. "And the others? You told them?"

"I didn't tell anyone, not even Lani. It just . . . what I saw was so strange, like no place I've been, so . . ."

"Big mana. You felt it."

"It was . . ."

Walana patted his arm.

"Don't you want to know what I saw? Where it was?"

She smiled. "I know all that. What I don't know is how you found it."

"You know? You know where it is?"

"Of course. Lani and I closed the entrance after Artemas Finch died. We pried down loose ceiling rock, blocked it real good. My dreams, your dreams, told me you would find it, but I couldn't imagine how. If there was another way in, I needed to know."

"Lani? Lani knew where it was? Why didn't she . . . ?"

"Lani was to help with your journey, not show you the way."

"Dan thought he saw the bird—*thought*. There's no proof. If we don't let people know about the *kohe* . . ."

"Look at it another way," said Walana. "If we tell the world, what'll happen? Someone will open the cave. The archaeologists will measure and film it, publish it in their books for everyone to see. Tourists will wander up, set babies in the *kohe,* snap pictures of them making doo-doo in it. Teenagers will cover the walls with graffiti. The fast-buck people will put water from the cave in tiki-shaped bottles to sell in Waikiki as a sex potion. Then the parks folks will want to put a chain-link fence around it. And our people? They can't agree on anything. They'll argue over who's holy enough to visit it. The hot-heads, the Sons of Pele? They'll arm themselves, guard it, try to keep everyone but themselves away, then no doubt shoot some tourist, and have a gun battle with the federal people. I don't need dreams to tell me that." Walana paused, shook her head, then looked up, toward the mountain summit. "Tutu Pele? Can you imagine how angry she would be if the *kohe* was desecrated? What would happen if it stirred, came to life? All that mana, power? Big trouble, all right."

"But Walana, if we don't speak out, they'll cut down the forest, make the valley into a golf course. Everything that happened . . . it would be for nothing."

"Not so fast. For nothing? You met your friend Caddy, got to know her, no? She found her sister's murderer, yes? That was what set you on your journey. And your other friends? Digger, Dan, Lani. You share a bond you'll never forget. And look at you. From trying to make quick money in a peeing contest . . ."

"Whoa. Who told you about that?"

"Doesn't matter, I know things. Were you going to charge your friend for helping find her sister's murderer? When you discovered the *kohe,* did you think about selling a map to the golf people? About auctioning pieces of it to collectors?" She ruffled his hair again. "No, you didn't. You came to me. I am proud of you."

"But the valley? Jeez, it's so beautiful. Thousands and thousands of years to make it that way, Caddy said. Clear water, huge trees, all those birds, butterflies. Not one beer can, a single cigarette butt, the whole time we were there. After Waikiki . . ."

"Don't give up yet. That's Tutu Pele's valley. She may be sleeping again, but she listens, and she acts when it suits her." Walana refilled Star's cup, tapped the platter of cookies. "Now, you tell me how you found the *kohe*. Everything."

He began from their first night above the valley, told her the whole story in detail—everything but his visit to Lani's love nest.

"Such a brave boy. You're sure you're not Hawaiian? Perhaps there was a Hawaiian great-grandfather you forgot about. *Ali'i?* A chief?"

He shook his head. "Haole through and through."

"Far as I'm concerned"—Walana stood—"you're honorary Hawaiian." She wrapped thick hands around his head and touched her nose to his.

Star blushed, felt his eyes water. He reached into his pocket for his bandanna and felt a small round object. He retrieved it. "Here." He held it on his palm for Walana to see. "One of the shiny black seed pearls I told you about that broke the spell, let me get away from the *kohe*. I wasn't sure you believed me, but this is one of them, all right."

Walana pinched it between forefinger and thumb, held it to the light, then pressed it in Star's palm. She closed his fingers around it, into a fist.

"You keep that," she said. "It has mana, will bring you good luck."

"But what is it?"

"Pele's tear. I gave Lani a pouchful to take into the valley. They were from Kilauea, Mauna Loa. During eruptions, Pele cries, we find her tears. To protect you, Lani put them in your sleeping bag before you left the nene reserve.

"One thing bothers me, though," she said with a scowl. "All these macadamia nut chocolate chip cookies here, and you only ate two. These aren't store bought, you know. I made them myself. What's the problem? Too salty, too sweet?"

"Delicious," he said, "better than before, honest." He finished the plateful, feeling at ease with the world for the first time in a very long while.

59

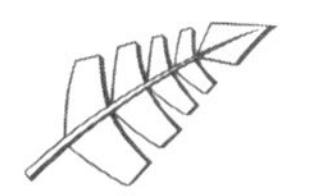

"Aha-ha-hum." Otto Grosz, the chairman of HydraCorp, cleared his throat.

The other board members sat, silent, eager for news.

"I know you've all been awaiting Stanley Fong's and my analysis of the Paradise Valley venture. There is bad news, and there is good news, of sorts."

Shuffling papers, shifting chairs, and whispering suggested the others had hoped for a more positive and conclusive prologue.

Mr. Grosz settled into his oversized chair, waved a hand for the others to be patient. "I know you would rather hear from Bernie Bergen, since this was his project . . ."

"You bet we would," said Mr. Tunalufu, the Samoan. "He talked us into this."

"Bernie suffered some misfortune," said Mr. Grosz. He nodded to the door at Baxter, Bernie's assistant. A moment later, Baxter and his preppy cohort, Sue Shaw, wheeled Bernie in on a gurney. Bernie was dressed, more or less, in his navy power suit. Baxter and Sue had slit the shirt, jacket, and trousers up the back and spread them over Bernie's prone body, disguising most of the gauze, except for Bernie's feet, head, and hands. A clip-on tie rested on Bernie's chest.

The board gasped, averted their eyes.

"Bernie," explained Mr. Grosz, "fell asleep in the sun by his swimming pool and is not his usual chipper self. But he insisted on being here."

Bernie said, "Gladabhrr."

"Speak up," said Mrs. Hamilberg, grating as ever.

"Mr. Bergen said, 'Glad to be here,' " said Baxter. "He can whisper, but it's difficult for him to speak. He's asked me to interpret."

"I know you've all heard about this damned eruption," said Mr. Grosz. "Lava flowed all the way from the top of Mauna Loa to our access road. Crossed it twice. Act of God, as they say in the insurance business, right, Stanley?"

Frowning Stanley Fong, of Pan-Pacific Insurance, nodded.

"Nproblm," said Bernie. Baxter leaned by the gurney, ear to Bernie's lips. "Mr. Bergen says no problem. Wait for it to cool. Won't be that long. Bulldoze over it, no one knows the difference."

"Ah," said Mr. Grosz, "but it *is* a problem, and sad to say, they *will* know the difference. And how do we know this eruption is over?"

"And how," added Stanley Fong, "do we know the next time the lava won't flow *into* Paradise Valley? I met with my people at Pan-Pacific, our financial underwriters, and they say: Cut your losses, dump the project, it's a lemon."

"Noooo!" from Bernie. Everyone heard that without Baxter's intervention. Bernie whispered again, Baxter spoke. "Wait a week or two, it will all be over."

"Pan-Pacific," said Stanley, "*is* willing to wait, then reevaluate. Ten years from now, minimum. I don't know about the rest of you, but thinking past the next quarter is difficult for me. Sit on this for ten years?"

"Noooo! Now," Bernie said.

"Here's the unfortunate scenario Stanley and I visualize," said Mr. Grosz. "You're a sales rep, hawking the condos. You drive in with your Mr. ex-CEO and his wife. They look out the car window and ask what the black stuff is, trailing down the mountain and across your road."

"Mr. Bergen says lie," interjected Baxter.

"Of course," said Mr. Grosz. "This is real estate, after all. But in this case, not so easy. You tell the truth, that this black stuff is from an active vent, that more could drop into the valley any day and eat up their million-dollar condo? No sale. So you lie? Tell them it's topsoil, spilling down from the forest. Or old flow, a hundred years old? Then there's another eruption, good-bye condo and maybe the grandkids, too, and they discover you lied. I smell accusations of fraud, some very unpleasant and expensive litigation. Gentlemen and ladies, we're skating on thin ice.

"But forget the lava for the moment. We have a more embarrassing dilemma. It seems our HydraCorp chief of security and contingency operations was a bit overzealous. He and two HydraCorp security guards visited the property armed to the teeth. The security chief *shot* an archaeologist *and* a bird-watcher, shot *at* a Hawaiian activist and a writer for *Pacific Rainbow* magazine. Moreover, the security guard tried to *rape* a geologist."

Coughs and sputters rounded the table.

Conservative Mr. Hashimoto spoke. "Assuming the security guard was a man, was this geologist, um, of the same gender?"

"No," said Mr. Grosz, "it was a woman. So we're talking straight rape here. But that's a small consolation."

"Trsspsrs," said Bernie. "Trespassers," clarified Baxter.

"Hardly gets us off the hook," said Mr. Grosz. "We kept the land transfer a secret, didn't post it off-limits. Besides which, our attorneys assure me Hawaiian law condones neither the murder nor the rape of trespassers."

"There is some good news," Stanley Fong said. "Apparently, the security chief and the rapist guard met their maker in Paradise Valley. The second guard vanished from the face of the earth. That means no trials, no unavoidable publicity."

"So"—Mr. Grosz thumped his palm on the rosewood table—"here's the bottom line. Stanley, I, and our attorneys visited the shot bird-watcher—publisher and owner of *Pacific Rainbow,* no less. He made a proposal. If we accept, he and the other victims will waive future liability and agree to say nothing to the media about their misadventures. There are strings, but strings that also resolve this knotty dilemma."

"Strnnks?" asked Bernie.

"Money, of course," said Mr. Tunalufu. "How much do they want?"

"Here it is," Grosz said. "Eight hundred thousand dollars remains of our original investment after the land purchase and road construction. Five hundred thousand of that is to be set aside, as I'll explain shortly. The balance goes to settle the shooting and raping claims, reflecting the severity of the injuries: two hundred thousand for the bird-watcher, seventy-five thou for the archaeologist, and twenty-five for the geologist."

"We're getting off cheap," said Mr. Gomes.

"Yes, pay it and run, our attorneys advise," Grosz said. "But there's more, and the shot bird-watcher holds an even bigger stick. He tells me there's an extinct bird—still living—and a high holy Hawaiian shrine in the valley. He has no proof, mind you, but the man assures me that if we reject their proposal and they bring suit, with the publicity resulting from the shootings and the attempted rape, he could create enough media attention to hold up our project for a long, long time. As well as sully HydraCorp's fair name."

"Did I hear 'extinct bird'?" asked Mr. Watanabe, the Hawaiian egg king and bird fancier.

Bernie moaned.

"So they say," said Mr. Grosz. "One of those shy ones Bernie told us about. But birds schmirds, and forget the shrines—all this is moot if we accept the second demand of the bird-watcher. Namely, that we magnanimously donate the Pali-uli land to the state of Hawai'i, to become a wildlife refuge."

"Noooo!"

"Ha!" "You must be kidding." "No way."

Otto Grosz ignored the plaintive wail, the sarcasm. "The Pali-uli Wilderness Refuge is the name the victims suggest. Further, we are to finish paving the road at HydraCorp's expense and provide a secured entry gate. And the five hundred thousand dollars I mentioned? That's to go for maintenance of fences and constructing a field station at the edge of the valley for bird study, the Pali-uli Bird-watch Lodge.

HydraCorp will also, out of the generosity of its heart, fund a full-time conservationist in the park—a woman, a Hawaiian."

"Wha, wha . . ." Bernie, trying to raise himself from the gurney, toppled his sliced power suit onto the floor. Baxter and Sue Shaw eased him back, rearranged the suit, repositioned the clip-on tie.

The other board members were grumbling as well at such capitulation, rumbling much like the torch-bearing townsfolk wending their way to Frankenstein Castle, collectively inarticulate, but of a mind in their discontent.

"What kind of giveaway is this?" Mr. Gomes finally shouted.

Otto Grosz and Stanley Fong both edged from the table and the angry board members. Stanley raised his hands. "Hear us out," he said. "The eruption leaves us without financing, because if our patron, Pan-Pacific, won't stand behind us, no one will. Do any of you want to pledge your personal wealth against so uncertain a venture?"

The townsfolk fell silent.

"Pay 'em off, sell the land fast," said Gomes.

"No. They won't accept their meager settlement without the rest of it, and they could sue us for millions, hold us up in court for years. Sell? With the eruption, challenges to the rezoning, the litigation, and the general stink these people threaten, we'd be lucky to find a buyer at any price."

"None of us," said Mr. Grosz, "nor Bernie—right, Bernie?—had any knowledge of the violent natures of our security people, but would you want to testify in court about HydraCorp's employment practices or past peccadilloes? This publisher hints at an ominous HydraCorp dossier. Who knows what skeletons might surface under courtroom scrutiny?"

The board members studied laps, watches, pencils, wood grain.

"So," said Grosz. "We become benefactors of the birds and the ferns, of the people of the great state of Hawai'i. We put this turkey behind us, write it off."

"No, no, noooo," from Bernie.

"Now," Grosz continued, "here's the good news. Another venture, one in which all of us but Bernie share—the rain forest logging in Indonesia—is turning a phenomenal profit. We can carry our Paradise Valley loss against the Indonesian gains, and still come out way ahead. Here in Hawai'i? We're heroes. Brass plaques and accolades: HydraCorp, the ecologists' friend. Watch the PR people for the Kaua'i resort turn our heroism into tourist dollars. Unbeatable advertising. Think of the sway we'll have with the state."

The board members nodded, smiled.

"Luzeverthin," said Bernie. Tears soaked the gauze at his cheeks.

"Mr. Bergen says he'll lose everything," said Baxter.

"Surely you have other profitable investments," said Dollie Yum. "When we brought you on board, Bernie Bergen, you assured us you could handle risk. Thrived on it, I recall you said. I don't mean to be unsympathetic, but this is a game of large stakes. You win some, you lose some."

Bernie whimpered.

"Be a man, Bernie," Grosz said. "We're not indifferent to your accomplishments. In fact, Stanley and I have had outside consultants working new business angles. They've come up with a proposal we think might be right down your alley—something to get you away from this Big Island debacle, back on your feet.

"With a goad from Hong Kong, capitalism is overrunning mainland China, and when China's teeming masses rise from their squalor, they'll demand a say in their destiny. Think of it: millions of managers, executives, rising entrepreneurs, all calling for what their Western counterparts take for granted: *golf*.

"Of course, it will be years before they can afford our standards, but we plan to meet their modest needs with HydraCorp's new venture: Econogolf.

"The plan is to build a prototype, no-frills golf resort on the Taiwanese island of Quemoy, on the doorstep of mainland China—wave the future under their noses. At present, most of Quemoy is military, underground. We got a ninety-nine-year lease on surface rights from the Taiwan government for a song. They'll provide cheap military construction, too. Mainland China and Taiwan will settle their differences sooner or later, and when the mainland Chinese make the great leap forward to a golfing nation, we'll be ready. Until then? You'll have lower-level Taiwanese, Japanese, and other Asian managers flocking to Econogolf for its bargain-basement memberships.

"What a challenge, Bernie. Proletarian golf. A new frontier."

Silence. Then a small smile lit Bernie's red, puffy, peeling face. Bernie remembered his one true love, his Chinese turtledove, Mai Ling, who had done her business for him in Hawai'i, then returned via Singapore to her native Taiwan. "Mayln." He said it again, "Mayln!" Oh, to see Mai Ling again, to hold her in his arms at last.

"What did he say?" screeched Mrs. Hamilberg.

"Good old Bernie," said Mr. Grosz. "If memory serves me right, I think Mai Lin is the sole country club on Taiwan. Disgraced and on his back, Bernie is negotiating with us for a membership. What do you say, HydraCorp? A company-paid membership for Bernie as a farewell, until Econogolf comes on line?"

"Hell, why not?" "For old times." "Hear, hear."

Bernie's smiles cracked the sun-parched skin at the corners of his mouth. "Mayln, Mayln, Mayln." He said it over and over, until they wheeled him away.

When Baxter rolled the gurney into Bernie's office, he found a disheveled man slumped against the wall, muttering, a nearly empty tumbler of bourbon on the floor beside him. In one pale, trembling hand he held a VHS tape.

Bernie croaked a "S'okay. That's my minister," and waved Baxter away.

The Reverend Jaycie Pitts lurched to his feet, leaned over the gurney, held the box for Bernie to see. It was a preproduction mock-up. The title, in English, French, and Japanese, said *The Colonel and Solome Do: Where's the Head of John the Baptist. Hot. Hot. Hot.* Gracing the cover was a fine photo of Reverend Jaycie, seated on a pillow, bright silk scarves draped across his shoulders, pants loose around skinny ankles, eyes rolled heavenward, an angelic smile on his flushed face. He cradled the head of his former Cheerleader for Jesus, little Josephine, in his bare lap with one hand, clutched a Bible with the other.

"This is the end for me here," Reverend Jaycie wailed. "Doom.

And on the mainland, in French Polynesia, Japan, New Zealand, Australia, Europe. Oh, Brother Bernie, what shall I do?"

Bernie was still smiling. "I don't see any Chinese printed on that tape box, Reverend," he whispered. "I hear there's still plenty of heathens praying for salvation in Taiwan. I know a great girl there, too. And five'll get you ten, she's got a friend."

60

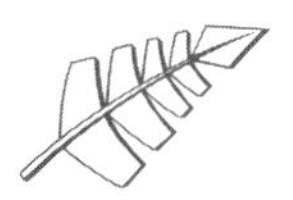

"HAPPY BIRTHDAY DEAR DORIS, HAPPY BIRTHDAY TO YOUUU."

Red crepe bunting blocked off the rear of Papa's for the partyers, but everyone up front sang along.

Papa set a flaming cake on the table. Doris huffed and puffed.

"Way to go," said Star. "Has this woman got a great set of lungs, or what?"

Teary-eyed, Doris cocked an eyebrow at him, then turned to Papa. "The top of that cake is solid wax. You're lucky the sprinklers didn't go off. How many are there, anyway?—and watch your answer."

"Thirty-nine. I hope that's not too many?"

Doris blew him a kiss.

"Speech. Speech."

"I don't know what to say. And all these presents. I'll tell you what the best is, before I open any of them. It's having my friends back from the Big Island in one piece. Or almost." She tweaked Digger's nose, punched Star in the shoulder. "And you, Mr. Publisher." She patted Dan, in a wheelchair, on the back of his hand. "And Papa's Lani, too."

"Tell them about Digger's present," Star said.

Doris blushed. Digger beamed. "Should I?" she asked Digger. He nodded. "This old geezer is coming into some unexpected money," she said.

"Workmen's compensation," Digger said. "Thanks to Dan."

"A toast," Dan said. "To HydraCorp, patron of archaeology and conservation."

Glasses raised, clinked.

"To the Pali-uli Wilderness Refuge," Caddy said, "and the Pali-uli Bird-watch Lodge. I'm glad I got back to Hawai'i in time for the party. It's good to be with you guys again."

"And to the Pali-uli Bird-watch Lodge superintendent-to-be," said Dan.

"Me, and the birds, and the plants, and no pigs," said Lani.

"You know I'll be over to see you," Dan said. "Soon as they let me out of this wheelchair, and HydraCorp finishes the road and the field station. A shame we never found the Kapo shrine. Maybe if you're there full-time, you'll have better luck than we did. And the bird?" Dan rang his fork on a water glass. "Everyone? Did you know I exposed a frame of the *'o'o* before I was shot? The bullet wrecked my camera, but the film came out. You want to see the photograph, the proof?" He pulled an eight-by-ten-inch color photo from an envelope. Each of the guests studied it, passed it along. It captured a beautiful blue sky, silhouetted treetops, and, among the distant leaves, a flying, blurry bird, dark as the trees.

Out of Dan's sight, the guests exchanged glances, shook their heads.

"Not easy to make out, I know," he said, "but that's what it is. I know it in these broken bones."

Papa dished out cake, ice cream, and two each of Walana's macadamia nut chocolate chip cookies, a present, brought by Lani from the Big Island.

"So, Doris, let's hear about this special present from Digger," Caddy said.

Doris blushed again. "As I said, the old geezer came into a pile of money, and decided to blow some of it on fieldwork, soon as he heals up, in French Polynesia. You know, Tahiti."

"More precisely, the island of Bora Bora," Digger said. "South Seas paradise."

"And Digger asked me to go along!"

Cheers. Applause.

Digger gave her a squeeze.

"I gave her a month off," said Papa.

"Star," said Dan. "I don't want you to feel left out. There's a present for you, too."

"For me?" Between fingers and thumb, Star twirled a small black stone bound with silver wire, hanging from a cord around his neck.

"For our hero?" Caddy asked.

"She saves my butt and calls me a hero," said Star. "Well, what is it?"

Dan waved through the window to Kuhio Avenue. They all looked, but saw nothing. "Star," he said, "you remember your old friend, the Reverend Jaycie Pitts?"

"The chicken man. The one who set up that guy to attack my car. Jeez, Dan, don't tell me you invited him here?"

"Hold on, my boy. A package arrived at the magazine, to the attention of the publisher—that's me, folks—from Papeete, Tahiti. It was a VHS tape, an advance copy for an edition soon to hit the market commercially. A blue movie, as we used to say, starring, guess who?"

"The Reverend? No!"

"Filmed with a hidden camera. The Reverend Pitts, under a pseudonym, but unmistakable, in flagrante delicto with one of his Cheerleaders for Jesus. Shocking stuff. A big surprise to the Reverend, I'm sure. I guess the producer figured *Pacific Rainbow* would run an exposé, give the film free publicity."

"Oh yeah. Do it," Star said. "Where's the tape? Papa? Do you have a VCR in back?"

"Patience, ace reporter," Dan said. "That's not the present. It turns out, your buddy, the Reverend, is planning to vamoose, close up shop, leave Hawai'i for good, fast. Not that *Pacific Rainbow* and I have forgotten your run-in. We've kept an eye on the Reverend Jaycie Pitts."

"And . . . ?" Star asked.

"Anticipating exposure, he's liquidating, plans to clear out before the you-know-what hits the fan. Our attorneys tracked him down, however, threatened a suit on your behalf—not that it would get anywhere, mind you—but they convinced him they could tie up his assets. To make a long story short, we struck a deal.

"Take a look outside."

Everyone's head turned. An interminably long car pulled to the curb, a superstretched Lincoln Town Car, lavender with dark windows, gold trim, and a foot-high golden cross hood ornament.

"It's the Leviathan," said Doris. "Everybody knows that car. It's the one the Reverend gets out of at the beginning of his TV show. It's Reverend Pitts."

"Jeez, Dan. The chicken man."

"The Reverend Jaycie Pitts coming here," said Papa. "Imagine."

"An apology," Doris said. "The Reverend's going to apologize to Star for making him Sinner of the Week and for the damage to his car."

"Not quite," said Dan. "That's one of my people driving. Here." He tossed a set of car keys and an envelope on the table. "Other set's in the car. The registration and title are in the envelope. It's your car now, boy, a let-me-off-the-hook present from the Reverend Jaycie Pitts."

Hoots. Claps on the back. Star stared at the car.

"I'll fix it up for you," said Scooter. "We'll goose up the engine, nose and deck that baby, lower her, make her look like a fat-assed submarine. . . ."

"When the party's over," Doris said, "I want a ride."

"And what about you, Caddy?" Dan asked. "Your book is finished, I understand. So it's back to the old grind? A shame you can't spend some time here, R and R, now that the excitement's behind us. You're welcome, you know. Angela and I would be pleased to put you up."

"Actually," she said, "I'm still on sabbatical. I'd planned some library research at UCLA, but, thanks to you, I came into a bit of a windfall myself, and I've grown quite fond of Hawai'i."

Star was still staring at the car. It extended nearly the full length of Papa's.

"I've been hearing all these stories," Caddy continued, "so I thought I might stay awhile, and"—she tapped Star on the shoulder—"you know—meet Mr. Lucky."

"What?" Star's eyes shifted from the car to Caddy. *"What?"*

"You heard me." Grinning. "Meet Mr. Lucky."

"Jeez."

ACKNOWLEDGMENTS

Hearty thanks to my agent, Eleanor Wood, and my editor, Bob Gleason, for their enthusiasm, confidence, and sage counsel. My friends at the fiction critique group of the Cincinnati Writers' Project provided invaluable advice as the story evolved. John Graham, Karen Jobalia, Patrick C. McCoy, Judy A. McCoy, and Ryck Neube kindly read the manuscript, to its benefit; Wildman Ryck was a willing and helpful sounding board from start to finish. I am grateful to Kauanoelehua Chang, Roxy Labourne, Steve O'Meara, M. Christine Valada, and C. Puanani Wilhelm for their assistance. Sherri Kempf gave me hugs when I needed them and kept the faith throughout. The Maui Writers Conference sharpened my learning curve, and the friendly people of the Aloha State made every visit a delight. *Mahalo,* Madame Pele.

A Woof! Woof! of gratitude to you all.

The Kapo site is real; its setting and location are fictionalized. Hawaiian, federal, and private agencies work conscientiously to preserve Hawai'i's cultural and biological heritage, a challenging job. Half the bird species living in Hawai'i before human arrival are now extinct; some thirty birds, including the nene, are currently threatened or endangered. The likelihood of finding a living Hawaiian *'o'o* is remote—but one may hope.